"Come On, Honey. I'll Show You Mine, If You Show Me Yours."

Hope closed her eyes and tried to get a handle on her suddenly topsy-turvy world, but lack of vision only made matters worse when a hot hand skated up her bare leg. Her eyes flashed open as she grabbed Colt's wrist.

"Stop." She tried to sound firm, but only came out sounding needy. She cleared her throat. "I mean it, Colt." Except it didn't really sound like she meant it.

Those sensual gray eyes stared back at her from beneath lowered lids. "Come on, honey," he coaxed as his fingers caressed the spot right above her knee. "I promise not to tell a single soul—I never did."

The man knew exactly what to say. Always had. A naughty outlaw who had no scruples about cornering a woman in an old Chevy while water cascaded down the windows like the best carwash fantasy she'd ever had? It was too much for one very ordinary woman to deal with.

So she gave in. Just a little. Just enough to let her eyes close in surrender. Just enough to lean into the mouth that trailed kisses down her neck and back up again.

Raves for
Going Cowboy Crazy

"Sexy, sassy fun!"   —Susan Andersen,
New York Times bestselling
author of Burning Up

"Katie Lane is a wonderful new voice in Western
romance fiction."   —Joan Johnston, *New York
Times* bestselling author of the
Bitter Creek and Hawk's Way series

"Katie Lane creates handsome cowboys with hearts as
big as Texas."   —Lori Wilde, *New York Times*
bestselling author of
The Welcome Home Garden Club

"Sexy Texas cowboys are Katie Lane's gift to her readers."
—R.C. Ryan, *New York Times* bestselling
author of *Montana Glory*

"A sparkling debut filled with Texas warmth and humor."
—Jane Graves, author of
Tall Tales and Wedding Veils

"Don't miss Katie Lane. You're gonna love her!"
—Christie Craig, author of
Don't Mess with Texas

Make Mine a Bad Boy

Also by Katie Lane

Going Cowboy Crazy

Make Mine a Bad Boy

KATIE LANE

FOREVER

NEW YORK   BOSTON

Copyright © 2011 by Cathleen Smith
Excerpt from *Going Cowboy Crazy* copyright © 2011 by Cathleen Smith
All rights reserved. Except as permitted under the U.S. Copyright Act of 1976, no part of this publication may be reproduced, distributed, or transmitted in any form or by any means, or stored in a database or retrieval system, without the prior written permission of the publisher.

Book design by TexTech, Inc.

Forever
Hachette Book Group
237 Park Avenue
New York, NY 10017
www.HachetteBookGroup.com

Forever is an imprint of Grand Central Publishing. The Forever name and logo is a trademark of Hachette Book Group, Inc.

The publisher is not responsible for websites (or their content) that are not owned by the publisher.

Printed in the United States of America

First Printing: June 2011

10 9 8 7 6 5 4 3 2 1

To my favorite heroines, my daughters,
Aubrey Lane and Tiffany Heather

Acknowledgments

Like my character, Hope Scroggs, I am blessed with people who believe in me. And I can't thank them enough for all their love and support:

My loving husband, Jamie; my beautiful daughters, Aubrey and Tiffany, and their wonderful men, John Sedberry and Donny Sevieri; and my precious granddaughters, Gabby and Sienna. You are my heart, and I am so proud of each and every one of you.

My mother-in-law, Kay Smith, for all her encouragement over the years.

My L-Sisters—Lori Tillery, for dropping everything when I needed help; Lu Loomis, for always being the voice of reason; and Linda Chambers, for all the giggly dinners.

And speaking of giggles, my favorite night of the month is book club night, when I get to flop down on a couch and drink wine and munch on snackies while discussing books with the divine Dog-eared Divas.

Then there are the lovely ladies of LERA, the Land of Enchantment Romance Authors, the best Romance

Writers of America chapter in the world. It is an honor to be part of a group of such talented writers. Go, Team Romance!

And thanks to all my Defined gym-rats. If I need an expert, I can always find one there. Thanks, Jeff Fauver, for all your custom bike expertise. I hope your custom bike kicks butt in Sturgis.

Last, but not least, a special thanks to my agent, Laura Bradford, for all her business savvy and the great title. And to Alex Logan, my editor, for all her hard work. I'm so lucky to have such a great team!

Make Mine a Bad Boy

Chapter One

IT WAS A DREAM. It had to be. Where else but in a dream could you be an observer at your own wedding? A silent spectator who watched as you stood in the front of a church filled to the rafters with all your family and friends and whispered your vows to a handsome cowboy you've loved for most of your life. A cowboy who kissed you as if his life depended on it, before he hurried you down the aisle and off to the reception, where he fed you champagne from his glass and cake from his fingers, before taking you in his strong arms and waltzing you toward happily ever after.

It was a dream.

Her dream.

"Hog, you gonna eat that piece of cake?"

And just like that the dream shattered into a nightmare.

Hope Marie Scroggs pulled her gaze from the dance floor and looked over at Kenny Gene, who was staring down at the half-eaten slice of wedding cake on her plate.

"'Cause if you ain't," he said, "I sure hate to see it go to waste." Without waiting for an answer, he speared the cake and crammed a forkful into his mouth, continuing to talk between chews. "That Josephine sure outdid herself this time. Who would've thought that raspberry jam would go so good with yeller cake?"

The fork came back toward her plate. But before he could stab another piece, his girlfriend, Twyla, slapped his hand, and the plastic fork sailed through the air, bounced off one of the ceramic pig centerpieces, and disappeared beneath the table.

"Kenny Gene, don't you be eatin' Hope's food! She needs all them noot-tur-ents!"

Hope didn't have a clue what Twyla was talking about, and she didn't care. All she wanted to do was recapture the dream. But it was too late. Too late to ignore the fact that she wasn't the one who whirled around on the dance floor in the arms of Slate Calhoun—the handsomest cowboy in West Texas.

But she should've been.

It should've been Hope dressed in her mama's three-tiered lace wedding dress. Hope who sipped from his clear plastic Solo cup. Hope who licked Josephine's Raspberry Jamboree Cake from those strong quarterback fingertips. It should have been her arms, looped over that lean cowboy frame, and her face tucked under that sexy black Stetson, awaiting a kiss from those sweet smiling lips.

Her.

Her.

Her.

Certainly not some damned Yankee who had come to Bramble, Texas, looking for her long-lost twin sister, only to steal that same sister's identity like a peach pie set out to cool. It wasn't fair, and it wasn't right. Not when Hope was the one who had done all the prep work. The one who suffered through all the cheerleading practices and home-coming parades and hog-calling contests, all to make her family and the townsfolk proud.

And then some citified wimp with ugly hair showed up, and their loyalties switched like Buford Floyd's gender, and she was expected to grin and bear it? To pretend that everything was just fine and dandy? To act like she didn't give a hoot that her life had just been spit out like a stream of tobacco juice to a sidewalk?

Her anger burned from the injustice of it all, and all she wanted to do was drop to the ground and throw a fit like she had as a child. If she'd thought it would work, she would have. But it was too late for that. The vows had been spoken, the marriage license signed.

Besides, she was Hope Marie Scroggs, the most popular girl in West Texas, and she wasn't about to let anyone know just how devastated she was that the dreams of her wedding day were being lived out by someone else.

Someone who, at that moment, looked over at her and smiled a bright, cheerful smile with white, even teeth that reflected the lights shooting off the huge disco ball hanging from the ceiling. How could some sugary sweet Disney princess have lived in the same womb with her for nine months? It made absolutely no sense whatsoever. Nor could Hope figure out why she smiled back—though it might have been more of a baring of teeth, because Faith's smile fizzled before Slate whirled her away.

"Your fangs are showin', honey." Her best friend, Shirlene, slipped into the folding chair next to her with a soft rustle of gold satin.

Since her daydream was already stomped to smithereens, Hope turned to Shirlene and lifted a brow at the mounds of flesh swelling over the top of her bridesmaid's dress.

"Better than havin' my boobs showin'," Hope retorted.

Shirlene didn't even attempt to tug up the strapless confection that put Hope's grotesque purple maid-of-honor's dress to shame. "Admit it. You've always been jealous of the girls." Shirlene flashed a bright smile at Kenny and Twyla as they got up and headed for the dance floor.

"The girls?" Hope's eyes widened. "Those aren't girls, Shirl. Broads, maybe, but not girls."

Shirlene laughed. "Okay, so you've always been jealous of the broads."

Hope shrugged. "If you had my teacups, you'd be jealous too."

"I don't know about that. I get pretty tired of lugging these suckers around."

"I'm sure Lyle doesn't mind helping out with that." She glanced around for Shirlene's husband. "Where is Lyle, anyway?"

"He's got a meetin' in the morning, so he wanted to get to bed early."

"A meetin' on a Sunday?"

For just a brief second, Shirlene's pretty green eyes turned sad before she looked away to fiddle with the purple ribbon tied around the fat ceramic pig, one of the same pigs that had been pulled out for every town celebration since they were made for Hope's fifteenth birthday. "That's the problem with marrying a wealthy man. They're so busy making money, they don't have time to make babies."

"Are you still trying?"

Shirlene shrugged as she retied the ribbon in a perfect bow. "Lyle thinks it's God's will."

"You could adopt, you know."

"I know, but maybe Lyle's right. Maybe this West Texas girl is a little too wild to be a good mama." Releasing her breath, she flopped back in the chair, causing her broads to jiggle like Aunt Mae's Jell-O mold. "Geez, we make a pathetic pair, don't we, Hog? Me a lonely, childless housewife and you a jilted woman."

Hope looked around before hissing under her breath. "I was not jilted, Shirl."

"I don't know what you would call it, Hog. Everyone in town was there when you agreed to marry Slate— regardless of the fact that he hadn't asked."

Hope's jaw tightened. "You know as well as everybody else that Slate proposed to me."

"Years ago. And we both know he was never serious." She hesitated and sent Hope a pointed look. "And if I remember correctly, neither were you."

Unable to look back at those perceptive green eyes, Hope stared out at the dance floor, where Slate continued to whirl her twin sister around. "I always planned on marrying Slate."

Shirlene snorted. "If I had a dime for every one of your plans, Hope, I'd be rich enough to lure the Dallas Cowboys away from Jerry Jones."

"As if you're not already."

"True." The contagious smile flashed as Shirlene reached over and picked up a champagne bottle. She filled a cup for each of them before lifting hers. "Here's to wild West Texas women—we might be down, but we'll never be out."

Finally giving in to a smile, Hope lifted her cup and tapped Shirlene's. "Damn straight." But before she could take a sip, the mayor, Harley Sutter, came chugging up and took the cup from her hand.

"No time for drinkin', Hope." He handed the cup to Shirlene and pulled Hope up from her chair. "Not when the entire town wants a dance with their sweetheart."

Since Hope had never been able to disappoint her hometown, she rolled her eyes at Shirlene and allowed Harley to pull her out to the dance floor. Unfortunately, the two-step had ended, and the band struck up one of those stupid wedding songs that only worked in a room filled with drunks. Still, she pinned on a smile and tried to act like she enjoyed impersonating a flustered chicken.

"Glad to see you so happy, Hope," Harley said as he flapped his arms above a belly that was more keg than six-pack. "You know what they say: 'Home is where the heart is.'"

Unless some Disney princess stole it right out from under your nose, Hope thought as Harley swung her right on over to Sheriff Sam Winslow.

"He's right, Hope," Sam said as he flapped. "Hollywood has had our sweetheart long enough. Though I bet they ain't gonna be real happy to lose such talent. That hemorrhoid commercial you did sure brought tears to my eyes. It had to be real hard to get such a look of complete discomfort." He swung her around. "But you sure nailed it, Hog. Myra raced out and got a tube that very night."

"A tube of what?" Rachel Dean stepped up.

"Hemorrhoid cream," Sam answered, before stepping away.

"Oh, honey." Rachel Dean clapped her man hands, then jerked Hope into a swing that almost snapped her spinal column. "I got hemorrhoids when I was pregnant. And I'm tellin' you right now, there ain't no cream on God's green earth that will help with that hellish burnin'."

Not wanting to talk about hemorrhoids or pregnancy, Hope gladly turned to her next partner, although her pinned-on smile slipped when she stared up into a pair of dreamy hazel eyes. As she struggled to regain her composure, the silly song ended and a waltz began.

"Could I have this dance, Miss Scroggs?" Slate asked.

The word *no* hovered on her lips. But, of course, she couldn't say no. Not unless she wanted him to know exactly how hurt she was.

"Only if you keep those big boots off my toes, Cowboy."

"I'll do my best." Slate flashed the sexy grin that made women melt. Hope didn't melt, but she felt thoroughly singed, or maybe just annoyed that she didn't get to claim the body that went with the smile.

His best turned out to be worse than Hope remembered. After only two steps, her toes were smashed under his boots, and she was forced to do what she'd always done when they danced: Take the lead. Except now he didn't follow as well as he used to.

"Listen, Hope," he said. "I realize this has been hard on you. You come back to Bramble expecting... well, I don't exactly know what you were expecting, but it sure couldn't have been a twin sister you didn't even know you had. Or a wedding that had been planned without you knowing— our wedding, no less." Slate chuckled. "Crazy townsfolk."

She looked away. "Yeah...crazy."

"But you want to know what is even crazier," he continued. "All it took was one look from Faith—or maybe a kiss that knocked my hat off—and I was a goner. A complete goner."

Hope wished that she was a goner. Gone from this man. And this room. And this town. If the pits of hell opened at that very moment and swallowed her up, it would be a relief.

But that didn't happen. So all she could do was guard her toes and try not to act like she gave a darn that her wedding plans had disintegrated just like her dreams of becoming a movie star. She was thankful when the slow ballad ended and Slate was pulled away as Harley bellowed, "Come on all you unhitched folks! It's time for the garter and bouquet toss!"

Hope tried to make a run for it, but the town pushed her forward, swarming around a chair that had been set up in the middle of the dance floor, a chair where her sister sat and waited for Slate to dip that head of sun-kissed hair and, using nothing but his teeth, tug the light blue garter down a leg identical to her own.

"I love a man who knows what to do with his mouth!" Rachel Dean yelled, and whooping and hollering broke out loud enough to shake the sturdy stone building.

With the town's attention focused elsewhere, Hope attempted to inch her way to the door. But she should've known better, especially when she had such an ornery best friend.

"Now don't be gettin' any ideas about leaving, Hog." Shirlene positioned her body between Hope and the exit. "Not when everyone expects you to get up there and catch that ugly bunch of silk flowers Darla hot-glued together."

"Ugly?" Darla clasped her hands to her chest. "Well, I'll have you know that I paid a pretty penny for those at Nothin' Over a Buck."

"Of course, you did, honey." Shirlene sent her a wink. "If anybody can stretch a buck, it's you."

The words seemed to pacify Darla, and she smiled

brightly as Shirlene slipped an arm around Hope and leaned down to speak in her ear.

"Now I know you want to go home and wallow in self-pity. But we both know that this town isn't going to let you get away with that. So just bite the bullet and get in there and do me proud." She gave her a loving pat on the back before she shoved her into the middle of the dance floor, and by the time Hope caught her balance, Shirlene had disappeared in the crowd of single ladies.

It was a pathetic group. There was Twyla, who had already been married three times. Rachel Dean, who came close, with two. The librarian, Ms. Murphy, who was smart enough to avoid marriage altogether, but still had to endure the crazy ritual every time someone had a wedding. Hope's two younger sisters, Jenna Jay and Tessa. And a couple other giggling girls.

Her twin sister stood to the side, holding her "Nothin' Over a Buck" bouquet and grinning like the seven dwarfs were all coming over to the castle for dinner. Of course, who wouldn't grin if she had just wrangled the best-looking man this side of the Mississippi while her sister was forced to fight for the leftovers?

Well, Hope wasn't fighting.

She was all fought out.

She didn't care if Darla's hot-glued flowers were made out of solid gold. She wasn't going to lift a finger to catch them. Not one finger.

"Ready?" Faith looked directly at her, and Hope experienced the same strange phenomenon that she always experienced when her twin sister looked at her. It was like looking into a mirror. Not just externally, but internally. Everything Hope felt was reflected right back at her. Hurt.

Confusion. Anger. Self-pity. It was all there in the familiar blue eyes.

Fortunately, Faith broke the connection by turning around and giving Hope something else to think about, like how to avoid the large bouquet of silk flowers that Faith launched over her shoulder.

Hope figured it wouldn't be hard, not when Twyla had perfected the wide-receiver dive that won her numerous silk-flower trophies and a bunch of good-for-nothing husbands. But as the bouquet sailed through the air, Twyla didn't move one underdeveloped muscle toward it. Nor did Rachel. Or Ms. Murphy. Or Jenna Jay. Or Tessa. Or any of the giggling girls. Instead, everyone just watched as the purple batch of flowers tumbled end over end, straight toward Hope.

She took a step back.

Then another.

But the bouquet just kept coming. If it hadn't been heading for her like a heat-seeking missile, she might've turned and run. But she wasn't about to take her eyes off Darla's creation, not when Hope's own maid-of-honor bouquet was a good solid five pounds of hardened hot glue. So, instead, Hope widened her stance and prepared to deflect the floral grenade with an arm.

It would've worked too, if her watch hadn't snagged the yard and a half of tulle netting surrounding the flowers, something Hope didn't realize until she lowered her arm and felt the dead weight.

Like a preschooler doing the hokey pokey, she shook her arm to try and get it loose. But the bouquet refused to budge. And after only a few seconds of crazy waving, she realized it was no use and let her arm drop. She expected a wave of catcalls and whistles, but what she got was complete silence.

Confused, she glanced up to find the entire roomful of people staring.

Except not at her.

Few things could pull the town's attention away from their sweetheart. Yet something had. Something that had nothing to do with ugly silk flowers and five pounds of hot glue. Something that so intrigued the town they had completely forgotten that Hope Scroggs existed.

A chill of foreboding tiptoed up Hope's spine, and her stomach tightened and gave a little heave as she slowly turned around.

Just that quickly, things went from bad to worse.

A man stood in the open doorway with his shoulder propped against the frame as if he didn't have a care in the world. As if he didn't stick out like a sore thumb from the other men, who were dressed in their Sunday best of western pants, heavily starched shirts, and polished cowboy boots.

This man looked like a desperado who'd come off a long, hard ride. Road dust covered his round-toed black biker boots with their thick soles and silver buckles, partially hidden by the tattered hem of his jeans, jeans so worn that they molded to all the right nooks and crannies, defining hard thighs and lean valleys. A basic black T-shirt was tucked into the jeans, stretching over miles of muscle and hugging the hard knots of his biceps.

But although he had a body that could tempt a Bible-banger on Sunday, it was his face that held Hope's attention, a face made up of tanned skin, hard angles, and a thin layer of black stubble. Come to think of it, every thing about the man was black—including his heart. Everything but those steel gray eyes, eyes that scanned the room as if looking for something.

Or someone.

Hope ducked behind Kenny Gene and stealthily peeked over his shoulder, watching as the man pushed away from the doorjamb and weaved around the tables— fortunately, in the opposite direction. The smart thing to do would be to slip out the door before he saw her. And she might've done just that if his fine butt in those buttery jeans hadn't distracted her.

It was a shame, a darned shame, that the man was such a mean, ornery lowlife.

A mean, ornery lowlife who stopped right in front of...

Faith?

It made no sense, but there he stood, those unemotional eyes drilling her sister with an intensity that caused the Disney smile to droop.

"It seems I missed the weddin'," he stated in a deep, silky voice that didn't match his rough exterior. "So I guess the only thing left to do"—those big biker hands slipped around Faith's waist—"is kiss the bride."

Then, before Hope's mouth could finish dropping open, he lowered his head and laid one on her twin sister. Not a gentlemanly peck, but a deep wet lip-lock that left little doubt that a tongue was involved. It was that tongue that forced Hope's true nature to return from the depressed, self-pitying cocoon it had been hiding in since learning that Slate was in love with Faith. That lying, conniving tongue caused Hope's long-withheld emotions to spew forth in a geyser of liberating anger.

"Colt Lomax!" Hope screamed, loud enough to shake the tiles from the ceiling, as she shoved her way through the crowd. "Get your filthy hands off my sister!"

Chapter Two

COLT LOMAX HAD SPENT MOST OF HIS LIFE in Bramble, Texas, angry. Angry over his daddy dying at such a young age. Angry that his mama couldn't pull herself together after his daddy's death and take proper care of him and his little sister. And angry that he had to grow up in a small town filled with small-minded people who only saw what they wanted to see.

But it wasn't anger Colt felt when he pulled away from the kiss. It was confusion. Confusion over the fact that the woman he thought he'd just kissed was the same woman racing toward him with murder in her big blue eyes. And since the look was a familiar one, Colt figured he'd made a mistake. But before he could figure out the extent of his mistake, Slate Calhoun's fist connected with his face and rang his bell.

Now, he had always accepted responsibility for his mistakes, along with a fitting punishment. But one punch was fitting, two was overkill. So when the next punch came at him, Colt was ready and easily deflected it with a raised arm. Unfortunately, this fist belonged to Hope. Her skinny forearm thumped against his so hard that he worried about fractured bones. But that concern was replaced with another when the bouquet of flowers that hung from her wrist clipped her in the chin, dropping her to his feet in a crumple of shiny purple material and a pile of glossy brown hair.

If fear hadn't gotten in the way, Colt might've seen the humor in having Hope Scroggs spilled over his boots like a religious fanatic at the foot of an idol. But there was no humor in the pale, limp arm flung over the gray-speckled tile floor. No humor in the satin-covered chest that didn't appear to rise and fall.

"Gee, Colt," Kenny Gene said. "I knew you didn't like Hope, but did you have to haul off and hit her?"

Stunned and slightly punch-drunk, it took Colt a moment to react—a moment that found Hope in Slate Calhoun's arms.

"Just put her down here, Slate." Jenna, Hope's mama, directed Slate over to a table where a couple of the women scurried to clear off the plastic plates and utensils and a ceramic pig that almost brought a smile to Colt's face.

But it was hard to smile when you had just knocked out a woman. And not just any woman, but the Sweetheart of Bramble, Texas. He was surprised that they hadn't tarred and feathered him by now. Probably because they were too concerned over their little Hope.

Although not as concerned as Colt.

Slate carefully laid Hope down as Jenna soaked a napkin in water and ran it over her face. The rest of the town moved in to huddle around her, and it took a few well-placed elbows for Colt to make his way to the front of the pack.

"She ain't dead, is she?" Kenny tipped his black cowboy hat up on his forehead and leaned closer as the knot in Colt's stomach tightened.

"Of course, she ain't dead," Rachel Dean said, although her man-sized hands were clutched to her chest in a very unconvincing way.

With her purple gown spread out around her and the bouquet resting on her chest, Hope looked like a fairytale princess. Not the one who slept, but the one who had been poisoned. Miles of rich dark hair framed a deathly white face. A face as familiar to Colt as his own, from her high forehead to the stubborn chin—a chin that now had a nasty-looking red knot.

What the hell was the matter with these country bumpkins anyway? Someone should be calling 911 or running to fetch Doc Mathers, not standing around like a bunch of hicks straight off the farm. But before Colt could voice his thoughts, Slate leaned over her, presenting a picture all too familiar.

Now the fairytale was complete. Slate and Hope. Star quarterback and homecoming queen. Colt waited for the prince of Bramble to kiss the princess awake, but instead Slate tapped her cheek in a way that didn't look all that princely.

"Come on now, wake up, Hog."

The nickname sent a stab of anger through Colt. But it was nothing compared to what he felt when those long, dark lashes fluttered open, and a dreamy smile slid across those rosy lips.

"Slate," Hope breathed with what could only be described as awed relief.

Slate grinned down at her. "What? Did Hollywood

turn you into a citified wimp? You used to take a punch a lot better than that, Hog."

Just that quickly, her smile slipped, and her gaze shot around the room until it hit Colt square in the gut. Those baby blues narrowed, and in one fluid motion, she swung her legs over the edge of the table and hopped down onto her scuffed brown cowboy boots.

"You hit me!" Hope yelled in a voice that made his head ache. She swung at him, but he caught her wrist, the bouquet of heavy-assed flowers cracking into his forearm with a painful thud.

Her other fist flew at the opposite side of his face, and he grabbed it too. With no hands left, her little cowboy boots started in, attacking his shins with a vengeance. It hurt like hell, but he wasn't about to let go of her hands, not in a room filled with heavy ceramic pigs. Of course, he didn't think about her knees until one came way too close for comfort.

Colt turned to the side to avoid having his voice changed three octaves and tried to figure out some way to contain the wildcat. Luckily, Hope's daddy, Burl, stepped up and placed a beefy arm around her waist, gently pulling her away.

"Settle down there, little girl, your mama's worried you're gonna hurt yourself."

Hurt herself? Colt was the one with a multitude of bruises. Not that anyone seemed to care. All eyes were on Hope, who still ranted and raved like a lunatic.

"You lowdown son of a snake! You smelly piece of Texas roadkill! You disreputable good-for-nothing motorcycle bum!"

It wasn't anything that he hadn't heard coming out of

Hope's mouth before, so he settled in and waited for her to run out of steam. He knew from experience that it could take awhile. But the rant was cut short when his baby sister pushed her way through the crowd.

"What in the world is going on here?" Shirlene sashayed over to Hope in her high heels and pretty gold dress. Next to Hope, she looked like an Amazon, a golden-haired Amazon with laughing green eyes. It had been only six months since he and Shirlene had met in Odessa to visit with their mama. Still, it looked as if his baby sister had grown even more beautiful since then.

As Shirlene set down the plastic cup of what looked like straight tequila, her gaze drifted down to the bouquet that dangled from Hope's arm. "Okay, so I see you caught the bouquet, but is that any reason to throw a temper tantrum? I mean, it's not like you're going to become Twyla."

"And just what is that supposed to mean, Shirlene Dalton?" Twyla huffed.

Shirlene lifted an eyebrow at the woman in the too-tight dress and piles of makeup. "Do I need to explain it, honey?" She turned back to Hope. "But it's only a bouquet, Hog. It's not like anyone's forcing you to get married."

"She ain't mad about the bouquet, Shirlene," Rachel Dean enlightened her. "She's mad because Colt knocked her out."

"Colt?" Shirlene turned and her gaze snagged him. "Colt!" In two steps, she was in his arms, and he had to say that it was nice to finally receive a warm welcome. "What are you doing here, honey?" she asked. She pulled back, all smiles, until her gaze settled on his lip. Then her face looked like a mama tiger that had just discovered her cub abused. "Who hit you?"

He tested his lip with his tongue and, tasting blood, used the back of his hand to wipe it off. "It's not a big deal. I made a mistake, is all." *More like numerous mistakes. The biggest was coming back to Bramble in the first place,* Colt thought.

"What kind of mistake?" Shirlene's eyes clouded with confusion. Colt knew exactly how she felt. He still wasn't quite sure what he had walked into.

"I think I can explain." Harley Sutter stepped up.

Harley was the mayor/judge/lawyer of Bramble, and as such, he had always taken it upon himself to be the town mouthpiece, a long-winded mouthpiece who could talk for days. Which was why Colt leaned back against the edge of the table and crossed his arms.

"It appears to me that this is a simple case of mistaken identity. Colt here—" Harley paused and gave Colt the disapproving look he'd always given him. "I thought you were in prison, son."

Colt tossed back his signature go-to-hell look. "I got out on good behavior."

Harley's eyes narrowed suspiciously before he rested his hands on a stomach that had seen too many nights of chicken-fried steak from Josephine's Diner and then continued. "Not being as perceptive as the rest of the town, Colt assumed that Faith was Hope." His gaze moved around the room. "Where is our little Faith, anyway?"

"Right here." The woman Colt had kissed stepped forward, and his eyes widened.

During the hoopla of the last few minutes, he'd convinced himself that, between lack of sleep and the hard ride, his mind had played a trick on him. But his mind hadn't tricked him at all. The blushing woman who stared back at him with innocent blue eyes looked identical to Hope—identical except for the short, honey-streaked brown hair that curled around her face.

"So you're Shirlene's brother," Faith said, without any twang whatsoever.

"Faith, this is my ornery brother, Colt Lomax," Shirlene made the introductions. "Colt, this is Faith Aldri—I mean, Faith Calhoun."

His gaze shot over to Hope, and their eyes locked for a brief second before she looked away. But a brief second was all he needed to read the turbulent emotions that swirled around in the endless blue eyes.

"It's nice to meet you, Colt," Faith said.

Since Colt had done a little more than meet her, he rubbed a hand over the back of his neck and stumbled through his mind for a way to apologize for cramming his tongue down her throat. "Nice to meet you, ma'am. And I'm real sorry about the confusion and all."

A tentative smile tipped the corners of her mouth, and she took a few steps closer. She looked so much like Hope that if he hadn't already been leaning against the table, he might've taken a few steps back.

"Apology accepted," she said in a voice so soft that he could barely hear her.

Colt cocked an eyebrow. She might look like Hope, but she sure didn't act like her. Hope had never accepted an apology from him in her life. Not that he'd ever given her one.

Those pretty eyes scrunched up. "Did you realize you're bleeding?" Before he could do more than nod, Faith jerked a couple napkins off a nearby table and dunked them in a cup. "I wish I had my disinfectant wipes, but this will have to do."

The first touch of the soaked napkins on his cut lip almost sent him straight through the ceiling tiles.

"Lord, woman!" He held a hand to his burning lip. "What the hell is on that?"

Her blue eyes widened before she glanced down at the napkin. "Water?"

"I think that would be Rachel Dean's Everclear, Faith," Slate said as he took the napkins from her hand. "But don't you worry, darlin', 150-proof liquor works just like your disinfectant wipes," his humor-filled eyes tracked over to Colt's, "just with a little more sting."

Faith shook her head, and the curls danced. "I'm so sorry...I thought—"

"Is someone going to tell me who hit my brother?" Shirlene cut in.

"I did," Slate stated.

Shirlene's eyes narrowed on him. But before she could let him have it, Rachel Dean jumped in.

"Only because he was kissin' Faith."

"More like devouring," Twyla added. "I got all hot and bothered just watchin'. 'Course after years in prison, a man must be pretty starved for female attention."

Something that sounded an awful lot like a growl came through Slate's teeth, and Colt braced himself for another go around. Although at this point, he would welcome a good fight. But his sister held up her hand before Slate could threw the next punch.

"So let me get this straight. Colt mistook Faith for Hope and laid one on her?" Shirlene asked. Without waiting for a reply, she started laughing like a crazy woman.

Always willing to laugh at a good joke, the town joined in. And, as annoyed as Colt was with the entire prison comment, he had to smile. The only person not laughing was Hope, whose eyes had turned as cold and icy as a North Dakota fishing pond in the dead of winter. And all that frigid hate was directed solely at him before she whirled and stomped off.

As usual, once Hope was gone, the townspeople didn't quite know what to do with themselves. Women looked at each other while men stuffed their hands in their pockets and studied the tiled floor. More than a few uncomfortable minutes passed before Harley took the bull by the horns.

"Well, what are we all standin' around for?" He nodded at Bud Mueller, who had always played a mean fiddle, and Bud hurried off, followed by the other band members. "Are we gonna let a little fight stop us from celebratin' Faith and Slate's weddin'?"

A chorus of *hell no*s rose up, and just that quickly, people dispersed, leaving Colt alone with his sister.

"Lord." Shirlene shook her head as she retrieved her cup and sat down at the table. "I leave for two seconds and miss all the good stuff."

"Believe me, it wasn't all that exciting." He sat down and grabbed a napkin and held it to his mouth.

"I guess after spending the last few years in prison, Bramble must seem awfully dull." Shirlene shot him a quirky little grin before she offered him her cup. When he shook his head, she pulled it back and took a deep drink. "I bet folks would be surprised to know you're such a teetotaler. Of course, folks would be surprised by a lot of things."

He sent her a warning look. "Things I'd just as soon you kept to yourself."

She ran a finger across her lips. "Sealed as tight as a drum."

Colt didn't need the reassurance. Shirlene could keep a secret. Which was a good thing, given their childhood.

Cradling the cup between her hands, she rested her elbows on the table. "So what brings you back to Bramble, big brother?"

"I missed my little sister."

She snorted. "I'd believe you, if it hadn't been eight years since you've been back."

"You got me." Colt winked at her before stretching the truth a little. "I'm on my way to Austin to deliver a bike and needed a bed for the night." Even though she was good at keeping secrets, there were still some things that she didn't need to know.

She sat up, splashing tequila on the gold satin of her dress. "One night? You're only staying one night?"

He hadn't even planned on staying that long. In fact, he hadn't planned on coming at all. One second, he was talking about a bike delivery, and the next thing he knew, he was passing by the WELCOME TO BRAMBLE sign on the same bike that should've been heading for Austin in a covered trailer.

"Hope is right," Shirlene huffed as she set down the cup and flopped back in the chair. "You are a lowdown motorcycle bum, Colt Lomax. The least you could do is stay a couple nights and keep your sister company."

"Lyle working a lot?"

"Too much."

Colt scowled. As much as he liked Shirlene's husband, the twenty-five-year age difference was still hard for him to swallow, especially when his sister didn't look all that happy. Of course, he could help with that. All he needed to do was stick around for a few days. Unfortunately, Colt had his own demons to deal with, and most of them resided right there in Bramble.

"I'll tell you what." He leaned his arms on the table. "How about if you come to Austin with me for a few days?"

"On the back of your chopper?"

He lifted one eyebrow. "I was thinking more of you meeting me there."

"Sort of like you meet me other places—you get there three days late and leave three days early. No, thanks. Besides, I don't want to go to Austin. I want you to stay right here with me in Bramble and do all the fun things we used to do as kids."

Fun things? Colt couldn't think of one fun thing he'd done as a kid. Still, not wanting to bust his sister's bubble, he held his tongue and let her continue.

"It will be just like old times, especially with Hope back in town. Except now, with Faith here, it will be double the fun. You're going to love Faith. She's Hope, but nice."

Colt laughed. "I gathered. So who is she?"

"Hope's twin sister, who Jenna gave away at birth."

The news surprised Colt. Not the twin part—that was obvious—but the giving away part. Jenna Scroggs had always been the perfect mother. The kind who baked cookies and played hide-and-go-seek and read books and bandaged scraped knees. The kind who was the complete opposite of Colt's and Shirlene's inattentive mama.

As if reading his thoughts, Shirlene nodded. "I know. It was hard for me to believe too. But I think people forget that she was only fifteen when she had Hope and Faith. She and Burl weren't married, or even out of high school. And you remember how hard it was for them back then. They were in the same boat as we were."

Not quite. Their boat had sailed, while he and Shirlene had remained behind.

"So how did Hope take the news that she had a twin?" he asked.

"Not well, especially when Slate ended up falling for Faith."

His gaze shifted to the dance floor, where half the town waltzed in a circle around the happy couple. While the sight gave him a certain satisfaction that justice had been served, a part of him almost felt betrayed. In a life where he had learned to count on nothing, Slate marrying Hope had been one of the few things he'd counted on. Which didn't explain his initial anger, or the kiss. But, years ago, Colt had given up trying to explain his behavior where Hope was concerned. Like Bramble, she brought out the worst in him.

Even knowing this, he still couldn't stop himself from scanning the crowd as he talked with Shirlene and all through the windy speech Harley made before the new-lyweds headed out the door. He continued looking for her long after the drunks sobered up, and the ceramic pigs were boxed away, and the plastic dishes were rolled inside the ugly purple tablecloths and tossed into the trash.

Funny, but Colt hadn't taken Hope for the type to turn tail and run. But that's exactly what it looked like she'd done. And maybe she had the right idea. Maybe the best thing for him to do would be to hop on his bike and get the hell out of Dodge. He didn't know why he'd stopped here, but nothing good would come of it. Bramble was a part of his past, and he needed to keep it that way. Shirlene would be upset, but he would make it up to her by spending the holidays with her—anywhere but Bramble.

Outside, he found the night had grown chilly. It would be a cold ride to Austin, but he didn't mind. While most people found comfort in a cozy home, out of the elements, Colt preferred the open road. No ties or responsibilities, just miles of blacktop and freedom.

Parked up on the sidewalk, right beneath the town hall's flagpole and right next to the dedication plaque, sat the custom chopper he'd been working on for the last few months. It was a slick machine with a hot custom paint job and chrome exhaust and wheels that gleamed in the light from the overhead streetlight like high-polished mirrors. It wasn't as fancy as some, but Colt had never gone for show as much as go. This baby had a 124-cubic-inch motor and a six-speed transmission, and just hearing it rev made Colt proud as hell.

After slipping on his leather jacket, he started up the bike and circled around the courtyard of the town hall. The loud, unbaffled engine had people stepping out the doors to investigate, his sister one of them. When Shirlene saw him, she didn't look surprised. Obviously, she knew him too well.

"Remember I love yew, big brother!" she yelled, over the throbbing noise. He might've paid more attention to the devious gleam in his sister's eyes if the woman in purple satin hadn't caught his attention.

Hope stood next to the big maple tree, her dress crumpled and her hair limp. In the shade of the tree, he couldn't see her eyes, but he didn't need to. Her arrogant stance said it all. The unyielding strength of such a little bit of sass made him smile. Even after her lifelong beau had chosen somebody else, Hope would not be defeated. He admired that about her. Would always admire it. He touched a hand to his forehead in a salute to both of the women who had made such an impression on his life.

Then he twisted the throttle and shot off the curb, the thick 240 mm back tire bouncing down to the asphalt. Unfortunately, that was as far as he got before Sheriff Winslow's patrol car came barreling around the corner with lights flashing and siren blaring to cut him off.

Chapter Three

"HOPE, HONEY?"

"Shit!" Hope slapped a hand to her chest and turned to her daddy, who sat at the table in the dark dining room. With her heart thumping guiltily, she plastered on a smile. "Oh, hi, Daddy. I didn't realize you were still up."

"Your mama's snorin' gets worse when she drinks, so I had trouble gettin' to sleep. What are you doin' up?"

"Uhhh," she tried not to glance back at the front door she'd been headed to. "I was just checking to see if Jenna Jay, Tessa, and Dallas got home okay."

"Jenna Jay slept over at her friend's house. And Tessa and your brother are passed out cold." Her daddy shook his head. "'Course, when I was younger I did the same thing—weddin's are a perfect excuse to tie one on."

Especially if the bride was supposed to be you, Hope thought. Unfortunately, every time that Hope had reached for a drink, she had been grabbed by one dancing fool or another.

Her father held up what appeared to be a half-eaten Ding Dong. "You care to join your old daddy?"

Unable to help herself, Hope glanced back at the door. "No, thank you, Daddy. Now that I know everyone's home safe and sound, I guess I'll head on back to bed. I wouldn't want to sleep through church tomorrow."

"I suppose you're right." Her daddy polished off the rest of the Ding Dong and then downed the last of his milk before he pushed back from the table. "Although if I want to get any shut-eye, I'll have to use my earplugs."

Since that would make escape much easier, Hope nodded. "That's a good idea, Daddy." She lifted a hand. "Well, good night." She hurried back down the dark hallway, but her father proved that he was still as quick on his size-fourteen feet as he'd been when he played high school football. Before she could close her bedroom door, his big frame filled the doorway.

"Your mama says you've been makin' lists again."

Damn. She knew she should've taken her trash out. Luckily, all that was written on the numerous crumpled pieces of paper were four words—*Hope's New Life Plan.*

Trying to make light of it, she chuckled. "You know I've always been a list-making fool, Daddy."

"And that's exactly what I told your mama—our little Hope Marie don't do nothin' without a list. But that didn't seem to make her feel any better. She thinks you're gettin' ready to run off again on some wild tangent." He paused and stared down at her for a few excruciating seconds. "Now I realize things didn't work out exactly like you had planned." He cleared his throat. "But me and your mama sure wish you'd stick around for awhile."

Touched, she stood on her tiptoes and gave him a hug. "I love you, Daddy."

"I love you, too, princess." He awkwardly patted her back, then turned and lumbered down the hallway.

Hope waited in the darkness of her room until she figured her daddy was ear-plugged and tucked in tight before she slipped out and headed for the front door.

The night air was cooler than she thought it would be. But she welcomed the stiff breeze that rustled the crisp autumn leaves of the elms and cottonwoods as she headed into town. As she walked, her father's words came back to her. No, her life hadn't turned out the way she had planned, and she couldn't figure out where things had gone wrong.

Her plan had made perfect sense. She would go to Hollywood and become a famous movie star while Slate stayed there and concentrated on his coaching career. Then, once she had fame and fortune, she would return to Bramble and marry the hometown hero, who would be more than happy to let her make the occasional blockbuster as long as she returned during football season.

Okay, so maybe she should've called more often. Or come back on weekends. But she had been terrified that Slate, and everyone else in town, would find out that while she'd shone on the performing arts stage at Bramble High, in L.A. she was just a mediocre actress with a thick Texas twang.

So she had stayed. Unable to accept defeat, Hope suffered through long, grueling auditions with rude, critical casting directors. She'd forked over hundreds for acting lessons and voice coaches and basically had tried to fit a country square into a Hollywood star. All while she hustled tables at any restaurant or bar that would put up with her taking off for auditions or jobs.

Not that she landed many jobs. Her biggest job had been the hemorrhoid commercial. And she'd only gotten it because the casting director was an extremely short guy who had trouble finding women his own size to date. She had to suffer through a boring dinner listening to the guy's many "accomplishments" before the commercial was filmed and she got the first check, a check that didn't stretch quite far enough.

Despite these challenges, she would probably still be in California if she hadn't completely lost her mind one night. Waking up alone in a cheap motel room had forced her into reevaluating her entire life plan and making a few minor adjustments. Like accepting the fact that she couldn't act and returning home to marry the man she was destined to be with—the kind of man who would never leave her or let her down.

When she returned to Bramble and was welcomed home like the prodigal daughter, Hope figured she'd made the right choice. After years of feeling like a piece of chewed-up gum on the sole of a flip-flop, it was an overwhelming relief to be back with people who loved and adored her—adored her so much that they had already planned her wedding. It seemed a little fast, but since that was why she came home, she couldn't very well back out. So she stepped up to the plate. Except, when she got ready to swing, she discovered someone else had hit the home run and won the game, someone who hadn't wasted five years trying to prove she was more than just a small-town girl. Someone who at that very moment was enjoying her honeymoon with Hope's only backup plan.

The thought riled Hope so much she forgot to pay attention to where she was walking and almost fell into the big pothole at the corner of Maple and Main. Sidestepping the hole, she hopped up on the sidewalk and headed down Main Street. Past the post office on the corner with the big red-and-blue mailbox out front—the same mailbox she and Shirlene had dropped their unfinished Popsicles into as kids, for which they had received a stern lecture from Miguel the Postmaster about federal crimes. Past the Halloween-decorated window of Sutter's Pharmacy, where she had bought her first tube of mascara. And past Duds N Such, where she and her sisters had browsed through racks of jeans while her daddy salivated over John Deere mowers.

With her old fuzzy slippers thumping softly against her heels, Hope continued down the street. Past the city park with its patchy grass that always needed more water and the small Catholic church that never quite caught on. Past Josephine's Diner, the pink-painted caboose where Hope had worked for years, serving up chicken-fried steak.

She didn't slow down until she reached the one-story brick building located on the other side of the town hall, a building that was completely dark—except for one tiny square of light.

The wind picked up, loosening a few strands of hair from her ponytail and rattling the chain against the town hall flagpole. A chill tiptoed down her spine, and she shivered. Given that she wore nothing but a skinny-strapped cami and thin cotton pajama bottoms in the middle of October, it wasn't surprising. Except the goose bumps that covered her bare arms didn't come from the outside temperature as much as from the cold knot that settled in the pit of her stomach, warning her of imminent danger.

And as she stood in front of the city jail, she knew exactly what that danger was.

Colt Lomax.

Just the name made her want to scream out a very nasty cuss word. She glared at the light spilling out from the small barred window. Why couldn't Shirlene just let her brother stop for a quick visit? Why did she have to have him arrested? The man was ornerier than a cornered jaguar, and prodding him only made him worse—something Hope knew from experience.

No, the best thing to do for a caged wild animal was to set it free.

Hope glanced around, then quickly headed down the path that led to the double-glassed doors of the jail. She didn't expect them to be locked, and she wasn't disappointed. No one in Bramble locked anything, probably because there wasn't anything in Bramble worth stealing.

Hurrying through the dark reception area, she made a quick stop in Sheriff Winslow's office and then headed down the dark hallway to the only jail cell.

Like any good Christian woman of Bramble, Hope knew the way. More than once, she'd come with her mama to deliver Bibles to the poor lost souls who found themselves behind bars. Not that Bramble had a lot of criminals. Most of the Bibles had gone to Elmer Tate, who slept it off in jail every time he got drunk rather than go home to his wife, who had a mean right hook. Despite his love of Jack Daniel's, Elmer was a nice man who would always drop the Bibles back at First Baptist so the women could redistribute them.

Being the town troublemaker, Colt had gotten his fair share of Bibles too. Though Lord only knew what he'd done with them.

At the end of the hallway, Hope pushed through another unlocked door and into the room that housed the jail. But how anyone could call it that was beyond her. Except for the bars, the cell looked like a country bed and breakfast. Up against one wall was a brass bed with fluffy down pillows, a wedding-ring quilt, and crisp, flowered sheets that matched the curtains on the window. The white porcelain toilet was sparkling clean and had an air freshener on the back and a fuzzy blue cover for the lid. The sink had a Dixie cup dispenser and small mirror hanging above it, a mirror Colt was using as he cleaned the blood from his lip.

The door clicked shut behind her, and he turned. And for a split second, Hope had the urge to run for her life. No wonder the folks of Bramble thought he'd been in prison. The man looked like he belonged behind bars—an unscrupulous outlaw who spent his days robbing trains and his nights stealing the hearts of loose women. Wind-tousled black hair fell almost to his shoulders, and the stubble on his square jaw looked even thicker than it had a few hours earlier. Those steely gray eyes stared back at her, the whites bloodshot from booze or lack of sleep, or possibly both.

Suddenly, she didn't feel cold anymore.

"Deliverin' Bibles, sweetheart?" The dark slashes of his eyebrows lifted. The sarcasm in his deep, smooth voice snapped her out of her outlaw fantasy and back to loser reality.

"As if reading the Bible would do your black soul any good." She pushed away from the door. "I'm here to get you out."

"A jailbreak? Funny, but I thought you were the reason I was here in the first place. Mean Colt Lomax beat up sweet little Hope Scroggs."

"Don't blame me, Lomax. I wasn't the one who got Sam after you. Not that you didn't deserve it, after hitting me." She felt only a second of remorse over the lie. She was well aware of what had hit her, but she just wasn't about to let Colt get off so easily. Not when he had hurt her plenty in her lifetime.

"A jailbreak, huh?" He took a few steps closer to the bars, and it was a challenge for her to keep from taking a step back. "So what's your plan? Dynamite? A bulldozer? A file pulled from those silken locks?"

"I was thinking more of a key." She held up the heavy key ring.

One corner of his mouth flirted with a smile. "A key. What an ingenious plan."

Ignoring his sarcasm, she walked over to the lock and started trying keys. It was a daunting task, considering there had to be enough keys there for every unlocked door in Bramble, so many that she had trouble remembering which ones she'd tried. Especially with Colt standing there watching.

"You're not kidding, are you?"

She glanced up into a pair of curious gray eyes. "I realize you skipped school more than you attended, but does it look like I'm kidding?"

Those eyes narrowed. "So what's in it for you?"

"What else? I get you out of my hair."

So quickly that she couldn't avoid it, he reached through the bars and snagged a lock of her hair that had fallen over her shoulder from the low ponytail.

"I guess a man could get lost in this." He rubbed it between his fingers.

The sight made her stomach do a crazy flip before she

jerked her hair back, leaving a few strands entwined in his rough biker fingers. "Stop screwing around."

"But I like screwing around." Those dark brows lifted. "Remember?"

Her face flushed hot. "Do you always have to be such a smartass?"

"Weren't those our roles in high school?" He pointed a finger at her. "Homecoming queen." He touched his chest. "Smartass."

"Loser, is more like it." She went back to the keys, but damned if she hadn't lost her place again.

Luckily, Colt had always been easily bored. After only a few minutes, he walked over to the bed, where he stretched out on Granny Lou's quilt and propped his hands behind his head. It was hard to take her eyes off all the miles of muscle that rippled the black cotton shirt and soft jeans.

"So are you cold?"

At his words, the keys slipped through her fingers and clanked to the floor as her gaze flashed back to his face.

"What?"

His head turned toward her, and those gray eyes slithered down to her chest. "Cold."

She glanced down to the beaded nipples that poked through the soft white cotton of her cami. She crossed her arms over her chest and glared back at him.

"You are a sick pervert, Colt Lomax."

He shrugged. "I only take what's offered."

Not wanting him to think she offered anything, she tugged the ponytail holder out and slipped it over her wrist before adjusting her hair over her chest.

"The hair should've been a dead giveaway," he stated.

She glanced over at him.

He had rolled to his side, his head propped up on his hand. "The mistake I made with your sister—I should've known you would never cut your hair."

Thankful to be off the subject of her boobs, Hope shrugged as she picked up the key ring and tried another key. "I thought about it once. I even went to a salon in L.A. with the intention of whacking it all off."

"What happened?"

"I chickened out."

There was a long pause before he spoke.

"I'm glad."

Her gaze shot over to him. She might've taken it as a compliment if she hadn't known better. "This coming from a man who used to refer to my hair as a matted possum pelt."

He flashed her a full-fledged smile. Since it wasn't something he did often, the blinding radiance took her by surprise. "And you think a skinned possum would look better?"

With her insides boiling, she went on the offensive. "As if I care what a lowlife motorcycle bum thinks. Why don't you get a job, Lomax, and quit being a blight on society?"

"Because I believe the fewer the responsibilities, the freer the man."

"And you are about the freest man I know," she said as she continued to try the keys. "Of course, you wouldn't be so free if you didn't have Lyle Dalton's money to spend."

"Is that where you think I get my money?"

She glanced up. "Isn't it?"

Seconds ticked by as he stared at her. Finally he relaxed back against the pillows and rested his hands over his chest. "You found me out, honey. Luckily, old Lyle doesn't seem to care."

The truth shouldn't have bothered her. But it did. Just another reason she needed to get him out of town as quickly as possible. Thankfully, the next key worked.

Twisting the lock open, she pulled back the barred door. "Come on. We don't have much time." She pulled the key out of the lock and moved over to the outer door. "Regardless of the wedding, the churchgoers get up bright and early on Sunday. But since you have never attended church, you probably don't know that."

"I go to church."

Hope turned to find him standing close behind her, his hand braced against the door that she'd just cracked open. It was one thing to have a row of bars separating her from all the testosterone-pumped maleness, and another to have it inches from her nose. Startled, she dropped the keys, and they slid out into the hallway.

"I call it the Church of Our Lady of the Highway." Colt released the heavy door, and it clicked closed as he tipped up her chin. "You should've put ice on it. It would've helped with the swelling."

"I did," she breathed, her voice betraying her quivery insides.

"By the looks of it, not long enough." He shook his head and gently brushed his thumb over the bump. "You never did have a lick of patience."

It took a second for Hope to find her voice. "Which is exactly why I want you out of this town as quickly as possible."

Colt leaned down, and his cheek brushed against hers in a slide of prickly heat. "Now why is that, I wonder?" His breath fell soft and warm against her ear, and everything inside her seemed to still in anticipation of what he'd do next.

Except he didn't do anything. He didn't have to. Just his mere presence was enough to make her head fill with thoughts that had no business being there. Naughty thoughts that involved the rugged outlaw in front of her and the soft mattress behind him.

She took a deep, steadying breath. But it was a mistake. While most guys in town doused themselves in whatever country-singer-endorsed cologne was popular at the time, Colt had always smelled like soap and detergent beneath a layer of grease and gasoline, a powerfully strong mixture that never failed to make Hope light-headed.

Although now the grease and gasoline weren't as strong as another scent—a raw masculinity lacking in his youth. It was this scent that drew her like a moth to a porch light on a hot summer night. But, refusing to get her wings singed, she slipped beneath his arm and stepped around him. In an attempt to slow her heart rate, she moved over to the sink and washed her hands.

"Still avoiding my touch, Hog?" he asked from behind her.

"At all costs." She tried to keep her voice even, but it still came out shaky and a little breathless. "And don't call me that. Only my friends call me that."

"And just where in the hell do you think they got it?"

Confused, Hope turned back to him, her hands dripping water on the rag rug in the center of the floor. If it was possible, he looked even more dangerous than he had only moments before.

"You're lying," she stated with a firmness that she didn't quite feel. "Slate made it up."

Colt studied her for only a few seconds before he tipped his head. "Of course, Slate. Who else would come up with such a sweet moniker for his girlfriend?" He rested a shoulder on the frame of the barred door. "So what does he call Faith? Frog . . . or maybe just Wife."

The arrow struck with a reverberating thunk.

"I'd shut up if I was you," she growled.

His eyes widened with innocence. "What? Did I hit a sore spot? Is Hope Scroggs a little pissed at her twin sister for stealing her boyfriend?"

Forgetting about drying her hands, she headed for the door. Unfortunately, his big body blocked it.

"Get out of my way," she ordered.

Colt shook his head. "Not until you fess up."

"There is nothing to fess up to."

He crossed his arms over his chest, bringing her attention to the tattoos that covered his arm from shirt sleeve to wrist. "How about being so pissed off your head is about ready to explode? You're practically shaking from all the suppressed anger. So go ahead. Let it out. Scream and rant and rave about how your life has been ruined because Slate Calhoun, the hero of Bramble, found someone he liked better."

"Shut up!"

"Or maybe he didn't find anyone he liked better. Maybe he just got tired of waiting around for you?"

"The only thing I'm going to let out is how much I hate you! You have always been a burr on my butt, Colt Lomax, and you still are!"

Hope ducked under his arm and would've made it past him if he hadn't grabbed a hank of her hair.

"Let me go!" she yelled, but he had always been a poor listener. He wrapped the strands around his fist and reeled her in. Hope refused to give in that easily, and she stretched out and grabbed onto one of the bars. Unfortunately, the bar she grabbed onto was connected to the door, and as she was tugged backwards, the door slammed closed behind them with a loud clang.

Her hair was released.

"Did you . . . ?"

Colt's words hung there until Hope let out a high-pitched squeal.

"No!" She raced over to the bars and jerked on them, but they didn't budge an inch. Not one inch. She searched around for the keys before she remembered that they were lying on the floor on the other side of the door.

She whirled around to let him have it, but stopped at the sight of him pulling his shirt up. It was hard to talk when confronted with a washboard stomach that she could play with a spoon.

"What are you doing?" she squeaked.

"Going to bed." The shirt inched higher before she snapped out of her sexual haze and jerked it back down.

"Have you lost your mind? We have to find a way out of here!" She looked around the tiny cell for anything that would help her escape. But she could find no use for a Dixie dispenser, a pile of *Field and Stream* magazines, or a crocheted doll toilet paper cover. And what infuriated her even more was that he didn't seem at all concerned about the situation, probably because he'd spent so much time behind these bars that it was like home to him.

"We?" He bounced down on the bed and propped his hands beneath his head, fortunately with his shirt still on. "Since I'm not the one who locked us in here, I don't see how that's my job."

"No! You were just the idiot who caused me to slam the door in the first place!"

He shrugged. "All right, I'll give you that one. So you want me to get us out of here?"

"Forget it!" She paced the cell, her slippers flopping. "Lord knows, I wouldn't want you to hurt yourself."

"If you say so, honey." He tugged the quilt up. "But could you turn out the light before you come to bed?"

"I'm not coming to bed. I'm going to find a way out of here if it kills me!" She sent him her most determined look. He must've read it perfectly, because he released a long, heavy sigh.

"Well, hell." In one fluid motion, he was off the bed, had the light off, and her hefted over his shoulder.

"Put me down!" She kicked and swung at him, but she couldn't do much damage in the two strides it took to get to the bed. He tossed her down on the mattress, and before she could sit up, he bounced down next to her and clamped an arm around her waist.

"Now believe me, honey, when I tell you that I've always found your temper tantrums entertaining. But after riding for close to twenty hours, getting my bell rung, my shins kicked, and tossed into jail for no damned good reason, my patience is running a little thin. So I think the smart thing for you to do right now is to be quiet and go to sleep."

"I'm not going to sleep with you!"

"Then don't sleep—I don't give a damn. But you're not getting out of this bed until the sun shines through that window up there."

She made one more attempt at getting loose, but he only tugged her closer and flung one very hard thigh over her legs.

"You are the same arrogant jerk you were in high school," she huffed.

"And you're the same spoiled brat."

"I'm not spoiled."

He stuffed a pillow under his head, while his other arm remained firmly tucked around her waist. "I don't know what you would call it. You have an entire town doing your bidding."

Accepting the fact that she wasn't going anywhere, she relaxed and allowed her arms to flop over the corded muscles of his forearm. "Not the entire town."

"No, I guess you're right." And with that, he pressed his face into her matted possum pelt and went to sleep.

Hope lay awake, trying to figure out how she had ended up in bed with Colt Lomax. Again.

Chapter Four

HOPE SCROGGS WAS a cuddle bug.

Who would've guessed it? Certainly not Colt. Not after a lifetime of watching the sassy, independent woman strut around Bramble as if she owned the place. Which she pretty much did. At least, every heart in Bramble belonged to Hope.

Except one—one lone heart that wasn't stupid enough to give itself to such a stubborn wildcat. No, his heart didn't belong to her, but other parts of his body could be persuaded to. Especially when she was plastered against his chest like a nice custom paint job, miles of rich brown hair spilling down his sides like bronze metallic flames. How did such a small woman grow hair so thick and gorgeous?

He gently ran his hand through the tangled mass. He could bathe in it, wrap himself in the satin strands twice over and drown beneath the silken waves. Bringing it to his nose, he breathed deeply. The scent, faint but familiar, was a mix between earthy woman and sweet berries. As far back as he could remember, Hope always smelled like berries. Smelled and tasted.

Smoothing the hair back from her face, he studied her lips. They were about as perfect a pair as he had seen. Not too plump and not to skinny, with two cute little peaks that just begged for some lovin'. And since he had never been a man to refuse a woman's plea, he leaned down and brushed his lips over hers. Not a deep kiss, just a settling of firm flesh against soft.

"Mmmm." She hummed against his mouth, sending a sizzling shaft of heat straight to his crotch.

Liking the direction things were heading, Colt deepened the kiss. But just as he was about to slip into all that warmth, her eyes blinked open. Up close, they were bluer than he remembered—a mixture of cobalt and azure that would elude the most talented artist's airbrush. They stared back at him, all sleep-drugged and baffled. And for a moment, he got lost. Unfortunately, a moment was all it took for her to remember where she was…and who he was. When she did, she pulled away, taking all that wet heat and mind-altering blue with her.

"You!"

He figured she was about to tack on a few descriptive words. But before she could, her gaze shifted up to the sun shining in through the window. Her eyes widened, and she scrambled off the bed and started searching for her slippers.

"Why did you let me sleep so late? They'll be here any minute to give you breakfast."

Since it looked like the fun was over, he rolled to his feet. "Eight o'clock on the dot. And with my stomach touching my backbone, I'm sure looking forward to some homemade biscuits and gravy."

"No!" She stared at him as if he had lost his mind. "Don't you see? I can't be found in here with you."

"You could always tell them you came to save my black soul." He moved over to the toilet and unzipped his pants.

"If we could just find a hairpin—" She hesitated at the first splash. "Are you...?"

At her shocked voice, he glanced over his shoulder into her bright red face.

"Draining the lizard? Emptying the fuel tank? Taking a piss—?"

"I get it!" She whirled around and started searching the corners as far from him as she could get.

He grinned. Sex would've been a lot funnier, but he had to admit that teasing Hope was pretty darned fun.

After using the bathroom, he washed his hands and rinsed out his mouth before he picked up the washcloth and cleaned away the blood that he'd missed the night before. The cut on his lip had started to scab over and in a few days wouldn't even be noticeable. He rubbed a hand over his beard. He could sure use a shave. He wondered how long Shirlene planned on keeping him locked up. Talk about a spoiled brat. Still, he had told her that he would stay the night, which was why he had gone along with Sheriff Winslow without a fight. If she wanted him to stay so badly that she had him tossed in jail, he figured he could at least give her a day.

One day wouldn't hurt anything.

He turned around to find Hope on her hands and knees, scouring every inch of the concrete floor. He had to give it to her. She was tenacious. Tenacious and damned sexy in the pink pajama bottoms sheer enough to see that she wasn't wearing any panties.

Offered such a nice view, he figured he had a few more

minutes to spare before he headed over to Shirlene's. He flopped down on the bed and stacked his hands behind his head. Hope had never had much in the boob department, but what she lacked up top she made up for downstairs with an ass so sweet and tight that it made his mouth water. It was a darn shame her tenacity paid off as quickly as it did.

"I found one!" She jumped up and held out what looked to be a skinny silver straight pin.

He squinted. "Uh, I hate to disappoint you, honey. But that's not going to work. A hairpin, maybe. A paper clip, even better. But a little bitty straight pin, no way."

Her eyes narrowed. "Being as how you spent more than a few nights here, I probably should take your word for it. Except you never were good at setting goals and achieving them."

"And just what goals would those be?"

"Any goals—sports—high school—college." She strutted over to the bars and squatted down, showing a hint of butt crack that caused all the moisture to evaporate from his mouth.

"The only things you put any effort in were motorcycles and women." She slipped the pin into the lock, and with each wiggle, the elastic waistband inched down, then back up.

Colt swallowed hard. What were they talking about?

"Not that the loose women in this town made you work real hard," she continued, although he no longer could comprehend a single word. Not with her pajamas playing peek-a-boo butt crack. She stretched even further and revealed so much butt cleavage that a moan escaped his lips.

She swiveled around. "What's wrong?"

He cleared his throat—twice—before he could speak.

"Nothing." He patted his stomach. "Just hungry, is all."

Sending him a skeptical look, Hope went back to lock-picking. "Is that all you can think about, Lomax—physical satisfaction?"

Pretty much. At least, that was all he could think about at the moment; the satisfaction of filling his hands with those sweet cheeks. Unfortunately, he had learned from past experience that giving into temptation was extremely bad for his health. Which meant he needed to get out of there before his body overruled his brain.

He sat up. "You about spent, honey?"

"No. I just about got it. All I need is a little more... Damn it!" She bent over and searched the floor, giving Colt a view that almost sent him to his knees.

Luckily, before he could start begging, she turned and flopped back against the bars, sending him a look that wasn't all that friendly.

"Is it too much to ask for you to get off your butt and help me out?"

He lifted his eyebrows. "You want me to help? Because I thought you had your heart set on doing it all by your lonesome."

Hope gritted her teeth. "The only thing I have my heart set on is getting you out of this town as quickly as possible and the hell away from me!"

"In that case." He rolled to his feet and walked over to the picture of the Texas state flag that hung on the wall. Reaching behind the frame, he felt around until he found the paper clip stuck in between the bricks.

"What are you doing?" she asked as he walked over with the stretched-out piece of wire.

"Granting your wish, honey." He winked at her before he knelt on the cold concrete and slipped his arm through the bars. It had been a lot easier when he was a skinny kid. Now that his biceps barely fit, it took a little more concentration. Which was close to impossible with Hope standing there tapping a foot.

"Are you telling me that you could've broken us out last night?"

"No." He wiggled the end of the paper clip in the lock.

"Don't you dare lie to me, Colt Lomax! Not when the proof is right in front of my eyes."

There was a click as the lock released, and he pushed the door open.

Straightening, Colt turned to her. "Now how could a no-account motorcycle bum break us out of jail when a spoiled control freak already had a plan?"

"Oooo!" Hope stomped her foot before she flopped past him. "You have always loved making a fool of me."

"Maybe because it's so easy to do."

"Easy for a troublemaker with mischief on his mind." She jerked open the outer door, her elbow jabbing him hard in the stomach. "And don't think I don't know that you were the one behind all those mean pranks that happened to me."

"I don't know what pranks you're talking about."

She bent over to pick up the keys. "The frogs in my bed. The garter snakes in my lunch box. The huge rubber pig on the homecoming semi. My bra hoisted up on the town hall flagpole. The live ammo in the prop gun of my senior play."

"Live ammo in a prop gun? You really think I'd be that devious?"

Hope glared over her shoulder as she stomped down the hallway. "I don't think so! I know!"

Colt followed her at a more leisurely pace, partly so she wouldn't see his grin and partly because he wasn't in any hurry. The night in Bramble hadn't been so bad after all. Although the company could've been a little sweeter. Of course, he had never liked things too sweet. He preferred his coffee black and bitter. His food spicy and hot.

And his women . . .

His gaze followed her cute little butt as it slipped into Sheriff Winslow's office, then back out again.

And his women warm and willing.

Something Hope would never be.

Outside the jailhouse, it was a nice autumn day. Not too hot and not too cool, with blue skies that stretched on forever. Summer in West Texas could be hot, dry, and brutal. But autumn made a man feel like hopping on a motorcycle and cruising down to Fredericksburg for some peaches or over to Austin for some good blues or down to San Antonio to mingle with the spirits of heroes.

Of course, in order to do that, you needed to have a motorcycle to hop on to. And looking around the parking lot, it didn't appear that he did.

"Where's my bike?"

The words were spoken more to himself than to Hope, who was already half a block away. It didn't take him long to catch up with her short legs and to step in front of her.

"Where's my bike?"

"How would I know?" She tried to sidestep him but he met her, steel toe to matted fur.

"So you were going to break me out of jail with no form of transportation?"

"I figured you could handle that part of the plan." She flipped a hand in the air. "Which was really crazy of me, considering you don't seem to be able to handle any part of any plan."

His eyebrows lifted. "I got us out, didn't I?"

"About four hours too late!" She whirled and started back down the street. As he watched those silly little slippers eat up the concrete, he realized she was probably right. He shouldn't have spent an hour alone with her, let alone four. Which didn't explain why he hurried to catch back up.

"Josie still make the best red chili this side of the Pecos?" It was a stupid thing to say, but with less than four hours of sleep and no coffee, it was the best he could come up with. It seemed to work, because she stopped and stared at him.

"Oh, no." She waggled a finger beneath his nose. "You're not eating breakfast here. You're finding your motorcycle and leaving, A-S-A-P."

"And just how do you expect me to find it when I don't know where the hell Sheriff Winslow put it?"

She thought for a moment before her eyes lit up. "Kenny drove it off."

"Kenny Gene got on my chopper!"

Since he had never been much of a yeller, Hope blinked. "How else do you think they were going to get it out of the middle of the street?"

He hadn't thought about that. He'd been too pissed off to do more than fantasize about getting his hands around his sister's neck. And Hope's. Agitated, he ran a hand through his hair, but he should've known better than to show any weakness around his arch nemesis.

"Aww, does the big, bad biker not like to share his toys?"

Damn straight, he didn't like to share his toys. Especially with some hick who didn't know the time and effort put into one of his bikes. But he wasn't about to let Hope know how pissed he was.

"So you think Kenny has it?"

"Probably." She started walking again. "Unless he wrapped it around a telephone pole." She shot a sly glance over her shoulder. "He was pretty drunk last night."

"Funny."

"I thought so." She grinned, showing off her crooked incisor. Besides her disposition, it was her only flaw. But Colt had never viewed it as such. For some reason, he found it endearing and extremely sexy.

"So are you going to give me a lift out to Kenny's?" he asked, in an attempt to get his rebellious mind on other things.

"Do I have a choice?"

"Not if you want me gone, you don't."

"Fine."

It was the first time Hope had ever conceded anything to him, and his enjoyment of the day increased tenfold—even if the concession had to do with getting rid of him.

And as they walked together down the uneven sidewalk, Colt took the time to look around.

Bramble had changed little over the years. There was the pharmacy, where he'd swiped more than his fair share of Fireballs and Bazooka bubble gum. The Duds N Such, where he drooled over a pair of lizard cowboy boots. And Josephine's Diner, where he worked every night after leaving Jones' Garage. But what *had* changed was his feeling about the town. What had once seemed as suffocating as a wet wool blanket now felt, if not welcoming, at least familiar.

"I guess they still have the Parade of Queens," he said as they walked along.

"According to Mama, every year."

"Minus the most popular homecoming queen."

Hope glanced over at him. "If you are referring to me, then yes. Although I hear my sister filled in for me this year."

He expected to see a thundercloud settle over her features. Instead, she laughed. It had been a while since he'd heard the deep, husky sound or felt the warmth it caused deep down in his belly.

"I have to say that's one thing I'll gladly give her," she said.

"Not the hog-calling trophies?"

"Are you kidding? I don't share my trophies with anyone," she mimicked his earlier response to Kenny riding his bike.

"I don't think hog-calling trophies are in the same league with eighty-thousand-dollar motorcycles."

She halted in mid-strut and stared up at him with eyes the same color as the sky above them. "Do you mean to tell me that motorcycle cost you close to a hundred thousand dollars?"

"It's worth that, and then some."

"Have you lost your mind, Colt Lomax?"

He grinned down at her and shrugged. "Some people think so."

"Hey, Hope!"

Startled, they turned and looked down the street.

Kenny Gene stood out in the parking lot of Josephine's Diner, a parking lot filled to the brim with dust-covered trucks and dinged-up American-made cars.

"Oh, hell," Hope grumbled under her breath, but it only took a second for her to recover and wave and smile like the true homecoming queen she was. "Hey, Kenny Gene! We was just talkin' about yew." She spread the Texas twang on thick as peanut butter. "You wouldn't know where Colt's motorcycle is, would yew?"

"Shore do!" he yelled back.

"And just where would that be, Kenny?" Colt asked.

"Well, hey, Colt! I didn't see you standin' there."

It wasn't surprising. Colt had always been invisible to the people of Bramble, especially when standing next to the town sweetheart.

"So where is it?" Hope asked.

"Where's what?"

Damn, Colt had forgotten how annoying the folks of Bramble could be.

"So where is my motorcycle, Kenny?"

"Oh, I can't tell you that. Shirlene would have my hide." His eyes narrowed. "Hey, ain't you supposed to be in the town jail?"

"I'm going to kill him," Hope said through her teeth.

"Only if you beat me to it." Colt stepped off the curb with every intention of grabbing Kenny up by his stiff western shirt and shaking the information out of him. Unfortunately, before he could, the mayor came out of Josephine's.

"Hope, honey, what in the world are you doing, standin' over there?" Harley waved his hand. "Come on over here and let me buy you some breakfast. At a time like this, we need to keep you well fed."

Confused, Colt looked over at Hope, but she didn't even spare him a glance as the bright fake smile slid back in place.

"Actually, Uncle Harley, Mama and Daddy are waitin' breakfast. So I need to get." As she backpedaled down the sidewalk, she spoke to Colt out of the side of her mouth. "Just keep walking, and when you get to the corner, run like hell."

Most people wouldn't understand her crazy talk. But after growing up in the town, Colt understood perfectly. One Bramble citizen was easily dealt with—two, almost impossible. Unfortunately, before he could follow her instructions, a brand-new black Lincoln Navigator came barreling down the street and zipped into the parking lot. The dust hadn't even settled before the door opened and a pair of bright turquoise stilettos slipped out.

"Well, good mornin', big brother." Shirlene strutted across the street in a tight pair of jeans, a huge concho belt, and a white blouse unbuttoned low enough to show off the hundred pounds of silver and turquoise wrapped around her neck. "I see you made it out of jail all right."

"No thanks to you." Colt crossed his arms and shot her an annoyed look.

"Now, honey." Shirlene batted those green eyes at him. "You aren't mad at me for forcing you to keep your promise, are you?"

He probably should be mad. The woman was too arrogant and controlling for her own good. But she had a point. He had promised to stay the night. And she was his baby sister, who he'd always had a soft spot for.

"Besides," she continued. "I knew you could get out anytime you wanted. In fact, what took you so long? I was hoping we could watch—" Those green eyes flickered over his shoulder and widened, but only for a split second. "Well, now, what do we have here?"

He glanced back to see Hope standing a few feet away, frozen in her spot. She looked all mussed and cute in her saggy pajama bottoms, her big eyes a little fearful at being caught by someone who knew how to put two and two together. For some reason, her fear prompted the need to rein in his sister.

"Quit being a brat, Shirlene, and tell me where you stashed my motorcycle."

Her gaze flickered back to him. "A brat? All I'm trying to figure out is why the Sweetheart of Bramble is wandering around in her pajamas with an escaped convict."

Colt really wanted to give his sister a good sock in the arm for bringing Harley's attention to the situation.

"What are you doin' with our little Hope?" Harley asked, not looking at all happy about the situation.

"Doing?" Hope finally entered the conversation, her voice sounding three pitches too high. "Nothing. We aren't doing a thing...I was just taking a walk and ran into him."

Shirlene tipped her head and smiled. "Sleepwalkin', were you, honey?"

With her hair all tangled and wild around her face, Hope did look like she just rolled out of bed. And she pretty much had—his bed. The thought brought a flash of heat to his crotch and, not wanting to embarrass himself, he tried to get his mind back on track.

"It doesn't matter what Hope is doing. Where's my bike?"

Shirlene flapped a hand, the morning sun refracting

off her huge diamonds. "Would you stop worrying about that bike? You'll get it back all safe and sound in a few days."

"A few days!" Both he and Hope spoke in unison.

As if on cue, Sheriff Winslow pulled up in his squad car and rolled down the window.

"You put the cell keys back, Shirlene?" When she only flashed her dimples, he turned to Colt. "Colt, I shore hope you ain't plannin' on causin' any more trouble. I'd hate to have to lock you up again."

"I sure hope so too, Sam." Shirlene threw Colt a sly look. "It breaks my heart to see my big brother behind bars. And I give you my word that I'll keep an eye on him. In fact, we were just headed over to Josephine's to have us a nice, hearty breakfast." She waltzed over to Hope and hooked an arm through hers. Hope put up a good fight, but in the end Colt's ornery baby sister prevailed and tugged her across the street.

Colt remained on the sidewalk with his arms crossed over his chest, debating whether or not he wanted to follow his sister or tell her and the entire town of Bramble to take a hike. But the truth was, with the bike delivery deadline a week out, he didn't have anywhere that he needed to be.

Still, he hadn't completely made up his mind until Hope shot him a wicked glare over her shoulder. A glare that grew even more poisonous when he couldn't help but grin. She turned back around, and he watched the wiggle of her butt beneath the thin cotton.

What were a few days?

Especially when it annoyed the hell out of the homecoming queen.

Chapter Five

THERE HADN'T BEEN anyone murdered in Bramble, Texas, since 1892, when the sheriff shot William Cates for attacking the mayor, after the mayor refused to pay him for the dedication plaque he'd made for the town hall.

But Hope was about to change that.

As she sat at the counter, awaiting a breakfast she hadn't ordered and didn't want, she eyeballed the knife Harley was using to spread the mound of whipped butter over his pancakes and calculated how long it would take to grab the knife, ram it through Shirlene's conniving heart, and get out the door before Sheriff Winslow could clear his gun from beneath the edge of the counter.

Of course, it didn't matter how quickly he cleared it. He didn't keep any bullets in it anyway. "Safety first" was the town motto. And people knew from experience that Sam wasn't someone who could carry a loaded weapon safely.

Still, the sheriff wouldn't need a gun to stop her. Especially when her truck sat at her parents' house. By the time she said good-bye to her sisters and brother, her mama made her bologna sandwiches for the trip, and her daddy checked the oil and the other fluids in the engine, the lynch mob would be in the front yard, amid her mother's whirling lawn ornaments.

So her murder plans would have to wait.

"...so I said to Mary Jean, you should be thankin' your lucky stars that Melvin ran off with your manicurist," Rachel Dean continued her nonstop chatter as she poured Shirlene a cup of coffee, coffee that smelled as good as it looked. "After two husbands, I can tell you men ain't all that."

Hope flipped her cup over and set it in the saucer.

"Maybe you just haven't had the right man," Colt spoke up for the first time since entering the diner. Not that it was easy to get a word in edgewise with the folks of Bramble. Especially Rachel Dean.

Rachel turned to Colt and studied him as if just realizing he sat there. A smile creased her weathered face, and she moved past Hope's empty cup, right on over to his.

"Well, it looks like you got yourself a golden tongue while you was in prison, Colt Lomax." She sent him a saucy wink as she poured his coffee. "And I can't say as I don't prefer it to that chip you carried around on your shoulder as a kid."

Since Colt had never taken criticism well, Hope waited for him to take offense. Instead, he gave Rachel a sexy, gray-eyed wink of his own before he took a sip of coffee and closed his eyes in euphoric satisfaction.

Annoyed that she wasn't experiencing the same enjoyment, Hope tapped a finger on the rim of her cup. But Rachel couldn't seem to take her eyes off Colt. Not that she could blame the woman, or any of the other women in the diner, who had lost interest in her food to stare at the man who exuded a raw, masculine sex appeal in his travel-worn clothes and dark scruffy stubble.

Like a regular at a local bar, Colt straddled the red vinyl stool, his knees almost touching the counter where his bare forearms rested. Tattoos snaked up the arm furthest from her, while the one closest boasted nothing more than hard, tanned muscle, covered in a sprinkling of silky black hair. The muscles led to a thick wrist and a hand scarred and calloused from tinkering with machines.

Hope watched as his hand lifted the white porcelain mug to his firm, unsmiling lips. But before he took a sip, the cup halted. She glanced up and found him watching her, his eyes bemused. Not wanting to appear guilty, she stared back. They gazed at one another for a few moments until his eyes lowered to her chest. His brows knotted.

"Rachel," he called, even though the woman wasn't more than six inches away. "You have a sweater or something for Hope to put on?"

Hope's eyes shot down to the front of her shirt, and she quickly crossed her arms as Rachel scurried to do his bidding.

Shirlene laughed. "If you didn't wander around half dressed, honey," she said as she stirred five packets of sugar substitute into her coffee, "your teacup handles wouldn't be showin'."

"Real funny, Shirl." But that didn't stop her from taking the ugly gray sweater and slipping it on—with the annoying help of one very cocky motorcycle bum.

"Nice to see you remember your manners, son," Harley said, before he leaned over the counter to whisper something in Rachel's ear. She nodded and moved back to stand in front of Hope.

"Manners is a nice thing for a man to have," Rachel said. "Neither one of my husbands had a manner one, although Homer always said a polite 'excuse me' after he burped or farted."

Colt choked on his coffee, but had the manners to whisper a quick "excuse me" before Rachel continued.

"But worse than that, in my opinion, is a man who don't take responsibility for his own actions." She lifted her nonexistent eyebrows at Hope, as if to convey some message Hope wasn't getting.

Nor was she getting any coffee.

"She's right," Sheriff Winslow chimed in from his spot further down the counter. "There's nothing lower than a scoundrel who won't own up to his mistakes."

Knowing the town could go on and on about something that had nothing to do with anything, Hope finally spoke up.

"Could I get some coffee?"

After topping off Colt's cup, Rachel held up the half-full pot. "You don't want this coffee, honey, it's been sittin' out too long." She dumped it in the sink and grabbed a pitcher of orange juice. "Now let me pour you a glass of OJ. All that vitamin C is much better for a body than caffeine."

"I don't want orange juice," Hope stated as Rachel set the glass down in front of her. "I want coffee."

Rachel's smile faltered, but only for a second. "Well, of course, you do. I'll just start another pot." Except she didn't move to start one; instead, she set the pitcher down and rested one big man hand on her hip and the other on the edge of the counter.

"Now I bet there's a lot of men out there in Hollywood who ain't got no idea how to treat a lady, especially someone as sweet as our little Hope." She leaned closer. "I bet you knew a few fellers like that, didn't you, Hog?"

The clink of forks on plates halted all at once, and Hope could've sworn the entire place leaned in. Even Colt's gaze settled on her.

She sent him a scalding look before she answered.

"A few."

"A few, like two?" Rachel asked. "Or is that a couple? I always get those two mixed up."

"A few is three," Cindy Lynn enlightened her from a table behind them. "And a couple is two. Like Ed and me are a couple."

"Unless she's at Bootlegger's," Shirlene mumbled under her breath. "Then her couple can expand to any man willing to give her the time of day."

"A few." Rachel's eyes turned worried. "That many, huh? Are you sure you couldn't narrow it down some?"

Harley leaned over from his end of the counter. "Well, now, I'm sure Hope doesn't want to talk about all the men she dated out in California. After all, there had to be a slew clamorin' for an opportunity to date the prettiest homecomin' queen we ever had."

Colt snorted.

"But what Rachel was askin'," Harley continued, "is if there was any one special. Anyone that might've made an impression on our little sweetheart."

With a pair of steel gray eyes pinned on her, Hope really wanted to come up with a name of someone really special. A name that would wipe the cocky smirk off Colt's whiskered outlaw face. But since she had been too busy in California trying to make ends meet, the only man she could come up with was her old roommate. Sheldon had only been a friend, but Colt didn't need to know that.

"Well . . . there was this one guy—"

"A movie star?" Twyla jumped in.

"Matthew McConaughey?" Cindy Lynn's voice almost wept with envy.

"Tommy Lee Jones?" Rachel Dean breathed.

"Sandra Bullock?" Kenny added. When everyone in the room shot him a surprised look, he smiled sheepishly. "Faith had an on-counter with her. I just figured it was worth a shot."

Hope didn't have a clue what Kenny was talking about, but then again, she never did. So instead of getting sucked into the craziness, she kept it simple.

"No, Sheldon is not a movie star."

"A pro quarterback?" Sheriff Winslow asked, and Hope couldn't help but smile at the mental image of Sheldon on a football field.

"No."

"A country western singer?" Cindy Lynn leaned around her poor whipped husband.

"Afraid not."

"Is he at least a Texan?" Harley said, and when Hope shook her head, he heaved a sigh and slumped back on the bar stool. "Well, I guess that settles that."

"It's not the end of the world, Harley," Rachel Dean said, as she slipped two plates down in front of Hope and Colt. "He can't be all that bad if our little Hope likes him." She pointed down at the plate and prodded. "Go ahead, honey, Josie made it just the way you like it—the eggs runny and the chili hot."

While Colt attacked the food like the starving convict he was, Hope stared at the two fried eggs swimming in a sea of brilliant red chili. The same red chili that had burned a hole in her stomach two weeks earlier.

God, she *had* become a wuss since leaving Texas.

She pushed the plate away. "I'm not feeling like chili today, Rachel."

Rachel only looked confused for a second before she jerked the plate back up, and then reached out and patted Hope's hand. "Take a few deep breaths, honey. It will pass."

"What will pass?" Colt turned to her, his fork poised in midair. "Are you sick?"

As Rachel walked off with her plate, Hope turned to Shirlene. "Is it my imagination, or has everyone completely lost their minds?"

Shirlene shot her a skeptical look. "You have been gone too long, honey. Since when have the people of this town had minds?" She took a couple bites of steak and eggs before she continued. "So what shall we do today? Everyone could come over to my house for a barbecue and margaritas. Or we could go out to Sutter Springs for a picnic. Or we could—"

"Find my motorcycle," Colt stated.

"I told you I'd get it back to you." Shirlene pointed her fork at him. "But is it too much to ask for a couple days? You would think that a man who owns—"

"Fine." He threw her a warning look. "I'll stay for a couple of days. But come Wednesday morning, I'm out of here."

"A week would be better."

"Don't push it, baby sister."

Her dimples flashed. "Wednesday it is."

It was hard for Hope to keep her mouth shut when she wanted to yell "No!" at the top of her lungs. She didn't want Colt to stay one hour longer, let alone three days. Unfortunately, there wasn't anything to do about it. Shirlene was too smart for her own good, and there wasn't any way that she would let Hope's objections go without a pisspot full of questions. Questions Hope wasn't about to answer...even if she could.

"Here you go, honey." Rachel set another plate down in front of her.

Hope stared down at the four saltine crackers and wondered if Rachel had sniffed too much diesel fuel from the clothes of her truck-driving husbands.

"What is this?" she asked.

"Crackers."

"I know they're crackers, but why are you giving them to me?"

"To settle your stomach." She winked. "Every mornin' for three entire months I ate nothin' but saltines and a little ginger ale. 'Course around lunchtime, I was right as rain and could swallow down an entire cow without stoppin' to spit out the hooves and horns. But until then, I couldn't look at real food or even smell it."

"What are you talking about, Rachel?"

"Oh, honey." Her eyes teared up. "I realize that at a time like this you'd just as soon not have a big bunch of people makin' a fuss over you. But we're family, Hope. And we love you. Even if you did run off to Hollywood and get yourself—"

"It's a mistake!"

Hope was still trying to piece together Rachel's words

when Faith's voice rang out through the diner. She swiveled around on the bar stool to find her sister standing by the door, looking all wild-eyed and sleep-tousled.

And annoyingly satisfied.

The satisfied part, no doubt, came from the handsome cowboy who stood directly behind her. Although he didn't look exactly happy to be there.

"It's all a mistake," Faith continued as she stepped into the diner in a cami and pajama bottoms very similar to Hope's. "Slate told me what you all think, and I take full responsibility for you thinking that because it was me who said it—although I didn't mean it the way it came out—I was just trying to explain to Slate why I had left Bramble without saying a word and I didn't realize everyone was listening and would assume what you've obviously assumed. But she's not." She held a hand to her chest. "Really."

There was an exchange of glances as if everyone knew what Faith was rambling about—everyone but Hope, Colt, and Shirlene. Shirlene seemed to fit the pieces together quick enough.

"Lordy." She fanned herself with one hand. "Things just keep getting more excitin' and more excitin'. Pretty soon I'll have to move just to get some rest."

"What are you mumbling about, Shirl?"

"I think you're about to find out, honey." She winked at Hope as Harley slipped off his bar stool.

Hitching up his pants, he moved over to Faith. "Now, I realize Hope's embarrassed about what happened, and being her sister, you want to keep her little secret, but you can't change our mind about something we heard with our own two ears."

"But you heard wrong!"

Hope had to give it to her. Faith could win a few hog-calling trophies of her own.

Harley's eyes squinted. "So are you tellin' us you lied?"

"Not lied, exactly. I just didn't explain things properly."

Slate stepped up and placed his arm around Faith. "Now, darlin', I know you want to set things straight and all, but I don't think now's the time or place. Why don't we go on back to Bubba's and continue where we left off before I went and opened my big mouth."

"No." She shook her head. "If I don't explain they'll continue to believe Hope's pregnant, and I can't let them—"

"What?" Hope came off the stool so quickly that her slipper got caught in the rung of the bar stool. And she would've hit the floor, just like Colt's coffee mug, if Shirlene hadn't reached out and grabbed Rachel's gray sweater and reeled her back in.

Rachel hurried around the counter, ignoring the broken shards. "Now, don't be gettin' yourself in a lather, honey." She fanned Hope with one hand, which created enough air to rival a ceiling fan. "It's not good for the babies."

"Babies?" Hope sat down hard on the bar stool and tried to keep from passing out.

"'Course, babies." Rachel fanned harder. "You're a twin, ain't you?"

"No." Faith raced over. "I told you, she's not pregnant. It was all just a misunderstanding. She threw up, and I just assumed she was pregnant."

Rachel nodded her head. "And that's a good assumption, honey. I threw up like the town drunk with both my kids."

"Except she's not pregnant,"

"Says who?" Harley said.

"Says me." Hope finally came out of her comatose state and stood back up to glare at her twin sister. "I gather I have you to thank for this mess?"

Faith's eyes widened, and she nodded.

Damn. A double murder was going to be more difficult. But before Hope could let her sister have it, Slate pulled Faith toward the door.

"Come on, darlin', I think you've straightened things out enough for one day."

"B-but," she stammered and sent Hope one last beseeching look before she disappeared out the door.

Once they were gone, Hope turned to the group. "I'm not pregnant," she stated firmly. "It was just a little misunderstanding between sisters."

"So you didn't throw up," Kenny jumped in.

"Yes, I threw up, but only because I ate red chili the night before."

"But, Hope," Twyla entered the conversation, "you grew up on red chili—"

"I'm not pregnant!" Hope screamed so loudly that the glasses rattled on the shelf behind the counter.

The town exchanged looks before Shirlene spoke up, her green eyes twinkling almost as much as Colt's were.

"I don't know, honey. Throwing up and bad mood swings, I'd say that about clenches it."

Shooting a murderous glare at her best friend, Hope

slapped Rachel's fanning hand out of the way and jumped up from the stool.

"Where are you going, Hog?" Kenny yelled as Hope headed for the door.

"To get me a cup of coffee and a loaded gun!"

The folks of Bramble waited for Shirlene and Colt to follow Hope out before they hurried over to the window.

"So what are we gonna do?" Kenny asked as he watched Hope cuss Shirlene up one side and down the other.

"I'm not sure," Harley stated. "But we can't let our little Hope raise a passel of children by herself." There was a long pause as Harley twirled the end of his mustache. Finally his eyes narrowed, and he looked over at Rachel.

"Rachel, isn't your cousin, Bear, a private eye?"

"He ain't a private eye, Harley. He's a bounty hunter."

Harley nodded. "Well, I'd say that's even better."

Chapter Six

COLT MISSED THE open road.

Shirlene's guesthouse was more than comfortable, and her Mexican cook sure knew her way around a kitchen, but comfort didn't compare to freedom. Which was why, before Shirlene rolled out of bed on Tuesday morning, he stole the keys to the Navigator and headed out on his own.

On the way into town, he made a few calls on his cell phone, a phone Shirlene had retrieved from the leather bags on his bike, along with his aviators and extra clothes. He wasn't much of a talker, so the calls only lasted a few minutes. Just long enough to make sure things were going smoothly back at his custom motorcycle shop in L.A.

Colt had started Desperado Customs six years earlier in an old, abandoned warehouse. With his ability to hand-form sheet metal into unparalleled designs, wealthy customers had quickly lined up to own the hottest bikes on the street. His talented group of designers and mechanics didn't build a lot of motorcycles, but the motorcycles they built were unique enough to attract a huge cult following.

The majority of his followers couldn't afford his bikes, but they were more than willing to shell out twenty bucks for a T-shirt or twelve for a ball cap. He made as much selling that crap as he did selling his motorcycles.

After checking in with the shop, he fiddled with the radio until he found a station that played soft rock, which was about as far from country as he was going to get in this neck of the woods. He was singing along with a Bob Seger tune when he drove past Bramble High School.

The school was small and looked even smaller compared to the huge football stadium next to it—a tribute to the town's dedication to the sport. Colt hadn't played football. Not because he hadn't wanted to, but because school and work didn't leave room for much else. But, occasionally, he would sneak into the games after he finished working at Josephine's, to watch Slate Calhoun throw winning touchdown passes while Hope cheered him on with high kicks and straddles.

It was after those games that he got into the most trouble.

Up ahead, the faded and chipped sign of Jones' Garage stuck out like a sore thumb against the gray skies, and Colt lifted his foot off the accelerator.

"Hey, Colt," Tyler met him as he stepped from the SUV. "I see you got some proper boots."

Colt looked down at the black lizard cowboy boots he'd purchased in Lubbock; a foolish whim egged on by a sassy sister. Luckily, he'd drawn a line at the snap-down plaid western shirt.

"Yeah, well, you know how it goes." He placed his hands on his hips and stared over at the garage, a garage he knew like the inside of a carburetor. "So I guess if I was to wander around a bit, I just might run into a custom bike."

Tyler grinned as he took the cap off the gas tank. "You might. But I sure hope you don't."

Colt arched an eyebrow. "I thought we were friends, T-bone."

"Sure are." He lifted the nozzle and slipped it in. "Which is why I hope you stick around for a while."

"And you and Shirl are about the only ones who feel that way."

Tyler spit out a stream of tobacco before wiping his mouth with the back of his hand. "And whose fault is that? I've never seen anyone work so hard to make folks dislike him."

"I didn't have to try all that hard."

"Nope." Tyler leaned against the side of the Navigator and crossed his arms while the tank filled. "You just had to be your obstinate self. If the town said white, you said black. Couple that with spending most of your free time bullying the town sweetheart, and that about did it." He returned his attention to the pump. "It was your choice, buddy. Always your choice."

Had it been? Funny, but it hadn't seemed that way so many years ago, when he was forced to scrap for everything he got. Growing up, he'd always thought it was the town that held him back, the town that kept him from being what he wanted to be. But he wondered if Tyler wasn't right. Maybe it hadn't been the town that held him back as much as his own belief that he would never be more than "that poor Lomax kid." Of course, it made no difference now.

Changing the subject, Colt nodded at the excavated lot next to the gas station. "Planning on expanding?"

"I thought about putting a car wash there, but that outfit on the interstate beat me to it." Tyler shook his head as he hooked the nozzle back in the pump. " 'Course I didn't really have the money for it, anyway. Things have been slow around here."

Colt took his wallet out of his pocket and handed Tyler the cash. "Thanks, Ty."

Tyler nodded. "You still tinkering around with motorcycles?"

"Pretty much," he said. "You still making babies with Missy Leigh?"

Tyler's smile was genuine and proud. "Pretty much."

Grinning, Colt walked around to the driver's door.

Tyler followed him. "If you stick around until Friday, we've got a play-off game. Best darned quarterback since Calhoun."

"Sounds like fun, but I'll be long gone by then." Colt opened the door and climbed in. But before he pulled away, he backed the truck up and checked inside all three open garage stalls, while Tyler stood there laughing.

"Take care of her, T-bone," he yelled through the open window.

Tyler nodded. "Will do, Colt."

After leaving the gas station, Colt decided to take a quick cruise through town before he headed back to Shirlene's. He thought about breakfast at Josephine's, but Shirlene's cook had fed him enough red and green chili to last him awhile. That, and he didn't much feel like listening to the people of Bramble talk their nonsense. Although he had enjoyed them razzing Hope about being pregnant with twins.

Hope pregnant. He shook his head and laughed.

Crazy townsfolk.

Of course, he hadn't been laughing at first. He'd been too stunned to laugh. Over the years, he'd thought of Hope in a lot of different scenarios. But pregnant wasn't one of them. Probably because babies weren't something he spent a lot of time thinking about.

Not that he didn't like babies. He liked babies just fine. His sister had been a baby once, and she had been kind of cute. Still, it had been a full-time job making sure that she didn't roll off the couch or play around electrical sockets or ram pennies in her mouth. And as she got older, there were more responsibilities. Like getting her out of bed, dressed, and fed before school. And making sure she washed behind her ears and did her homework before she watched TV. And keeping all the boys away from her when she finally outgrew being a tomboy and turned into a hormonal teenager.

It had been a relief when she married Lyle and settled down.

But that didn't mean that Colt had stopped worrying about her. In the last couple days, he'd noticed that she was drinking more than usual. He figured it had to do with Lyle being gone so much. Lomax women didn't do well without their men—his mama was a perfect example. Which was why he planned on talking to Lyle about staying home more often and keeping his wife from drowning her lonely heart in a bottle of Jose Cuervo.

With his thoughts wrapped up in Shirlene, he barely noticed the woman who stepped off the curb to flag him down until he almost ran her over. He slammed on the brakes, and the tires squealed to a stop inches from her scuffed cowboy boots.

He didn't have to read her lips. Even with the windows closed, her voice carried.

"Oh. It's you."

With a thunderous look, Hope turned and stomped back over to her beat-up truck, parked next to the curb in front of the Food Mart. Biting back a smile, Colt pulled into a space and got out. Even with the gray clouds that rumbled overhead, the day somehow seemed brighter.

"You need somethin', honey?" he asked politely, although he had to admit a little gleefully.

Completely ignoring him, Hope struggled with the big box of groceries that sat on the sidewalk next to her truck, the same truck she'd had eight years ago.

He walked over and leaned against the open tailgate. "You sure you don't need any help? That's a mighty big box for such a little thing." He drew the word *thing* out into a nice Texas *thaaang*.

"I'm good," she growled between clenched teeth.

His gaze traveled over the swells of her bottom in the thin cotton dress. "No doubt about that, honey."

The box thumped down, and glass bottles rattled as she turned to glare at him. "Don't you have something else to do, Lomax? Like maybe find a hundred-thousand-dollar motorcycle so you can get the hell out of town and quit harassing me?"

"I hate to bring this to your attention, but I wasn't the one who flagged you down."

"I didn't flag you down! I flagged Shirlene down!"

With his arms crossed, Colt shrugged. "Well, one Lomax is as good as the other."

"A few days ago, I might've argued the point. But after all the stunts your sister has pulled recently, I'll have to agree with you on that one. I don't know why I flagged her down in the first place." She turned back to the box.

It would've been easy to leave her there. In Bramble, someone would show up to help her out. But *easy* wasn't in Colt's vocabulary. Besides, it wasn't like he had anything else to do.

Pushing away from the tailgate, he bodily picked Hope up and set her out of the way, taking only a second to notice the way his hands spanned her trim waist.

"Darn you, Lomax, I told you I don't need your help!"

"I know. But you're going to get it anyway." He picked up the box and hefted it into the back of the truck, next to the other boxes of food. "Burl training for the pie-eating contest?"

"Funny." She tried to shove him out of the way to close the tailgate, but he wasn't having it.

"So where are you taking all this?"

She glared at him for only a few seconds before she answered. "Out to Grover Road."

His eyebrows shot up at the mention of his old neighborhood. "I thought the church only handed out boxes at Christmas?"

"They do, but I thought they might need something to tide them over. So I called Shirlene, and she called Ed and told him to charge whatever I wanted."

It was so like Hope. Whether delivering Bibles or food for the hungry, Hope never let the people of her town go without. The realization brought with it a wave of warmth that settled all nice and cozy in his stomach. Although the look she sent him was anything but.

"So do you mind moving so I can get out of here before it starts to rain?"

On cue, a rumble of thunder drew their eyes up to the dark sky.

"You got a tarp?" he asked. When she didn't answer, he looked away from the nebulous clouds into annoyed baby blue. "I'll take that as a no." He reached back in and pulled the large box out.

"Give me that back! I don't need any help." She tried to take the box from him, but he held tight.

"I don't doubt that for a minute, sweetheart. But you ever tasted soggy cereal?" When she looked confused, he glanced up at the sky. "Because in about three minutes that's exactly what you're going be handing out to those kids if you don't let me get the rest of these boxes inside that SUV."

"Fine." She released the box and stepped out of his way. "But if you hadn't nosed in, I could've made it."

"Doubtful." He placed the box in the back of the Navigator and turned to find her standing there with another one. He went to take it from her, but she refused to let go.

"You really can't help yourself, can you?" He lifted a brow at her. "Now let go and let me do it."

"Or what?" Her blue eyes snapped, and he would've laughed at her stubbornness if the store owner's wife, Jeannie Mitchell, hadn't raced out the front door.

"Hope, I thought I told you to wait until Ed got off the phone before you loaded those boxes. You want to give those babies bad backs?"

Colt laughed, and Hope's eyes narrowed as she released the box. "I hope Kenny Gene is riding your motorcycle all over the countryside."

Mentally cussing Kenny, Colt loaded the rest of the boxes while Jeannie stood on the sidewalk and watched with a confused look on her face.

"I sure never thought I'd see the day when Colt Lomax did charity work."

"Actually, I'm just takin' these back to Shirlene's." He winked at her as he slammed the hatch. "But I fig ure you're the type of woman a man can trust with all his secrets."

Jeannie blushed to the roots of her bright-red hair. "Rachel was right. You have turned into quite a sweet talker since you've been in prison, Colt Lomax." Her smile got even bigger when he walked around and held open the door for Hope.

"Fake talker is more like it," Hope mumbled beneath her breath as she slipped inside, flashing a good amount of tanned legs before she jerked down the hem of her flower-printed dress.

Smiling almost as big as Jeannie, Colt slammed the truck door behind her.

Grover Road sat north of the town dump and south of the junkyard, although it looked more like an extension of both. Around a dozen trailers sat in the midst of rusted-out cars and trucks and piles of old mattresses. And each pathetic home looked the same, a rectangular box of aluminum siding with cracked windows, tires on the roof, and lopsided steps leading up to torn screen doors.

"It's weird, isn't it," Hope voiced his thoughts. "I mean, everything looks the same, except not. I don't remember the trailers being so small." She glanced over at him. "Did we really live here?"

Raw emotion rumbled through Colt like the dark clouds that had yet to produce rain, and he struggled with the strong desire to crank the wheel and head back to town. Instead he slouched down in the seat and tried to get his shoulders to relax. "I lived here a lot longer than you did."

She studied him for a few more seconds before she looked away. "Mama said to leave the boxes beneath the steps. Folks like it better that way."

He nodded in agreement. The one time the church ladies arrived with their Christmas charity box, he'd been so ashamed that he'd refused it, tossing in a few belligerent cuss words for good measure. Later on, when the other kids had fruit snacks for their lunches and Shirlene didn't, he'd regretted his bad behavior. But by that time, it was too late. Which seemed to be the story of his life. Hot temper followed by rash behavior followed by a whole lot of regret.

"Just pull in here," Hope directed him into a weedy lot.

"Does old man Smith still live here?"

"No, Mama told me he died a few years back."

Maneuvering the SUV around the junk and weeds, Colt parked by the door. "He was sure a mean old bird. Every time I moved, he called the sheriff out."

She glanced over. "And I'm sure sweet little Colt Lomax didn't do a thing to deserve it."

His gaze took in the filthy front window with the huge crack spidering across it. "Okay, so maybe I did occasionally deserve it, but the guy was a jerk."

Whether the guy was a jerk or not, dead or not, that didn't stop Colt from pulling out his wallet when Hope wasn't looking and slipping a hundred beneath the snap top of an oatmeal box. Not that the money would go to fix the crack Colt had made in the window, but it made him feel better.

"You think they'll find it before it rains?" Hope asked, as he slid the box under the sloping metal steps.

"It should be okay here until they do."

They placed boxes at eight more trailers, and Colt recognized a few more cracks in the windows and shelled out a few more hundreds, although at the last one, a pit bull almost chewed clean through his brand-new cowboy boot before he could get the box placed under the stairs.

"Nice boots, by the way," Hope yelled as they raced back to the truck. "Flashy but nice."

"You should talk." He jumped behind the wheel and slammed the door before the dog could get his head in. "Weren't you the one who asked for those hideous pink boots for Christmas that year? Whatever happened to those, anyway?"

"I lost them," Hope stated, before directing him to the next trailer.

It was funny, but he almost didn't recognize his childhood home—funny because nothing much had changed. The yard was still cluttered with beat-up vehicles and old motorcycle frames. And the trailer still had rust spots and dangling screens, along with a wooden door with a fist-sized dent in the middle.

"Damn," Colt breathed as he pulled in behind the old Ford truck without any tires, windows, or doors. "Does someone actually live here?"

"No." When he shot her a questioning look, she grinned. "I just thought you might like to take a walk down memory lane."

"Gee, thanks." He looked around. "Why hasn't anybody in town come out here to clean things up?"

"Probably because the one time Marty Clines tried it, you chased him off with a hammer."

"Still, they should raze the place."

"The place? Or your memories?"

His gaze shot over to her serious blue eyes. "Both." He reached for the gear shift. But before he could pop it into reverse, Hope had her door open.

"Come on, let's look around."

"I had eighteen years to look around," Colt stated. "And believe me that was plenty."

She leaned in the open door. "I dare you."

"Double dog?"

"Triple."

Never one to refuse a dare, he got out, leading the way down the worn path that led to the broken-down steps. But when he tried the door, it refused to open.

"You've got to be kidding!" He jiggled the handle in disbelief.

"Ironic, ain't it?" Hope stood at the bottom of the steps, smirking like all get out. The wind kicked up, sending the mane of hair flying around her upturned face and molding the soft fabric of her dress to her small breasts and flat stomach. "The only locked door in Bramble and it's Colt Lomax's."

She giggled, and then the giggle turned to out-and-out laughter. And no one laughed like Hope. She laughed like she yelled, loud and uninhibited with her head thrown back and her arms crossed over her stomach. But while her yelling could bust an eardrum, her laughter had a mellow huskiness that filled Colt with a warm contentment.

He didn't know how long he stood there staring at her, or how long he would've continued to do so, if her laughter hadn't suddenly died and her gaze lifted up to the skies.

"Gully-washer," she stated, but not soon enough for either one of them to escape the deluge of water that suddenly dropped from the sky without one drip of warning. One second they were completely dry and the next soaking wet.

Most women would've been squealing their heads off. But not Hope. Her laughter returned, and she did a quick little spin in her scuffed cowboy boots.

"Come on," Colt yelled as he took the steps in one leap, the racket of raindrops against aluminum deafening. He tried to shield her with his body and steer her toward the truck, but Hope had other plans and raced around the piles of junk toward the large elm tree.

When he finally caught up with her, she was struggling with the rusted door of the old Chevy. He wanted to jerk her stubborn body up and carry her back to the comfortable, heated seats of the Navigator, but instead, he reached out and added his strength to the door, then held it while she clamored in on the torn seat. Soaked to the skin, he climbed in behind her.

"Have you lost your mind, woman?" He slammed the door and scraped the wet hair back from his face.

"I just wanted to see if it was still here," she said, all out of breath. "Besides, a little rain never hurt anyone."

"A little?" Colt turned to her. The sight that greeted him brought a smile to his lips. "You look like a drowned rat." He reached out and smoothed back a rope of wet hair.

"And what makes you think you don't," Hope tossed back, her gaze locked on his chest. It remained there for only a second before she turned to the rain-drenched windshield. "I'm surprised no one has broken it out."

"Believe me, it was quite a temptation."

She glanced over at him. "So why didn't you?"

Staring at the water that rushed in tiny waves down the

solid sheet of glass, he only shrugged. "I guess because it was the only play equipment Shirlene had. She used to love climbing behind the wheel and traveling all over the world."

"I know," she said. "I traveled with her."

Hope was right. She had been there, sitting in the front seat next to Shirlene while Colt was busy taking apart some old piece of junk in the yard. Those were the days before her life got better. *Before high school cliques. And before Slate Calhoun,* Colt thought.

"Don't act like you didn't like playing in here too." She sent him a smug smile before latching on to the big steering wheel and turning it back and forth. "Where do you want to go? New York? California? Paris?"

Unfortunately, the thoughts of Slate and high school had soured his disposition and the rebellious, belligerent kid he thought was long gone reared his ugly head.

"Come on now, Hope, don't tell me you've forgotten what we used to play."

She stopped twisting the steering wheel, and her hands tightened on the hard plastic. But she refused to look at him.

Rain or no rain, he should've pushed open the door and climbed out. But Colt had never known when to leave well enough alone. Or when to leave Hope alone, for that matter. His gaze followed a drop of rainwater that trickled down one flushed cheek, over a stubborn jaw, and along her soft throat to disappear beneath the damp collar of the flowered dress.

"Come on, honey," he breathed as his arm stretched out along the back of the seat. "I'll show you mine, if you show me yours."

Chapter Seven

"I DON'T KNOW WHAT YOU'RE TALKING ABOUT," Hope said as her gaze remained locked on the water cascading down the windshield.

Colt slid closer, blocking her view with miles of wet black T-shirt. She now understood why men were so enthralled with wet T-shirt contests. Wet cotton made for some mouth-watering fantasies, especially when shrink-wrapped to the hard, chiseled body in front of her.

As her gaze got stuck on the tiny beaded nipples topping each perfectly sculptured pectoral muscle, her breathing grew uneven. The seat was big enough that she could move back. Except that a strange paralysis had settled over her, and she couldn't move if she wanted to, especially when his hand came to rest on the steering wheel and his other on the back of her neck. A chill spread through her body, which brought his droopy-lidded gaze sliding down her soaked dress.

"Sure you do," he whispered, as his breath wafted over her face. It smelled of mint toothpaste and cool rain. "You know exactly what I'm talking about—sophomore year behind the girl's locker room."

Hope closed her eyes and tried to get a handle on her suddenly topsy-turvy world, but lack of vision only made matters worse when a hot hand skated up her bare leg. Her eyes flashed open as she grabbed his wrist.

"Stop." She tried to sound firm, but only came out sounding needy. She cleared her throat. "I mean it, Colt." Except it didn't really sound like she meant it.

Those sensual gray eyes stared back at her from beneath lowered lids. "Come on, honey," he coaxed as his fingers caressed the spot right above her knee. "Just a little peek." He leaned over, and his cheek brushed against hers, not as prickly as it had been in jail, but prickly enough to cause more chill bumps. "I promise not to tell a single soul—I never did."

The man knew exactly what to say. Always had. If he took a notion, he could tempt a nun from her habit. Hope was no nun, but she could count on one hand the times she'd had sex in the last year. So how could she fend off a desperado like Colt Lomax? A naughty outlaw who had no scruples about cornering her in an old Chevy while water cascaded down the windows like the best carwash fantasy she'd ever had?

So she gave in. Just a little. Just enough to let her eyes close in surrender. Just enough to lean into the mouth that trailed kisses down her neck. Just enough to loosen the grip she had on his hand.

But she refused to let it go. She might be sex-deprived, but she wasn't stupid. Although that didn't seem to stop his fingers from moving. In fact, her hand just went along for the ride, clinging tight to his wrist as he stoked a line of fire up her thigh. He caught the damp material of her dress on the way up, baring her legs to the chill of the air and the warmth of his fingers. Fingers that hesitated for a brief heart-dropping second before skating over the satiny smoothness of her panties.

She moaned and pulled back, needing air in the worst possible way. Releasing his hold on her neck, he allowed her the freedom, his gaze settling on her mouth for a moment before dropping down to the quivering need between her legs. He stared for sizzling seconds—a full mind-blowing minute.

"I have to say," his voice came out even more husky than normal as a finger flicked over her most quivery part of all. "I might even like these better than the cotton heart ones you wore in high school." He inched the dress even higher, until part of her stomach and hipbones were bared to his greedy gray eyes. His gaze returned to hers, all heat and desire.

"You want to get real naughty, baby?"

When put that way, she did.

She really did.

So she nodded and waited. Waited for those wonderfully talented fingers to dip into her panties and put out the fire that burned out of control. Except instead of diving in, he removed his hands and settled back against the door.

"So show me," he stated, his eyes smoldering.

She knew what he wanted; she just didn't know if she could give it to him. Never in her life had she stripped in front of a man. Pathetic but true. She might be loud and controlling, but she had always been modest about showing her bits and pieces. Which is why she had never collected any Mardi Gras beads to hang off her rearview mirror, or sunbathed topless, or chosen nude acting roles.

And those things had only dealt with her bits. Her pieces were an entirely different matter.

If she'd been thinking right, she would've jerked down the hem of her dress and called it a day. But she wasn't thinking right. After spending the last few weeks feeling like the most undesirable woman on the face of the earth, beneath his hot gray eyes she suddenly felt like the most desirable. And even though she knew it was a big mistake, she couldn't seem to help herself. There was something about Colt Lomax that brought out the naughty girl in her—that made her want to take a walk on the wild side. Or dive smack dab into an entire pool of wicked.

She just refused to be the only one making a fool of herself.

"Only if you show me yours."

Surprise flashed in his eyes before they steamed back up.

"Lead the way."

Now that she was the main attraction, crazy things started popping into her head. *I wish I'd taken the time to shave this morning. Or trim. Or even fluff and spritz with some intoxicating perfume. I wish I owned intoxicating perfume. Something that would make up for the lack of hair sculpturing. Would a big bad biker prefer Brazilian or native? Or maybe somewhere in between—a wild Brazilian—*

"I hate to hurry you, honey," Colt's voice interrupted her rambling thoughts. "But if you don't show me something soon, what I have to show you might not be all that impressive."

Her gaze flickered down to the bulge beneath soft damp denim, and she blushed. When she glanced back up, a smart-aleck grin creased his face. Which annoyed her. She might not be an expert in the art of seduction, but she wasn't a naïve schoolgirl anymore. If he wanted to play wicked, she could oblige him as well as any other woman.

Hooking her thumbs in the elastic of her panties, she slowly inched down the material, her fingers cupping her inner thighs and her thumbs forming a V around her moist—getting moister by the second—center. She kept her eyes on him, while he kept his eyes lowered, the heat of his gaze burning through his dark, thick lashes. She lifted her hips off the torn leather and slipped the satin down her thighs. The springs of the old seat squeaked, but not loud enough to cover Colt's intake of breath.

She dropped her hips back to the seat, allowing the hem of the dress to fall over her lap as she struggled to get the panties over her cowboy boots. It wasn't easy. And after getting one boot out, she gave up and left the scrap of satin dangling off the top of the other.

"Next time it might be easier, honey, if you just don't wear panties." Colt's voice strummed across her.

"There won't be a next time."

His hot gaze lifted. "Then I guess we better make this good." The *good* came out all sexy and sizzling as his eyes lowered to the spot between her legs.

But before she lifted her dress, she took a quick glance around. The rain had ended as quickly as it came, leaving behind sparkling rivers that trailed down the steamed-over windows. If she couldn't see out, no one could see in. So she leaned back against the opposite door and slowly eased up the dress. The soft fabric brushed against the tops of her thighs, teasing the throbbing spot between her legs before coming to rest just above her hipbones.

Colt's breath hissed through his teeth, and Hope glanced up. He hadn't moved, but his body seemed tighter than before, his hands clenched in fists on the knees of his faded jeans.

"Spread them," he said in a breathy groan.

Slowly, she separated her knees, settling one bent leg up on the seat and allowing the other to loll against the steering wheel. He didn't touch her, but he didn't need to. His gaze stroked over her most private parts like hot, skilled fingers as his breath grew more uneven. Her breathing followed his, and soon the air grew thick with restrained desire.

"Now you." Her voice came out needy and desperate.

Without taking his eyes off her, he slid a hand to the button on his jeans and flipped it open. Tooth by brass tooth, the zipper eased down over the hard fist of denim to reveal black cotton stretched to the limits. With a few simple adjustments, he was released, and it was Hope's turn to greedily eat him up with her eyes. His penis was smooth and hard with tiny veins pumping through it and a broad tip that held a trace of moisture. Her mouth went dry, and her heart did a funny little two-step.

"Nice," she croaked.

"Thank you. You want to touch it?"

She glanced up expecting to see a cocky smile, but instead there was only serious heat. She swallowed and tried to remember why she wasn't going to let things go any further than a little naughty fun. Of course, the day after was never fun. Especially when you had to confront the man you had naughty fun with.

Except she wouldn't have to confront Colt.

He was leaving.

Tomorrow.

So basically all she had to do was hide out for one day. How hard could that be? Of course, sex was out of the question. But touching was well within the parameters of naughty without getting nasty. And with the way she was feeling, it wouldn't take much naughty to send her right over the edge. Except about the time she leaned in to accept his offer, a cherub face pressed against the steamed-up, water-splashed glass.

"Kid!" she screamed as she drew her legs together and shoved down her dress.

"Now, honey," Colt sat up and reached for her. "I've got that covered. I never play without a raincoat handy."

"I'm not talking about me getting pregnant, you idiot!" She slapped at his hands. "I'm talking about a real kid!" She waved a finger at the window. "A kid who just saw my pieces!" She fumbled around for her panties, but when she shoved her other boot through the hole, the satin ripped clean in half.

Colt looked back at the window behind him. The kid was gone, but the face imprint was still there.

"Shit!"

While Hope stuffed her ruined panties in her boot, he readjusted. Although he had a hard time getting his zipper up.

"Damn it, I thought you told me nobody lived here!"

"That's what Mama said. And they probably don't." She leaned up and wiped a circle in the steam. "It's probably some kid from another trailer."

"Well, why the hell isn't he in school?"

"How would I know? Do I look like the principal?"

Once he had his jeans zipped and buttoned, it only

took a second for his temper to cool. And only another for him to chuckle.

"Well, I guess that's what we get for being naughty."

"Real funny." Hope glared at him. "Now we have to figure out how to get out of here without him seeing us."

The smile slipped. "Afraid to be caught with the Bad Boy of Bramble?"

She shot him a smug grin. "No more than you should be worried about being caught in a compromising position with a woman expecting twins."

"Point taken." He made his own circle in the steam. "Well, it looks like he's gone now. No doubt scared by that hog-calling squeal of yours."

"You are just a hoot a minute, Lomax." She shoved open the door and cautiously stepped out.

The rain had completely stopped, although it still dripped from the overhanging branches of the elm. Shaking out her damp dress, Hope looked around, but all she saw were piles of dripping junk. She was about to tell Colt that the coast was clear, when a black dog came bounding through the hedge that separated the property from the lot next door, quickly followed by her twin sister.

"Hope?" Those sweet-as-blueberry-pie eyes blinked in confusion. "What are you doing here?"

She slammed the door in Colt's face, just as Buster slapped his muddy paws on her chest and bathed her face in dog slobbers. She pushed him down, and, having been taught at an early age that the best defense was a good offense, she threw the question back. "What are you doing?"

Faith blinked. "I was trying to get Buster to come in out of the rain when I heard you yell." She looked back at the car. "Is someone in there?"

"No."

"But I think I see—"

"A little rain won't hurt a dog," Hope cut her off as she reached down and pushed Buster away from the door where he'd started to whine. "So quit fretting about Buster and get back inside before you catch your death."

"But..."

"No ifs, ands, or buts." She flapped her hands. "Go on with you. Mama would kill me if I let you get even a sniffle."

Stubbornness obviously ran in the family because Faith didn't move a muscle, except for the ones around those innocent eyes that she squinted at the car. But fortunately, after only a few seconds she gave up and looked back at Hope.

"I'm sorry about the baby thing."

A simple *sorry* didn't come close to making up for the last few days of hell Hope had had to endure. Between pregnancy advice and people fighting over shower dates, Hope was about ready to blow this town regardless of whether or not she had money or a plan. But since an angry tirade would only prolong the conversation, she had little choice than to accept.

"Apology accepted." She tried to brush the mud off the front of her dress. "Well, you better get inside, and I better get going."

"But what about Shirlene's brother?"

Hope's head came up, but she refused to look behind her. "What are you talking about? Everyone knows I wouldn't be caught dead with Colt Lomax."

Faith leaned closer and squinted even harder. "Are you sure? Because that looks exactly like the man I met

Saturday night, and the one I saw with you and Shirlene at the diner."

Releasing her breath in one drawn-out sigh of frustration, Hope turned back to the car. Sure enough, the steam had evaporated enough to see Colt sitting there, as clear as day. He stared back at her with one dark eyebrow hiked up along with a corner of his sexy mouth. Wasn't the man even smart enough to duck?

"Well, good mornin'," he drawled as he stepped from the car and squatted down to scratch a wiggling Buster. "Nothin' like a little rain shower to liven things up."

Faith might be a little princess, but she was no dummy. Her gaze swept over Colt's rain-soaked body, then back to Hope, then over to the car, and then back to Hope. And just that quickly, the sun rose in those wide blue eyes along with the biggest, most disgusting smile Hope had ever seen in her life.

"Well, good morning, yourself." If people could pop from happiness, Faith was about to bust like an over-inflated balloon. "So what brings you here, Mr. Lomax?"

"Kindness and charity, Mrs. Calhoun," Colt said with a smile almost as big. "I'm helping Hope deliver food boxes."

Faith looked back at her. "How sweet."

Hope's desire to pick up the rusted crowbar at her feet and use it to wipe off both white-toothed smiles was almost too much to bear, especially when Colt continued to enjoy himself at her expense.

"That's a mighty pretty dress you got on, Mrs. Calhoun."

Since it was almost an exact duplicate of Hope's—minus the mud—she threw him a glare as Faith blushed and held out the soft fabric.

"Why, thank you, but please call me Faith."

Yes, please.

Colt shook his head. "Well, I'd love to, but my mama would have my hide if I showed such disrespect to such a fine married lady."

Hope wanted to show them both disrespect and leave their butts in the dust of Shirlene's Navigator. Unfortunately, the keys were in the pocket of Colt's wet jeans. Besides, before she left, Hope had to convince her sister that she had no reason to be grinning like a Disney princess after all the wicked stepmothers had been banished to another kingdom.

"I sure hope you weren't delivering boxes in that thing," Faith said with just a tad bit too much innocence.

"No, ma'am." Colt leaned an arm on the roof of the Chevy. "Even I couldn't get this thing to run."

She nodded, and Hope wondered if maybe she would leave it at that. But she should've known better.

"So if it doesn't run, what were you doing?"

Hope opened her mouth to reply, but nothing came out. Damn! Where was a brain when you needed it.

"We were just reliving old times," Colt helped her out. "I used to live here, and Hope lived next door."

Faith's eyes widened, and she turned to Hope. "I didn't realize this was where you and Shirlene grew up. You lived in Bubba's trailer?"

Colt's gaze snapped over to Hope's, and she explained to both of them. "Some guy named Bubba Wilkes bought it off Daddy for a hunting lodge, and now my sister and Slate are living in it while Slate builds his house."

Colt smiled and turned to Faith. "So welcome to the world of trailer trash, Mrs. Calhoun."

Faith didn't seem the least bit concerned about the negative connotation. "Thank you. I have to say, it was a little overwhelming at first, but now I love my little trailer. I'll be sad when we move out this Saturday."

"Slate's new house is finished?" Hope asked, suddenly consumed with resentment.

"Everyone in town chipped in to help." Faith's eyes twinkled with happiness. "It's been like a dream come true."

Yeah, my dream, Hope thought.

Faith nodded back in the direction of Bubba's trailer. "Why don't you come over and I'll make you some tea." She glanced back at the car. "That's if you're finished ... talking."

"No," Hope said.

Colt's eyebrows lifted. "We're not done ... talkin', honey?"

Hope's eyes narrowed as Buster came back over and sniffed around her boots. "No, I mean we don't have time for tea. We need to finish delivering the boxes."

"But I thought—"

"Try not to think, Lomax. Your brain can't take the sudden exercise."

He chuckled before demonstrating the manners that Hope had lacked. "Thanks for the invite, Mrs. Calhoun, but Hope's right. We need to finish delivering the boxes before we get another gully washer. But maybe next time."

"I'd like that. You're coming to the game on Friday, aren't you?"

"I'm afraid not," Colt said. "The open road calls."

"That's too bad." Faith sounded truly upset as she glanced at Buster, who trotted back to her. "Buster, what do you have?" She reached down and tugged something from his mouth, and Hope stared in horror as her sister lifted her tattered blue panties up. "What in the world?"

Colt's shout of laughter had Hope whirling and stomping off, and he was still laughing when he caught up to her.

"Real funny, Lomax," she fumed as she waited for him to pull the keys from his pocket.

"Come on, Hope. Lighten up." He chuckled as he fought with the wet denim. "You're not mad your sister caught us as much as you're mad about her moving into a house you wanted—with the man you wanted. You need to work on hiding your jealousy, honey."

"At least I'm not a kiss-ass." She kicked at a rusted tin can as she mimicked him. "Good mornin', Mrs. Calhoun. What a pretty dress you've got on, Mrs. Calhoun."

"I wasn't kissing ass. It is a pretty dress." He pressed the button on the key ring, but the locks clicking up could not drown out her grumble. She reached for the door handle, but the locks clicked back down before she could open the door.

"Don't tell me you're jealous of the compliments I gave your sister," he stated with the grin still in his voice.

"Not hardly." She jiggled the handle, refusing to turn around and face him.

"Are you sure?" He moved up closer, caging her in by resting his hands on the roof of the Navigator. "Because I'm sure I could come up with something to compliment you on. Although with all that mud, it's not going to be easy...or the wet doggy smell wafting off you." He grunted when she elbowed him in the stomach. "Now don't go gettin' all bent out of shape, honey. That wet, matted Rastafarian-looking hair isn't so ugly." This time he sidestepped the elbow, although he didn't remove his arms. "No, seriously. There are times when you don't look so bad...times when you look—"

He cut off suddenly. And when he spoke again, his voice held awe and deep-felt emotion.

"Beautiful. Breathtakingly beautiful."

Something inside her went very still at the words. Still and wobbly, all at the same time. Probably because Colt had never complimented her in his life, and she didn't realize how much those simple words would mean. Especially coming from his mouth. Slowly, she turned and lifted her eyes to him.

But, obviously embarrassed, he refused to look at her, his gaze pinned to a spot over the top of the Navigator.

"I've never seen anything like it," he continued as she blushed. "I mean I've seen parts before, but nothing like..."

Parts? He had to be talking about what she'd shown him in the car. And while it wasn't exactly what she wanted to hear, it was nice to know he'd been so impressed. Although she refused to think about how many other parts he'd seen.

"But seeing that beautiful V-twin housed in its original package..."

Okay, V-twin was a little weird, but coming from a mechanic, probably not so much.

"And those rocker boxes."

Boxes. Last time she checked, she only had one.

Confused, she finally spoke up. "Rocker boxes?"

His gaze flickered down for only a second before flickering back up. "Just look at it." His arms dropped as he pointed a finger over the top of the Navigator.

Hope had to climb up on the running board to see what

he was pointing at. An old rusty motorcycle leaned up against a dinged-up washing machine, and it didn't take a rocket scientist to figure out which one Colt was talking about.

"A motorcycle," she fumed as she turned to him. "You've been talking about a motorcycle?"

He looked back at her in shock. "That's not just a motorcycle, honey. That's a 1941 Harley Knucklehead."

Anger bubbled up inside her, and when his gaze snapped back to the rusty piece of crap, she jumped down and jerked the keys out of his hand. But it took her starting the SUV for Colt to finally snap out of his daze.

"Hey, what are you doing?" He reached for the door handle, and she quickly locked the doors. But she did crack the window.

"What am I doing?" She smiled sweetly. "I'm leaving you with the most breathtakingly beautiful piece of machinery you've ever seen." She popped the truck into reverse. "You knucklehead."

Chapter Eight

THE MOTORCYCLE WAS A CLASSIC. A perfect example of American ingenuity.

Named for the V-twin engine's rocker boxes that looked like lined-up knuckles on a fist, the Knucklehead was one of the fastest bikes of its time. With its wraparound oil tank, teardrop gas tank, and rocker covers, it became the model for all Harleys that followed.

Colt didn't know how it had ended up in a pile of junk. All he knew was that it hadn't been there when he lived in the trailer. He wouldn't have missed a gem like this. Which meant someone had dumped it there. Someone who didn't understand the value of such a bike. And if that was the case . . . finders keepers, losers weepers. Especially since Shirlene's husband, Lyle, still owned the property that the bike sat on.

"So you gonna chop it?" Tyler asked.

"I'm not sure." Colt ran a hand over the cracked leather of the sprung saddle seat. "It's a beauty just like it is."

"A beautiful pile of shit." Tyler shot a stream of tobacco juice out the open door of the garage.

"That coming from a man who drools over old Ford pickups."

"I guess everyone has their weaknesses. And yours has always been motorcycles. But good luck getting this one to run."

Colt glanced up. "Are you doubting my skills, T-bone?"

"Nope." Tyler adjusted the wad of tobacco in his lip. "I'm just remembering that other Harley you brought in."

Colt shook his head. "No comparison. That was a screwed up piece of crap, and I was all of fifteen."

Tyler placed his hands in his back pockets and smirked. "Still, it never reached the corner."

"This one will reach the corner and then some," Colt said, just as the rusted bolt he'd been trying to get off the engine case broke off in his socket wrench. He removed the bolt, to Tyler's chuckle.

"Now that's a pretty motorcycle." Tyler nodded at the custom chopper he had wheeled into the garage just that morning. Like Colt had figured, his bike had been hidden in the back shed. Parked next to the old Harley, it gleamed like a jewel of shiny chrome and metallic blue paint.

"So I thought you were leaving today," Tyler commented, as he leaned against a stack of tires.

"I am. Just as soon as I get this thing running." Colt sprayed more Liquid Wrench on the next bolt before he applied the socket wrench, but after a few fruitless minutes, he figured he would need to pull out Tyler's acetylene torch to get it loose.

"So you're staying a few months, are you?"

He sent Tyler an annoyed look. "A day, at the most."

"If you say so."

"I say so."

The words came out sounding pretty childish, and Tyler grinned as he walked back inside to answer the ringing phone.

Once he was gone, Colt tossed down the wrench and ran a hand through his hair. Tyler was right; it was going to take more than a day to get the bike running. With the rust and corrosion, it might take most of a year. So instead of sitting on the greasy garage floor, dirtying up the only pair of jeans he'd brought, he should be making arrangements to have the Knucklehead hauled back to his shop in L.A. where he had all the proper equipment to fix it.

Except something didn't feel right about using modern tools on a classic piece of history. The Knucklehead shouldn't be thrust into the twenty-first century so brutally, but rather babied in the small garage where Colt had taken apart his first carburetor with nothing more than a screwdriver and a pair of pliers, welded his first frame with a hand-held gas torch, and sanded his first gas tank, using nothing but a strip of 220-grit sandpaper and a little elbow grease.

Not that he planned on staying there until the bike was completely restored. But he had a few more days before he had to be in Austin. A few more days to spend with Shirlene, and a few more days to try to get inside a pair of satin panties that were as blue as the Texas bluebonnets that lined the highway to San Antonio.

Just the thought of what that strip of blue covered left him hotter than a tailpipe after an all-day ride. Which wasn't good. He had no business playing such naughty games with Hope. Hope was trouble with a capital T. Or more like tempting with a capital T. A temptation he needed to ignore if he wanted to keep his life as carefree as it was. Hope carried way too much baggage. Not only was she the town sweetheart, but she still had her heart set on catching someone like Calhoun—a hometown hero deeply rooted in Texas soil. And Colt was about as far from that as a man could get.

Of course, she might have her heart set on a respectable Texas boy, but her body seemed to like wild motorcycle bums just fine. And since that was the case, what was wrong with him offering her a little comfort after losing her lifelong beau? They were both consenting adults.

"Hey, mister. That's my motorcycle you're messin' with."

Colt looked up at the shadowy figure slouched in the open doorway of one garage stall. Taking the sunglasses out of the collar of his shirt, Colt slipped them on and studied the young boy in the beat-up cowboy boots, holey jeans, and stretched-out Spider-Man T-shirt. His hair was a bright strawberry blond that shot out in all directions like he hadn't combed it in a week, and his face still held the remnants of breakfast. Or possibly supper. Colt placed him at around ten or eleven, although he didn't know enough about kids to be sure.

"Did you hear me, mister?" The kid took two steps closer. "That's my motorcycle."

"Really?" Colt got to his feet and stretched out the kinks in his knees. "And I assume you have the papers to prove that."

His sunburned brow knotted as his dirty chin tipped up. "I don't need no papers. It's mine."

"Then what was it doing on Lyle Dalton's property?"

"I don't know nothin' about no Lyle Dalton. I was ridin' it down the road, and it ran out of gas, so I rolled it up into a yard."

Colt's eyebrows shot up. "Riding it down the road?" His gaze returned to the motorcycle that looked as if it hadn't been started since Kennedy was in office. "Is that so?"

"Yeah. And I was about to come and get it. Except you stole it before I could. And now I see that you busted it up." He pointed one grubby finger at the broken off bolt. "That's gonna cost ya."

Colt couldn't help but grin, which made the boy's big brown eyes turn even angrier.

"Are you makin' fun of me?"

"No, sir." Colt shook his head. "Although that has to be the worst lie I've ever heard. This motorcycle hasn't run for a good forty years and was probably on my brother-in-law's property for the last five."

"That's a lie!" The boy doubled up his fists. "I found it at the dump, and I rolled it home a week ago!"

Colt's eyes widened. The bike weighed five times more than the kid did, but for some reason, he didn't doubt for a minute that the scrappy kid had achieved such a feat. Especially if he lived out on Grover Road. Tough times made for tough kids. And if that was the case, then the whole finders keepers thing worked against Colt.

Unless the kid liked money more than he liked machines.

"Calm down." Colt held up a hand. "I didn't realize the Knucklehead belonged to you. How about if I give you a thousand for it?"

The kid seemed to stare right through him with eyes way too observant for such a small fry. Then, before Colt could even sweeten the deal, the boy whipped out a cell phone from his back jeans pocket.

"How do you spell that? N-U—"

"K-N," Colt supplied, stunned by the agility of the thumbs that flew over the keypad. When the kid finished punching buttons, he held up the phone with a wide grin, showing off a chipped front tooth.

"More like thirty thousand."

Colt's eyebrows hiked up at the number flashed at him. "For a running bike with all the original parts, not a rusted piece of scrap metal I'm not even sure I can get to run."

The kid gave him another steely-eyed look before his gaze wandered over to the gleaming chopper. "You make that bike?"

"Yes, but I had a little help."

"How much they pay you for something like that?"

"Enough."

"You know Jesse James?"

Colt hesitated, wondering how much he should tell the kid. Figuring it didn't make any difference, he answered truthfully. "I do."

With boots that appeared to be too big for his feet slapping against the concrete floor, the kid moved around the custom bike, examining it from all angles. "I'll tell you what, I'll trade you, even steven."

Colt bit back a smile. "'Fraid not, buddy. That one's already sold."

"I'm not your buddy," he stated as he flipped a leg over the bike.

"Oh, no, you don't." Within two steps, Colt had the kid off the bike and back on the floor.

"Don't touch me!" The boy jerked back, almost dropping his phone.

"Then don't climb on my bike without asking."

His bottom lip protruded. "Well, now I ain't gonna sell you my bike at all." Slipping the phone back into his jeans pocket, he grabbed the handlebars and used the slanted heel of one boot to kick at the kickstand.

Since the bike wasn't his, all Colt could do was watch. But it wasn't easy, not when he had to fight down the urge to jump in front of the bike and fight over it like he was fighting for a Tonka truck at a playground. Instead, he pulled his wallet from his back pocket and took out a twenty, which was about all he had left after dropping the hundreds out at Grover Road.

"I'll tell you what." Colt tried not to beg. "Take this as earnest money, and then, if I can get it running, I'll have it appraised and give your parents thirty percent of whatever the appraisal turns out to be."

The kid stopped kicking and turned to him, his eyes riveted to the money. "Ninety percent, and we got a deal."

Colt had to give it to the kid. He was a wheeler and a dealer.

"Fifty and that's final."

"Seventy, and I get to help."

"Oh, no. I don't need some kid running around getting in my way. Besides, shouldn't you be in school?"

"I'm homeschooled." The reply came almost too quickly.

Colt's gaze narrowed on the innocent-looking face. No kid on Grover Road had ever been homeschooled that he knew of. Of course, no kid had an expensive cell phone with Internet access either. Obviously things had changed in the last eight years. Still, he wasn't about to have some obstinate little kid bugging him nonstop while he tried to work.

"Sixty, and you stay the heck away from the garage."

"Fine," he grumbled as he stuck out one grubby hand. "But I get to ride it once it's finished."

"Not in my lifetime." Colt smacked the twenty into his palm. "Now get out of here and let me work."

The kid stared at the money for a few seconds before he stuffed it in his front pocket.

"You better make sure there are no holes," Colt advised, before he sat back down next to the motorcycle.

"There ain't," he said. Out of the corner of his eye, Colt watched as the kid felt around in his pocket.

While Colt went back to work on the bike, the boy meandered around the garage with his hands stuffed in his pockets before he came back to sit on the other side of the Knucklehead. "I'm named after him, you know."

"Who?" he asked without looking up.

"Jesse James—the outlaw, not the motorcycle dude."

Colt shook his head.

It figured.

He felt like he'd just been held up.

Chapter Nine

A WEST TEXAS football game was something to behold—not necessarily the game itself as much as the insanity of the fans who attended it. The Bramble High Football Stadium looked as if a huge purple paintball had been dropped from overhead, splattering sweatshirts and jackets, hair and faces, and even bare man-boobs and beer bellies with the dark, vibrant color. Of course, this wasn't just any game. This was a play-off game, the first in a series that could lead to a state championship and another year added to the WELCOME TO BRAMBLE sign at the city limits. Pennants flew, pompoms waved, and balloons floated amid the chattering, excited folks of Bramble.

But since the game had yet to start, the town's attention wasn't on the field as much as it was on Hope, as she made her way up the steps of the stadium.

"Hey, Hope!" Kenny Gene blasted his air horn, and Hope's heart almost jumped out of her chest.

"Hope, honey, don't be sittin' too close to the field," Rachel Dean yelled from her spot right behind the band. Her purple foil wig glittered in the stadium lights as she pointed two huge foam fingers straight at Hope like a double-barreled shotgun. "Some of Jimmy Daniels punts can go a little haywire, and we don't want you goin' into an early labor."

"Early would definitely be the word for it," Shirlene said from behind her.

Hope glanced back at her best friend. As usual, Shirlene was dolled up like a blonde bombshell—hair curled and fluffed, makeup artfully applied, and enough gold and diamonds to warrant an armed escort. And everything she wore, from the sky-high heels to the down jacket, was a deep Bramble High purple. Hope, on the other hand, had done nothing more than run a brush through her hair and slap on a sweatshirt.

Purple, of course.

"Up here, girls," her mother yelled, shaking her cowbell to get their attention.

Hope didn't particularly want to sit next to her mama, not when her mama was still convinced she was pregnant and nothing Hope said would change her mind. Jenna Scroggs had been a smothering mother before, but it was nothing compared to what she was now. They hadn't even reached her row, when Jenna started in.

"Hope Marie, don't tell me you forgot to bring a jacket? If I told you once, I've told you a thousand times—don't forget your jacket. And now ain't the time to catch a chill."

Since the jacket Hope had worn to every game since she was fifteen was now being worn by the woman sitting next to her mother, all she could do was shrug, which wasn't enough for her mama.

"Burl, take off your coat and give it to Hope. I don't want her catchin' a chill."

"I don't want Daddy's coat," she said, a little too loudly. "I'm not cold. In fact, I'm burning up." She was burning up, burning up with jealousy over an ugly purple letterman's jacket with more than a few state championship patches on the leather sleeves.

"Leave her be, Jenna," Darla butted in from the next row up, where she sat with her husband, Billy Joe. "I thought I would boil alive with my first one. Tyson was like havin' my own little heatin' pad tucked right inside my belly. Billy Joe swears we saved hundreds on our utility bills that year."

"She's right," Billy Joe agreed. "I didn't even need no blanket when snuggled up next to her."

Shirlene laughed. And since her friend thought the situation was so amusing, Hope shoved her into the row so she would be the one to sit next to Slate's coat and closer to her overprotective mother.

"Temper, temper, honey," Shirlene whispered back at her. "You don't want to hurt the twins, do ya?"

"Shut up, Shirl." Hope sat down on the purple-and-gold blanket that her mother had spread all the way down the bleachers, even though the only children living in Bramble were Hope and Faith. After the wedding, Hope's brother, Dallas, had headed back to the University of Texas in Austin. Jenna Jay had gone back to Texas Tech in Lubbock, and Tessa had returned to her job in Amarillo. Lucky ducks.

"Hi," Faith spoke so softly Hope could hardly hear her over the crowd's building excitement.

"Hi, honey," Shirlene patted Faith's Wrangler-covered knee. "You all packed up and ready to move into that gorgeous new home of yours?"

"There wasn't really that much to pack."

"Well, give it a few months, and I'm sure you'll have as much crap as I do."

"Doubtful," Hope grumbled.

Shirlene shot her a snide look before she got even. " 'Course, crap or no crap, Hope and I will be there bright and early in the mornin' to help you move into your dream home."

"Really?" Faith leaned over and looked at Hope with enough wide-eyed gratitude to fill Cinderella's castle.

"What are sisters for," Hope said as sincerely as a jilted woman could. But Faith wasn't so easily fooled, and after only a second of staring into Hope's eyes, she glanced down at Slate's letterman's jacket, and all that Disney happiness fizzled right out of her.

"Of course, if you'd rather not help, I understand."

"Hope not help out a member of Bramble?" Shirlene sounded horrified. "Why that's like asking a wide-mouthed bass not to swim." She shot a warning look at Hope. "Isn't that right, Hog?"

"I'll be there with bells on," Hope said, although this time she refused to look her sister in the eye. Fortunately, Faith didn't push it and instead turned to answer a question her mama had asked.

"Just you wait, Shirl," Hope spoke under her breath. "Your day will come."

"My day has already come and gone, honey. The town loved to gossip about all my sexual exploits before I married Lyle, but after the weddin' no one seemed the least bit interested." She opened her huge purple designer purse and pulled out a bag of microwave popcorn. "Of course, I can't say as I blame them. Married life is about as boring as it gets."

Hope took a handful of popcorn. "Lyle still out of town?"

"Yes. And I have to tell you, I'm starting to get worried."

Hope choked on a kernel, and Shirlene tapped her on the back while her mama leaned over with a concerned look. After catching her breath, Hope waited for her mother to sit back before she whispered, "You think he's cheating?"

Shirlene's green eyes widened. "Of course not. Why would a man cheat when he could come home to this?" She fanned French-manicured nails down the front of the tight purple sweater. "No, I think it's something worse."

"What could be worse?"

"Try *no money*."

"Dalton Oil's in financial trouble—"

Shirlene slapped a hand over Hope's mouth before glancing around. "Would you keep it down, honey? We don't want a riot on our hands, do we?" After releasing Hope's mouth, Shirlene dove into the popcorn, as if she hadn't just brought up her husband's financial ruin.

"So what makes you think there's a problem?"

"Last time I was in Austin shopping, I had two of my credit cards rejected."

Hope snorted. "With the way you shop, Shirl, that's not a big deal. You probably just spent over the limit."

"Over a hundred-thousand-dollar limit? I'm a big spender, honey, but not that big. Which means Lyle isn't paying them off like he used to every month—which means something isn't right."

"Why don't you ask him about it?"

"I have, and he just keeps telling me not to worry my pretty little head over it."

"I hate to bring this up, Shirl." Hope leaned over for another handful of popcorn. "But isn't that what you wanted when you married him? You told me you never wanted to worry about money again."

"I guess you're right." Shirlene nibbled a few kernels before she turned to Hope. "But what if I should be worried? What if the well ran dry—literally?"

It was a terrifying thought. Dalton Oil employed half the town. If it went under, Bramble would too. It had happened to other small towns when their main source of income fell prey to a weak economy. But Hope couldn't believe that could happen to her beloved town—not when oil was what made the world go round.

"It's probably not as bad as you think," Hope tried to rationalize. "Maybe Lyle just got too busy and forgot to pay the credit cards off. And now that you brought it to his attention, I bet it's already been taken care of."

"Probably," Shirlene said, in between bites, although she didn't sound convinced. "But when I go to Midland for your baby shower decorations, I'm definitely taking cash."

Another kernel got stuck in Hope's throat, but this time a blast of disbelief shot it back out, and it sailed down three rows to land in Sue Ellen's purple spray-painted hair.

"Baby shower?" Hope shook her head. "Oh, no, you are not throwing me a baby shower, Shirl."

"Why, of course I am, honey. What kind of a best friend do you take me for?"

Before Hope could tell her exactly what kind of friend she took her for, the announcer's voice blasted through the speakers.

"Please stand for our national anthem!"

"I mean it, Shirl," Hope said as she stood and placed

a hand over her heart. "This foolishness has gone on long enough, and I'm certainly not going to let the good people of this town spend their hard-earned money on things I'll never use."

"Who says you'll never use them. You want kids, don't you?"

Hope had wanted kids. Cute little blonde-headed mini-quarterbacks and petite, brunette starlets, but that plan had gone to hell in her sister's handcart. Now all she wanted was to cuss out Shirlene, along with an entire town of people who refused to accept the truth.

Unfortunately, she was forced to drop the conversation when the Bramble High ROTC took the field; if there was one thing the folks of Bramble didn't put up with, it was disrespecting the American flag. And after the honor guard marched off the field, the roar of the crowd grew deafening as the team tore through the paper banner.

Slate was the last one to step through the tattered remnants. Without a hat, his hair shone like liquid gold in the bright stadium lights. When he reached the benches, he looked up at the crowd, his eyes searching until his gaze caught hers. Suddenly she was back in high school, standing on the sidelines in her cheerleading uniform, awaiting a smile and a wink from the most popular boy in school.

Except this time, his gaze moved on quickly, and she became nothing more than an observer to the warm, loving smile that he sent her sister, a sister who reciprocated with a blown kiss that Hope could've sworn made Slate blush.

The cheers grew louder, and Hope jerked her gaze away, only to be caught in the stormy depths of a pair of eyes she hadn't planned on seeing again.

Ever.

The pain in her heart moved to her butt.

Colt Lomax stood at the bottom of the bleachers in a tight black T-shirt that made him stand out in the sea of purple like the black sheep he was. He casually leaned against the concrete wall that ran in front of the stands, one biker boot crossed over the other and a worn leather jacket hooked over his tattooed arm.

He didn't look at her with loving warmth. More like steamy lust. Steamy lust that caused her breath to hitch and her heart to thump wildly. This man would never blush if she threw him a kiss; more than likely he would catch it and place it somewhere really nasty.

The pervert.

Of course, he wasn't the only pervert in the stands. Every time she was alone with the man, she broke every moral instilled in her since birth. Even now her body heated from the message in those devilish silver eyes.

If you show me yours, I'll show you mine.

"Colt Lomax!"

Hope jumped guiltily when Shirlene stood up and yelled.

"Quit blockin' the view and get your cocky butt up here!"

His eyes remained on Hope for a brief second more before he pushed away from the wall and ambled up the steps. Without asking permission, he sat down on the end of the bleachers, sandwiching Hope between his broad shoulders and Shirlene's puffy down jacket.

Faith leaned over and smiled down the row at him. "I thought you were leaving, Colt."

"Change of plans," he merely stated, before he reached over to grab a handful of popcorn, his bare arm brushing against Hope's boob in the process. She pulled back, only to run into Billy Joe's knees.

"Pardon me," she choked out, before sitting back up.

Meanwhile, Colt munched the popcorn as if nothing was amiss, although when he reached for the next handful, Hope quickly crossed her arms over her chest. One corner of his mouth twitched, but he didn't say a word.

With Colt sitting there smirking, she thought it would be hard to concentrate on the game. But it didn't take long for her to get caught up in the thrill of competition, especially when the Bulldogs' lanky quarterback had an arm that would make pro scouts drool.

The kid's talent quickly turned the game into a rout, so much so that Hope's attention began to wander. Unfortunately, it didn't wander very far. In fact, no more than a few inches, to the man who sat with his arms propped on his hard thighs and his gaze riveted to the field.

His dark hair didn't shine like liquid gold in the stadium lights, but rather gleamed like Shirlene's polished onyx kitchen countertops as it spilled over the ribbed neck of his black T-shirt. A T-shirt that stretched over broad shoulders and lean back muscles, stopping just short of the waistband of his jeans. A very tiny bit of skin peeked out, just enough to make Hope swallow hard and shiver.

He glanced over. "Are you cold?"

Since she wasn't about to claim otherwise, she nodded and, within seconds, found herself engulfed in the folds of his thick leather jacket.

"No, really..." She tried to slip it off, but her mother jumped in.

"Don't be rude, Hope Marie."

Not wanting to cause a scene, she acquiesced and

slipped her arms into the smooth satin lining. It smelled of him—raw and dangerous, something she tried not to notice as her gaze returned to the game. But only a few seconds later, her eyes left the green of the field to stare down at the tattooed arm resting on one knee.

It was the first chance she'd had to study the tattoo up close—in the Chevy, her mind had been riveted on a different part of his anatomy. Still, the blue-ink design was so cluttered and detailed it took her a few minutes to figure out what it was.

A snake coiled around the corded muscles of his forearm, its opened-fanged mouth poised over the huge knot of Colt's biceps and its rattle curled around his wrist like the watch he never wore. Along the diamond-backed reptilian body, other tattoos jutted out. The front forks and tire of a motorcycle. A banner with "Desperado" written across it. A tombstone with his father's initials. The Texas state flag. A queen of diamonds playing card. A thorny rose. And at the very top, peeking out from beneath the tight sleeve of his shirt, was some kind of snarling animal.

A wolverine?

A javelina?

Hope leaned closer. But before she could figure it out, his arm moved from beneath her nose, and she glanced up into Colt's curious, gray eyes. Caught in the act, there wasn't much she could do.

"What kind of animal is that?" She pointed.

"A rattlesnake."

"Not that one. The one—" Before she could finish, he jumped up.

"I'm headed to the snack bar. Anybody want anything?"

"More than you can carry, big brother." Shirlene quickly

got up to go with him. Surprised that Shirlene would leave a football game for food, Hope glanced back at the field, only to discover it was halftime. Where had the time gone? There was no way she had been looking at Colt for an entire quarter. But as the band performed their marching routine, she realized she'd done just that.

Stunned by the revelation, she didn't pay much attention when Emma Jean flopped down next to her and started chattering up a storm.

"...and she's only been doin' this for a couple months, but I think she's got real talent, and I just know with your expert Hollywood advice she can go on to great things—possibly even a hemorrhoid commercial." Emma Jean pointed out at the field. "Look, there she is! Isn't that the cutest little outfit you've ever seen in your life? I wanted to get it in the school colors, but wouldn't you know it, it only comes in red, white, and blue—which is almost as good."

A little girl strutted out on the field in a white cowboy hat and a sequined outfit with a blue star on the front. She wore little white boots with huge blue tassels and red sequined cuffs around her wrists. Hope had to admit that she looked cute and was about to say so, when she noticed Emma Jean's husband, Chester, following behind her, holding two batons and a blowtorch.

"Oh, no." Hope shook her head. "I don't think this is a good idea, Emma. Especially if she's only been doing this for a couple months. I mean, I'll be more than happy to help her anyway I can—"

Before she could finish, the blowtorch flamed, and the batons were lit and handed to the little girl, who didn't look the least bit worried. Obviously, she'd done this before. But that didn't stop Hope from leaning forward in fear.

The band struck up "You Are My Sunshine," and flaming batons took flight. And darned if the little girl didn't manage to toss and twirl those burning sticks like a pro. Impressed and relieved, Hope stood and clapped and whooped as loudly as the rest of the crowd as the performance ended in a blur of whirling fire and a cute little hat-tipping bow. The batons were handed off to her daddy, who was beaming like any proud papa should.

Hope sat back down and sighed in relief.

It was a tad bit premature, because while Chester had brought something to light the batons with, he'd failed to bring anything to put them out. And while most people might snuff them on the ground, football turf was as sacred as the Shroud of Turin to the people of West Texas. So he stood there with the flaming sticks, uncertain what to do or where to go. Things might've turned out alright if the team hadn't come out of the locker room, forcing the band to leave the field.

Hope had never been in the marching band, but she'd listened to enough practices to know members did not get out of line for anything less than a natural disaster. And these kids had learned the lesson well. Without breaking file once, they marched right past those flaming batons as if they weren't there—eyes straight ahead and instruments held vertically in front of them as a drummer tapped out a beat.

Chester did his best to avoid bare faces and hands, and it was easy to see where his daughter got her baton-twirling skill. As the tuba section left the field, it looked as if a catastrophe had been avoided. It wasn't until the

band members took the steps back up to the bleachers that
Hope noticed the flaming poof on the cap of a trombonist.

"Fire!" Hope hollered at the top of her lungs and pointed
down at the kid.

Everyone froze.

Everyone except Colt, who was headed back from the
snack bar. Retaining the 64 oz. Big Slurp, he handed the
tray of nachos off to Shirlene before knocking the hat to
the ground and stomping out the fire with one big biker
boot.

Hope might've commented to Emma Jean about his
quick reflexes if her attention hadn't been caught by the
giant of a man who had just entered the stadium behind
Colt.

It had been years since she'd seen Rachel Dean's
cousin Bear, and she had forgotten how appropriately he'd
been nicknamed. Bear stood a good head and a half taller
than the other men who were filing back into the stands
with their nachos and drinks.

Except Bear wasn't carrying a cardboard tray of goodies. Instead, his huge paw was clamped over the shoulder
of the short man that he pushed in front of him. A man
Hope recognized immediately.

"Sheldon?" Hope spoke more loudly than she
intended, her voice quieting the mutters that had started
after the fire had been put out.

Bear looked up and grinned broadly, flashing an
incomplete set of tobacco-stained teeth. "See, Harley," he
yelled as he shoved poor Sheldon up the stairs. "I told you
I would find the baby's daddy!"

Chapter Ten

"Too bad Sheldon didn't turn out to be the daddy," Kenny Gene said as he piled his paper plate high with food the women of Bramble had brought to feed the crowd that had showed up to move Slate and Faith into their new home. "Besides that sissy fit of tears he broke into when he saw Hope, I kinda liked the little feller."

Standing beneath a cedar tree behind Slate and Faith's just-completed house, Colt couldn't help feeling a little annoyed. He might not want to be part of the daddy-hunt, but it was a little ego-deflating that he didn't even rate above a man who wore orange pants and used more hair products than Twyla. If Sheldon was straight, Colt would eat Kenny Gene's hat.

He took another bite from his own heaping plate of food, while he continued to eavesdrop on the group of townsfolk clustered around the long table.

"Still," Sheriff Winslow wiped the barbecue sauce off his chin with the edge of the paper napkin tucked into the collar of his uniform shirt, "since Hope insisted we throw this one back, Harley says the hunt is still on." He glanced over at Bear, who sat at the end of the table in front of two heaping plates. "But this time, Bear, try to pick out one who doesn't act like Darla's nephew."

"I'll do my best, Sam," Bear said, over the sparerib he'd been annihilating.

At that point, Colt probably could've stepped in and tried to set things straight about Hope not being pregnant. It would be the right thing to do. But Colt had never done the right thing where Hope was concerned, and it seemed a shame to start now.

His gaze wandered through the crowd until he found her. She wore jeans today. Not tight Wranglers, but worn jeans with a relaxed fit that hung low on her hips, along with a long-sleeved navy T-shirt with the name of a California surf shop printed on the front, and a pair of flip-flops that showed off her pretty pink-painted toenails.

The October sun had reddened her nose and deepened the tan of her cheeks, a tan that had been brought to his attention in the front seat of the beat-up Chevy. And in the last few days, he'd thought of little else but the tiny triangle of pale skin Hope had revealed beneath her panties. Even now, he had to do a little covert adjusting at just the thought of Hope in the tiny bikini that had left that triangle. The kind of bikini with ties that took only a swift tug to undo.

Hope glanced up, and he got lost in the blue of her eyes. A blue that turned all dark and sensual, as if she, too, was thinking about their naughty fun. Of course, her eyes didn't remain sensual for long. It only took a few blinks before the passion turned to annoyance.

But her sass made Colt even hotter, and he tossed the remainder of his food into the trash bag taped onto the table, with the intention of joining the group of townsfolk that she was talking with. But before he could make his way through the crowd, a strawberry blond head of hair caught his attention, and he looked over to see Jesse stuffing his face with a hot dog, the ketchup dripping off the end onto his Batman T-shirt.

"Hey, Kenny," Colt said. "You know that kid?"

Kenny looked up from his plate at Colt and registered surprise. "Hey, Colt, when did you get here?" He glanced around. "What kid?"

"The one over by the hot dogs—Jesse."

Kenny's eyes landed on the boy, who had moved on to the chicken wings. "Sure, everyone knows Jesse. I bought Twyla one of them stand-up hair dryers from him that made her happier than a pig in mud."

Sam Winslow jumped in. "He sold me a wet vac that had more suction than a ten-dollar hooker—" He shut up when Darla walked past. "Anyway, that thing was well worth the thirty dollars I gave him."

Colt couldn't help but grin at the kid who was now munching on a wing. No wonder Jesse could afford the fancy cell phone. The kid was a real shyster.

"What does his father do?" Colt asked.

"He doesn't have a daddy," Sam said. "Just a mama that works nights at that truck stop on 87."

"I thought she worked cleaning rooms at a hotel in Lamesa," Kenny leaned over the table and snagged a cookie. "Least ways that's what Jesse's big sister told me when she picked up the money for that hair dryer—pretty thing, but not real friendly."

The thought of a single mom working two jobs made Colt reevaluate the deal he'd made with Jesse. Of course, knowing how prideful people on Grover could be, he couldn't just hand the woman a check. But once he finished the bike, he could jack up the appraisal.

"Would you look at our little Hope," Sam pulled Colt's attention away from Jesse. "It looks like she's back to her old self."

Sure enough, Hope was giving Harley Sutter an earful. At first, Colt thought she was ranting about her gay friend getting kidnapped. But when he walked over, he realized she was rattling off from a list that she held in one hand.

"...and the storefronts along Main need some paint. And we could use another stoplight to keep the out-of-towners from speeding—I was thinking right on Spruce, near Josephine's, since it might pull in more business. And what happened to that hotel chain building a hotel in Bramble?" She tapped the list. "Oh, and there's a pothole on the corner of Maple and Main that needs fixing."

Harley chuckled, and his mustache twitched. "Now that's the goddaughter I remember—always trying to take my job."

Hope snorted. "Not hardly, Uncle Harley. I just wanted to point out some things that need fixing."

"All things I've noticed for myself. But money has been a little tight the last couple years. And with Dalton Oil cuttin' back, it doesn't look like it's going to get better anytime soon."

"Cutting back?" Hope's eyes turned concerned.

Harley patted her shoulder. "Nothing to get upset about. Just a little tightenin' of the belt, from what I hear."

Since Desperado Customs also had to cut back on spending from time to time, Colt wasn't concerned about Lyle's company. But Hope wasn't so easily pacified.

"Will anyone lose their jobs?"

"Of course not. They probably won't hand out Wal-Mart gift cards for Christmas this year, is all."

Colt could tell by the look on her face that Hope didn't completely believe him. But she allowed Harley to change the conversation to the upcoming Halloween carnival and Thanksgiving Day Parade. Colt didn't really care about carnivals or parades. He only had a day before he left town, and he planned on spending it trying to get in Hope's panties. But it wasn't easy to distract a woman who was as single-minded as Hope. His own mind had about exhausted itself, when Slate and Faith showed up.

Faith led her husband by the hand, as if she was forcing him to do something he really didn't want to. And Colt figured out what that something was when Slate opened his mouth.

"I want to thank you for helping out, Colt." He glanced over at his wife. "If I'd known how many different configurations a couch could be put in, I would've bought a couple of beanbag chairs and been done with it."

"Shush, you." Faith swatted at him, and then laughed when Slate pulled her into his arms and snuggled her neck.

The open show of affection had Colt glancing over into Hope's hurt eyes. He couldn't really blame her. The guy had built a house with his own two hands. Damn, you couldn't get any more perfect than that. Hope had the right to be bent out of shape, and having it shoved in her face at every turn couldn't be easy...something that might play right into Colt's hands.

"You're welcome," Colt said. "But I probably should get going." He turned to Hope. "Since my ornery sister seems to have left already, did you need a lift?"

Without a moment's hesitation, she answered. "If it's no problem."

"No problem, at all." Colt tried to contain his smile, while Faith didn't even attempt to hide her enthusiasm for the idea.

"If you're riding on Colt's motorcycle, you'll need some boots," she offered, before she scurried back inside.

The cowboy boots were bright red and sexy as hell. Colt had a hard time keeping his eyes off them as Hope braided her hair and waited for him to pull the helmet and leather jacket out of the side bags he used when traveling.

"I don't need the jacket," she stated.

"Believe me, you'll feel differently after a few minutes in a fifty-mile-an-hour wind."

Surprisingly, she didn't argue, but slipped her arms into the jacket that he held out. Once she had it zipped, he handed her the helmet. It was too big, but it would have to do. She struggled with lacing the strap, so he brushed her hands aside and did it for her. But the feel of the soft skin beneath her chin distracted him so much that it took him a couple tries.

"It's a pretty bike," she said, her breath falling over his face, all warm and sweet.

But it wasn't her breath that left him feeling like he had just planted the American flag on the moon. It was on the tip of his tongue to tell her that he had built the bike, was involved from its conception to the last spit and polish. But before he could, her mouth quirked up in a smirk.

"Not eighty thousand pretty," she completely deflated him, "but pretty."

"I guess I'm just a sucker." He jerked the helmet strap tight before he walked around the bike to flip down the passenger foot pegs. Most choppers didn't have pegs or a small removable leather seat that fit over the back fender. But his client had a wife, although Colt wasn't sure for how long, after the woman spent a few hours straddling the hard metal.

Colt didn't plan on riding that long. Just long enough to get Hope somewhere less populated.

After climbing on the bike, he turned and helped her on. Then he flipped down the visor on her helmet before he took his aviators from the collar of his shirt and slipped them on.

"You ready?"

"Yes," came her muffled reply.

He turned the electric switch on the chrome analog dash and punched the starter. The engine roared to life, and the loud throb soothed his bruised ego as he settled back on the form-fitting leather seat and released the clutch. He eased the slick machine over the gravel drive and out onto the blacktop. Hope's hands rested on her knees, until the bike bounced over the edge of the asphalt, and then she quickly latched on to his waist.

He smiled.

Okay, so maybe a passenger wasn't such a bad thing.

Colt took his time on the side roads, cruising no faster than thirty. But when he turned onto the highway, he twisted the throttle, and the bike took flight. Hope slid back before her arms and thighs tightened, and she slid back up, the edge of the visor bumping against his head. Of course, a sledgehammer could've dropped from the sky and he wouldn't have cared, not with those sweet thighs locked around him. Heat emanated from the spot pressed against his lower back, taking the chill right out of the wind that whistled past them.

The pretty autumn scenery took a backseat to hot

images of tanned thighs spread wide and waiting. Desire knotted in his stomach, and his crotch started to throb more intensely than the engine. He tried to keep his mind on the road, but it was difficult with two soft hands inches from the brain he was now using.

Hope seemed to be falling right into his plans to get her into bed; now all he had to do was figure out what bed. He didn't think she'd go willingly back to Shirlene's guesthouse. Nor could he take her back to her house. Not when Jenna and Burl could arrive home at any minute. And a hotel was a good fifty miles away.

That left only one other place.

He expected Hope to start yelling and pounding his back when he turned off the highway—even an unbaffled motor was no match for a champion hog caller. But, strangely enough, she didn't show any signs of protest.

The road to Sutter Springs was unpaved, and it took all his concentration to finagle the bike around the ruts. Once there, he pulled under the big cottonwood and cut the engine. Before she could ask what they were doing, he quickly tried to come up with a feasible excuse.

"Since you're not used to riding, I thought you might need a little break."

She slipped off the back of the bike, taking those sweet thighs with her.

"Geez." She rubbed her butt. "You really need to come up with a better backseat."

With his eyes glued to the way the soft denim clung to the sweet hills, he couldn't comment.

Undoing the strap beneath her chin, she pulled the helmet off. "You would think with as much as the bike cost, they could add a little more cushion." She slipped off the jacket and placed it, and the helmet, on the seat. Then she stretched her hands over her head, showing off a strip of tanned stomach that finished off the moisture in his mouth.

Colt turned away, hoping to get some kind of control over his out-of-control libido. "Custom choppers aren't really made for passengers."

"Then who invented the little seat?"

"A guy who was hoping to get lucky."

"Well, you didn't get lucky, Lomax." She moved over to the shade cast by the shimmering gold leaves of the cottonwood tree.

Finally able to move without causing himself pain, he pulled out a rain poncho from one of the side bags and walked over to spread it out under the tree.

"So why are you still here?" she asked, once they were both seated on the poncho. "I thought you would be long gone by now."

Leaning back on his elbows, he cocked a brow at her. "I could ask you the same thing, especially when it seems painful for you to be around your sister and Slate."

"It's not painful," Hope snapped.

"Really?"

"Okay." She crossed her arms and looked away. "So it's a little painful. So what? I'll get over it."

He reached out and grabbed a blade of buffalo grass and placed it in his mouth. "I don't doubt it for a minute, especially since you've lived five years without him."

"That was different."

He shrugged. "Well, I'm not an expert, but true love seems like it would get a little antsy after five years."

"You're right. You're not an expert." Hope shot him a

snide look. "Did you ever even have a girlfriend—and I'm not talking about one-nighters."

He tipped his head. "You sure you don't want to talk about one-nighters? Because some of the best times I've had have been one-nighters."

He didn't expect her to take the bait. Hope had always had a selective memory. He only wished he could be as fortunate, but with those glossy lips in front of him, memories sizzled through his brain as if they had happened only yesterday.

"Never mind," she said as she turned and looked at the horizon. "I should've known I couldn't have a normal conversation with you."

"A few."

Hope looked back.

"I've had a few girlfriends, but nothing serious," Colt said, truthfully. "And what about you? And I'm not talking about gay roommates."

"Who said Sheldon was gay?" When his eyebrows hiked up, she conceded. "Okay, but he's also a very nice guy who helped me out when I first arrived in L.A. and who didn't deserve to be dragged halfway across the country by a crazy bounty hunter. I'll be shocked if he doesn't sue the entire town."

"He won't. From what I could tell, he has a major crush on Bear. Besides, Shirlene pampered the hell out of him and flew him home first-class." He pulled the blade of grass out of his mouth and tossed it away. "So what happened in L.A.?"

It hadn't been hard to figure out that Hollywood hadn't been kind to Hope. He had dated his fair share of women with stars in their eyes and had listened to countless horror stories of tough casting directors and endless auditions.

Most never made it past a few commercials or a couple lines in a B-movie. It wasn't anything to be ashamed of. But Hope wasn't one to own up to defeat. Which was why he was shocked when she answered so honestly.

"I sucked."

A snorted laugh popped out of his mouth and earned him a vicious look from her sky blue eyes.

"Don't get all feisty." He held up a hand. "I wasn't laughing at you. I was laughing at your choice of words."

"I don't know why," Hope said. "Those were the exact words you used after my debut performance in *Annie Get Your Gun*. Are you telling me you lied?"

"I might've stretched the truth a little. You weren't that bad." When she glanced over at him with a look of disbelief, he added, "I mean, some parts weren't so bad—the scenes where you didn't look terrified."

"I wasn't terrified. I was merely nervous. And who wouldn't be nervous when the gun in their hand held a live round?"

"Come on, Hope," he pressed, "be honest. The only reason you took drama your senior year was because Shirlene wanted to. And the only reason you ended up as Annie was because Shirlene got the flu and couldn't do it. Still, I might've believed you stumbled onto your one true passion if I hadn't been sitting in the audience that night. The girl I saw up on the stage looked like she was about to throw up—and not from happiness."

"I did throw up," she stated. "Right in the back of the wagon Daryl Watts loaned to the drama department."

He laughed, and this time she joined in. The sun had dipped even lower, low enough to spill beneath the aging leaves of the cottonwood, gilding her face and catching the natural highlights in the lock of hair that had come undone from her braid. *Cute* and *sassy* had always been the words that came to mind when he thought of Hope. But now the word *beautiful* joined the list.

And the realization caused him to sober.

Just as quickly, she stopped laughing and tipped her head to one side in confusion. "What?"

Since the entire beautiful thing was out of the question, he pointed to the speck of barbecue sauce just below her bottom lip. "You've got something right there."

She swiped at her chin. "Did I get it?"

Being a man of few words, he reached out and took care of it himself. At the first touch of her soft skin, his finger lingered, then took a detour up to her mouth. Her lips opened, and a hot, moist puff of air caressed his finger, sending a shaft of heat straight to his stomach...and lower.

Cradling her jaw in his hand, he tipped her chin up with his thumb and leaned in.

"I think we missed a spot," he breathed, before he lowered his mouth for a deep taste.

He expected some sort of refusal. Hope had never come easy. But instead, her mouth opened in sweet surrender, offering up spicy heat that, if he hadn't been sitting, would've brought him to his knees. He took full advantage, sweeping his tongue into the warm recesses and coaxing her tongue into a sensual dance of give and take. But soon the connection of mouth and hand were not enough, and he crawled closer, bringing her up with him as he came to his knees.

She accommodated their differences in height by hooking her arms around his neck and straining closer as his hands slipped down to the sweet blue-jeaned cheeks he'd spent the last few nights dreaming of. Or possibly the last fifteen years. The firm flesh filled his palms as he pressed her closer to the hardened fly of his jeans.

The snap and zipper of her jeans came undone without a hitch or argument, and within seconds, he had his hands beneath the denim. He stroked and teased each cheek until she quivered in his arms like the golden leaves overhead. And still it wasn't enough. Patience had always been one of his virtues, but he wanted her naked. And he wanted her naked now.

The T-shirt slipped easily over her head, but the front snap of her bra took more than a few tries. Finally it slipped open, and he pulled back to look at what he'd exposed.

Sweet Lord.

He'd been right. She did own a teeny bikini. Two tiny white triangles encased sweet dollops of crème topped with deep raspberry nipples.

"Don't you dare laugh, Lomax," she said in a shy whisper.

"Oh, honey," he breathed as he lifted two very shaky hands and slipped off the thin pink bra straps from her shoulders. "As God is my witness, these are the most beautiful things I've ever seen." His hands slid over each one, cradling the softness. "The most beautiful things..." Unable to resist, he dipped his head and gave one small beaded nipple a gentle kiss. "Beautiful..."

"Colt," she groaned, and her hand came to rest on the back of his neck, pulling him closer as her head fell back.

He swept his tongue over the rigid tip, circling it a few delicious times before pulling it into his mouth.

"I want you," she stated as her fingers restlessly fluttered through his hair.

"And I want you too, baby." He continued to sip and stroke. "More than you will ever know."

"No." Her fists closed around his hair, and she tugged hard enough to bring tears to his eyes. "Now. I want you now."

Well, if she insisted.

His mind struggled with the logistics.

Hard ground.

Rough tree.

Small bike.

The ground won out. But before he could do more than kiss his way up her neck, a noise broke through his lust. A noise he instantly recognized as a truck engine—undeniably Chevy.

Shit.

Easing back, he took a moment to absorb the glorious bounty of Hope's bare-chested surrender. The soft breasts and wet peaks gilded in golden sunlight. The curved waist and tanned stomach sloping down to the opened V of her jeans and the tantalizing peek of white lace. The sexual droop of those blue eyes as they stared back at him. It took every ounce of willpower he had to reach down for the bra and slip it back on.

"What?" She blinked back to reality, and saying good-bye to those lust-filled eyes was like a swift kick in the gut.

"Company," he croaked, desire still high in his throat.

"Company!" She grabbed at the bra as the truck engine grew louder.

"Look, honey," he tried to keep the desperation out of his voice. "Why don't we go on back to Shirlene's? I've got the guesthouse all to myself—"

"Not a chance, Lomax," she stated with so much vehemence it left no hope.

No Hope, at all.

Chapter Eleven

"Isn't this the most fun y'all have ever had?"

Faith and Hope exchanged dubious glances as Shirlene came out of the kitchen carrying a large tray of brownies and drinks. Dressed in cow pajamas with a tiara perched around her high ponytail, she looked like a little girl. A little girl with over-developed breasts and no clear idea of what constituted fun.

"I can't believe you both wanted milk over margaritas." She plopped the tray down on the glass-topped coffee table, sloshing milk and green liquid over the rims of the tall glasses. "It's like you share the same addled brain."

"Not hardly," Hope said, although it was weird that she and Faith had said "milk" at the exact same time.

"I don't know what you would call it." Shirlene took the margarita glass and flopped down on the couch next to Faith. "Not only do y'all speak at the same time, but you've got that whole twin dress-alike thing down pat."

...A twin dress-alike thing that had really started to annoy Hope. Every time she turned around, Faith was wearing the same outfit that she was. And every day it became Hope's goal to screw things up by switching outfits a couple times before leaving the house, but damned if she still didn't come face-to-face with her mirror image. Thank God the woman had short hair. Although in the last few weeks, it seemed to have gotten longer.

"Of course, I think it's absolutely adorable," Shirlene continued, her eyes twinkling back at Hope. "I mean, just look at you two."

Hope glared down at the flannel pajamas with the silly flying pigs on them. "Adorable if you're seven."

Picking up a brownie, Shirlene sent Hope a wounded look. "You mean you don't like the pajamas I bought you, Hope?"

"Of course, she likes them," Faith hurried to smooth things over. "She just..."

"She just feels ridiculous sitting here in a pair of ugly pig pajamas with a dumb tiara on her head," Hope grumbled.

"You don't like the tiaras I brought?" It was her sister's turn to look hurt, except her look wasn't fabricated.

But even though she'd started to feel some kind of big-sister sensitivity toward Faith, Hope refused to backpedal. Not when at any time, Colt Lomax could come waltzing into the house and have enough ammunition to amuse himself for a good month. Not that she cared what Colt thought. It was just that...she cared what Colt thought. And had always cared what he thought. Be it about her pink cowboy boots or her acting ability, Colt's opinion mattered. It shouldn't, but damned if it didn't.

"No, I think they're dumb." Hope reached up to pluck the tiara off her head, but Shirlene had french-braided the thing right to her scalp.

"Now, honey, don't be such a party pooper." Shirlene lifted the plate of brownies and offered them to her. "Here, have some chocolate. I read it's good for mood swings."

"I'm not having mood swings, Shirl," Hope said as she tried to twist the tiara free. "Geez!" She gave up and flopped back on the couch, glaring at both of the grinning fools. "What was I thinking, accepting an invitation to a slumber party at your house, Shirl?"

"You were thinking about how much fun we used to have at sleepovers." Shirlene set the plate back down. "And you'd be having fun now, if you'd pull that corn cob out of your butt." Lifting the margarita glass, she took a big sip before she winked. "Come on, Hope, let loose and get a little wild."

Get a little wild? Oh, Hope had gotten a little wild, which was exactly why she sat there as tight as a brand-new pair of boots. Because a little wild was no longer enough. She wanted to go hog wild with a certain dark-headed, nimble-fingered motorcycle bum. A motorcycle bum who was only yards away. So close that her mind kept bringing up images of smoldering eyes, tight wet T-shirts, and warm, skilled lips.

Reaching out, Hope snagged a brownie off the plate and bit into it. The rich chocolate melted between her tongue and the roof of her mouth, but it did nothing to alleviate her cravings.

"So?" Shirlene pulled her bare feet up on the couch and tucked them under her. "What should we do now? Watch a chick flick? Paint our toenails—which Faith looks like she desperately needs? Or play a little Truth or Dare?"

Since Truth or Dare was the last thing Hope wanted to

play, she quickly tried to answer, but ended up choking on a chunk of brownie as Faith took the bait.

"Truth or Dare? I've always wanted to play that game."

"Then Truth or Dare it is," Shirlene said, before looking at Hope, who had finally dislodged the brownie. "Since Faith hasn't played, I'll go first. Start me off, Hog."

Resigned, Hope flopped back on the couch. "I don't know why I have to ask, you always choose Dare."

"I do not, so quit stalling."

"Fine. Truth or Dare?"

"Dare."

Hope rolled her eyes and wondered why in the world she had chosen such an annoying woman as her best friend.

Reaching for another brownie, Hope tried to think up a good dare. It wasn't easy. Not when Shirlene loved dares as much as her outlaw brother. She could have Shirlene strip off her cow pajama top and race around the outside of the house three times, but Shirl had never much minded getting naked. Nor did she mind making a fool of herself. In fact, Shirlene was up for just about anything.

Well...maybe not anything.

"All right." Hope smiled evilly. "I dare you to attend First Baptist every Sunday for the next month."

That got a rise out of her friend, and her size nine feet hit the Oriental rug beneath the coffee table with a thump.

"You know full well, Hope Marie Scroggs, that it has to be something I can do tonight—not next Sunday or the Sunday after. Besides, if folks caught me at church, they'd figure hell froze over and start sinnin' up a storm."

While Hope tried to come up with another dare, Faith spoke in her quiet voice. "How about not drinking for the rest of the night?"

Hope choked on the drink that she'd just taken, and milk rushed up her nose. But since this time it was at Shirlene's expense, she didn't mind so much.

"Oh, no, honey." Shirlene held up a hand. "That's not a good dare."

"It's not?"

"Oh, no, you want to suggest things like stripping naked and singing 'Copacabana' at the top of your lungs out in the front yard, or making me wear my panties on my head—stuff like that."

"Actually, I think that's a brilliant dare," Hope said. "In fact, that's the dare. No booze for the rest of the night." She reached out and picked up the margarita with every intention of downing it herself. But the thought of mixing chocolate, milk, and lime didn't sit well, so instead, she emptied it in the potted plant that sat on the end table next to her.

"That was a waste of fine liquor," Shirlene stated, with the first frown Hope had seen all night.

"I doubt that." She smiled innocently. "In this house, I'm sure the plant will thrive."

Shirlene's green eyes snapped. "Okay, Miss Smartie Pants, you're up. Truth or Dare?"

It was a conundrum. Hope had quite a few truths that she wasn't willing to share. Of course, if she chose Dare, she had little doubt she would be racing around outside without a shirt on. Normally that wouldn't be a big deal, especially with Lyle out of town. But now there was a guest in the guesthouse. A guest who needed no encouragement in that direction. Especially when he thought her small breasts were the most beautiful things he'd ever seen.

Heat infused Hope's body at the mere thought of those appreciative gray eyes, and she had a hard time getting out the answer.

"Truth," she said, but when she noticed the devilish glint in Shirlene's eyes, she quickly added. "But it's Faith's turn to come up with the question."

"She came up with the dare."

"No. She suggested the dare. I was the one who gave it."

Shirlene flopped back on the couch. "Fine. But make it good, honey."

Only a few seconds passed before Faith spoke. "Do you hate me for marrying Slate?"

Damn. Hope had been willing to answer anything but that. Well, maybe not anything. There were a few questions that could be worse—much worse. Still, this one was pretty bad. She studied one pink flying pig on the knee of her pajamas as she searched for the truth. Did she hate her sister? She hated spinach. Hated raisins cooked in anything. And pretty much hated Cindy Lynn. Or, at least, strongly disliked her. But what she felt for her twin sister wasn't close to any of those things. In fact, since coming home, she hadn't had much of a chance to figure out how she felt about Faith. Not when she'd been too busy trying to keep all her emotions bottled up, including her desire for a certain biker.

She looked over at the woman who sat across from her. A sweet little Disney princess in flannel pig jammies who wore her emotions on her face like a downtown L.A. billboard. A woman who, at every turn, had offered her friendship and love, even after Hope had ignored her and hit her in the nose and pretty much treated her like a stray dog with fleas.

How could she hate someone like that? Especially when it wasn't Faith's fault that Slate fell in love with her. If it was anyone's fault, it was Hope's. She was the one who left Slate on his own for five years.

And if she truly loved him, why *had* she left him for so long?

She released her breath in one long huff. "No, I don't hate you."

"You don't?" Faith leaned up on the couch and gave Hope one of those laser stares. "Because sometimes it feels like you..."

"Are an ass," Hope finished for her. She looked her straight in the eyes, even if it did give her the willies. "Look, I guess I've just been feeling sorry for myself, and I took it out on you."

It was a lame excuse, but once the words were out, Hope realized they were the truth. She had been feeling sorry for herself, and Faith was the easiest scapegoat. A Disney princess scapegoat who wasn't to blame for a backup plan gone south.

A brilliant smile lit Faith's face. "So Slate *was* just your backup plan."

Hope's gaze snapped over to Shirlene, who was smiling broadly. "Don't look at me, honey. I didn't tell her that."

But if Shirlene hadn't told her that, then who had?

"And I'm not a Disney princess."

Hope's eyes swept back to her sister, and her mouth dropped open. "How did you...?"

"Just a guess," she said brightly, before she reached for a brownie. "So is it my turn now?"

Shirlene needed no further encouragement to jump back into slumber-party mode. "Truth or Dare, honey?"

Faith looked away from Hope, who was still trying to decide if her sister had just picked her brain as clean as a shucked ear of corn. "Well, since I'd rather not run around the house naked, I guess Truth," Faith said.

Shirlene looked thoroughly disappointed. "I should've gotten y'all chicken pajamas. Especially since Faith doesn't look like the type to have any good secrets." She tapped a fingernail to her chin as her devious mind worked. "All right, honey, tell us something you haven't even told Slate."

Since Shirlene was right, and Faith wasn't the type to have any juicy secrets, Hope figured it would be something like she put an extra pinch of salt in Slate's beef stew. Or used milk on his cereal a day after the expiration date. Or used his razor on her legs.

But her sister surprised her again.

"I think I might be pregnant." Her entire face lit up like she'd just found the other glass slipper in her pocket. "I mean, it's only been a few weeks since we kind of forgot to use protection, but I just have this feeling. And I know it's stupid. I mean, who feels like they're pregnant after only a couple weeks? And that's why I haven't mentioned it to Slate—because it *is* so stupid." Finally realizing the other two occupants of the room weren't exactly bubbling over with enthusiasm, her smile wilted. "I guess I should've chosen Dare."

As usual, Shirlene was the first to snap out of it. "Why, honey, that's wonderful news." She shot a glance over at Hope. "Isn't it, Hope?"

"Yeah." Hope tried for a smile, but it didn't quite reach her mouth. "Wonderful."

Shirlene lowered her eyebrows at her before she turned back to Faith. "So, honey, why haven't you just gone and gotten one of those tests? Now you can pretty much tell if you're pregnant as soon as the swimmer hits the pool."

"I was going to, but I haven't had a chance to drive to Odessa, and there was no way I could get it here without the entire town knowing. You know how crazy they will get when word gets out."

"Yeah." Hope couldn't help the snide reply.

"Now, Hog." Shirlene flapped a hand. "That's all water under the bridge. Although don't you think it's rather ironic? I mean, the town thinks you're pregnant and actually it might be Faith."

"Real ironic, Shirl."

But Shirlene chose to ignore her sarcasm as she hopped up from the couch. "Come on, girls. Faith has just given us our next fun activity."

Hope had had all the fun she could take for one night. Still, she followed Faith and Shirlene down the long hallway and through the master suite to the master bathroom. Though some people might find the room gaudy, it reminded Hope of Shirlene. Bold and beautiful. The walls were covered in golden-hued tile that had been cut and refigured into intricate patterns that ran along the double sinks and into the glassed-in steam shower. On the floor, darker-toned tiles formed a multi-pointed star that encircled a spa-sized tub with a Tuscan chandelier hanging overhead.

"I'm not hopping in the tub with you two," Hope stated. "It's big, but it's not that big."

"Don't be silly," Shirlene said as she opened one of the cabinets next to the vanity. "We'll get naked in the Jacuzzi later." She pulled out a small box, then another one, and then another, until eight boxes were lined up on the counter.

"What in the world, Shirl?" Hope walked over and picked one up. It only took a glance to figure out what it was. The physical display of her friend's desperation brought a lump to her throat, and she set the box back down without saying a word.

"Now stop acting so morbid." Shirlene waved a hand at her. "Especially when I'm almost an entire year younger than both of you and have plenty of time to get pregnant."

"You're trying to get pregnant, Shirlene?" Faith asked, her eyes suddenly wide and concerned as she studied the boxes. "If I had known, I never—"

"Shush up. Just because I can't get pregnant doesn't mean I can't be happy for people who do." She tore open a box and pulled out the plastic-wrapped device. Using her teeth, she tore open the package and pulled out the flat white stick. "Okay, so here's how it works. You pee on this lower part, then we wait a few seconds and see if a blue line shows up."

"That's it?" Faith accepted the stick from Shirlene.

"That's it. Of course, the first few times I did it, I wasn't sure what I was looking for—" She stopped. "In fact," she grabbed another box and opened it, "it probably would be best if we had something to compare it to. You know, positive versus negative."

Faith nodded. "I think that would make me feel better."

While Shirlene opened another package, Hope sat down on the ledge that ran around the tub.

"Don't go gettin' all comfortable, honey." Shirlene tapped the stick on her arm. "You're up."

"What?" She jumped up and immediately started shaking her head. "Oh, no, I'm not peeing on some stick for a comparison. After what the town's put me through,

I refuse to do anything that deals with babies." And she would've stuck to her guns, if the pained look that entered Shirlene's clear green eyes had only been an act.

"Fine!" Hope grabbed the stick and headed for the toilet, slamming the door behind her. No more than thirty seconds passed before she was back out.

"Here." She shoved the stick at Shirlene, who shook her head.

"I'm not touchin' that thang. Put it down on the vanity." She looked at Faith. "Go on, honey. If grumpy Hope can do it, so can you."

But suddenly Faith was hesitant.

"What if Slate doesn't want a baby? I mean, we haven't really talked about it. I mean, we talked about kids but not about having them so soon. And what if—"

Hope didn't know why she stepped up. Maybe she just wanted to shut her up. Or maybe she just couldn't stand to see her sister so upset.

"Are you kidding me? Slate has loved kids ever since I can remember. Just look at how much he loves coaching. Besides, wasn't he the one who forgot the contraception in the first place?" When Faith nodded, Hope herded her toward the bathroom. "So what makes you think he didn't plan it? Besides, I didn't pee on a stick for nothing."

Once Faith stepped into the bathroom and closed the door, Hope turned to Shirlene, who sent her a soft smile.

"You're a good person, Hog."

"Not really." Hope walked over and sat down on the edge of the tub. "Inside I'm seething with jealousy."

Sitting down next to her, Shirlene rested her pile of blonde hair on Hope's shoulder. "Me too, girlfriend. Me too."

Luckily, Faith took a lot longer than Hope did, which gave them both plenty of time to feel sorry for themselves. By the time she came out, they had ditched the baby blues and were engrossed with the precautions on the back of one box.

"Who would shove this thing up their butt?" Hope asked.

"I guess someone who thought they were going to have a butthead for a kid," Shirlene replied, and they both fell against each other laughing as Faith stood holding the test like it was a lit stick of dynamite.

"Just set it on the counter, honey," Shirlene directed, after she caught her breath. "It doesn't take more than a few seconds."

Faith bent over the vanity. "So what am I looking for again?"

"A blue line," Shirlene said before pointing to the next warning and giggling against Hope's shoulder.

"So if there is a blue line, I'm not pregnant?" She leaned closer.

"No, that means you *are* pregnant."

"Does it start with a blue line and then fade out if you're not?"

Sending Hope a look that said Faith might be a few eggs short of a dozen, Shirlene got up and walked over to the vanity.

"See that blue line?" Shirlene pointed down to the stick on the counter, and Faith nodded. "That means you're knocked up. Congratulations, honey."

"But that's not mine." Faith lifted the stick she still held in her hand with an identical bright blue line. "This is."

Chapter Twelve

STAYING AWAY FROM the main house wasn't easy. Not when one slumber party fantasy after another kept popping into Colt's brain. The only thing that kept him from becoming a Peeping Tom was his sister. There was no way he wanted to catch her doing anything kinky. That was the nice thing about fantasies. You could invite whomever you wanted to the party. And at his sleepover, all he wanted was a matched set of twins. Twins wearing nothing but tiny see-through panties and a few strategically placed down feathers from their pillow fight. Of course, both twins looked exactly alike, right down to their butt-length hair.

With his hands tucked beneath his head, he stared up at the ceiling in Shirlene's guesthouse and let the fantasy play out.

Ooops! One twin took a direct hit from the other one's pillow and bounced down to the bed, sweet breasts jiggling. Thrown off balance, the other twin fell on top of her in a tangle of tanned limbs and silky hair. Amid girlish giggles and fun, bare skin brushes bare skin and lips might... accidentally collide. And once that happens, an innocent curiosity might get the best of them and they might—

A knock on the door jerked his attention back to reality, although it did nothing to soften the raging hard-on that stretched out the black cotton of his boxer briefs. Nothing short of a dip in Lake Michigan in late winter would do that. Rolling to his feet, he searched around for his jeans, wondering why someone was knocking at his door at one o'clock in the morning—and not knocking as much as pounding.

"Hold on," he called as he pulled up his jeans and hurried to the door, zipping them as he went. As he crossed the small sitting room, he banged his big toe on a chair leg and was still cussing when he opened the door. But the f-bomb fizzled when he saw who it was.

Hope stood in the darkened doorway with straggly pieces of hair framing her face and a tiara perched lopsided on her head. The flannel pajamas with the scary flying pigs were as far from see-though panties as a person could get, although the prospect of getting his hands on a flesh-and-blood woman made up for his disappointment in attire. Unfortunately, before the spider could welcome the fly into his web, she hauled off and punched him right in the nose.

"Damn it!" He pulled back and covered his throbbing nose with one hand. "What the hell was that for?" While he checked for blood and broken cartilage, she shoved her way past him and started ranting and raving in her hog-calling voice.

"How about for being a good-for-nothing, incompetent idiot!" She waved her hands around as she paced. "Don't worry about a thing, honey! I've got everything under control, sweetheart! I'm all suited up!"

Having worked herself up into a frenzy, Hope whirled around and came back at him with clenched fists.

But he wasn't about to be a punching bag without an explanation.

"Hold up there, wildcat." Colt grabbed her wrists and held her back. It wasn't easy. She was as mad as a hornet. But he couldn't figure out why. There was no way she could've tuned in to his twin fantasies. Although when she stopped struggling, he read more fear in those blue eyes than anger. And since fear wasn't something he'd seen in Hope's eyes often, he started to get worried. His worry tripled when those pretty blue eyes blinked as if fighting back tears.

His grip on her wrists loosened. "What happened, honey? Is Shirlene hurt? Faith?"

Her eyes narrowed as two words came out of her mouth. Two words he couldn't quite make out over the buzzing in his ears—a buzzing that grew louder as he stared down at the woman in front of him.

For a second, he wondered if he was dreaming—if he had nodded off during the twin fantasy and would wake up in the morning, sighing in relief. But then a foot stomped down hard on his toes and the dream bubble burst.

"Are you listening to me? I'm pregnant!"

The sudden increase in volume had him dropping her wrists and pressing his fingertips to his temples. Or maybe it was the words that had his head throbbing.

"Well, aren't you going to say anything?" she asked.

Lifting his head, he looked into those fear-filled eyes

for one brief moment before he turned and walked over to the mini bar. After switching on the light above the cabinet, he started searching. Wine. No. Vodka. No. Whiskey. Most definitely. He poured a good two fingers and downed it in one gulp before he poured another one and did the same.

"Great," she spoke from behind him. "My child's father is a drunk."

He might've poured himself a third if the entire "child's father" thing hadn't brought the whiskey back up his throat. With a hand braced on the bar, he swallowed hard as his eyes stung like hell.

"Now you see how I felt," Hope said. "Except you didn't have to find out the news while two women stared back at you."

Colt turned around. "Shirlene and Faith?" What girls did at slumber parties took a mean curve. "But why would you..."

"Faith thought she might be pregnant, so your sister pulled out her entire drugstore of pregnancy tests. I was supposed to be the constant in her little experiment." Her laughter held no humor whatsoever as she flopped down on the sofa. "Some constant."

"But those things aren't foolproof. Are they?"

"Ninty-seven percent accurate." She looked up at him. "One percent less than your raincoat."

"Shit." Colt ran a hand through his hair as he paced over to the sliding glass doors that led out to the pool. The pool was closed for the winter, but it didn't matter. He couldn't see anything beyond his own disbelief. He turned back around. "Maybe you should take another one—just to be sure."

"I did. After Shirlene and Faith fell asleep, I used up her entire inventory. I've now been told I'm pregnant by blue lines, green dots, and one very annoying word." She swallowed hard. "Pregnant."

The air left his lungs in one long rush, and his knees finally gave out, and he flopped down in the closest chair. There were a thousand things to say, too many for him to dissect at the moment, so he chose to say nothing. He just sat there with the whiskey churning in his stomach and his eyes pinned on the swirls in the rug beneath his bare toes.

Pregnant? He could understand getting the news after being in a serious relationship, but one quickie in a hotel room didn't seem worth the burden that had now been placed on his doorstep. Of course, most of the blame was his. He was the one who had gone looking for her after Shirlene had called, worried because she hadn't heard from Hope in weeks. He had been the one who rented the hotel room close to the club where she worked so he wouldn't have to make the long trip back to his house on Hermosa Beach so late at night. And he had been the one unable to control his desires long enough to consider the consequences of fumbling around in the dark with a condom that had been in his wallet for a good month and had endured more than its fair share of road time.

"Aren't you going to ask if its yours?" Hope spoke almost as softly as her sister. Colt looked up. In the dim light put out by the mini bar, she looked small and childlike, all curled up on the couch in those silly pig pajamas with the crooked tiara.

"It's mine," he stated without hesitation.

They stared at one another for a few seconds before

they both turned away. The front door stood open, and only the occasional chirp of crickets broke the thick, heavy silence. He didn't know how long they sat there, both lost in their own thoughts, before he finally spoke.

"So what do you want to do?"

She fiddled with one of the buttons that ran down the front of the pajamas. "I don't know, but I don't think I can get an abortion. What do you want to do?" she shot back.

The question shouldn't have taken him by surprise, but it did. Probably because the shock had yet to wear off. A baby. His baby.

He swallowed and tried to think. Do? What did he want to do? A variety of things popped into his head. Drink the rest of the whiskey and move onto the vodka and wine. Sue the condom company. Stomp over to Shirlene's and yell at her for asking him to check on Hope in L.A. in the first place. Hop on his bike and pretend this never happened.

Except it had happened, and there was no way to pretend otherwise.

So what did he want to do?

He didn't have a clue. The only thing he knew for certain was he didn't want to have a baby. He wasn't ready for something like that. Like Hope said, he was an irresponsible motorcycle bum and proud of it. A motorcycle bum who spent half the year in a garage and the other half touring the country on a custom chopper that only had room for one. One lone rider, who stopped when he wanted. Not when a woman needed to take a pee, or a kid screamed for release from the confining contraption he'd been buckled into.

That was the way it was and that was the way Colt liked it.

There were a few times he felt lonely, but certainly not lonely for a baby. But now he didn't have much of a choice. There was a child—his child—therefore he needed to give Hope an answer. Or if he couldn't come up with one, he needed to at least be honest about that.

He ran a hand through his hair. "I don't know. I haven't ever really thought about babies."

"And you think I have?" Her words held a lot of anger, no doubt because he'd taken so long to answer.

Feeling a little tense himself, his gaze snapped over to her. "Come off it, Hope. That's all you and Shirlene talked about when you were growing up. Weddings and babies."

"With Slate! Never with some motorcycle bum who can't keep a foolproof condom in his wallet!"

Just like that, the situation turned nasty.

He tipped his head. "Funny, but you didn't seem to be too worried about that in the Motel 6."

"Because you seduced me!"

"Seduced you?" He arched a brow. "Was that before or after you sucked my tongue down your throat?"

"You ass!" Hope jumped up. "I should've known it was useless to come here expecting you to take any kind of responsibility for your actions." She started for the door, but he got up and blocked her way.

"Oh, I take full responsibility for my actions. I had no business taking you back to my hotel room, but I'll be damned if I take full responsibility for what happened after. You were just as hot as I was for it, baby. And don't you ever forget it."

"How can I? I'll carry that mistake around for the next eight months!"

The word *mistake* caused his temper to flare. "And that's what really chaps your ass, isn't it? It will be hard to pretend to the people of this town that you hate my guts with my child growing in your stomach."

"Your child?" She tapped her chest. "You mean, my child."

"So now you're going to claim immaculate conception?" He snorted. "The people of this town are stupid, but I don't think they're going to fall for that."

"Well, they certainly won't think you're the daddy! Sandra Bullock won out over you!"

"Then why are you here?" Colt finally released all his anger and frustration. "If you're going to walk around pretending I'm not the father, what the hell are you doing asking me what I want to do? If that's the case, you can damn well figure it out on your own."

"I hate you, Colt Lomax! I hate you so much!" She shoved him out of the way. "And I will figure it out on my own. I don't need anything from you."

The door slammed closed behind her, and Colt stared at it as he whispered, "No. And you never have."

Chapter Thirteen

IN THE TIME it took her to cross Shirlene's lawn and slip back into the dark house, Hope's anger had turned to a hard knot of anxiety. Needing to do anything to prevent complete hysteria, she felt her way to the kitchen, where she rifled through the drawers until she found a pen and pad. Switching on the lights over the breakfast bar, she sat down on a stool and started writing.

> **Reasons I'm Not Pregnant**
> 1. *My period is always late.*
> 2. *I'm not sick in the mornings.*
> 3. *My breasts are not tender.*
> 4. *I feel exactly the same as I did two months ago.*
> 5. —

She paused for only a brief second before writing the next sentence, pressing so hard it tore the paper.

It was only one time! One measly time that I haven't even given a second thought to!!!!

But even as she dropped the pen and flopped her head

down upon her folded arms, Hope realized it was a lie. She'd given more than a second thought to that night in L.A. As much as she'd tried to forget it, it had been carefully preserved in her brain like a Turner Classic, waiting for just such a moment of weakness to be pulled from the vault and replayed in all its digitally mastered glory.

"See ya, Sweetie," Phoenix, one of the strippers at Tittly Wink's, called out before she climbed into her brand-new Porsche.

"See ya." Hope waved as she hurried across the parking lot to her old beat-up Chevy truck. In her haste to get back to her apartment after the long night on her feet, Hope hadn't even taken the time to remove her blonde wig, something she didn't realize until the cold breeze blew the short strands across her face.

"Got any change?"

Hope almost jumped out of her black sports bra when a man materialized out of the darkness.

"Geez, Marty." She held a hand to her chest. "You scared the crap out of me."

"Sorry, Hope." He pushed back his long, greasy dreadlocks with a dirty, sun-damaged hand. "I figured you saw me."

She probably should have. In his flowered board shorts and parka, he was hard to miss.

"It's not a big deal," she said as she searched through her purse for some change. Unfortunately, all she came up with was a linty orange Tic-Tac. Even Marty looked disappointed as he stared down at her open palm. But his eyes lit up when a ten-dollar bill suddenly appeared over Hope's shoulder. Grabbing the ten, Marty popped the

Tic-Tac in his mouth and offered up a "God Bless You" before hurrying off.

Hope turned to thank the man who offered the bill for his generosity, and ended up looking into a pair of cool, steel gray eyes she remembered well.

"Living dangerously, honey?"

After five years of walking through a parched desert of surfer dudes and arrogant actors, the familiar twang blended with the husky male timbre poured over her like a cool West Texas rain shower. But she only had a moment to drink it in before the implications of Colt Lomax finding her working at a dump of a strip club smacked her right between the eyes.

If Colt knew, so would the entire town of Bramble.

Hoping it was all just some weird coincidence, Hope tried to bluff her way through it.

"Did you need something, sir?" She mimicked the hard tones of all her California neighbors.

His eyes narrowed. "Yeah, I need something all right. I need you to tell me what the hell you think you're doing!"

She swallowed hard and tried to keep her eyes off the chest muscles that strained against the black cotton of his T-shirt. Muscles that had gotten much more pronounced in the last eight years.

"Doing? I don't know what you're talking about. You must have me confused with someone else." She went to walk past him, but he grabbed her arm.

"Cut the shit, Hope."

"Hope?" She stared down at the sexy tattoo on his arm. "I'm afraid I don't know anyone by that name. My name is . . . Pumpkin."

The name popped out before she could stop it. Damn Shirlene and her theory that the best stripper names were made up using the name of your first pet. What was the matter with her? What if he remembered Pumpkin? Her pony had been very cute and very memorable.

"Fine. We'll play it your way." He jerked a twenty out of his pocket and slipped it in the front of her sports bra. His eyebrows lifted at the extra padding. "I think that's the going rate, isn't it?"

Before she could say a word, he bent down and hefted her over his shoulder.

"What do you think you're doing?" she yelled, as she pummeled his hard butt with her fists.

"I'm collecting my lap dance."

"But I'm off work!"

"Consider it overtime."

His long strides made it much harder to land a punch, although that didn't stop her from trying. While she flailed her arms aimlessly, she looked around for one of the many bouncers who worked at the club. Unfortunately, they were all inside, having their usual after-hours drink with the boss. And while she had been searching for change to give Marty, all of her dancer buddies had left. Which meant there was no one to stop Colt but Hope.

She gave it her best shot, but the guy's butt and legs felt like they were made of wrought iron. During one wild screaming tangent, the wig came off and her hair swept down to tangle in his legs.

"Nice hair, Pumpkin," he gloated.

And since the jig was up, she gave in.

"Colt Lomax, you good-for-nothing piece of Texas roadkill, put me down!"

"Now, there's the sassy little Hope I remembered. I thought I'd lost you forever."

"You're going to lose your teeth, if you don't put me down," she yelled so loudly, her voice echoed down the alley they passed. But he only laughed and kept going.

She didn't have a clue where he was taking her, but it took him long enough to get there. He walked a good half block with her screaming and fighting all the way. In another neighborhood, someone would've called the police. But here, calling the police was like inviting an anteater into an anthill.

Finally, he turned into a parking lot, and she glanced up at the brightly lit sign. "Oh, no. If you think I'm going into a hotel room with you, Colt Lomax, you can think again."

Except in a matter of minutes that was exactly where she found herself, bouncing on a flimsy mattress while Colt stood over her, looking none too happy. "Have you lost your mind?" She scrambled off the bed on the opposite side.

He swept his jet black hair off his forehead before resting his hands on his hips. "Funny, but I was about to ask you the same thing."

She tried not to fidget under the intense look, but it was hard when her heart thumped so loudly in her ears. "I wasn't the one who kidnapped a person and is holding them hostage in a cheap hotel room."

"No, you're just the person dressed up like a hooker and working at a strip club."

"I'm not dressed up like a hooker." Hope tried to defend her clothing, but even she knew it was a losing battle.

"Really?" His gaze ran over her, starting at the hem of the short black skirt and moving up her bare quivering belly to the low neckline of the sports bra, where two squares of toilet paper now hung out. "What would you call it?"

"A waitress's uniform."

The stiffness eased from his shoulders. "Waitress?"

She placed her hands on her hips, mimicking his stance. "What difference does it make to you, anyway? You never have approved of anything I wear. My cheerleading skirt was too short, my pink boots too bright, my homecoming gown too low. What are you, my daddy?"

His steel eyes flickered. "I liked the uniform you wore when you worked at Josephine's."

Her hands dropped. "You've got to be kidding. That ugly thing came down past my knees."

"It was decent."

"Decent? This coming from a man who dated Marcy Henderson."

The grin was real this time. "I guess Marcy didn't exactly dress decent, did she?"

The smile did something to her stomach. Something she tried to ignore. But it was hard to ignore the fact that this was a man who knew her—had known her ever since she was born. Colt might be annoying as hell, but he was as close to home as she had gotten in more than a year. And she missed home. Missed it more than she had realized until that moment.

Flopping down on the end of the bed, she unbuckled the skinny black straps of one of her high heels and slipped it off to massage her aching toes. "Talk about a hooker. That girl screwed anything with pants on. And why you dated her, I'll never know."

His hands dropped from his hips, and he moved around the end of the bed and took a seat next to her. "Because I was a horny young kid, and she would screw anything with pants on."

Rolling her eyes, Hope switched feet and unbuckled her other shoe. "I'll tell you one thing, the running shoes I got to wear at Josephine's sure beat these to hell and back." The shoe slipped to the floor, and she rubbed her sore arch and groaned. "Lord, that feels good."

"Here." He reached out and grabbed her foot.

"You are not touching my feet, Lomax." She tried to pull her foot back, but he refused to let go. And once those strong fingers started to move, any resistance she might've had was completely snuffed out.

"Scoot back," he ordered, and she quickly complied.

Once she was stretched out with her head tucked against a pillow, he lifted her foot to his lap and started in earnest. For a motorcycle bum, he knew his way around a foot. His thumb dug into her arch while his fingers massaged the instep. And when he stretched her toes back, she moaned and dug her head back into the pillow.

"Feel good?" he asked.

She could only nod. Although his next words brought her out of her physical utopia.

"So why are you working there?"

A thousand smartass remarks filled her mind, but instead she told the truth. Foot massages would make one hell of an interrogation tool.

"I need the money."

"It's hard to believe you couldn't find a better place to work." He pulled on her pinkie toe, and she died and went to heaven.

"Don't tell me you haven't spent your fair share of time in strip clubs—tonight being a perfect example. Of course, you got there a little late, didn't you?"

There was a moment of hesitation before he spoke. "I wasn't there for the strippers."

She leaned up on her elbows and stared at the ebony hair curled around the strong column of his neck. "Don't tell me you were there for the eight-dollar Dr Peppers."

He glanced back at her. "I was looking for you."

"Me? But why?"

Still holding her foot, he shifted around on the bed. "Shirlene has been worried about you, so I told her I'd look you up."

Hope's stomach dropped, and she tugged her foot away from him.

"So now you know." She tipped up her chin with as much defiance as she could muster. "Now you can call Shirlene—and whoever else you want to—and tell them that Hope Scroggs isn't a budding actress after all...just a barmaid at a sleazy strip club in L.A."

She expected some snide remark, but instead he just stared back at her with emotionless eyes. And somehow that seemed worse.

"Go home, Hope."

She shook her head. "I can't."

"Damn it!" In one swift movement, Colt came up off the bed. His eyes were no longer cool and emotionless as he strode around to stand over her. "Why can't you ever just let things go? You don't belong here. You've never belonged here. You belong back in Bramble—back with Slate Calhoun. So accept it and get your ass back there!"

Hope sat up on the bed, her own anger bubbling to the

surface. "That's easy for you to say. But I don't see you going back."

"Because I was never the town favorite. I was that poor Lomax kid, remember? And who the hell in their right mind would want to deal with that every day of their lives? But you are Hope Scroggs, loved by every man, woman, and child—"

"And that's the point. I can't go back there when they believed in me—when they think I'm the next Sandra Bullock. How can I possibly live with myself if I disappointed them?"

Tears welled up in her eyes, and she tried to push them back. It was bad enough that Colt had discovered her working at a strip club; she didn't want him thinking she had turned into a crybaby too. Except her body refused to listen to her brain, and the tears splashed down her rouged cheeks like her apartment's drippy faucet.

"Admit it, Hope," Colt sat down next to her. "It's not about the town as much as it is your own stubborn pride."

"B-but I thought I had it all figured out," she sobbed. "I m-made numerous lists."

"You and your damned lists." Releasing an exasperated sigh, Colt slipped an arm around her and tugged her close. "Sometimes things can't be planned, Hope. Sometimes things just aren't meant to be."

His show of kindness only made her cry harder. Tucked against his chest, she sobbed out all her anger, hurt, and frustration from the last five years. When she was finally spent, she remained there—a lifeless piece of quivery female.

After a while, his hand lifted from her shoulder and stroked her hair. "How did you manage to get all this up in that wig?"

"It wasn't easy," she said, her voice clogged with tears and snot.

A chuckle rumbled through his chest. "Pumpkin. I had my doubts until you mentioned that ornery old pony."

"He wasn't ornery."

"I don't know what you'd call it. He bit me every time I tried to pet him."

"Probably because he knew a mean kid when he saw one."

He laughed. "Probably." He continued to stroke her hair, and she continued to let him. How long had it been since someone had touched her like this? It seemed like a lifetime. And she didn't want it to end. Unfortunately, her nose started to drip, and no amount of sniffing would keep it contained. So she grabbed the toilet paper that hung from the sports bra and loudly blew her nose. She didn't realize how it must've looked until she glanced up into twinkling gray eyes.

"So that's what that's for."

"Very funny." She tried to tear off the used piece but only succeeded in pulling out more. Like a line of silk scarves from a clown's sleeve, the paper kept coming and coming as Colt's eyebrows hiked further and further up his forehead. Completely humiliated, she dropped her hand.

"It's not my fault that men tip better if you're blonde with big boobs."

"No, I guess not." He gathered up the toilet paper, then slipped his hand beneath the bra to get the rest. When his knuckle brushed her nipple, she sucked in her breath and jerked back.

"Sorry," he said as his hand popped out with the wad

of tissue. Except he didn't look very sorry. Those gray eyes gleamed with a devilish light. "Here." He tipped up her chin and wiped beneath her eyes. "You look like you've been in a fight."

"I have."

"Now, honey, that didn't even come close to some of the zingers we've had in the past. Remember the time I told you that you kissed like a three-year-old?" He chuckled. "I thought you were going to tear my head off and spit in my neck."

"I think you have that memory a little screwed up, Lomax. I was the one who told you that you kissed like a three-year-old, and you were the one who got upset."

His eyes filled with smoky heat. "Well, maybe we should see if I've improved."

"I don't..."

The words dropped along with her stomach as his mouth dipped toward her. He didn't move fast. In fact, she had plenty of time to stop him—to tell him that she had no need to test his kisses. Except she didn't want to stop him. It was insane. But she had always been a little insane where Colt Lomax was concerned. And as soon as those warm lips touched hers, she gave herself up to that insanity.

His lips swept over hers with a raw sensuality that held nothing back. No one kissed better than Colt. It was as if she was a goblet of water and he was a parched man in the desert. His hands cradled her face as his lips took deep thirsty pulls. Then, as if not completely quenched, he changed angles to drink some more.

She answered him with deep, thorough kisses of her own, her hands fisted in the cotton that stretched over his chest. Releasing her lips, his hands slipped to the back of her neck as he kissed his way toward her ear. Her breath fell out in heaving gasps as she fought for the oxygen he'd taken. This outlaw. This desperado who had stolen her will to fight. But the sports bra stopped him cold.

"How the hell do you get this thing off?"

She smiled at his impatience, although it faded at the thought of him seeing her breasts. They had never been her best attributes, and she wasn't about to show them to a man who had found so many flaws. But that didn't mean she didn't want to feel those big biker hands on her.

So she leaned over and turned off the lamp before stretching the bra up over her head. His hands were on her before she even got her head through the stretchy Lycra.

"Jesus," he sighed as he filled his hands.

He gently squeezed before he slid his palms up the sides and over the rigid peaks. As he stroked and teased, he leaned over and gave her another deep kiss, pushing her back to the mattress. Once he had aligned his body to hers, he pulled away from her lips and trailed hot, wet kisses down her neck and along her bare shoulders, before using that talented mouth and tongue on her breasts. Beneath his lavish attention, Hope felt as well-endowed as any one of her dancer friends. And luckier, much luckier, that Colt was the one doing the lavishing. Of course, she forgot all about what he was doing to her breasts when his fingers skated up one trembling thigh and slipped beneath her skirt.

It took all of three flicks to send her skyrocketing.

"Did you just...?" Colt's breath fell soft against her nipple. "Damn, baby."

Her orgasm seemed to incite his passion, and his

foreplay became more frantic, his need more evident. He left her for a time to strip off his clothes. There was little light in the room, so she could only imagine the articles being removed. The popping of cotton stitches. The thud of a heavy boot. The metal zing of a zipper. And then he was back—hard biceps cradling her hips—a solid wall of muscles pressed against her lower legs.

He didn't remove her skirt but merely pushed it higher as his breath fell hot and moist against her panties, panties that were no match for his deft fingers. Once they were gone, his familiar voice reached through her sexual haze.

"Let me turn on the light, Hope. I want to see you."

"No." She waggled her head on the pillow. Light might wake her from this dream, and she wasn't ready for that.

Not yet.

Acquiescing, his fingers traced up her bare thighs, then back down again before they stopped at her knees to press them apart. She waited, listening to the sound of his breath as it fell rough and heavy from his lungs. Anticipation grew, and she jumped when his hot, wet mouth settled over her.

He was gentle at first. A sweep of tongue. A sip of lips. But slowly he settled into a tempo that brought her back to the edge again. Her thighs closed around his head, and her hips lifted. But before she could take flight, he pulled away. Not that it was easy to unclench her fingers and squeeze past her thighs.

"Easy, baby," he said. "I'm not going to leave you hanging."

Then he moved up her body, and she felt the hot length of him, nudging for entry. Opening her legs wider, she angled her hips and welcomed him home. Although at the first deep thrust, reality broke through her sexual haze, and she pressed a hand to his chest.

"I'm not on birth control."

He leaned down and kissed her, his lips tasting musky and sweet. "No worries. I'm already suited up, honey."

On the word *honey,* he drove deep, taking her breath and reality with it. He stretched her to the limit, filling a space deep inside. A space she'd forgotten existed. With each thrust, the emptiness and loneliness of the last five years receded.

She tried to savor everything at once. The deep, satisfying stretch. The brush of his hips on each thrust. The strength of his arms braced beside her head. The sound of his breath as he neared climax. But it was too much for her mind and heart to absorb, so she closed her eyes and sank into her own universe of pleasure.

Soon after, Hope fell into a dreamless sleep. And when she awoke, Colt was gone. No good-bye. No note. Just the indentation of his head in the pillow next to her, along with the scent no other man could duplicate.

Chapter Fourteen

COLT DIDN'T KNOW where he was going when he left Shirlene's. All he knew was he needed to ride. So that's what he did. Without glancing at mile markers or highway signs, or worrying about putting mileage on a bike that wasn't his, he rode. Rode until his butt ached and his back throbbed. Rode through the frigid, appendage-numbing cold of the dark night to the cool dampness of the early morning. The only time he stopped was to get gas, use the bathroom, and down an energy drink before heading back out to the long stretch of blacktop that gave him solace when nothing else could.

When he finally arrived in Austin, he pulled into a restaurant, where he drank numerous cups of coffee in an attempt to defrost. Unfortunately, once his body had thawed, his mind still remained frozen, and he found himself watching the other occupants of the restaurant in a dazed kind of trance.

An older couple complained about the service and haggled over the bill. A young man sat and punched the keypad of his phone, using just his thumbs, while across the table his girlfriend did the same. A woman struggled to keep her two toddlers from ripping open the little jam containers and tipping over creamers while she tried to pacify her crying baby in the high chair. It turned out to be an impossible job, and finally she sat back in the booth and let all hell break loose.

Her gaze swept over to Colt, and they stared at one another for a few seconds, both defeated and at a loss for what to do.

Finally, Colt got enough gumption to call the man who had bought the custom bike and set up a time for delivery.

Travis Mossman's house was nothing short of spectacular: A sprawling estate on Lake Austin with a three-story main house and a scattering of outbuildings that included a boathouse, two guest cottages, and a huge garage that stored a variety of vintage cars and motorcycles.

If Colt hadn't been comatose, he might've been impressed, if not with the estate, at least with the nice collection of Harleys, Indians, and one Victory. But with no sleep and the effects of the coffee wearing off, his mind could barely stay focused on Travis as he walked around the bike Colt had brought, and looked at it from all different angles.

Compared to the classics, it wasn't all that impressive. Still, Colt was glad he'd taken the time to stop at a car wash and clean off the road grime. The chrome and custom paint sparkled in the sunlight that spilled in through the open doors of the garage.

"Impressive." Travis ran his hand over the custom paint job, admiring the tribal-blade graphics that ran over the tank and fenders. "I knew just by talking with you that you knew what you were doing—which is why I gave you *carte blanche*—but this is more than I expected. The detail is amazing."

Colt liked the man and was glad he had his approval. Over the last few months, they'd built a long-distance relationship, their discussions moving from bikes to the trials of growing up in small Texas towns. On the phone, Travis had come across as an honest, upstanding kind of guy who you wanted to count among your friends. And meeting him in person only confirmed this belief. His blue eyes were direct, his smile genuine, and his handshake firm. He was a few inches taller than Colt and about twenty pounds lighter, his body slim and fit. Even with the silver threaded through his dark hair, Colt didn't figure he was much over forty-five.

"Thanks," Colt said. "I've got a good group of guys working with me."

Travis finally looked up from the bike. He studied Colt for a few minutes before speaking. "Tough ride?"

Rubbing a hand over his day's growth of beard, Colt figured he probably should've hosed himself off at the car wash as well. "Yeah."

"I thought you were going to trailer the bike from L.A."

That had been the plan until the night at the Motel 6 threw him off course—was still throwing him off course.

"I wanted to test it on the highway before delivery." It was a lame excuse, but Travis didn't question it.

"So how did she do?"

"She'll go the distance."

Travis looked back at the bike, and for a moment, his eyes glazed over as if he was out on the road right then, instead of standing with both feet on the pristine epoxy floor.

"I look forward to that." The way Mossman said it made it seem like a dream more than a reality.

"Grandpa!"

Colt turned to watch as two bright-eyed kids raced across the immaculate lawn. Since there was no one else around, Colt figured he'd made a mistake in calculating Travis's age. Obviously, the man took as good care of himself as he did of his vehicles.

"Whoa there, partners." Travis reached down and lifted the little blonde-headed girl into his arms before he placed an arm around the bigger boy. "Colt, I'd like you to meet my grandkids, Lily and Daniel. Lily and Danny, this is Mr. Lomax."

The little girl shyly tucked her head into her grandfather's neck, while the boy stretched out a hand.

"It's nice to meet you, sir."

Travis smiled proudly as Colt gave the small hand a shake.

"Nice to meet you, Daniel."

Once the introductions were out of the way, Daniel didn't waste any time relaying his message. "Mima says lunch is ready, and you need to pull your head out of your tailpipe and come and eat before she gives it to Rufus."

"She said that, did she?" Travis's blue eyes sparkled with suppressed laugher. "Well then, I guess you better run back in and tell that ornery woman I'm on my way, and I'm bringing Mr. Lomax with me."

Once the kids were racing back across the manicured lawn, Colt held up a hand. "I really appreciate the offer, but I need to be getting back."

In truth, he didn't know where he was getting back to. The long road trip should've cleared his mind, but instead he felt more confused than ever. Hell, he hadn't even arranged for transportation after dropping off the bike. The original plan had been to take a cab to the airport and fly back to L.A., but the original plan had been shot to hell when he veered off the interstate and ended up in Bramble. Of course, his trip to Bramble hadn't really changed things. Even if he hadn't gone, Hope would still be pregnant with his child.

His child.

The words left him feeling like he had the first time he'd been knocked off a surfboard, struggling underwater with no clue which direction to swim in to find air. Unaware of Colt's dazed state, Travis pressed his offer.

"Nonsense, after that long trip, you might as well stay the night. We've got more guest rooms than relatives, and Sissy loves company about as much as she loves to harp at me."

"Thanks, but I can't." Colt pulled out his cell phone. "I'll just call a cab and wait out here."

For the first time since meeting him, Travis's tone carried a hint of the tough businessman he was. "Being from Texas, you should know Texans never pull out a checkbook on an empty stomach. Besides, once we've eaten, I have no problem driving you wherever you need to go."

Once Travis put it that way, Colt didn't really have a choice. So he nodded and followed him up to the house. Even with the high ceilings and massive windows, there was a cozy charm to the home that made a person feel immediately comfortable and welcome. Or maybe it wasn't the house as much as the people who lived there.

Sissy Mossman, as hospitable as her husband, was a sturdy cowgirl with flaming red hair that reminded Colt of his sister's before she had gone blonde. Though she wasn't as pretty as Shirl, there was a softness to Sissy's hazel eyes that Colt found soothing as he sat at the long dining room table and ate lunch.

"Would you like more salad, Colt?" she offered.

"Yes, ma'am." He didn't really want more, but he had always had a problem saying no to motherly women, and Sissy Mossman was as motherly as you could get. As they ate, she wiped mouths, refilled milk glasses, and cut up food into small bites for her grandchildren.

"Such nice manners, but *Sissy* will do just fine." She passed the bowl down.

"Yes, ma'am," popped out before he could stop it. Travis and Sissy laughed, which set the kids to giggling.

The kids were well-mannered and pretty cute. Daniel reminded Colt of Jesse, although he carried a youthful innocence in his blue eyes that Jesse was lacking. Youthful innocence was something kids lost early out on Grover Road. Still, both boys had the same interest in motorcycles, and Daniel spent most of the time asking questions about the customs Colt had built. Comfortable with the topic, Colt didn't mind answering his questions, but the conversation soon dwindled when it moved to monster trucks—a subject he knew little about.

The little girl, on the other hand, just sat there and stared at him with eyes the color of Texas sage and as big as the dinner plates they ate off of, which was why he was so surprised when she suddenly appeared at his side.

"You got whiskers."

Startled, he choked on the bite of chocolate chip bunt cake he'd just placed in his mouth. After forcing the chunk down with a few swallows of water, he nodded.

"Are they scratchy?" she asked.

He glanced over at Travis and Sissy, but they just smiled back like a couple of idiots. So he improvised.

"Would you like to feel them?"

She nodded, and Colt leaned down so she could slide a tiny soft hand over his jaw. When she giggled, he couldn't help but smile back at her and wink. That was all it took. Without a word, she climbed up on his lap and remained there while he tried to finish his dessert. Her small, crayon-scented body didn't make him all that uncomfortable. Shirlene had sat on his lap when she was little. He had just forgotten how nice it felt.

When the kids were excused from the table, Sissy ushered him into the living room, where a fire took the chill off the autumn day. Between the deep couch cushions, the full stomach, and the crackling cedar, Colt had a hard time keeping his eyes open, let alone keeping up the conversation.

"So you grew up in Bramble?" Sissy asked, as she took a seat on the couch next to her husband. The arm he hooked over her shoulder seemed as natural an action to him as breathing.

"We went through Bramble," Travis said, before turning to his wife. "Remember, honey, it was when we made that trip up to Roswell so Travis Jr. could see the aliens. Hell, that must've been ten years ago."

"Closer to twenty-five," she stated. "T.J. couldn't have been more than ten. And of course, I remember. How could I forget? You left our youngest daughter at the gas station."

"Now that wasn't entirely my fault. I thought she was still sleeping in the back of the camper. How was

I supposed to know she had gotten out when I wasn't looking?"

Sissy glanced over at Colt and shook her head. "Poor little thing, by the time we realized she was missing, we were halfway to Roswell. Luckily, the nice man working at the gas station took care of her." She glanced over at Travis. "What was his name? Smith? No, Johnson?"

"Jones," Colt supplied, surprised at what a small world it was. "Tinker Jones. I grew up with his son, Tyler. He runs the gas station now while his father and mother travel around in their motor home."

"Jones. Of course." Sissy smiled at the memory. "By the time we got back, he had taken Shelly over to this cute little train caboose diner and gotten her an ice cream. With three older brothers to contend with in the back of the camper, I think she was happy to get the short reprieve."

"That would be Josephine's," Colt said. "And it's still there, crooked stovepipe and all."

Sissy smiled. "That's what I love about small towns. They never change. It's like a time capsule that you dig up every time you go home. But instead of things, it's places that bring back all the happy memories."

Happy memories? He had never thought of Bramble in that way. But in the last few weeks, more happy memories had surfaced than bad. The taste of good red chili burning its way down your throat and the icy cold of a drugstore chocolate ripple ice cream cone. A rainy afternoon spent inside an old Chevy and the feel of the late afternoon sun on your neck on the way to Sutter Springs.

No, the memories weren't all bad. And Sissy was right; in a big city, things were constantly changing. Buildings coming down and more going up. Businesses failing and others taking their place. But in Bramble, things had stayed constant. And there *was* something nice about that.

"I think I told you about growing up in a small town just east of San Antonio," Travis continued. "Not more than a grease spot on the highway. And I tell you, I couldn't wait to get out of there and shake the dust of that town off."

"The dust," Sissy asked. "Or the girl?"

"Now, honey, I think that we've been over this. I was young and stupid."

"You sure were."

Travis looked over at Colt and rolled his eyes. "Anyway, the point I was trying to make is that no matter how much money I have or how big my house is, I'll always be that small-town boy."

Sissy leaned up and kissed his cheek. "And six grown kids and five grandkids later, I'm still your small-town girl."

Six? If the thought of one kid left Colt stunned, six with five grandkids was downright mind-boggling. How did a man get six kids? A faulty condom was a start. But six faulty condoms constituted a learning disability.

"I never thought I'd go back to my hometown to live," Travis continued. "But lately, I've been thinking about buying some land there and building a house."

"You have?" Sissy turned to him. "Why haven't you said anything?"

"I thought you would think it was stupid. I mean, we have three houses already."

"Oh, honey." She leaned her head on his shoulder. "I think it's a wonderful idea. And with our mamas and daddy getting older, we can be right there to help out if they need us."

While they continued the conversation, Colt leaned his head back on the couch and studied the cracking fire. He thought he'd only closed his eyes for a second, but when he opened them, the light had changed in the room, and Travis was the only one there.

As he sat up, Travis lowered the edge of the newspaper that he was reading and looked over at him.

"Sleep well?"

Colt rubbed a hand over his face. "I didn't mean to sleep at all. What time is it?"

"Around three." Travis nodded at the coffee table. "I've got your check right here. But before you head out, I thought you might want to talk a little."

Thinking it was about the bike, he said, "I sent you all the specs, and if you have any questions, all you need to do is call me."

"I'm not talking about the bike, Colt." He folded the newspaper and set it aside. "I'm talking about what has you strung as tight as a fiddle bow. And don't give me any bull that nothing's wrong. The man I've talked to on the phone for the last few months is not the same man who blew in here looking like the wrath of God. Hell, you no more than glanced at my collection—talk about a bruised ego." Travis flashed a grin. "Normally, I wouldn't push my nose into someone's business, but I feel like we've known each other for years. Not just from the phone conversations and e-mails, but through your designs and our mutual love of bikes."

Colt ran a hand through his hair. He had felt the same connection, which was one of the reasons that he had wanted to personally deliver the bike. He had wanted to meet Travis Mossman—to see the man behind the voice. But that was before his life had taken an unexpected curve. Still, the man deserved some kind of an explanation for his sudden wild appearance. And a rough road trip wasn't going to do it.

Especially when Travis asked, "So who's Hope?"

"How do you know about Hope?"

"You talk in your sleep. Luckily, the grandkids are outside with Sissy or they would've gotten an earful." Colt actually blushed as Travis continued. "Since I already know you're not married, I assume she's a girlfriend."

What would you call the mother of your child? Girlfriend didn't seem like enough. Of course, in Hope's case, it was too much. Except there was nothing else to call her.

"Yes."

"And you got her in trouble?"

Damn, how much did he talk in his sleep?

Colt blew out his breath and fell back on the couch cushions. "I guess you could say that."

"So what are you going to do about it?"

"I don't have a clue."

"I've shoveled enough bullshit in my day to recognize it when I see it. You know what to do, you're just too afraid to say it out loud. Afraid if you do that someone will hold you to it."

"If you're talking about marriage, you can think again."

Travis leaned over, his forearms on his knees. "I wasn't talking about marriage, but it's obvious you've been thinking about it."

Had he? Colt hadn't thought that he'd been thinking

about anything, but perhaps a part of his brain had been working without his realizing it. An illogical part of his brain. Marriage to Hope was out of the question. They could barely have a conversation without fighting.

"So you don't have feelings for the girl?" Travis continued his interrogation.

"What do you mean?"

Travis shot him a look that pretty much called him out on the idiotic question. Colt tried to backpedal, except there was no place to backpedal to.

"I . . . she's . . . there is this . . . Hell, I don't know."

The grin on Travis' face was downright annoying, and the glare Colt sent him must've said so, because he quickly held up a hand.

"Believe me, I'm not laughing at you . . . okay, so maybe I am. But it's nice to know I'm not the only idiot when it comes to women. I think it must have to do with being born in a small town. With everyone butting into your business, you get it in your head that when you grow up you'd rather go it alone."

Colt snorted. "I wouldn't exactly call a wife, six kids, and five grandkids going it alone."

The grin deepened. "No, I guess you wouldn't, but before I got married that was exactly what I had convinced myself I wanted to do. I left town and traveled around the country, until I ended up back in Texas working on an oil rig and pretending like I was having the time of my life. And then I ran into the girl I'd left behind. I tried to act like the big shot I wasn't, but she looked straight through me and called me a liar right to my face. God, how I hated her. It took me a good year of trying to convince myself I didn't need her before I realized she was exactly what I

needed. Of course, by that time, she'd found somebody
else."

"So the girl wasn't Sissy?"

"Of course she was. A little thing like a fiancé doesn't
stop a Texan when he's made up his mind. I begged like
a two-year-old in a candy store—a whole lot of tears and
a whole bunch of promises to be the best husband she'd
ever want. Of course, if she didn't love me, I guess no
amount of begging would've gotten her to leave that idiot
and marry me."

Colt had been so wrapped up in the story that he hadn't
realized they'd come full circle. All the way back to
marriage.

"I think your situation was a little different than mine.
Hope doesn't love me. And I sure as hell don't love her."

Travis glanced behind him before he spoke in a low
whisper. "Just between you and me, I didn't exactly love
Sissy either." When Colt sent him a surprised look, he
quickly continued. "To be honest, my head has always
been a little behind my heart. I suppose my heart knew,
even when we were dating in high school, but my head
didn't realize how much I loved her until about six months
into the marriage."

"So why did you marry her?"

He released his breath. "Because I couldn't stand the
thought of her marrying Michael Beaudine."

Jealousy was something Colt could identify with.
Growing up, he'd been jealous of just about everyone
in town. But as an adult, he felt as if he'd conquered the
emotion. The image of Slate and Faith's wedding popped
into his mind. Okay, so maybe he hadn't conquered
it. Of course, it wasn't jealousy that had caused him to

belligerently kiss the bride as much as a bruised ego at the thought that Hope had fled from his bed straight into Slate's arms. And now he wondered if his ego had been responsible for his sleeping with Hope in the first place: The poor Lomax kid finally gets the homecoming queen.

Except it hadn't felt like his ego.

It had just felt right.

"Listen," Colt got to his feet, "I need to be going."

Travis stood. "Had enough of my advice, have you?" When Colt didn't reply, he only smiled. "Well, marriage or no marriage, I don't doubt for a minute that you'll take care of your own. From the way you talk about your sister, I'd say you've had some practice."

"A little," Colt hedged. He reached for the check on the table, then pulled his wallet from his pocket and slipped it inside. When he glanced back up, the smile was gone from Travis's face, replaced with a look that made Colt suddenly wary.

"Listen, Colt," he said, "I probably don't have any business bringing this up. Being a business man yourself, you realize how quickly gossip can get out of hand." He paused as if carefully considering his next words. "But I think you should be aware of the rumors that are going around about Dalton Oil."

The haze that had settled over Colt's mind lifted, and he became alert.

"What have you heard?"

Travis released his breath. "That the gulf oil well Lyle invested in didn't produce, and he's having a hard time paying back his loans. Companies are already talking about getting their hands on Dalton—companies I wouldn't wish on my worst enemy." When Colt didn't comment, he continued. "Look, I've only met Lyle a few times, but he struck me as an honest man. If he decides he needs some investors, I know of a good company that might be interested—C Corp. And if there's anything else I can do..."

"I need a ride to the airport." Colt finally spoke.

With a nod, Travis reached down and picked up a set of keys off the coffee table.

"A man's got to do what a man's got to do."

Chapter Fifteen

NEVER ONE TO wallow in self-pity for too long, Hope spent the following week on the list of things that needed to be done in town while she clung to the thin thread of hope that pregnancy tests were as faulty as condoms.

The pothole was her first project. It wasn't hard to talk some of the highway construction guys into stopping by for a free lunch at Josephine's. Then, while they were filling up on biscuits and gravy, she used a little country charm to convince them to fix the hole at the corner of Maple and Main on their way back to work.

The next day, she lit a fire under Harley and had him call the hotel chain to find out if they were still considering building a hotel in Bramble. After spending a good half hour trying to bridge the language barrier between India and Texas, he was transferred to the corporate office where he spoke to a vice president who beat around the bush more than Uncle Harley before he informed them that Slumber Suites had decided Bramble was a bad risk.

The news was discouraging, but it didn't slow Hope down. On Thursday, she stopped by the hardware store to see if Ralph would donate some paint for the store-fronts. Unfortunately, he had already donated ten gallons of purple paint to paint the town hall for Faith and Slate's wedding. Hope had just stepped out of the hardware store on her way to go talk to Rye Pickett to see if they had any paint left over when Bear's big black Dodge truck pulled up.

After Sheldon, she thought the town would give up on their craziness. Obviously, she'd been wrong. But at least this time, the man Bear had with him didn't look terrified. In fact, he looked quite pleased with himself.

"Hey, Texas!" Her agent, Ryan Seever, hopped up on the sidewalk and engulfed her in a hug. After she had inhaled a lungful of his expensive cologne, he pulled back and gave her one of those smiles that only convinced people who didn't know him. "So this is where you've been hiding out."

Hope barely acknowledged the greeting before she turned her narrowed gaze on Bear. His beady eyes widened with fear, and he took a few steps back, stumbling over a crack in the sidewalk.

"Now, Hog, I didn't force him. This here feller wanted to come see you."

"That's exactly right, Bear." Ryan reached out and slapped the mountain of a man on the back. "I take full responsibility."

Since Ryan had never taken responsibility for anything, Hope grew even more suspicious about his presence in Bramble. But she wasn't about to question him, not when they had started to draw a crowd.

Traffic had slowed to a snail's pace, and people were stepping out of the businesses up and down Main Street to stare at her and Ryan like they were bugs beneath a microscope. The women looked hopeful, as if waiting for her and Ryan to declare their undying love, while the men just looked mean. When riled, Texans could be extremely unpredictable. And even if she and Ryan hadn't ended on the best of terms, she didn't want to see the man riddled with buckshot because they thought he'd deserted Hope and his baby.

Another lowlife was responsible for that—a lowlife who she hoped was getting pelted with golf ball–sized hailstones on whatever highway he was traveling down.

Pinning on a smile, Hope hooked an arm through Ryan's and steered him down the street. As they walked along, she made the introductions.

"Hey, y'all, this here is my Hollywood agent, Ryan Seever, who just stopped by to see how I was gettin' on. Isn't he the sweetest?"

The entire Hollywood agent thing seemed to work. The women looked thoroughly depressed and the men seemed disappointed that they didn't have an excuse to whip out their guns.

But it didn't take long for Ryan to change their expressions. Always the charmer, he greeted the townsfolk as if he and Hope were walking the red carpet. And by the time they had reached Josephine's Diner, he had the men laughing at his jokes and the women convinced they were all movie starlets just waiting to be discovered.

Even Rachel Dean fell under his spell when she brought their menus and water to the corner booth. Hope couldn't blame her. Ryan had done the same thing to Hope when she first landed in L.A. It took her years to read through the layer of charming fluff and get to the egomaniac center.

"A Hollywood agent," Rachel beamed. "Now ain't that somethin'. I guess you've met plenty of stars. You know that Angelina Joe Lee? I like her movies and all, but if that skinny little gal didn't have those lips weighin' her down, she'd blow clean away in a puff a wind."

Despite the Botox injections that left his skin scarily tight, Ryan's smile actually looked real.

"I couldn't agree more, Rachel. I think the days of skinny leading ladies are behind us. People want their heroines made of sturdier stuff." He winked at her. "Now, I bet a woman like you would make a great action hero and could take down an entire third-world country of terrorists without even blinking an eye."

Rachel blushed to the roots of her salt-and-pepper hair. "Well, I don't know about that. But I've taken down a few steers in my day. And one time, when my first husband got a little too drunk for his own good, I had to wrangle him into a kitchen chair and duct-tape him until he sobered up." She stared off and shook her head. "Although I feel real bad about that. The hair on his wrists and ankles never did grow back."

Knowing the conversation would only get crazier, Hope jumped in. "Could you get us a couple of diet Dr Peppers, Rachel?"

"Shore thing, honey." She gave Hope a direct look. "I guess this ain't the one, either." When Hope shook her head, Rachel's shoulders drooped and she walked away, muttering to herself.

When Rachel was gone, Hope turned back to Ryan.

"Okay. What are you doing here?"

Shaking his head, Ryan stared out the window. "Unbelievable. It's like Mayberry on crack."

The accurate description almost had Hope smiling. "I mean it, Ryan. Cut the crap and explain to me what caused a man who delights in traveling first class to ride across country with Bear."

He flipped open the menu and scanned it. "Surprisingly, it wasn't really that bad—and since someone forgot to pay their cell phone bill, it was the only way to get a hold of you." His eyebrows shot up. "Frog legs? People actually eat frog legs?"

"Only when they're in season," she said, dryly. "So why would you want to talk to me, when you dropped me as a client?"

Setting down the menu, he released his breath in a long sigh. "Fine. I made a mistake. I was thinking leading lady, when I should've been thinking…" he waved a hand at the window, "reality star." A smile flashed. "I have a job for you."

Since it wasn't something she'd heard often, it took her a moment for his words to sink in. "A job on a reality show? You mean like the ones who run around half-naked, drinking from tree-bark bowls and foraging for beetles to eat? I think I'll pass."

"You would be lucky to get on that show." He pulled out his cell phone and started texting while he talked. "But no, it's not quite as intense. All you'll have to do is what you've been doing for the last few years."

"Fail?"

He didn't even crack a smile as his thumbs flicked over the small screen. "Exactly. Except you'll get paid for it. It's tentatively called *Hollywood Dreams,* and it will follow the story of five different people who are trying to make it big in Hollywood. The producers are looking for unique actors who have their own distinct personality. And I immediately thought of you. I sent them the audition tape you did for that criminal show, and they loved it."

Hope's eyes narrowed. "The one where I played the corpse?"

"That's the one."

"But I couldn't get my eyelids to stop twitching."

Ryan shrugged. "They obviously know talent when they see it."

She reached out and jerked the phone out of his hands. When he looked up, she shot him a skeptical look.

"Okay," he said as he leaned back in the booth, "so maybe they're not looking for talent as much as entertainment. And what could be more entertaining than a feisty little Texan with a cute country twang? The audience is going to eat you up like *crème brûlée.*"

He leaned up and started rattling off the details of production dates and offers, but Hope wasn't listening. Her mind had finally settled back on the one thing she didn't want to think about. The one thing that kept her from jumping up and down with excitement over the fact that her goal of becoming an actress was within her grasp.

Fate was more than cruel; it was downright devious.

"...so they loved the tape, but they want to meet you in person. When I found out where you were hiding out, I called them back and scheduled a meeting for the end of next week. I figure that will give you plenty of time to tie up any loose ends you have here."

Loose ends? She had more than loose ends. It seemed her entire life had come unraveled.

"So when do you think you can leave?" he asked, just as Rachel walked up with their drinks.

"You feelin' okay, sugar?" Rachel's gaze dropped to the hand Hope rested on her stomach—a hand she hadn't even known was there. "You want me to get you some of them saltines?"

Hope shook her head. "I'm okay," she said, although she did feel slightly nauseated. But crackers weren't going to help.

The bell jingled over the door, and both she and Rachel turned to look at the three men who stepped in. It was clear that they were strangers to the area. Instead of finding a place to sit down, they stood just inside the door, waiting to be seated. They wore business casual attire—creased pants, lightly starched shirts, and high-polished laced shoes. If Hope's mind hadn't still been on Ryan's offer, she might've given the three men's presence in Bramble more thought. Instead, she turned back around as Rachel went over to greet them.

"I could be pregnant, Ryan," Hope stated. The words came out much easier than she expected.

Ryan had gone back to tapping out messages on his phone and didn't even glance up.

"Did you hear me? There's a good chance I'm pregnant."

He held up a finger; then, after punching the screen one more time, he set the phone down and looked at her. "Bear might not be a big talker, but I got that much out of him. And he was terribly disappointed to learn I hadn't seen you in over six months." A grin tipped up one corner of his mouth. "I take it the father is still on the loose?"

"Long gone."

"Good." A sly smile eased over his face. "There is nothing more appealing to an audience than a single mom who is struggling to feed her child." The smile turned blinding. "The producers are going to love it."

Ryan might not have a sincere bone in his body, but he knew the business inside and out. And if he thought the producers wouldn't care that she was pregnant, Hope believed him. What she couldn't believe was that all her prayers had suddenly been answered and all she could do was sit there and stare at him. Was she crazy? This was her chance, her chance to become—if not an awarding-winning actress—at least rich and famous. And she would be a fool not to take it.

"I have an appointment on Monday, but I can leave anytime after that." She forced the words out of her suddenly dry throat.

"Good." Ryan patted her hand. "I think this is going to work out well for both of us." He slipped out of the booth. "I need to go to the bathroom and make a few calls." He motioned at his drink. "While I'm gone, do you think you could get me a cappuccino or maybe some carrot juice? Carbonation sucks all the elasticity right out of your skin."

Her gaze wandered over his taut, spray-tanned face.

"I'll see what I can do."

But once he was gone, Hope didn't wave Rachel over. Instead, she just sat there staring out the window.

Bramble Elementary had just gotten out. Kids raced by with backpacks flopping, while other children meandered at a slower pace, stopping to kick an aluminum can down the gutter or peer in the window of Duds N Such while moms waited on almost every street corner to greet their children with warm hugs and bright enthusiasm for whatever they pulled from their backpacks.

Moms who didn't look terrified at just the thought of motherhood.

"...as far as I'm concerned we shouldn't have any problem whatsoever taking over Dalton."

The words cut into Hope's thoughts, and she quickly turned her head to stare at the bald spot of the man who sat in the booth directly behind her.

"I agree. The guy is so deep in debt—" The dark-headed man in the ivory dress shirt, seated on the other side of the booth, stopped talking when he noticed Hope peeking over his friend's shoulder.

Caught eavesdropping, Hope's eyes widened. But she recovered quickly. "Mercy sakes." She jumped up and glanced down at her bare wrist. "Would you look at the time? It seems my breaks are over before they even start." She gave them all a sassy wink. "Now you boys don't go anywhere, and I'll be right back to take your orders."

They looked more than a little confused as she hurried across the room and slipped behind the counter.

"You change your mind about them saltines, honey?" Rachel asked as she poured some coffee for Rossie Owens.

"Actually," Hope grabbed an apron off a hook by the door that lead to the kitchen and tied it around her waist, "I had a spurt of energy. And since you're so busy, I thought I'd help you out."

Rachel's face scrunched up as she looked around the near-empty diner. "Well, that's real nice of you, honey. But I think I've got it covered."

"Now, I won't hear any more about it." Hope steered Rachel around the counter to the bar stool next to Rossie. "You just sit right down there and take a load off those bunions of yours."

"Well, they have been hurtin' a little today." Rachel sighed as she took a seat.

"You tell her, Hog," Rossie said. "She works way too much for her own good."

As Rachel blushed, Hope moved back around the counter and quickly filled three glasses with water. But before she lifted the plastic tray, she grabbed a handful of napkins from the dispenser and shoved them in her bra. She adjusted each cup, flipped open two snaps on her shirt, and then picked the tray back up.

When she turned, both Rossie and Rachel were staring at her like two dogs looking at a rabid cat. She flashed them a weak smile before she walked back to the table, adding a little extra wiggle to her hips.

"So where you boys from?" She laid the accent on nice and thick as she handed out the water.

"San Ramon," the balding guy said, with an appreciative gleam in his eyes. Since it appeared that he was the most talkative of the bunch, Hope tucked the tray under her arm and moved over to his side of the booth.

"San Ramon? Ain't that in Mexico?"

They laughed, all except for the dark-headed unfriendly one.

"California," the skinny man with glasses finally spoke up.

She widened her eyes. "Don't tell me, y'all work in movies. 'Cause you're sure good-lookin' enough."

There was more laughter before the balding man answered. "We work for Pacific Coastal Energy."

Hope's smile dropped, but only for a second. "No foolin'? Is that like Red Bull? I tried one of those drinks once and stayed up for most of the night with more energy than a cat on a hot tin roof. You plannin' on sellin' that stuff here? 'Cause I know a few lazy cowboys who could sure use a little energy."

The balding man started to speak, but the dark-headed man cut him off. "We're just passing through, ma'am."

"Well, I hope you enjoy your stay in Bramble." She took out the pad and pen from the apron pocket. "So what can I get y'all?"

It was a good thing that Hope could take orders in her sleep, because her mind was a whirl, trying to piece together the information she'd just learned. She didn't have a clue why executives from Pacific Coastal Energy were thinking about taking over Dalton Oil, but she wasn't about to let it happen.

"I'll have that right out," she said as she headed back to the counter.

In no time at all, she had placed their orders with Josephine, stripped off the apron, and headed for the door. On the way out, she ran into Ryan, coming back from the bathroom. But she didn't stop to talk.

Hollywood would have to wait. Her Mayberry was in trouble.

Chapter Sixteen

"MR. DALTON," LYLE's secretary's voice came over the intercom speaker. "Hope Scroggs is on line two. I tried to tell her that you were still in a meeting, but this is the sixth time she's called in the last hour, so I thought it must be important."

Suddenly alert, Colt dropped the document he'd been trying to decipher and sat up so quickly that he almost toppled headfirst out of the leather conference chair. He didn't know why, but he suddenly felt as if he'd just been caught ditching class. And for a second, he had the strong urge to jump up and run like hell.

Which was just plain juvenile. Especially since there was no way Hope knew that he was at Dalton Oil's corporate office in Houston. And even if she did, so what? He was an adult who could go where he wanted to go and do what he wanted to do.

Still, that didn't stop Colt from pressing a finger to his lips when Lyle picked up the phone, which resulted in a bemused look from his brother-in-law.

"Hey, Little Bit," Lyle said, although his haggard face didn't match the jovial tone. "What a nice surprise—"

Before he could even finish, Hope cut him off. Colt couldn't make out what she was saying, but it wasn't hard to detect her anxiety. An anxiety that quickly changed Colt's fear of discovery into something much more terrifying. With his heart banging against his rib cage, he leaned over the conference table with every intention of jerking the phone out of Lyle's hand and finding out just what had Hope so upset. But before he could, Lyle spoke up.

"Now, Hope, honey, just because you overheard some guys from Pacific Coastal talking about buying—okay, taking over—Dalton Oil that's no reason to think we're going under. Companies try to buy out the competition all the time. That's just good business."

Colt flopped back in the chair and released his breath as Lyle continued to talk.

"So stop worrying your little head over things like that. Right now, the only thing I want you thinking about is names for those sweet babies." After a long pause, Lyle pressed the receiver closer to his ear. "Hope? You still there, honey?" There was a muffled reply, and Lyle quickly ended the call. "Well, I better get back to work so Shirlene can have some spending money. Say 'hi' to your mama and daddy for me."

After he hung up the phone, Lyle leaned back in his leather chair and rubbed his eyes. "I sure hate to lie to that little gal. But I can't chance her letting it slip to someone in town. Not when panic will only make things worse."

The intricate details of business had never been Colt's strong suit—he much preferred using his hands to his mind—but from what he'd ascertained in the last week, things couldn't get much worse for Dalton Oil. Due to bad investments and dropping oil prices, the company was as close to bankruptcy as a company could get, and it was only a matter of time before they went under. Still, Lyle looked so haggard and defeated, Colt couldn't bring himself to point that out.

"And I'll tell you one thing," Lyle continued. "If I ever run into the cowardly dog that got Hope pregnant, he'll rue the day he defiled our little sweetheart."

Colt was already ruing the day. Unfortunately, there was no way to go back and undefile. Which was why he was using the excuse of Dalton Oil's troubles to hide out, like the cowardly dog he was.

Rising up from the chair, he walked over to the floor-to-ceiling windows and stared out at the Houston skyscrapers.

"So Pacific Coastal showed up in Bramble," Colt mused.

"I figured it was only a matter of time before the vultures started to circle."

Colt turned back around. "Pretty soon they won't be circling—they'll be picking our bones." When Lyle didn't say anything, he continued. "I realize you want to keep the company in the family, Lyle, but instead of letting a group of money-grubbing sharks get their hands on Dalton by paying off the debt with seventy cents on the dollar, we should be looking for an honest company who might be willing to buy us out with a fair deal."

Lyle released his breath and slumped back. "You're probably right. It's just damned hard to let go of a business that has been in the family for close to a hundred years."

Figuring he'd made his point, Colt turned back to the

window and stared at the rows of lit windows. "Doesn't anyone go home in this town?"

"Time is money."

"If that's the case, then we should've made a bundle in the last week." When Lyle didn't say anything, Colt glanced over his shoulder. His brother-in-law was watching him with a look that made Colt extremely uncomfortable.

"Damned if you haven't surprised the hell out of me, Colt Lomax."

"I have a tendency to do that to people," Colt said, dryly.

Lyle chuckled. "I meant it as a compliment. I don't know what I would've done without your help this last week."

"I didn't do all that much."

"I disagree, but even if you hadn't lifted a finger, it was nice having family around—someone who cares about Bramble as much as I do."

Not wanting Lyle to get the wrong idea, Colt enlightened him. "I didn't do it for Bramble, Lyle. I did it for Shirlene." He turned back around. "And if you want the support of your family, why haven't you told my sister? I understand you not wanting the town to know about the company's trouble, but Shirlene is your wife."

Lyle swallowed. "I planned on telling her this weekend when she flew out, but then she started talking about Hope and Faith being pregnant..." His shoulders drooped. "If you could've seen that great big smile pinned on her face the entire time she talked about the baby shower she's planning, it would've broken your heart—especially knowing how much she wants a baby of her own." He looked up at Colt. "And damned if I could add to her misery."

Colt had never paid much attention when his sister had talked about having kids. Somehow the news that she wanted a baby so desperately made him feel even guiltier now for not wanting his.

"Still, I wouldn't want to be around when she finds out you've been keeping secrets from her," Colt said. "And the news will be out soon enough."

Instead of commenting, his brother-in-law just sat there, staring out at the glittering cityscape. For the first time since Colt had known him, he looked all of his fifty-six years and then some. His face looked drawn and his eyes were bloodshot from lack of sleep.

"I have to fix this, Colt," he said in a wary voice. "Not just for the folks of Bramble, but for the other employees of Dalton Oil and their families." He covered his face with both hands. "I couldn't live with myself if I let them down, especially since I'm the one responsible."

Colt had never been much of a touchy-feely kind of guy, but he couldn't help walking over and resting a hand on Lyle's shoulder.

"You haven't let anyone down. In fact, I've never seen a man work so hard to save a company." He gave him a couple awkward pats. "But there's nothing else you can do for now. So why don't you go home for the weekend and relax a little? Take that sister of mine out dancing at Bootlegger's. Or just kick back at the house and fill up on some of Cristina's cooking."

Lyle dropped his hands and shook his head. "I never was any good at dancing—or kicking back. Besides, you're right. Instead of sitting here waiting for the buzzards to land, I need to find a company worthy of Dalton. Didn't you tell me that Travis Mossman mentioned a company that was interested in us?"

"C-Corp." Colt walked back over to his chair and pulled up a file on the laptop. "It's a relatively new company. They started with farm equipment, then somehow ended up with land just south of San Antonio that was rich in natural gas. Two brothers own it." He glanced back up. "You want me to give them a call?"

It took Lyle less than a second to nod. "But if they're planning on sending anyone out to look things over, you might want to tell them to stay out of Bramble. Hope won't fall for my cock-and-bull story again." He grinned. "She's sure a firecracker, isn't she? You won't find another person in all of Texas who's more willing to fight for Bramble than our little Hope."

Colt glanced over at him. "I don't know about that. If it hadn't been for you and your family, Bramble would've turned into a ghost town long ago."

The smile dropped. "Which is why I can't give up, Colt."

"I know." Colt nodded.

A moment of awkward silence passed before Lyle leaned up and straightened the papers littering the tabletop. "And what about your own company? I guess you'll be headed back to L.A. soon."

It made sense. Colt had spoken with his office manager just that morning, and she'd informed him that his desk was piled high with project designs and part orders that needed his immediate attention. But for some reason he couldn't bring himself to leave the state of Texas, even if Hope had made it perfectly clear that she could handle things just fine without him.

When Colt didn't answer, Lyle cleared his throat. "I guess you wouldn't consider going back to Bramble for a few days? It would sure make me feel better knowing you were there, watching over the town."

"Watching over the town?" Colt's eyebrows lifted. "You do realize I'm the same delinquent that broke most of the storefront windows on Main Street."

Lyle laughed. "Do whatever you want to the windows, Colt, just watch out for my gal."

It was late by the time they finished working. Since Lyle had recently sold the penthouse, they were both staying in a hotel downtown. But while Lyle took a cab back, Colt decided to walk. He needed the fresh air to clear his mind of all the information and numbers that ran through it.

The streets were crowded with men in business suits and women in nice dresses and heels on their way to dinner or to get a drink. Colt could've used a few stiff drinks himself. But as always, he stifled the urge.

At the corner, he ran into a group of women dressed in skimpy costumes. There was a blonde vampire. A brunette French maid. And a very nasty-looking Little Red Riding Hood redhead who gave him a bold once-over as he stopped to wait for traffic. As he stared back at her, it took him a moment to make sense of the costumes. With the turbulent events of the past week, he'd forgotten all about the holiday. Now he remembered Shirlene talking about selling tickets at the Halloween carnival.

The annual event was a big deal in Bramble, and one of the few things Colt had enjoyed growing up. He loved the caramel apples. Got a real kick out of watching the mayor get soaked in the dunk tank. And anticipated a good scare in the haunted house. The only thing he hadn't enjoyed was watching Hope dressed up like a witch and passing out kisses for a dollar. Every horny guy for miles around would line up in front of the booth, awaiting a brush from those soft lips.

Everyone but Colt.

It became as big a challenge as the ring toss to see if he could resist pulling a dollar from his pocket and stepping in line. Of course, he never did completely resist. Sooner or later, he'd made sure that he took much more than a dollar's worth.

The light changed, and Colt waited for the ladies to step off the curb before he followed behind them. Halfway across the street, Little Red turned and blew him a kiss from her scarlet-painted lips.

He acknowledged the gesture with a smile, even though storybook characters had never been his thing.

Colt had always preferred witches.

Chapter Seventeen

"YOU'VE GOT TO be kidding me!" Hope's gaze narrowed on her twin sister, who wore the exact same costume as she had on—from the pointed black hat and purple sparkly wig to the purple-and-black–striped tights. The only things different were their boots. Faith's boots were black, while Hope wore the red ones she'd yet to return to her sister.

"Did you buy your costume in Lubbock?" Faith asked, as she came around the back of the carnival fishing booth.

"No. I've had it for ten years. Which makes it even freakier." Hope gave her sister's witch costume one final glare before going back to taping string on the end of the skinny dowel rods that they were using as fishing poles.

"It is freaky, isn't it?" Faith picked up a dowel from the box and started helping Hope. "It's like we have a telepathic connection. Sometimes I know what you're thinking without you even opening your mouth. Like at Shirlene's house."

"That was nothing more than a coincidence."

"I don't know about that. Since then, I've done a little research, and there are dozens of articles online about twins being connected mentally. And you have to admit it's strange the way we keep dressing alike."

Hope snorted. "*Strange* isn't the word I'd use—more like ridiculous. What woman in her right mind wants to dress exactly like someone else?" At the long stretch of silence, Hope glanced up into Faith's big, innocent eyes.

I can't help it. I like everyone knowing we're sisters.

"As if people couldn't figure out we're sisters without the clothes," Hope said, as she reached for another dowel. She had just pulled one out of the box when Faith grabbed her arm and squealed.

"You did it! You read my mind!"

The dowel clattered to the floor as Hope turned to her sister.

"What are you talking about?"

"I didn't say a word about me liking people knowing we're sisters, and yet you knew what I was thinking."

Hope's brow knotted. "But I heard..."

"Exactly." Faith smiled as if talking mice had just finished her trousseau. "That's exactly how it works with me; like you're in my head, talking. Go ahead, think of anything. In fact, make it something I wouldn't know about in a million years."

Since she really wanted to prove her sister wrong, Hope searched through her mind for something really obscure to throw at her. Faith concentrated on her for only a second before her face scrunched up in bewilderment. And Hope couldn't help but smile triumphantly.

But the smile faded quickly enough.

"Pumpkin?" Faith tipped her head in confusion. "Colt likes pumpkins?" Suddenly those eyes flashed open wide. "Colt and you? He's the father—"

Hope slapped a hand over her sister's mouth just as Shirlene came sashaying up to the booth in a gypsy costume, complete with black wig, silk scarves, and enough jewelry to sink the *Titanic* long before it reached the iceberg.

"So which witch is which?" Shirlene teased.

Since Hope had just spilled the biggest secret of her life to a woman with a face that was as easy to read as a first grade primer, it took a moment to collect herself. Dropping her hand from her sister's mouth, Hope sent her one stern warning look before she turned to her best friend.

"Real funny, Shirl," she said, with just the right amount of sarcasm.

"Well, that settles that." Shirlene pointed a red nail at Hope. "Wicked witch." She pointed at Faith. "Good witch. Although the good witch looks like someone just landed a house on all her munchkins. You okay, honey?"

Hope knew if she didn't get Shirlene out of there quickly, she would find out what a good-for-nothing piece of roadkill her brother really was.

"Of course, she's not okay, Shirl." Hope pulled a folding chair over and pushed her sister down, tugging the brim of the witch's hat low enough to shadow Faith's stunned face. "She's pregnant." She patted her sister none too gently on the shoulder. "Now you just sit right there and rest, Sis, while me and Shirlene go on back and finish getting the prizes ready."

A suspicious look settled over Shirlene's face, but after only a few brief seconds, she followed Hope behind the cardboard waves that Hope's mama had made.

"I'm mad at you, you know," Shirlene said, as she

flopped down in one of the chairs, her numerous bracelets and necklaces jangling.

Fearing Shirlene was much more perceptive than she'd thought, Hope moved over to the box of prizes and tried not to act guilty.

"For what?"

"For avoiding me for the last week."

Hope heaved a sigh of relief and sat down in the other chair. "I wasn't avoiding you. I was just busy, is all. Besides, if anyone should be mad, it's me at you for suggesting the stupid experiment in the first place."

"And just how was I supposed to know you two are Fertile Myrtles?" Shirlene said. "Especially when my best friend fails to tell me she's been doing the dirty deed with some guy out in California. The last I heard you were living with Sheldon."

Hope grabbed a bottle of bubbles and wrapped a rubber band around the cap, which would make it easier to attach the paper clip fishhook to when the kids tossed it over the waves.

When Hope didn't answer, Shirlene spoke up. "Don't tell me you changed his sexual preference."

"No. It wasn't Sheldon. The reason I didn't tell you is because it was just a one-night stand."

Shirlene shot her a skeptical look. "Since when does Hope Scroggs have one-night stands?"

"I can be as slutty as the next person," she defended herself. It was a lie, and the look on Shirlene's face said as much. There was only one man who brought out the major slut in her. An untrustworthy bum who didn't have two pennies to rub together or a responsible bone in his body.

"And I'm gathering it wasn't your spray-tanned agent." Shirlene snagged a bag of Tootsie Rolls out of the box and opened them.

"No. Ryan has only one love affair going and that's with himself."

Shirlene unwrapped a candy and popped it into her mouth. "So why is the man still here? I hear he's staying with Harley and signing people up with his agency right and left. He even has Twyla dreaming of her own reality television show."

The news didn't surprise Hope. It seemed Ryan felt as if Bramble was a sea of reality shows just waiting to make him millions. Fortunately, he had a flight out tomorrow morning. She would be glad to see him go. Not only because she didn't want him spilling the beans about the reality show until she got it, but because his presence reminded her that it wouldn't be long before she would have to return to California.

"So what are you going to do?" Shirlene asked, and Hope didn't need to be a mind reader to know what she was talking about. She stared down at the huge cardboard box of toys and did what she'd been doing since the slumber party—clung desperately to a false sense of hope.

"Maybe I'm not pregnant. Maybe I have an infection or something that threw the tests off."

"I guess it's a possibility." Shirlene offered Hope a Tootsie Roll before opening another one for herself. "Are you going to see a doctor?"

"Monday in Midland."

Without a second's hesitation, Shirlene asked, "You want me to go with you?"

Knowing how difficult a trip to the obstetrician's

would be for her friend, Hope shook her head. "Thanks, but I can handle it." She reached out and took her hand. "If I could trade places with you, you know I would."

"I know, honey." Shirlene squeezed her hand. "But as my mama always says, all things happen for a reason."

The words of wisdom didn't make Hope feel any better, and if the forlorn look on Shirlene's face was any indication, they hadn't worked for her either.

She was happy when Shirlene popped the candy in her mouth and changed the subject. "So when do you have to work the kissing booth?"

"Not until later. Cindy Lynn wants to make sure everyone is here."

"Well, can you blame her? Everyone in town believes the slow economy has to do with you not being here to dish out your good-luck kisses."

"Did somebody mention kisses?" Slate's voice came over the ocean waves, and when Shirlene and Hope got up, they found the two newlyweds kissing.

With so many other things to worry about, it didn't bother Hope as much as she thought it would. In fact, she couldn't control the desire to do a little devilish teasing. Without hesitation, Hope walked around the cardboard waves. "How could you, Slate?" She tried to blink up a couple of tears before her sister gave it away. But Faith surprised her by turning on Slate and socking him in the arm.

"Yeah, watch it, Calhoun!"

Confused, Slate glanced down at Hope's red boots before he apologized to Faith. "Sorry, Hog." He reached for Hope, but she held up a hand.

"Don't be mauling on me, cowboy."

He glanced back at Faith, and his forehead knotted. "This isn't funny, y'all."

But it was. So funny, all three women burst out laughing.

The kissing booth turned out to be twice as profitable as the fishing booth, but not nearly as much fun. After Hope sat down on the hard stool, a line formed clear out the gymnasium door and into the foyer. It wouldn't have taken so long if all the townsfolk expected was a peck on the cheek, but everyone had something to say—whether Hope wanted to hear it or not.

"Don't lift your hands over your head or the baby will be born with the cord wrapped around its neck."

"You date anyone else out in California? Maybe a Dallas Cowboy who stopped by Disneyland in between games?"

"Get out of bed on the right side, you'll have girls. Get out on the left, and it's boys for shore."

"What about one of those Texan actors? That Owen Wilson feller? Ethan Hawke? Matthew McConaughey?"

Hope tried to hold it together, but the craziness started to take its toll. And after what seemed like the five-hundredth kiss, she started grabbing the money, giving a quick peck and moving on to the next person, leaving the previous one still trying to get his words in edgewise.

Around nine o'clock, Kenny Gene stepped up to the booth, although she didn't know it until he lifted the white sheet and grinned back at her. He hooked the sheet over one of the pointed bull horns attached to his hat.

"Get it? Bull-sheet."

Hope had to admit it was clever, but she still thought Josephine's extra-crispy fried chicken leg deserved the best costume ribbon. Especially since the crumpled butcher paper looked so painful to walk in.

"So, Hope," Kenny grinned. "I was thinkin' that along with a kiss you might let me rub your belly—you know like one of them fat Buddhas? That way I'll get triple the luck."

Hope grabbed the dollar from his hand and slapped it in the cashbox before she leaned over and gave him the quickest kiss of the night. He started to complain, when Ryan came flapping up in a black cape and plastic vampire teeth. The costume was appropriate. If anyone could suck blood out of a person, it was her agent.

"Bella, Edward vants to suck your blood," he slurred as he flipped the cape around her and pressed the cold plastic fangs against her neck. When she shoved him back and sent him a warning look, Kenny jumped into the conversation.

"She ain't sellin' blood. She's sellin' kisses. And I thought your name was Ryan."

Ryan slipped the fangs out of his mouth. "Kisses?" He flashed a blinding smile. "God, I love this town." Before Hope could stop him, he pulled the wallet out of his back pocket and flipped it open. "Do you take debit or credit?"

Hope rolled her eyes at the gold American Express card shoved in front of her face. "Sorry, cash only," she said.

His smooth brow knotted. "You're kidding!" When she only stared back at him, he shrugged and slipped the card back into his wallet. "Then I guess you'll have to trust that I'm good for it."

"Sort of like you were good for the residual checks on my commercial?"

"Now, Texas," he tossed her an innocent look, "I couldn't help it if one of those checks got lost in the mail. And you did end up getting all your money."

She arched an eyebrow. "Yeah, after I almost got kicked out of my apartment."

Ryan held up a hand. "Fine." He flipped the wallet back open. "I've got an emergency hundred in here that I'm more than willing to give to your little charity. It's the least I can do for my new star client."

"You gonna give a hun-nerd dollars for a kiss from Hope?" Kenny jumped back into the conversation. "I hate to say this, but I just got one and a dollar's pushin' it."

Ryan pointed a finger. "Kenny Gene, right?" When Kenny nodded, he continued his brown-nosing. "Love the costume, man."

Annoyed, Hope reached out and jerked the hundred out of his hand and placed it in the cashbox. "Thanks, man." She slipped off the stool, ready to end her time in the kissing booth.

"Hey," Ryan said. "What about my kiss?"

"You'll have to trust that I'm good for it," she said, as she looked around for her witch's hat.

"Now, Hope," Kenny refused to keep his mouth shut. "That ain't very fair."

"What's not fair, Kenny Gene?" Rachel waddled up in her extra crispy costume.

"Hope's Hollywood agent just gave her a hun-nerd for a kiss, and Hope ain't even gonna give him a peck on the cheek— hell, for a hun-nerd, she should at least slip him the tongue."

"A hundred dollars?" Twyla joined the group in a saloon-girl cancan costume that was more appropriate for an adult party than for a kid's carnival. "Why, that's twenty haircuts."

"Fifteen six-packs of beer," Rye Pickett stated, as if he hadn't failed out of math four years running.

"Around forty cans of Spam," Rachel added.

"Forty?" Kenny looked truly shocked as he shot a glance over at Hope that said there was no way one of her kisses was worth forty cans of Spam.

Giving up on finding her hat, Hope stepped around the back of the booth with every intention of leaving the insanity far behind her. But Ryan was there, waiting with a devious twinkle in his eye and a pitiful whipped-puppy look on his face. No wonder he had become an agent; he was a worse actor than she was. Still, he had the town suckered.

"Oh, come on, Hope," Kenny pleaded. "Give the poor feller a break."

Realizing there was no way around it, Hope gave in. Besides it was for a good cause. All the money from the kissing booth went for new band uniforms, and Hope felt somehow responsible for the singed poof on the trombonist's cap, although it had been Colt who stomped it flat.

With the thought darkening her mood, she might've jerked Ryan over a little too hard for his kiss on the cheek. But her sympathy died when the sly dog swiveled his head and planted a kiss right on her lips. Surprisingly, they were as cold as a vampire's, cold and rather clammy, with the distinct flavor of Frito pie. But before Hope could pull back and give Ryan a piece of her mind, he was gone—like completely removed from her line of sight.

And it took only a second to locate him, dangling from a fist attached to a tattooed arm. For an instant, Hope felt relief. The instant right before she remembered that the man standing before her with a choke hold on Ryan's throat was the same man who had run off like a lizard with his tail on fire. A man who hadn't called or tried to contact her in over a week.

"Put him down," Hope yelled.

Colt glanced over at her, and his eyes narrowed. "You know this man?"

"Know him," Rachel Dean teased. "After a kiss like that, I'd say she knows him pretty well."

"Yeah," Twyla joined in. "You sure he ain't the daddy of your babies, Hope?"

"She's got a point, Hog," Kenny said. "Who else but a man in love would offer a hun-nerd for one kiss?"

There was a moment when Colt's grip tightened so much that Hope wondered if he was actually going to snuff the life right out of Ryan. But then his fingers relaxed, and Ryan slithered to the floor. Colt glanced back at Hope for one brief second before he tossed something to the floor and walked away. Rushing over, Hope knelt down to ask Ryan if he was okay, but the words got stuck in her throat when her gaze drifted down.

There on the high-polished wood of the gymnasium floor was one crumpled dollar bill.

Chapter Eighteen

COLT SHOULD LEAVE. He was pissed. And when he was pissed, he always did stupid things. Things he would regret later. Except his feet weren't listening to his head, and he continued to lean in the doorway of the auxiliary gym and glare at the vampire who had just offered Hope a bite of his caramel apple.

Colt hadn't known what to expect when he returned to Bramble, but it certainly wasn't another man. For some crazy reason, he had been convinced there was only one man in Hope's life to worry about—Slate. Now he had to reevaluate his entire way of thinking, and it didn't exactly sit well.

A gay roommate he could laugh off. A heterosexual Hollywood agent was not so funny. Especially when Colt wasn't buying his story. No agent Colt had ever met would waste his time driving hundreds of miles just to check on one of his clients. That was what cell phones were for. Which meant the man was here for a different reason. A reason that had Colt's temper boiling and his stomach knotted in a tight fist, a fist that tightened when Ryan leaned over to whisper something in Hope's ear.

Just that quickly, Colt realized he'd been wrong. He wouldn't regret wiping the fake blood off the man's chin with his fist. Not now or later.

"Hollywood agent, my ass," he growled under his breath. But obviously not low enough.

"I know what you mean, sugar buns. I couldn't believe it either."

It took an effort for Colt to pull his gaze away from Hope and over to Marcy Henderson. Now here was something Colt regretted already. He had no business latching on to Marcy like a spurned teenage boy. But there he stood, staring into a pair of eyes that held the same sexual invitation that had been there for as long as he'd known her.

"Hope has always stretched the truth," Marcy continued in a high-pitched voice that grated on his nerves. "But after talking with Ryan, I realized she wasn't lying after all. Ryan is an honest-to-goodness Hollywood agent." She placed a hand on her chest, drawing Colt's attention to the ample breasts that swelled above the low neckline of her tight sweater. "In fact, he offered me a part in one of those horror movies. 'Course I never was much of a screamer... least ways, not out of bed."

She paused as her gaze slid over Colt. "It's sure hot for October, don't you think, sugar? I swear I'm about ready to incinerate." Leaning over, she pressed her breasts against his folded arms. "What say, we go on back to my trailer and have us a nice cold beer? If I remember correctly, you always did like a cold one... followed by a lot of heat."

He had to admit the breasts felt nice. Unfortunately, they were accompanied by the overpowering smell of cheap perfume. Still, when he glanced up and noticed

Hope watching, he seized the opportunity as any spurned teenage boy would.

"Well, that sure sounds like fun, honey." His hands slid around her waist as he sent her a smoldering look. "But I've had a hard week, so I think I'm going to head back to Shirlene's and get some sleep."

"Sleep?" She looked thoroughly confused at the mixed signals he was sending her. "Since when do you sleep, Colt Lomax?"

Noting that Hope had gotten up from the table and was now walking off, he released Marcy. "Since I turned thirty." He tried to soften the rejection with a wink. "But how about if I drive you home?" It was the least he could do after using her to appease his wounded ego.

"No, thanks." Marcy shot him an annoyed look as she smoothed down her pink sweater. "I might be over thirty, but I ain't dead yet." With a flip of her fifties poodle skirt, she strutted over to a group of cowboys, who seemed more than happy to see her.

Once she was gone, Colt glanced around, but Hope was nowhere to be found. It was probably for the best. With the way he felt, he didn't need to confront her tonight. He slipped out the door and walked down the short hallway to the main gym. The carnival was winding down, and most of the booths had closed. But still people were reluctant to call it a night and stood around talking, as their children raced up and down the bleachers, hyped up on the sweets they'd consumed.

Colt weaved his way through the crowd on his way to the doors without much notice, which was why he was surprised when the tall, lanky kid who played quarterback for Bramble High stopped him.

"You're Colt Lomax, right?" When Colt nodded, the kid introduced himself. "I'm Austin Reeves."

Colt took his hand and gave it a brief shake. No wonder the kid could handle a football with such ease; his hands were the size of dinner plates. "I hear the Bulldogs are headed for state. Congratulations."

He grinned. "Thank you, sir. We've got a great team of guys." He held out a folded orange napkin. "The witch wanted me to give you this."

"The witch?" Colt took the napkin and glanced around. Hope stood just inside the doors that led out to the courtyard. Except she now wore a witch's hat that placed half her face in shadow. But he had no difficulty seeing the daring smile before she turned and disappeared through the doors.

Thanking Austin with a nod, Colt followed after her, flipping the napkin open and reading it as he went. When he got outside, Hope was already hurrying across the courtyard—her purple hair and black dress fluttering in the cool October breeze before she slipped inside the main building.

The note had said she wanted to talk. Obviously, she didn't want to be overheard by anyone in town. Or maybe she just didn't want her boyfriend to find out. The thought annoyed him, and he quickened his step, jerking open the door and taking the stairs to the second level two at a time.

When he reached the designated classroom, his gaze was caught by a cuss word scratched into the metal of one of the lockers that lined the hallway. The locker hadn't belonged to him, but the angry word did. The awkwardly written letters brought back a flood of memories—memories of a loner who had never quite fit in.

The room was dark when he stepped inside. The only light spilled in from the hallway. But even that disappeared when the door eased shut behind him. He took a few steps into the room, only to bump into a desk.

He muttered an oath as he stepped back and rubbed his thigh. He waited for Hope to laugh, but all he heard was the tick-tick of a clock. And all he could see was the shadowy outline of desks.

Obviously, Hope wasn't finished leading him a merry chase.

But Colt was finished. The long week in Houston, coupled with his anger, had left him too tired to keep up with a wildcat. So he turned back to the door with every intention of calling it a night, except that just as he reached for the doorknob, it was pulled open by a witch—minus the hat.

"Look, Hope, I don't have the time or the patience for any more of your games," Colt stated. But even as he said it, he stepped back to allow her entry.

"Funny, but I was just going to say the exact same thing." She strode into the room with her normal sass, and he couldn't help reaching out to stop her before she smacked into the same desk as he had.

She wasn't exactly grateful for the help. With something that sounded like a snarl, she jerked away from him.

"Don't touch me."

He held up his hands. "Don't worry, sweetheart. That's the last thing I want to do."

"So what do you want?" She headed back to the door, and he watched her feel around for the light switch.

"What do I want?" He sat down on the top of a desk and crossed his arms. "I thought this conversation was going to include what you wanted. Child support. A new minivan. A house to keep your Hollywood boyfriend in the style he expects."

Giving up on the light switch, she turned to him. "As if I would waste my time asking for those things from a motorcycle bum. Lyle's money has you living in some kind of a dream world, Lomax. At least in high school, you accepted who you were."

"Accepted? Did I have a choice? This town gave me my role, and I was expected to play it."

"And you're still doing a great job. Colt Lomax the big, bad boy with the nasty chip on his shoulder who runs off at the first sign of trouble." She turned and walked to the front of the class. Obviously, her eyes had adjusted to the darkness, because she didn't run into anything. Unlike Colt, who banged his shin on a desk leg after no more than two steps. He bit back a cuss word and hobbled over to the opposite side of the teacher's desk.

"I came back, didn't I?"

"Yeah, a week later!" She pulled off her wig and tossed it down on the desk.

"What do you want from me, Hope? You want me to be the big hero—the one who saves the day with a game-winning touchdown? Because if that's the case, you've got the wrong man. I'm not ever going to be Slate." He stepped around the desk. "It's too bad that Faith had to show up. If she hadn't, you would now be married to the only man who's ever been good enough for you." He paused. "Of course, that doesn't explain your relationship with your agent. Come to think of it, maybe I should be asking for a paternity test, seeing as how you seem to get around more than Marcy."

The slap that she gave him rang his bell. He was so dazed and confused that it took him a moment to realize she had headed for the door. She already had it opened by the time he reached her.

"Oh, no, you don't." He slammed the door closed and spun her around. "You wanted to talk, so talk."

"Why, you bastard!" Hope pushed at his chest. "Get your hands off me."

"After seeing you with your agent, I thought you liked being pawed."

Hope stopped trying to pull away. "You should talk! If I'd known you still haven't grown up enough to avoid women like Marcy, I never would've had sex with you in the first place. Now, not only do I have to worry about being pregnant, but I also have to worry about what I might've caught."

"Worried about being pregnant?" He stared down at her, trying to make out her features in the darkness. "Are you telling me that you're not sure?"

He couldn't see her face clearly, but he could hear her swallow.

"I refuse to believe it until my doctor's appointment in Midland."

"You sure as hell sounded positive when you busted into Shirlene's guesthouse, screaming at the top of your lungs." He took a step back and ran a hand through his hair. "Do you know the hell you put me through in the last week?"

"You think it's been easy for me?"

"From my vantage point, it looks like you've been whooping it up with your Hollywood boyfriend."

"He's not my boyfriend."

"So what is he to you?" he couldn't stop himself from asking.

"None of your business."

He didn't know what annoyed him more: her refusal to define her relationship with her agent or her refusal to accept she was pregnant with his child. Whichever it was, it had his back up and his temper high. Before she could utter more than a startled squeak, he jerked her up and kissed her.

After their hateful words, the heat of Hope's response took him by surprise. She held nothing back, answering his passion with a raw energy that left him slightly dazed. Her sweet tongue dipped inside his mouth, demanding attention, and he gave it, sucking and stroking until her moan resounded in his ears. Pulling away from the kiss, he sipped a path to her ear.

"What is he to you, Hope?" Colt whispered. "Can he cause you to tremble like this?" He sucked on a tender spot, and when she quivered in reaction, his hand slipped down and cupped her through the thin black dress. "Or ache like this?"

Her hands slid up from his chest, and he had just started to enjoy the feel of her fingers caressing his scalp when they closed around his hair and yanked so hard that he saw stars. Before he could recover, she opened the door and slipped out. He went after her, but she hadn't lettered in track for nothing, and by the time he caught up with her, she had reached the gym.

Colt grabbed her arm and cut to the chase. "When's your doctor's appointment?"

Hope turned on him, her eyes narrowed. "Why?"

"Because I want to be there."

She smiled smugly. "Sort of like you were there for me this past week?"

"When?" he repeated. But before she could answer, Hope's mama yelled across the gym.

"Colt, quit teasing Hope. She needs to help me get these boxes in the car."

Colt had always respected Jenna, but he refused to release Hope until she answered him. As if sensing his determination, it didn't take her long to give in.

"Nine on Monday."

Colt nodded. "I'll pick you up at seven."

Across the gym, a group of townsfolk watched as Hope jerked her arm away from Colt and hurried over to help her mama.

"It was the most pathetic thing I've ever seen in my life." Rachel scratched at a spot under her arm where the crumpled butcher paper of her costume had started to itch. "Hope stuffin' her bra full of napkins in an attempt to attract those foreigners' attention just broke my heart clean in two—which is why I sent Bear straight back to California. We need to find that daddy before Hope hooks up with some loser."

"I couldn't agree more, Rachel," Harley said, his mustache drooping from the time spent in the dunk tank. "But I don't think we can wait any longer. We got babies to think about, and we sure don't want people talkin' about our little Hope. Which means we need to give up on findin' the real daddy and start lookin' for a home-grown boy to do the job."

"You mean like a step-daddy?" Kenny asked.

"That's exactly what I mean."

"But who?" Sheriff Winslow jumped in as he watched Colt turn and walk out of the gym. "Hope is real picky about her men."

"I don't know," Harley said. "But if we keep our eyes open, it will come to us."

Chapter Nineteen

"HOPE SCROGGS?"

Instead of the female obstetrician Hope expected to see, Jimmy Higgins walked into the room with her chart, flashing a set of teeth that could no longer eat corn on the cob through a picket fence.

"How the hell have you been, honey?" He gave her a big hug as if she wasn't as naked as the day she was born beneath the thin cotton gown.

Struck speechless, all Hope could do was stare back at him.

"Danged if you don't look exactly the same as you did in high school." He pointed a finger at her. "Remember when we had Crazy Fifties Day and we won the jitterbug contest? Never could figure out why you chose me as a partner when you were dating Slate. But I guess he won out in the long run." He winked at her. "Congratulations, Mrs. Calhoun, you're going to have a baby."

Suddenly, having Jimmy for a doctor took a backseat to the news. After seven positive home pregnancy tests, the chances of her not being pregnant had been slim to none. Still, she had clung to that one tiny thread of hope like a lifeline. And now, just that quickly, "Bucky" Higgins had clipped the thread, and she went tumbling head over heels into the black abyss. Luckily, Bucky had finally noticed the other person in the room and didn't see her inappropriate reaction.

"Colt Lomax?" He glanced back at Hope, then back to Colt, and still the light didn't go on. "I guess Slate is busy coaching that state championship football team, huh? Well, it's good to see you, man. I saw your name in *Street Chopper Magazine*—"

"The baby is mine," Colt stated. Even in her comatose state, Hope wanted to reach out and slug him.

Bucky's eyes widened, but he quickly collected himself. "Well, didn't I just put my foot in it?" He walked over to the sink and set down the chart before turning on the water.

"I guess I shouldn't be surprised," he continued as he scoured his hands with soap. "You two were always like vinegar and oil. And all it takes is a little shakin' to get things mixed up. And it looks like you two got shaken up pretty well." He chuckled. "Colt and Hope married. Now isn't that just a kicker?"

Drying his hands on a paper towel, Bucky turned around and finally took note of their solemn faces.

"Would you look at me, runnin' off at the mouth like an idiot? You're not here to visit. You're here to find out about your baby." He cleared his throat and reached for the chart. When he spoke again, he sounded more like a doctor, instead of a babbling idiot. "So, using the information Hope wrote down on the questionnaire, I have her at six weeks with a due date of June tenth. Right before it gets too hot for a little extra weight."

He winked at Hope, but all she could do was stare back at him.

June tenth. Only five days before her own birthday. It seemed entirely too close.

"So have you experienced any morning sickness or dizziness?" Bucky set the chart back down.

She shook her head, even though at the moment she felt a little sick and light-headed.

"Good. Some women breeze right through pregnancy without a hitch. And I don't doubt for a minute that our sassy little Hope here will be one of those." He walked back over, and, taking her hand, eased her back on the table before he spread the sheet over her legs. "You two living back in Bramble?"

She started to explain the situation, but then realized she couldn't explain the unexplainable. So she was somewhat relieved when Colt kept it simple.

"Yes."

Bucky nodded. "If Doc Mathers ever retires, I might just move back there myself. It's a good place to raise a family. Although I need to pay off my student loans before my wife and I even think about kids. Kids are expensive." He lifted one of her feet and placed it in a stirrup before he moved to the other side.

"Before you leave, make sure to get the maternity packet from Katie. It gives you all the information you'll need—what exercise is good, what vitamins you'll need to start taking, and what food and drugs to avoid. And, of course, if you have any questions, don't hesitate to call me. After all, we're like family." He hooked the low stool on casters with his foot and pulled it toward him before he disappeared from sight.

Until that moment, Hope had been too busy thinking about the baby to pay much attention to what Bucky was doing. Even when the sheet started to lift, it took her a second to react. Fortunately, Colt's reaction was much faster. He reached over and jerked down the sheet, and at the same time, used a boot to shove the stool clear across the room.

"Whoa there, Bucky. What do you think you're doing?" Colt stepped in front of the table.

By the time Hope got her feet out of the stirrups and peeked around, Bucky wore the same look on his face that had been there thirteen years earlier when she'd dragged him out on the dance floor so she would have a chance at the trophy instead of no chance with Two-Left-Feet Calhoun.

"A p-pelvic examination," Bucky sputtered.

"If that includes looking at Hope naked—I don't think so, Buck."

"But I'm a doctor."

"And I'm a biker who's about ready to kick some MD ass."

Hope waited for Bucky to take offense, but she'd forgotten how good-natured the man was. After only a few seconds, a grin spread across his freckled face.

"Fair enough, Colt." He got up off the stool. "Doctor or no doctor, I wouldn't want a man looking at my wife either. We have a woman on staff, and if you're willing to wait, I'll have her come in."

"We'll wait," Colt said, without giving Hope a chance to speak. Not that she could have. Between Bucky and the baby, she was pretty speechless.

The other doctor wasn't as nice as Bucky, but Hope

didn't care, as long as she wasn't someone Hope had done algebra homework with. When she was finished, she helped Hope sit up.

"Everything looks fine, so unless you have any questions, we'll see you in another month."

"A month?" Colt took a step forward. "Isn't that a little long to wait? And what do you mean, unless something comes up? What would come up?"

The doctor walked over and started washing her hands at the sink. "I mean, if she should experience anything out of the ordinary—cramping, bleeding, or—"

"Which is exactly why I think a month is too long. Anything can go wrong in a month." Colt shook his head. "No, we'll be back next Monday."

The doctor looked at Hope and winked as if they shared some special secret about the idiocy of men. "Of course, if you'd like to come back in a week—"

"A month is fine." Hope finally found her voice, although it shook as much as her hands, clutched in her lap.

"Very good," the doctor said.

Once the door clicked closed behind her, Hope just sat there, unsure of what to say or do. And Colt didn't seem much better. With his hands shoved deep in his pockets, he wandered around, looking at the charts on the walls.

"You okay?" he asked.

"Yeah," she lied. "But we shouldn't have told Bucky."

Colt glanced over at her. "You still think we can keep it a secret?" He looked back at the diagram of fetal development. "It. Is that what you call something the size of a lima bean?"

"I don't know." She got up off the table and proceeded to get dressed, no longer concerned about Colt being in the same room. Not that he paid any attention. His gaze was riveted on the lima bean.

"Have you thought about names?" he asked.

She swallowed. "No."

"Well, until we do, I'm going to call it Pumpkin Seed."

Her heart, which had been beating so quickly, seemed to freeze up in her chest as her gaze snapped over to him. "I don't think we should name…it. Not until we figure out what to do."

He turned away from the poster, his brow knotted. "What do you mean?" The confusion cleared, and his eyes narrowed. "We're not getting an abortion."

As if it was the most important thing to do at the moment, she carefully folded the gown. "No, but that doesn't mean I'm going to keep…it."

His gray eyes filled with disbelief, but before he could reply, the cute little nurse poked her head in, and the conversation was put on hold while she gave them the maternity packet and directed them back to the receptionist's desk, where Colt paid the bill, using a credit card.

A credit card paid for by Lyle Dalton, no doubt, Hope thought. The idea of his using someone else's money on their child angered her, although she was no angrier than he seemed to be. As soon as they pulled away from the parking lot, he started in.

"So that's it? You want to give Pumpkin Seed away?"

"Stop it!" She turned to him, the seatbelt cutting into her shoulder. "Stop calling it Pumpkin Seed!"

"It's not an 'it,' Hope! It's something!" He ran a hand through his hair as he returned his gaze to the road. "It's something."

"I know it's something. But it's something inside my

body. My body!" She thumped herself in the chest so hard that it hurt.

"And because of that, I don't have a choice. Is that what you're saying?"

Realizing she was being a raving idiot, she fell back against the seat and took a deep breath. "No, that's not what I'm saying. I'm saying, we need to consider all the options and make an intelligent decision. A decision using all the facts."

"Like what? The fact that you hate my guts?" He glanced over at her, his eyes shielded behind the dark green lenses of his sunglasses.

Hope started to say that she didn't hate his guts. That as much as she wanted to, her emotions didn't come close to hate. But she stopped herself. That kind of revelation would only cause more hurt and pain. And it was already painful enough.

"How about the fact that neither one of us has a job?"

"I have a job."

She shot him an annoyed look. "Riding around on a motorcycle bought by someone else is not a job, Colt. It's a pastime. Which means, if I don't get this reality show, I'll be living with my parents. And Mama and Daddy have no business helping me raise a child after they just sent their last one off to college."

"Reality show?" Colt glanced over at her. "Is that why your agent showed up? He wants you to go back to California for a job?"

She nodded. "Ryan thinks I've got a pretty good chance of getting it. I guess I'll find out when I fly back next week."

There was a long pause before Colt spoke. "So that's

what this is about. You finally have a chance to achieve your dream, and you don't want my baby screwing it up."

Hope pressed her fingers to her throbbing temples. "Can't we have one conversation where we aren't at one another's throats? This isn't about me or you, Colt. It's about an innocent life that deserves the best we can give it."

"So what's the problem? If you become a big reality star, you'll have plenty of money to spend on a baby."

"It's not just about the money. It's about giving our child a nurturing home—a home with two loving parents." She turned away. "Given your childhood, I thought you would understand how important that is."

"I survived," he growled.

"Exactly." She turned back to him. "But I don't want my child to just survive. And I don't want my baby being raised by a nanny because I'm working day and night, or being neglected by a father who can't unglue his butt from a motorcycle seat. I want my child to feel safe and secure, surrounded by a loving mother and father."

Colt's gaze narrowed on her. "You've already decided, haven't you?"

He was right. All the time that she thought she was just walking around in a daze, her mind had already been working on a plan—a plan that made perfect sense.

"She'll love the baby as her own," she whispered.

He pulled up to the stoplight and turned to her. "She?" He studied her for a second before his eyes widened. "Faith? You're going to give Pumpkin Seed to Faith and Slate?" When she shook her head, it didn't take long for the logical answer to come. Colt fell back against the seat and released his breath in a slow, painful sigh. "Shirlene."

Leaning as far toward him as the seat belt would allow, Hope tried to justify her decision. "She wants a baby so desperately, Colt. If you could've seen all those home pregnancy tests she'd hoarded, it would've broken your heart. And with us, all it took was one time with one faulty condom." She looked out the windshield, but saw nothing. "And maybe that's why it happened. Maybe it's God's plan. I'd be like a surrogate mother. It would even have her genes."

Colt just sat there with a hand hooked over the steering wheel and his gaze riveted to the stoplight. It changed to green, but still he didn't go, not until a car honked behind him.

"Have you told her?" he asked, once they were moving again.

"No. She's been disappointed so many times, I want to be sure."

He nodded. "Good. I think you should wait until you're further along."

"So you think that's what we should do?"

"We?" He glanced over at her. "Am I now in the equation?"

Suddenly exhausted, Hope leaned her head back against the headrest and closed her eyes. "If you can figure out another option, Colt, I'm willing to listen."

It seemed like they drove for miles before he finally spoke.

"No. I can't think of a thing."

Chapter Twenty

A STIFF WIND blew through Jones' Garage, making the concrete floor Colt sat on feel even colder than it was. Still, he wasn't ready to go back to Shirlene's. Not even for a blazing fire and a steamy cup of coffee. He needed the comfort of being wrist-deep in crankshafts and carburetors, pistons and rods.

Working on a motorcycle was almost as soothing as riding one, and after the doctor's visit, Colt needed all the soothing that he could get. He wasn't freaked out about the confirmation of Hope's pregnancy. Even without it, he'd come to terms with her having a baby. What upset him the most was the idea of giving that baby away. Which was crazy. As much as he might want to deny it, Hope was right. He was a motorcycle bum. A rich motorcycle bum, but a bum just the same. A bum who enjoyed his freedom and the open road. A bum who had no place in his life for a child.

So why did he feel as if someone had kicked him in the solar plexus with a steel-toed boot? Probably because, while staring at the diagram of the different stages of fetal development, the baby had suddenly become something more than just a big mistake.

It had become a small miracle.

His miracle.

Pumpkin Seed.

The words were more than just a silly name to tease Hope with. They held part of the past and a piece of the future. And damned if he didn't struggle with the thought of giving Pumpkin Seed away, even if it was to his own sister. A sister he would walk through fire for. A sister who wanted a child more than anything else in the world.

"Hey. Where's your cool chopper?"

Colt glanced up from the Knucklehead to see Jesse standing in the doorway of the garage, looking more ragged than usual. Today he wore a plain white T-shirt. At least, it had started out white. Now it looked worse than the rag sitting on the floor by Colt's knee. Jesse's hair was sleep-mussed, but his eyes were alert as they tracked around the garage.

"I delivered it," Colt said. "Where's your coat?"

"I ain't cold." Almost as soon as the words were out, he shivered.

Shaking his head, Colt pointed to the leather jacket hooked over a tire jack. "Put it on."

"I ain't—"

"Put it on," he ordered, before he turned back to the bike. He thought the kid would continue to argue, but instead, a few minutes later, he appeared on the other side of the bike with the jacket hanging off his bony shoulders.

"You ain't fixed it yet?"

Great. All Colt needed was another person thinking he was incompetent.

"No, I haven't fixed it yet."

Jesse flopped down on the other side of the bike, but he leaned in close enough for Colt to see his freckled face between the teardrop gas tank and the front tire. "I ain't gonna wait around for the money forever, you know."

"Speaking of which . . . what did you do with the money I gave you?"

"That ain't none of your business." Jesse swiped at his nose.

"It is if you want to see any more."

His face grew more belligerent than usual. "I gave it to my mom."

"Is this the same mom who homeschools you, even with two jobs?"

There was a long pause before the kid answered. "My big sister homeschools me while my mom works."

Kenny had mentioned that Jesse had a sister, so it seemed feasible. "Then you should be home studying instead of hanging around here."

"It's recess."

Colt couldn't help but laugh. "Fine, but don't touch anything. I don't want you messing anything up."

The kid snorted. "Like I could make this bike any uglier."

The morning went by quickly. Colt probably should've sent the kid home, but the kid's constant questions about motorcycles took his mind off his own problems, although after about an hour Jesse's questions brought him full circle.

"You got kids?"

Colt swallowed. "No."

"How come?"

"Because," he hedged.

The answer didn't suffice. "Because you don't want any?"

It was funny how kids could get straight to the heart of things. He hadn't wanted kids. At least, he thought he hadn't. But now he wanted one. One tiny little seed.

"No, I want kids." He stopped working and wiped his hands off on the rag. Through the opening in the bike, he watched Jesse's face scrunch up in thought.

"How many?"

He got to his feet. "I don't know."

"Four's a good number."

Shaking his head, Colt walked over to the soda machine. "Yeah, four is a nice even number." He dug through his pocket for some change.

"You got a wife?" Jesse came over to stand next to him. Colt hadn't realized how small the kid was until that moment. As he studied him, he readjusted his first age estimate. The kid couldn't be more than eight or nine—too young to be wandering around by himself.

"No, I don't have a wife." His gaze narrowed. "How old are you?"

"Old enough." He punched a button on the machine as if the money Colt had put in was for him. When the grape soda rolled out, he grabbed it up. "My sister's real pretty."

Colt crossed his arms and glared down at the kid. "Stop stalling and answer the question."

He popped the top. "Twelve."

Colt lifted an eyebrow.

"Ten." He took a deep guzzle, then burped loudly. "And Mia's really nice. Well, sometimes she's nice. When she ain't yellin' at me about doing my homework."

"Speaking of homework," Colt searched his pockets

for more quarters, but only came up with three linty nickels and five pennies, "I think it's time for you to get back to yours."

"I ain't ready."

"Too bad." Colt moved toward the office. "After I get some caffeine, I'm driving you home."

Shooting him a belligerent look, Jesse tipped up the can and guzzled the drink.

"Hey, Colt," Tyler greeted him as he stepped inside the small office. "How's the bike coming?"

"Not well." He handed him a dollar. "Could you give me some quarters?"

"So you still think it's going to make it to the corner?" Tyler opened up the cash register and exchanged the money.

Colt wasn't so sure anymore, but he refused to voice his doubt. "It will take some time, is all. But right now, I'm going to drive Jesse home."

Tyler laughed. "That kid is a pistol, isn't he?"

"More like a pain in my butt."

Unfortunately, by the time he and Tyler got back out in the garage, the pain-in-the-butt kid was nowhere to be found and Colt's leather jacket hung back over the tire jack.

"Looks like he had other plans," Tyler said.

Colt pulled the keys to Shirlene's Navigator out of his pocket with every intention of going after the boy, but before he could, a long motor home pulled up in front of the station.

He glanced over at Tyler, who had a big grin on his face.

"The old man got in last night, but he swore me to secrecy. Said he wanted to surprise you."

Colt felt a lot more than surprised as Tinker, Tyler's daddy, stepped down from the driver's side. A wall of unexplainable emotions welled up inside him, and something that felt a lot like tears filled his eyes. Luckily, he had a strong wind to blame them on.

"If I hadn't just had my eyes checked," Mr. Jones drawled around the huge lump of tobacco in his mouth, "I would think they was playin' tricks on me."

"No, sir." Colt stepped forward and stretched out his hand to the man who, despite a balder head, had changed very little over the years. "A sharper set of eyes I've yet to run into."

Tinker walked past the hand and enfolded Colt in a bear hug. "You ain't gonna get away with that, Colt Lomax. Not after you practically lived in my garage."

Tinker Jones had gotten shorter, or maybe Colt had gotten taller. But it didn't matter if he'd shrunk a good three feet, it was comforting to be enveloped against a body that smelled like Ben-Gay and Josie's fried onions.

"How you doin', boy?" Jones whacked him twice on the back before he eased away. His kind eyes pierced right through Colt. And with raw emotion clogging Colt's throat, it was difficult to get the words out.

"Good, sir."

What was the matter with him, anyway? Yeah, Mr. Jones had been like a father to him, but that didn't mean he had to get all weepy-eyed. He was Colt Lomax, the kid who never cried, even when he had something to cry about. But damned if he could get a handle on the feelings that welled up inside him.

"Come on. Let's get out of this wind." Mr. Jones ushered Colt in front of him. "Hell, no wonder I don't want to live here. The summers are too hot and the winters could blow you plum away."

"Well, you better not head out on the road until after the holidays or your grandkids and Missy will have my hide," Tyler said, as he started to follow them back into the garage. But his father stopped him by tossing him the keys to the RV.

"Ty, I was hopin' you'd give her a once-over. After thousands of miles of road, she might need a little pamperin'."

Tyler's gaze locked with his father's for only a second before he nodded. "Sure thing, Daddy. I just made some coffee; you and Colt help yourselves."

Once they were inside the office, Mr. Jones took the lopsided chair next to the cluttered desk and pointed to the chair opposite. "So what's goin' on with you?"

"Same old." Colt remained standing, leaning a shoulder on the doorjamb in as casual a manner as he could muster. "Business is good, but I spend a lot of time on the road."

"I'm not talkin' about business, boy. I figured you were doin' all right when you had that big old motor home delivered to my doorstep."

"I didn't—"

Mr. Jones held up a hand, a hand that had guided Colt toward the straight and narrow, even when he fought against it. "Don't give me that, boy. Who else would be pigheaded enough to think he owed me something? Besides, I never entered no sweepstakes for an RV."

Colt pushed away from the doorway and walked over to the front windows. "I do owe you. You were the one who gave me a job at twelve when no one else would. The one who taught me all about engines. And the one who bought my books when I started those satellite college courses. Some stupid motor home doesn't repay that."

"Any debt you owed me was paid in full, son, the moment you succeeded. That's all a man ever expects from his kids." The chair squeaked. "So let's dispense with the bullshit and get onto the reason you look like someone shot your best huntin' dog."

Colt laughed. "I never owned a hunting dog."

"No, I guess you didn't. You had enough on your plate without addin' an animal. This isn't about Shirlene, is it?"

"No," Colt said, even though his sister played a part. After years of trying to give her everything she needed— or wanted—he had finally stumbled upon something he couldn't bring himself to give away. Not even to her.

"Then I guess that leaves Hope."

Colt whirled around and stared at the old guy. "What?"

"Not what." His bushy white eyebrows lifted. "But who. And you heard me the first time."

"I heard you, but that doesn't mean I understand what she has to do with my hangdog look—not that I have a hangdog look—but if I did, she wouldn't have anything to do with it."

Tinker shook his head. "You still playin' that game, boy? Because at thirty-two, it has to be gettin' old."

"I don't know what you're talking about, old man."

A grin split Tinker's face, showing off the wad of tobacco. "Sure you do. It's the game where you act like you don't like Hope."

Oh, that game.

"After growing up with three brothers, I know it ain't easy for men to put their feelings in words," Tinker continued. "Which is why we do stupid things to get our girl's attention—like poppin' wheelies and doin' handstands."

Since Colt had never done a wheelie or a handstand for any girl, he quirked an eyebrow.

"I busted out three teeth showing off for Martha on my bike. Most embarrassin' day of my life." He shook his head at the memory. "'Course, you chose pranks over showin' off. The pig snout on the homecoming semi. The live ammo in that there stage gun."

"I did not put—"

Tinker held up his hand. "Not here, nor there. What matters is what you do now. And if you tell me you've hoisted her bra back up on the town hall flagpole, I'm going to warm your butt just like the last time."

Colt hadn't hoisted her bra. It was worse. He'd gotten her pregnant. Now instead of dealing with a few moments of humiliation, she got to spend a lifetime wallowing in it. And he was to blame.

Again.

Moving over to the chair, Colt flopped down and ran a hand over his face. "I got her pregnant."

Until that moment, he had placed equal blame on Hope, but now he realized that most lay at his doorstep. He was the one who knew how old the condom was, and still he had gone ahead. And maybe, subconsciously, he had wanted her to get pregnant. All in an effort to get Hope to notice him.

God, he wished he had just done a handstand.

The chair squeaked as Mr. Jones leaned back. "I figured as much when Tyler told me about the baby. Of course, he's convinced, along with the town, that it's somebody out in California who did the deed. The blame fools don't even seem to know that's the same place you live."

Colt looked over at him. "So you want me to stand up and touch my toes or lean over the counter?"

"I reckon you're a little too old for a whuppin'. Besides, that kind of mistake takes two people. Two people to mate, two people to create."

"One person to hate," he mumbled under his breath, but not low enough.

"And who would that person be?"

"We both know who it is. And I can't blame her. Not after everything I've done to her."

Mr. Jones sat back and laughed.

It wasn't quite the reaction Colt expected. "I'm glad you find it so amusing," he said, without humor.

"It's amusing that men can be so damned stupid where women are concerned, especially when women wear their hearts right out on their sleeves for anyone who takes a notion to see. Men are just too busy worryin' about their own egos to take the time to look."

"Meaning?"

"Meaning, that girl has had a thing for you since you were both knee-high to a grasshopper."

"I think you've got me confused with Slate."

Those bushy brows lowered. "Don't go callin' me senile, boy, or I'll change my mind about that whuppin'. I know who Slate is, and I know who you are. And that girl didn't like Slate for anything more than a boy to soothe her ego after you'd bruised it to hell and back."

Colt stared at Tinker with disbelief. "But he was the town hero."

"So?"

"So she was the sweetheart. It made sense."

"'Course it did, which is why an entire town played into it. But whose fault was that, Colt? You didn't exactly give them another choice."

It was the same thing Tyler had told him, and Colt had started to wonder if maybe they didn't have a point. The thought rumbled around in his head while Mr. Jones swiveled in the chair and started rummaging around in one of the desk drawers.

"Since Tyler has always been a bit of a packrat, I figure it's got to be around here somewhere—here it is." He lifted a small rectangular photograph from the drawer. He studied it for a few seconds before swiveling back around and holding it out for Colt. "I took it with the new camera Martha had gotten me for my birthday that year. I guess you must've been around fifteen, which would've made Hope..."

"Thirteen," Colt supplied, as he took the picture.

It had been taken from the doorway of the office. It was a close-up of two young kids: a dark-headed boy, who sat cross-legged in front of a motorcycle, his gaze intent on what he was doing, and a brown-headed girl, who sat just beyond. The angle caught his profile, the large nose and unruly hair that fell over his forehead. But it was the girl's face that was the focal point of the photo. A pretty little girl with a sprinkling of freckles across her button nose and a blush of womanhood across her high cheeks. She stared intently, not at the engine of the 250 Yamaha, but at the boy who worked on it.

In those eyes, Colt saw something that shook him to the core of his being.

"Tell me now that she didn't like you," Mr. Jones said. "And every time I looked out, that's exactly what I saw."

Colt stared at the picture, afraid to take his eyes off it. Afraid it might change if he did.

"What do you want, Colt?" Mr. Jones asked. "It's an easy question, boy."

It was an easy question. At least, it had been an easy question a month ago. Then he could've answered with one word: freedom. Freedom to go where he wanted to go and do what he wanted to do. But looking down at the picture, he realized that freedom didn't come close to holding the same allure as a pair of adoring eyes the color of a West Texas sky.

"It doesn't matter what I want." Colt started to hand back the photo, but found he couldn't quite bring himself to do it. "This was taken a long time ago. She doesn't feel the same way anymore."

Mr. Jones eyes narrowed. "But what if you're wrong, son?"

Chapter Twenty-one

"MARRY ME, HOG!"

Hope turned to the carload of teenagers who slowly drove past her as she walked down Main Street. With a roll of her eyes, she addressed the kid who hung out the back window with his hand over his heart.

"Call me when you're old enough to shave."

The kid rubbed his baby soft chin. "That could be years."

"I'll wait," she hollered back.

The boy grinned and blew her a kiss as the car picked up speed.

"What's the count?" Hope's mama, Jenna, stepped out the door of the Feed and Seed and took the can of purple paint Hope had been delivering for the storefront.

"Jonas Murphy was twenty-one, so I guess that makes Anthony twenty-two." Jenna held out a Styrofoam cup to Hope. "It's decaf."

Hope accepted it and took a heavenly sip before answering. "Either way, it's absolutely ridiculous."

"Now, I agree that the flowers and gifts have gotten

a little out of hand—last night your daddy couldn't even find the remote with all the boxes of candy and vases of flowers—but not every girl can claim twenty-two marriage proposals. That has to be some kind of a record."

"A record I have no desire to have." Hope sat down on the bench under the window, and her mother set down the can of paint and joined her.

"It just shows how much the people of this town love you, Hope Marie. They just don't want you raising that baby all by yourself."

At the mention of the baby, Hope's chest tightened and tears threatened. She tried to hide the reaction by taking another sip of coffee, but when she glanced back up, her mama was studying her with a concerned look.

"It's okay to be scared, honey," her mama said. "Having a baby is a scary thing, especially when you haven't planned it."

The week before, Hope would've agreed with her mother. She had been scared about being pregnant and raising a child by herself. But after her decision to give the baby away, she wasn't scared as much as...in pain. She felt as if a huge anvil had been placed on her chest. And day by day, it grew heavier and heavier, until she wondered if her ribs would hold beneath the pressure.

It made no sense whatsoever. She had thought it all out and made dozens of lists, and all the pieces fit perfectly together. But if that was the case, then why did it feel so wrong?

"Was it hard?" she asked around the lump in her throat.

Thinking Hope was asking about motherhood, her mama jumped right in.

"Yes, it was hard. At fifteen, I didn't have a clue what

to do with a colicky baby or a husband who would rather be out with his friends. And I couldn't blame him, not when he had the responsibility of putting a roof over our heads and food in our stomachs."

"So why did you keep me?"

Her mama stared off across the street. "When two babies came out instead of one, I guess I took it as a sign— a sign that God wanted me to have one for my own."

Hope set the Styrofoam cup down on the sidewalk. "Were you ever sorry?"

"Sorry for giving Faith away? Or sorry for keeping you?"

"Both, I guess."

Seconds ticked by before her mama finally spoke. "I wish I could tell you that I regretted one but not the other. But the truth is, there were times I wished I had Faith with me and times I wished I didn't have you—like when all my friends were going out and I was stuck at home because your daddy was working swing shift and I couldn't afford a babysitter. Or when we didn't have money to get me a new pair of jeans or a pretty new shirt because we had to buy diapers. Or when I couldn't buy you a new Easter dress for church."

She shook her head. "Of course, those thoughts blew in and out of my young brain like the unpredictable West Texas rain—they were gone as quickly as they came. All it would take is you snugglin' close to me, your breath all sweet and warm against my throat, and I figured I'd made the right choice after all. Then I'd start feeling bad about Faith."

This time Hope couldn't fight back the wall of depression that seemed to engulf her. Tears welled up in her eyes, and her voice shook. "But how did you live with all those conflicting emotions?"

Noting her tears, her mama reached out and pulled her close. "Awww, honey, you just take things day by day. That's how all folks do it. And it all worked out. You both turned out to be intelligent young women any mother would be proud of."

Hope pressed her face against her mother's neck. "I don't see how you can be proud of me."

Pulling back, her mama stared down at her in disbelief. "How could I not be proud of you, Hope Marie? You have always been a perfect child—slightly stubborn and controlling, but a hard worker, a loving daughter, and a good human being. What more could I ask for?"

"How about my having enough smarts to stay away from the wrong man," she sniffed.

It was the first time Hope had even come close to acknowledging her condition, and her mama's eyes filled with relief.

Reaching out, she smoothed the hair off Hope's forehead. "I'll reserve my opinion about the father of my grandchild until I get to meet him. All things have a way of working out in the wash."

Hope got to her feet. "That's doubtful, Mama, given that my machine is broken."

Her mother chuckled as she stood. "Well, I guess I better get back inside and make sure Marty's not playing those silly games on his phone instead of taking inventory. If his daddy catches him at it again, that boy is going to get his ears boxed but good."

The bell on the door jangled as her mother opened it. "I'd tell you to go home and take a nap—you look tired, honey—but you never have listened worth a hoot." The door jangled closed behind her.

Once she was gone, Hope wondered if her mama wasn't right. She was tired, so tired that she wanted to curl up on the bench and sleep—sleep until the nightmare of the next eight months was over.

"Uhhh...hey there, Hope."

The deep, slowly spoken words pulled her attention over to a large farmer in a faded pair of overalls. Hope had always had a soft spot for Ethan Miller, so she flashed a smile and quickly got to her feet.

"Hi, Ethan. What brings you to town?"

His face was sunburned, but it got even redder as he stared down at the scuffed toes of his boots. "Uhhh... well, I...brought you somethin'." He tugged on the leash that he had wrapped around one platter-sized hand, and a baby pig trotted out from behind his legs.

"This here is Sherman. Uhhh...he's house-broke and don't eat much. Though he does like an occasional roll in the mud."

Other men had offered Hope live gifts, but she had been able to reject them with a few teasing jokes. But Ethan wasn't a person who understood teasing, not when the kids in school had been so cruel about his size and awkwardness. And Hope hadn't become his champion all those years ago to hurt his feelings now. Even if a baby pig was the last thing she needed.

"Thank you, Ethan." She accepted the leash and knelt down to let the pig bump her with his snout. "He's adorable."

A grin appeared for a brief second before he continued. "Uhhh...so I was thinkin'." He paused and swallowed hard. "That's if you don't have your sights set on someone else..."

When he took another pause, Hope searched for anything to keep him from continuing. Accepting a pig was one thing, but a marriage proposal was something else entirely. Fortunately, before he could do more than utter another "uhhh," Colt walked up.

She hadn't talked to him since the day of the doctor's visit. And suddenly she felt as shy and embarrassed as Ethan. Or maybe just guilty about being the type of woman who was willing to give away their child.

"Nice pig," Colt said, but he merely glanced at the pig before his intense gaze settled back on Hope.

Disconcerted, she scrambled to her feet. "Sherman. His name is Sherman."

"Hey, Sherman." Colt leaned down and scratched the pig's back until it snuffled with delight and rooted against his legs. With a laugh, he straightened and reached a hand out to Ethan. "How you doing, Ethan? Your mama still make the best chocolate chip cookies this side of the Pecos?"

"She shore does, Colt," Ethan replied without hesitation. "But I would've thought that you got your fill of them all those nights we worked late at Josephine's."

"Not even close. If it wasn't for your mama packing food for me, I wouldn't have had the energy to stay awake." Colt glanced between the two of them. "I didn't interrupt anything important, did I?"

"No!" Hope jumped in before Ethan could start stammering again. "Ethan just brought me a present."

One dark eyebrow hiked up as Colt looked down at the pig.

"Well, I guess I better get on back." Ethan nodded at Colt before looking over at Hope. "Uhhh...bye, Hope."

"Good-bye, Ethan. And thank you so much for Sherman."

"You're shore welcome." He ambled back down the street.

When he was gone, Hope flopped down on the bench and stared at the pig, which had tipped over her cup of coffee and was now licking the liquid off the concrete.

"Is coffee good for pigs?" Colt asked as he took a seat next to her.

"It's decaf." She hooked the end of the leash over the arm of the bench.

After watching the pig polish off the last drop, Colt glanced over at her. "Another marriage bribe?"

"Yes, but thankfully Ethan didn't get to the actual proposal." She turned to him. "You washed dishes at Josephine's with Ethan? How come I never saw you?"

"Probably because I showed up after you were gone." He grabbed the leash and pulled Sherman away from the blob of gum that the pig was trying to get up off the sidewalk. "And I didn't do dishes, I cleaned the toilets."

Confused, she stared at him. "But I thought your mama cleaned—you helped her?"

He looked away, and she watched his Adam's apple rise and fall. "I didn't help my mother, Hope. I did it for her because she was too drunk to do it herself."

Drunk? Hope didn't have a lot of memories of Abby Lomax, but what she did have weren't of a falling-down drunk. Mrs. Lomax had been quiet and soft-spoken with hair as jet black as her son's and eyes as green as Shirlene's. She moved slower than Hope's mama and wasn't much of a housekeeper or a cook. But once she had helped Hope and Shirlene make Kleenex dresses for their Barbies and, another time, paper chains for their Christmas trees. Although, now that Hope thought about it, there was that time Mrs. Lomax had taken a nap by the front steps. And the time she came outside while they were playing in the Chevy in nothing but her bra and panties. And it did explain why she looked so tired and sick in the mornings. And why Hope had never been invited to spend the night.

Hope tried to think of something to say, but there was nothing to say. Especially when staring into those beautiful gray eyes. She knew a lot of Colts—the Cocky Colt, the Teasing Colt, the Spiteful Colt—but the honest, sincere man sitting next to her, she didn't recognize.

But before Hope could make sense of his behavior, her mama came out of the Feed and Seed looking worried and flustered. "Your daddy just called. They've laid off a bunch of people at Dalton."

"What?" Hope jumped up, and Colt had to grab her to keep her from tripping over the pig's leash. "Daddy? Did they lay off Daddy?"

"No," her mama shook her head. "But they laid off fifty others."

"Fifty." Hope felt her knees give out. Luckily, Colt still held on to her.

"Jenna, why don't you take Hope on home?" He pulled the cell phone from his back pocket. "I'll call Lyle and find out what's going on."

"I'm not going home." Hope pulled away from him. She had let Lyle get away with his lies once; she wasn't about to do it again. "I'm staying right here until I get some answers."

"And it looks like you're not the only one." Her mama

nodded at the cars that had started to fill the parking lot of Josephine's Diner.

Colt sighed and ran a hand through his hair. "Fine." He handed the leash to her mama, who looked surprised to find a pig on the end of it. "But I don't want you adding to the panic, Hope. If the town is going to pull out of this, we need to keep cool heads."

"This coming from the biggest hothead in Bramble."

He flashed her a warning look as they started across the street. "I mean it, Hope. People will be hysterical enough as it is."

The diner was packed by the time they walked through the door. And Colt was right; there was mass hysteria. Everyone seemed to be talking at once. Harley's mustache was bouncing. Sheriff Winslow's mouth was flapping. And Rachel Dean looked like she hadn't come up for air in a good hour.

"Get their attention, Hope, and keep it," Colt instructed, as he punched a button on his phone.

Hope looked around at the panicked townspeople. "And just how do you suggest I do that?"

"I'm sure the Sweetheart of Bramble will think of something. All I need is five minutes to talk with Lyle and figure out what's going on, and I don't want a lynch mob forming before I do." Without waiting for a reply, he headed back out the door.

Hope stared at the mayhem for only a second before she let out the hog call that had won her five trophies and an honorable mention. When it stopped resounding from the walls, every person in Josephine's had turned to her. But now that she had their attention, she didn't have a clue what to say.

"Hi, y'all." She smiled brightly.

"Sorry, Hope," Harley held up a hand, "we don't have time for pleasantries. Dalton Oil just laid off fifty workers."

"Oh." She chewed on her lip as she struggled to come up with something to say to that. When they started to turn away, she blurted out the first thing she could think of. "Well, I guess that's much more important than the identity of my baby's father."

Rachel hurried out from behind the counter. "Now, honey, I'm sure Harley didn't realize what you wanted to talk about. Of course, we have time to listen to our sweetheart." She patted the red vinyl of an empty bar stool. "Now you just come right on over here and tell us all about that lowlife who did you wrong."

Hope sent everyone a weak smile as she made her way through the silent crowd. "Are you sure? Because what I have to say can wait."

"Of course, she's sure," Twyla pushed her way to the front of the group once Hope was seated. "So go ahead, Hog, give us all of the dirty details."

With every eye pinned on her, Hope cleared her throat. But nothing came out.

"Oh, you poor thing," Rachel said. "Let me get you some water."

Thankful for being handed another stall tactic, Hope waited patiently for Rachel to fill a glass, and then took her time drinking every last drop.

Once the glass was empty, Darla jumped back in. "So who is it? Someone you met in California?"

"Yes." She glanced out the side window where Colt was talking on his phone. "In fact, I ran into him at the place I worked."

"I knew it!" Twyla almost jumped out of her skintight Wranglers. "The daddy is a movie star."

"A movie star?" Rachel stared at Hope with confusion. "But why didn't you just say that in the first place, honey. It sure would've saved us a lot time."

Suddenly stuck between a lie and a hard spot, Hope could only stammer. "Well, I...I..."

Darla jumped back in. "No doubt, she was worried that her name would be splashed all over those rag magazines."

Rachel's confusion cleared. "You're right. I remember when Daryl's two-headed hog got on the front cover. There were so many phone calls and people stoppin' by unannounced that the poor man was forced to sell it to a travelin' carnival, just so he could get a wink of sleep. And I know for a fact he's regretted it ever since. Daryl loved Mizty and Bitzy like they was his own kids." She patted Hope's knee. "But there's no need to worry about that, honey. If anyone can keep a secret, we can."

"She right, Hope," Cindy Lynn leaned in closer. "Is it Matthew McConaughey?"

Fortunately, before Hope had to answer, Colt stepped back in the door, his hair tousled and windblown. He was dressed like he always was—in a black T-shirt and faded jeans. But there was something different about him. Something that Hope couldn't quite put her finger on.

"I just got off the phone with Lyle Dalton." Colt's deep, smooth voice pulled everyone's attention away from Hope. With every eye on him, he continued. "He's right in the middle of some important negotiations and can't fly back, but I know he's doing everything he can to fix this."

"He's a little late, ain't he?" Joe Mitchell said, and a grumble of agreement went through the crowd.

Colt turned to look at the older man. "I can understand you being upset, Joe, seeing as how all three of your sons work at Dalton. But you've known Lyle all his life—gone fishing with him and enjoyed his hospitality on more than one occasion—so if anyone knows how hard the man works or how much he loves the folks of Bramble, it should be you."

Joe looked away, then nodded. "I suppose I do," he confessed.

"Seeing as how you just got out of prison, how do you know so much about it, Colt?" Rye Pickett asked.

Colt didn't even blink. "Because I spent last week in Houston at the corporate offices, going over the books with Lyle."

Hope sat up straighter. Colt had been in Houston helping Lyle? For a moment, she was angry that he had kept such a secret. But looking around the room at the panicked faces, she quickly understood why.

"I'm not going to lie to you," Colt said. "Dalton Oil is in financial trouble. Which is why Lyle's negotiating with another company to buy Dalton. Meanwhile, he's assured me that everyone laid off will receive a severance package to tide them over until they get another job."

"A job where?" Rye Pickett asked. "If Dalton don't get bought, there ain't gonna be no jobs."

It was a good point, and the crowd's grumbling grew louder. But before panic could set back in, Hope slipped off her stool and walked over to stand next to Colt.

"Dalton Oil has been around for longer than most of the people in this room," she stated. "So let's not go and put the cart before the horse. If Colt says Lyle is doing everything he can to set thing straight, I believe him.

Besides, this isn't just Lyle's problem. If Dalton Oil is going to survive, then we all need to work together."

"But how can we help, Hope?" Kenny Gene pushed his way to the front. "Most of us don't know nothin' about business."

Colt's gaze swept over the crowd. "We can start by not panicking. And we can rally around the families who did have a member laid off." His voice rose, strong and sure. "And we can do what all good Texans do when their backs are against the wall."

"What's that?" Harley asked.

Colt winked at Hope before giving the group one of his rare smiles. "We fight."

Chapter Twenty-two

LOST JOBS, OR a town's complete financial ruin, weren't enough to keep true Texans from a football game. Especially a state championship. So on Friday afternoon, the entire town of Bramble loaded up their cowbells, face paint, and pompoms into chartered buses and caravanned down to San Antonio, where they checked into a Best Western to prepare themselves for the game the following day.

The Houston team pitted against Bramble High turned out to be the size of pro football players with helmets covered in award emblems for basically being a bunch of badasses. In the first half, the Central High Cougars scored three times while the Bulldogs scored only once. Still, the Dawgs held them to field goals and went into the locker room at halftime down by only two.

When her daddy and mama got up to go to the concession stand, Hope's gaze drifted down two rows to where Colt sat with Shirlene. The stiff breeze played in the silk of his dark hair, fluttering it around his strong profile and the flipped-up collar of his worn leather jacket. He turned to laugh at something Shirlene said, and his gaze caught hers, impaling her in smoky gray.

It was funny how one piece of information could change an entire image. The knowledge that Colt's mama had been an alcoholic was all it took to make the pieces fit together. Colt's anger and delinquent behavior. His desire to leave Bramble and all its bad memories. His passion for the open road and a carefree lifestyle. Everything made sense now.

"It's so admirable the way Colt has stepped up to help out the town."

The softly spoken words pulled Hope's gaze away from Colt to Faith's wide blue eyes.

"Slate said that Colt is even trying to get other businesses to relocate to Bramble—just in case there are more layoffs," her sister continued.

Hope had heard the same thing, and was more than surprised that Colt had so many business connections. It was a shame that Hope wouldn't be around to see if any panned out. She started to question her sister about the businesses when Faith pulled her crazy mind-reading thing.

"So when are you leaving?" she asked.

After glancing around, Hope sent her sister a warning look. "Would you keep it down?"

"Why? Are you planning on skipping town without telling anyone?"

That was exactly what Hope planned on doing. Things would work out so much simpler if she left the following week, and Shirlene just ended up adopting a baby in eight months. Hope would tell people eventually, but for now, the town had enough to worry about.

"It's for the best," Hope said.

"For who? You're miserable about giving up your baby to Shirlene."

It was hell having your brain picked clean, and even worse having all your emotions put into words.

"I assume you have a better plan," Hope said, keeping her eyes on the field and her miserable emotions to herself.

"You can marry Colt."

"What?" Hope's gaze snapped over to her sister, who looked as if she hadn't just dropped a bomb of atomic proportions. "Have you lost your mind?"

"You tell me." Faith leaned closer and stared back at her sister.

The image that flashed into Hope's brain was like a Disney storybook ending, complete with a dark-headed prince, a set of laughing twins, and a princess who looked ready to pop with happiness.

Stunned, Hope looked away. "You *have* lost your mind."

"Why?" Faith lowered her voice. "If Colt's the father of your child, it only makes sense."

"Sense to someone who lives in a fairytale. Believe me when I tell you that the last thing that Colt wants is to be saddled with a kid and a wife."

"But maybe he just needs the right motivation to change," Faith said, her big eyes pleading. "Maybe you two just need to spend more time together, talking things through."

An image of the note Austin had given her on Halloween night popped into Hope's mind, and her gaze narrowed on her sister. "You." She pointed a finger, and

Faith's eyes got as big as saucers. "You're the one who sent me that note—not Colt."

"Okay, so I admit it." Faith held a hand to her chest. "But only because I truly believe that you and Colt belong together—"

Hope slapped a hand over Faith's mouth as their parents maneuvered their way along the row. She might've squeezed a little too tightly, because her sister's eyes watered. But Faith deserved a lot more than that. And although Hope was forced to keep her words to herself, she couldn't help sending her sister a telepathic warning: *Stay out of my business, you little conniving matchmaker.*

The answer came back loud and clear. *No.*

In the third quarter, the Cougars ran one in for six, but the extra point was no good, and the Bulldogs answered with a sixty-yard drive down the field that resulted in a field goal. With the score fifteen to ten with less than twenty seconds on the clock, things didn't look good for Hope's alma mater. But she should've known that Slate and his team had worked too hard to give up easily. Third down and thirty yards from the end zone, Austin threw a perfect spiral straight into the hands of his wide receiver, who raced over the goal line to win the game with only seconds to spare.

The people from Bramble were a small portion of the forty thousand in attendance at the Alamodome. But size didn't diminish the volume level as pandemonium broke out on the field and in the stands. The townsfolk jumped and screamed and hugged and smeared face paint from one end of the bleachers to the other. Rachel Dean squalled like a baby. Harley howled up at the bright afternoon sun. Shirlene's broads fairly jumped out of her tight sweater as her feet left the ground. And Faith squealed like her prince had just slain the biggest dragon.

Hope was kissed and hugged and passed around like a jug of moonshine at the end of Prohibition. But even as she reveled in the victory, her mind kept returning to a happily-ever-after that included two loving parents and a couple of smiling babies.

"Cowboy, you still suck at dancing," Hope stated, as Slate clumsily maneuvered her around the dance floor of the San Antonio honky-tonk where the town of Bramble had chosen to celebrate.

"And, darlin', you still try to lead." Slate twirled her under his arm and ended up bumping her head with his forearm and catching a piece of her hair on the pearl snap of his cuff.

Untangling her hair, she steered him back into the two-step. "You're right, which is why we will never amount to much on the dance floor."

He sent her a cocky grin. "But you still love me."

"Yes." Hope laughed. "I still love you." Looking up into those familiar hazel eyes, she said what she'd wanted to say all through the celebration dinner at the Golden Corral. "I'm proud of you, Slate Calhoun."

Those eyes widened before he reached up and yanked on her hair.

"Ouch!" Hope glared at him as he flashed a smile.

"Just checking to make sure you're Hope Scroggs."

Rubbing her scalp, she grumbled. "That's the last time I give you a compliment, cowboy."

"Good." Slate made the turn and stepped on her toe. "You don't want me to get a big head, do you?"

"As if your head isn't already the size of Texas."

His smile almost blinded her. "Well, whose wouldn't be? I mean, I've got the prettiest wife this side of the Mississippi—a baby on the way—a state football title—and the Sweetheart of Bramble, Texas, proud of me. What more could a man ask for?"

Releasing a loud country yee-haw, Slate picked her up and swung her around, with no consideration for the people who danced around them.

"Put me down, you crazy fool," Hope said as she clung to his neck and laughed.

But he didn't pay her a lick of attention. No telling how long he would've kept going if Colt and Faith hadn't danced past. Slate released Hope so fast that she almost landed on her butt as he reached out and tapped Colt on the shoulder. When they stopped, Slate took off his black Stetson and pressed it over his heart.

"What do you say, Mrs. Calhoun? Can I have this dance for the rest of my life?"

It was one of the corniest lines Hope had ever heard, but Faith didn't seem to realize that. Grinning as if she'd just been awakened from a thirty-year nap, she slipped into his arms. "I think that could be arranged, darlin'."

Hope watched as they waltzed off to a country swing. She waited for the pain of loss to return, but instead all she felt was a rising wave of relief. Relief that Slate had been smart enough to figure out their relationship long before she had.

"So do you want to dance or throw a fit because Faith took your best beau?"

Hope shot Colt a skeptical look. "Since when do you dance?" When he only shrugged, she let him off the hook.

"How about we wait for another waltz? It looked like you could count to three, but a western swing is a little more complicated."

"I think I can handle it." Colt grabbed her hand before she could get off the floor.

"You sure, because I can't lead you through—"

"Shut up, Hope."

And before Hope could continue to argue, she was being whirled around like a top—their arms twisting and untwisting in so many configurations she had trouble keeping up. His style was a cross between the Dallas Push and the Houston Whip with an added spark that was solely Colt—cocky dipped in a whole lot of wild. But not one time did he bump her head or catch her hair or lose the beat of the music as his boots shuffled around her. His grip was firm but not too firm, and he never jerked or pulled, only directed with a sureness that left her light-headed and breathless. When the song ended, he reeled her in to his hard-muscled chest and dipped her low.

Panting like the winner of the Kentucky Derby that had been ridden by a competent jockey who knew exactly how hard to push, she stared up at him in stunned disbelief.

"Where did you learn to dance like that?"

The look he sent her was one of complete indifference. "My mama liked to dance."

As he released her from the cuddle wrap, Hope's eyes welled up. The entire pregnancy weeping thing was really starting to annoy her. Every time she turned around, tears threatened. And she was getting darned sick of it. Unfortunately, there was nothing to do about it, especially when she couldn't shake the image of Colt dancing with his mama in the tiny front room of their trailer.

Luckily, a two-step started, and Colt swept her into the quick-quick-slow before she could make a fool of herself. His two-step was even better than his swing. His steps perfectly matched hers, with the dexterity to pull her into promenades and spins without losing track of the beat. The few times she tried to take the lead, Colt twirled her around until she was so dizzy all she could do was cling. And after a while, she relinquished all desire to lead and let Colt take her where he would. He took her to a heaven of dizzying polkas, and smooth two-steps, and slow, tranquil waltzes.

It was midnight when the folks of Bramble started to load back up on the buses to return to the hotel. Hope headed to the bathroom, surprised at how disappointed she felt that the night was over so quickly. She had just locked the bathroom stall, when someone jostled the handle.

"It's taken," she said. And after a little more jostling, whoever it was slipped back out the door.

Unconcerned by an obvious drunk's behavior, Hope finished using the bathroom. But when she tried to get out, the door wouldn't budge. Since it wasn't the first time she'd had trouble getting out of a bathroom stall, she spent a little time jiggling and jimmying until she realized that whatever was holding the door had nothing to do with the latch.

Hope thought about crawling underneath. But after working in a strip club, she knew the disgusting stuff that could end up on a bathroom floor. So instead, she yelled at the top of her lungs until a waitress came running in and unbuckled the slender belt that had been looped between the handle of Hope's stall and the hinge of the one next to it.

By the time Hope washed her hands and came out of the bathroom, she wasn't the least bit surprised to find Colt waiting.

"Faith said you weren't feeling good." He pushed away from the wall that he was leaning against. "You okay?"

"I guess the buses are long gone," she said through gritted teeth.

Colt's eyes widened fractionally before he nodded. "But I don't mind giving you a ride back to the hotel."

For a moment, Hope had to fight back the strong desire to chase the bus down so she could strangle her sister with her own belt. But once she got her anger under control, she tossed the belt into the nearest trash can and grabbed Colt's hand.

"Let's dance."

That's exactly what they did. They danced until they were sweaty and thirsty, then downed some water and danced some more. They couldn't have a conversation without fighting, but on the dance floor they had found a perfect harmony.

"I never would've believed it," she leaned her head on his chest and listened to the steady thump of his heart as the band struck up the last song of the evening.

He adjusted his hands around her waist and pulled her closer. Close enough that the fly of his zipper brushed her belt buckle. "Believed what?"

"That Colt Lomax is the best darned dancer I've ever danced with."

"Better than Bucky Higgins?" He rested his cheek on the top of her head.

"No comparison." She smoothed a hand over his shoulder and down to his biceps. His bare skin was hot and moist, his muscles hard and exciting. "Why didn't you ever ask me to dance?"

His fingers slipped beneath the hem of her T-shirt and stroked along the waistband of her jeans, sending a tiny shiver up her spine. "Maybe because you were always dancing with Slate."

"Liar."

She could feel his grin against her head. "Okay. So maybe I was afraid you'd say no."

"I wouldn't have."

"Now who's lying."

She laughed. "Okay, so I probably would've said no, but only because I would've thought it was some kind of trick."

"Smart girl."

Pulling her head back, Hope hooked her arms around his neck and fingered the silky hair that curled up on his shoulders. "Bad boy."

A smile tipped one side of Colt's mouth as those beautiful gray eyes stared back at her. "Sometimes bad can be really good."

His hands slipped under her shirt, and his fingers trailed lightly up and down her spine. She probably should've pulled away; their caresses had moved beyond dancing to something much more dangerous. But he was right—sometimes bad could feel really good. As they continued to sway to the music, she allowed his hands to wander along her flushed skin as she stared back at the man who was so different from the belligerent boy who wore a scowl a mile wide.

Although the eyes were the same. The same hungry gray. And now as then, she couldn't bring herself to look away. In the stormy depths, she'd found a reflection of her own soul. A soul that wanted so desperately to be loved, not for the image a town had concocted, but for itself.

The music continued, and their boots slowly swept back and forth against the wood floor. When they couldn't take the truth in each other's eyes a moment more, Colt dipped his head and kissed her. The first heated brush of his lips had her trembling, and his fingers tightened as he pulled her closer. Standing on tiptoes, she aligned her body to his. And with every step they took, a wonderful heat built beneath the friction of blue jeans. A moan vibrated between their lips—a hum of need and desire. Colt broke away first, his eyes two glittering coals beneath the fringe of dark lashes. He stared down at her mouth for only a second before he unhooked her hands from around his neck and pulled her from the dance floor.

Outside the bar, the night was cool and windy. He tucked his leather jacket around her and sheltered her body as they hurried across the parking lot to Shirlene's SUV.

Inside, she tried to think past her thumping heart and aching center. But once he'd slipped the seat belt around her, he kissed her again until there was nothing left in her head but desire.

No telling how long they would've remained there if a cold wind hadn't blown into the SUV, causing her to shiver. Colt pulled back and gave her one more heated look before he slammed the door and moved around to the driver's side. He slipped behind the wheel with the ease of a man who could master any mechanical vehicle and quickly backed the truck out.

Once he was out of the parking lot, he reached over and took her hand, bringing it to the console between them. She thought the space would cool her down, but the man was as gifted a hand holder as he was a kisser. With their fingers linked, his thumb caressed her palm with a back-and-forth stroke that left her nothing more than a quivering puddle on the heated leather.

They didn't talk on the ride to the hotel, nor did Colt waste any time getting there. He weaved in and out of traffic and on and off freeways like a NASCAR veteran. When they arrived, he whipped the truck into the first empty space and was around to her side before she could even unhook her seat belt. Not that she could've unhooked it with her hands shaking so badly, but he didn't even give her a chance to try before he released the clasp and had her in his arms.

Pressing her back against the truck, he gave her another deep kiss and pulled her up against the ridged fly of his jeans. Then, before she could do more than moan, he released her and was guiding her across the parking lot toward the hotel.

The lobby was empty except for the same desk clerk who had worked the previous night. He greeted them, then discreetly turned away. Before the elevator doors had closed completely, Colt had her back against the wall. This time his hand slipped beneath her shirt and wasted no time. With a twist, her bra was open and her breast covered in one hot palm.

"Colt," she breathed against his shoulder. "Someone could see us."

"I don't give a shit." His calloused thumb brushed over her nipple. And just that quickly, Hope didn't give a shit either.

Of course, she did when the doors opened, and Rachel

Dean was standing on the other side in a large floral muu-muu with her thin gray hair rolled up in sponge curlers and a full bucket of ice in her hands.

"Hey, Colt." She smiled at him as if his hand wasn't stuck under Hope's shirt. "The ice machine on my floor was clean out of ice and, with these damned hot flashes, I need a big glass of ice water handy at all times." She stepped into the elevator and punched a button. "Y'all just gettin' in?"

"Yes," Hope croaked as she tried to shove Colt away, but he didn't seem in any hurry to comply. Although his hand did slip from her breast to her hip.

"Well, I tell you one thing," Rachel continued, seemingly unaware of what was taking place right in front of her. "You can sure cut up a dance floor, Colt. Surprised the hell out of the entire town, seeing as y'all couldn't get along for more than two minutes without the fur flyin'. 'Course dancin' doesn't have to involve talkin', which is how I got roped into marryin' my second husband. Good dancer—bad talker."

The doors slid open, and Hope squealed as Colt scooped her up in his arms and walked off the elevator, moving right past an open-mouthed Rachel.

"And just what do you think you're doin', Colt Lomax?" she yelled after them.

"Taking Hope to bed," he called back.

Rachel's deep, manly laughter followed them all the way to his room.

Chapter Twenty-three

BY THE TIME Colt kicked the door to his room closed, the sweet agreeable woman he'd danced with was replaced with the spitfire he grew up with.

"Have you lost your mind, Lomax?" Hope's fist connected with his shoulder, the bony knuckles worse than any frogger he'd received in grade school. "What possessed you to tell Rachel Dean that? By morning, everyone will know you brought me to your room." She went to sock him again, but before she could, he tossed her down to the king-sized bed.

"And so what if they do? It's not the first time we've been caught in a compromising position. And you know as well as I do that the people of Bramble can't put two and two together without a calculator." He sat down on the edge of the bed to pull off his boots. "Although, I have to admit, it was strange that Rachel noticed me before she noticed the homecoming queen."

One of Hope's cowboy boots dropped to the floor by his foot.

"Not so strange, given your performance at Josephine's

the other night," she said as she toed off the other boot. "I think the town is starting to view you as their champion."

He laughed and was surprised when Hope didn't join in. He glanced back to find her sitting cross-legged on the bed, her eyes confused.

"What do you mean put two and two together?" she asked.

It would've been easy to hedge around the question. But after talking with Tinker Jones, Colt had come to a few conclusions: 1. An old photograph wasn't something to pin your hopes on. 2. It was time to cut through the bullshit and start being honest.

He propped his knee up on the bed as he turned to her. "About this thing we have for each other."

"A thing? What are you talking about? I've never had a thing for you."

"Really? And what would you call this?" His gaze dropped to her unclasped bra that stuck out of the neckline of her black shirt.

Those blue eyes stared back at him for only a second before her chin grew stubborn. "A mistake." She started to scoot off the bed, but he caught her.

"A mistake we can't seem to stop making." He took her chin in his hand, tipping it up. "And why is that?"

Her throat convulsed as she swallowed. "I...I don't know what you're talking about."

"And I think you do. I think you're just too stubborn to say it." He smoothed a strand of hair off her forehead. "Admit it, Hope. You have a thing for a lowlife motor-cycle bum, a lowlife motorcycle bum who isn't afraid of overprotective townsfolk or big linebacker daddies. Who isn't afraid to take what he wants." He leaned down and brushed his lips over hers. "Even if it's from the Sweetheart of Bramble, Texas."

She blinked before staring back at him with wide blue eyes. "Are you saying you want me, Colt Lomax?"

"I'm saying I want you, Hope Scroggs." He bit at her plump bottom lip, and then licked it better. "Have wanted you ever since I can remember. And you want me, which was why you kept showing up wherever I was, begging for something I was more than willing to give you." His tongue swept over her earlobe, and he felt the tremor that ran through her body all the way down to his soul.

"Very funny theory, Lomax," she breathed.

"No, it's not funny," he whispered. "Not funny at all."

Similar to their dancing, their lips effortlessly slipped into a slow sliding waltz that quickly progressed to a hungry salsa that had them both fighting for air. Easing her back to the mattress, he took her wrists in his hands and pulled her arms above her head. He liked the feel of having Hope stretched out before him, a compact feast spread out for his taking. And he took—took deep kisses and soft nips and long, wet forages that left him hard and begging for more.

When his mouth was no longer enough, he released her wrists and slipped a hand over one perfect breast. Through the cotton of her shirt, her nipple stood proud and hard. He gently brushed his thumb back and forth until she moaned into his mouth and arched her back up off the mattress. He pulled away from the kiss and lowered his mouth to her breast. At the first touch of his lips, her fingers scraped through his hair and encased his head, holding it firm while she rode his thigh.

Her enthusiasm incited him, and he stripped off her

shirt and went for naked flesh. Her breasts were plump and soft. And while he cradled and stroked, he sipped at each sweet peak until her fingers tightened against his scalp.

"Colt."

His name on her lips had him returning for another deep kiss before his hand slipped down to the button of her jeans. Once the zipper was down, he slid two fingers past the elastic band of her panties. The wet heat that greeted him was pretty much his undoing; the need to take things slow was obliterated by the need to be deep inside her. He might've taken her right then, if her jeans had cooperated. But the tight denim refused to slip over her hips, and he was forced to get to his feet and grab each pant leg. As he tugged, she giggled.

"You think this is funny, do you?" He cocked an eyebrow at her.

"Hilarious." Hope answered with a cocked brow of her own. "I thought the Bad Boy of Bramble would be a little more skilled at removing women's clothing."

He sent her an annoyed look as he tugged, but the jeans refused to budge, which sent Hope into another peal of laughter.

"I could use a little help here," Colt stated, although he couldn't help but smile at the picture she presented. Miles of wild hair played peek-a-boo with sweet naked breasts. At that moment, his entire world was contained in the tiny, five-foot-nothing body stretched out before him, and there wasn't a damned thing he could do about it.

Her laughter subsided, and with a sassy grin, she pushed her jeans over her hips.

It was the first time he'd seen her completely naked and, in the gold lamplight, she was as beautiful as he knew she would be. Though small, her body was perfectly proportioned, from the high breasts to the soles of her petite feet. Her legs and arms were lean and toned. Her stomach smooth and flat with an inny belly button he had wanted to lick since the rainy day in the old Chevy. But it was the small strip of hair between her legs that grabbed his attention and held it.

"You're so damned beautiful," he croaked, his voice thick with passion.

Her gaze lifted to his and, in those deep blue eyes, he saw gratitude and something he couldn't quite put his finger on. Something that made his stomach light and his heart seize.

As he stripped out of his clothes, her eyes turned hot and steamy. His stomach tightened, not only with desire, but with the strong need to be the only man to light this fire in her eyes. But she soon started a fire of her own when she scooted across the bed and took him in hand. His knees buckled, and he would've landed on the floor, if he hadn't reached out and grabbed onto the headboard.

Inching closer, she slipped her legs on either side of his, offering up a delectable view of all her hidden places—but the view was interrupted by a flash of heat that blinded him when she leaned forward and took him in her mouth.

His world tipped on its axis, and he didn't know if he was still standing or flat on his back. Her lips slipped down toward the base of his shaft before sliding back up with enough suction to cause his eyes to roll back in his head. The entire time, her hand kept up a nice steady stroke, while her other hand did a number on his balls. But seconds from orgasm, she lifted her head.

"Am I doing this right?"

He blinked and tried to figure out where he was. "Huh?"

"Am I doing this right?"

He was brought back to earth by a pair of insecure blue eyes. Since Hope had never been insecure about anything, he ignored the raw need that pulsed between his legs and tried to reassure her.

"Oh, baby. You are doing it just right." He cradled her chin and leaned down to give her a kiss. "In fact, so right that if I don't get inside you pretty soon, I'm going to be the first man to expire from lust."

Her smile flashed bright. "Really?"

"Really." Colt lowered a knee to the bed and followed her down.

Once there, he took his time sipping from her lips while his fingers stroked over her breasts and down her sweet body. When her hips pumped up to greet him, he dipped inside the wet heat and flicked her clitoris with his thumb until she begged for release.

Pulling back, he reached for his wallet on the night-stand. But just as he slipped the condom out, she stopped him.

"Don't you think it's a little late for that?"

He glanced back at her, and she shrugged.

"I mean, if you have something—"

His brain finally broke through his passion, and he shook his head. "No." He tossed the condom back down on the nightstand and rolled back to her side. "I don't have anything. I just forgot, is all." He smoothed her hair back. "I didn't hurt you, did I? I mean, this won't hurt you, right?"

She ran a finger over his chin. "Except for a few razor

burns, I think I'll be okay. Although if you don't get in me soon, I might just expire from lust."

He moved over her, cradling her head between his forearms. "Well, we can't have that. Now can we?"

"No, we can't—" She sucked in her breath as he entered her.

He knew how she felt. He had never been inside a woman skin on skin, and the pleasure was so intense that he almost lost it right there. He took a few seconds to name the parts of a motorcycle engine before he slowly started to move. As with dancing, their bodies quickly got in sync, and the slow strokes soon quickened to deep thrusts that had him seconds away from a mind-blowing orgasm. He tried to slow things down, but his stubborn Hope wasn't having it. Her legs locked around his waist, and her nails sank into his shoulders.

"Harder," she breathed. "Harder."

Complying, Colt rode her hard and fast until he reached a point where he didn't care if she joined him or not. Luckily, right before he went over the edge, she tightened around him, pulling him in after her. The orgasm crashed over him like a California wave at high tide, sucking him down into a maelstrom of intense sensation. When he finally surfaced, blue eyes sparkled back at him with what could only be described as pure feline satisfaction.

"You're heavy," she said as she smoothed the hair off his damp forehead.

He rolled to her side and stroked a hand down her stomach. "You okay?"

"Yes. But next time I better get on top."

He shot her a surprised look. "Next time?"

A quirky little smile tipped her mouth. "You don't think you can tell a woman you want her, and have wanted her for most of your life, and then kick her out after only once, do you? I thought a lowdown good-for-nothing biker would have more stamina than that."

His face cracked open with happiness. "Well, honey." He brushed the back of his fingers down the center of her chest and then around each breast, stopping to give each sweet peak a gentle caress before moving on. "I guess if I'm forced, I can find the strength somewhere."

The phone woke Colt out of the first sound sleep he'd had in months. He thought about ignoring it, especially when the woman in his arms wiggled her smooth naked butt against him. But then the numbers on the digital clock caught his attention, and he realized they had slept away half of the morning. Which wasn't shocking, considering they hadn't gone to bed until after four.

Carefully moving his arm out from under Hope, he leaned over her and grabbed the receiver. "Hello."

"Hey, big brother," Shirlene's voice came through loud and clear. Almost too loud and clear. "The buses are getting ready to pull out. But, lo and behold, no one can locate Hope. You wouldn't know where she is, would you? Burl and Jenna are about ready to call out the Texas Rangers."

He glanced down at Hope, who still slept like the dead.

Shit. This wasn't going to be good. But he couldn't see any way around it.

"She's with me."

There was a long pause where he didn't hear a sound, almost as if the mouthpiece had been covered, before she came back on.

"Burl's on his way up."

"What?" Colt scrambled for the covers, as if that was going to make a difference when Hope's daddy plowed through the door,

Shirlene laughed. "Just kiddin'. Burl and Jenna's bus already left."

As his heart tried to find an even cadence, he gritted his teeth. "Shirlene, I'm going to bust your butt when I get a hold of you."

"Now is that any way to repay a loving sister who lied through her teeth for you? If I hadn't told Burl that Hope spent the night in my room last night, your ass would be grass right now, big brother. Especially after Rachel Dean said she saw you two together last night." Another pause. "Hope is alive, isn't she? I would hate to think of my best friend lying in a bathtub wrapped in a shower curtain, waiting to be dumped in the San Antonio River."

"Funny, Shirl." Relieved that he wasn't going to have to deal with Hope's pissed-off daddy, Colt leaned back against the pillows and stroked his fingers through Hope's hair. "So are you heading out on the bus?"

"Actually, I thought I'd head over to Houston and see if I can get that workaholic husband of mine to take a couple nights off." There was another pause before she spoke. "It doesn't look good, does it, Colt?"

Even though he spent most of his life sheltering his sister from life's brutal realities, he answered her truthfully. "No. Even if Dalton gets bought out, I don't see how they'll avoid more layoffs. Which is why we need to entice other companies to make their home in Bramble."

"Companies like Desperado Customs?"

At one time, he would've laughed at the absurd notion

of returning to a town he'd wanted so desperately to leave. But he wasn't laughing now.

When he didn't answer, his sister continued. "Look, Colt, I've tried to keep my nose out of whatever has been going on with you and Hope all these years. But Hope is my best friend, and she's going through a hard time right now. So if you're just using her for a little entertainment while you're in town..."

Colt's fingers hesitated in the silky strands of Hope's hair, and for the first time, he owned up to his true feelings. "You should know, Shirl, I've always cared about Hope."

"I know, but you can still hurt someone you care about."

It was a truth that he and Shirlene had learned at an early age. Their daddy had cared about them and he died, leaving behind a woman who couldn't think through the pain. And consequently, she had hurt Shirlene and Colt by not being able to control a disease that almost destroyed their family.

The sound of a horn honking came through the receiver. "My cab's here," Shirlene said. "So I guess I'll see you back in Bramble, big brother."

"Only if I don't see you first, little sister."

The phone clicked, and he leaned over and hung it up.

Settling back against the pillows, Colt looked down at the woman who slept on her stomach next to him. Light filtered in through the crack in the curtains and fell over one bare shoulder and the smooth tanned skin of the arm that dangled off the edge of the bed. The heap of wild brown hair completely covered her face, and he reached out and smoothed it back. Her mouth lay open against the pillow, and without the thick hair to mute them, Colt could hear her soft snores. The sound made him smile, and he slipped back down in the bed and snuggled next to her, curling an arm around her waist.

Against the white of the sheet, the blue ink of his tattoo stood out. It had taken two years to complete and numerous painful hours beneath a tattoo artist's needle. The rattlesnake had been the first—a coiled symbol for fate and its ability to strike at any moment. The chopper and the banner with "Desperado" written across it came after the sale of his first custom bike. The Texas state flag on a night he'd missed home. And the tombstone with his father's initials and the date he'd been killed in the car accident were done on a night when he'd missed being a father's son. Shirlene had picked out the queen of diamonds playing card when she met him in Vegas one weekend. And, since she had talked him into a diamond bracelet the same night, it seemed fitting. As was the rose, a tribute to his beautiful mama and a relationship filled with its share of thorns.

But the tattoo that held Colt's attention was the one of the snarling hog with the tiara hooked over one ear. A hog with wide eyes staring out over a cute little snout. So obviously different from the others, the tattoo had been a conversation starter on more than one occasion. Although not one person had ever gotten an answer for why he had tattooed a mean-looking, tiara-wearing pig on his arm.

Probably because Colt didn't have one.

He hadn't been drunk or drugged or even slightly road-weary when he had drawn the design for the tattoo artist. But once it was there, he wished it gone. For instead of a humorous joke, it became a painful reminder of something he wanted but couldn't have.

He wanted Hope. Not just her body, but all of her. He wanted her quick wit and hot temper. Her strong moral beliefs and loyalty. Her stubborn streak and kind heart. He wanted her hero worship and her smiles. And he wanted her babies.

But mostly, he wanted her love.

He didn't delude himself that she felt the same way about him as she had when she was thirteen. But one thing was certain, Hope desired him. If he could only figure out a way to keep her in his bed, there might be a chance that the Bad Boy of Bramble would end up with the homecoming queen after all.

Chapter Twenty-four

"ALL RIGHT THEN," Cindy Lynn said. Since she didn't have the little wooden mallet she normally used when presiding over meetings, she tapped one purple acrylic nail on Shirlene's onyx countertop. "Darla will be responsible for decorations."

Just the thought of the silk-flower and hot-glue nightmare that Hope's and Faith's baby shower had just turned into should've sent Hope screaming from Shirlene's beautiful mansion like the hounds of hell were after her. The only reason it didn't was because she had more important things to worry about.

Like the financial stability of her town.

The future of her baby.

And the complete loss of her mind.

"Now who would like to volunteer to be in charge of the games?" Cindy Lynn asked the group.

"Me!" Twyla madly waved her hand and, before Cindy could even call on her, started rambling. "I've got this really cute poopy-diaper game where you melt different kinds of mini-candy bars in Pampers and then everyone has to open up the diaper and try to figure out what candy bar poop is in it."

"Oh, I played that one," Rachel Dean talked around the little spinach quiche she'd just popped in her mouth. "And it's harder than you think. The only one I got right was the Baby Ruth. But only because it looked just like my little Johnny's after he'd eaten corn."

Faith choked on her iced tea, and Hope slapped her on the back a little harder than she should have. But she was still mad about her sister's deceitful matchmaking tactics.

"I'm not lookin' at baby poop," Darla spoke up.

"It's not baby poop, silly." Twyla flapped a hand. "It's chocolate candy bar—" She stopped in mid-sentence, although her mouth still hung open, as if she wanted to finish but just didn't have enough air to do it. Wondering what had caused her reaction, Hope glanced behind her, and her own breath caught.

Colt Lomax walked into the kitchen from the garage. He was talking on his cell phone, completely unaware of the women sitting across the room at the breakfast bar. Women who were all transfixed by the hot body clad in running shorts and a tight black T-shirt. And Hope couldn't blame them. Not when she couldn't pull her own gaze away.

"I'm not planning on firing anyone, Juan. The people who don't want to transfer can stay in L.A." He pulled open the refrigerator and took out a container of orange juice. Then, holding the phone to his ear, he opened the cap and chugged the juice, straight from the bottle. A drop dripped down his whiskered chin, then plopped to the strip of hard chest above his shirt's V-neck. He swiped it off, causing Cindy Lynn to release a sigh that made

Hope want to reach over and rip out her high, tightly curled ponytail.

With the plastic bottle inches from his mouth, Colt turned to them. His surprised gaze swept over the group until it landed on Hope. Then it wasn't surprise as much as heat that settled in his steel gray orbs.

A smile tipped up the corners of his mouth. A wicked smile that spoke of sweaty sheets and carnal knowledge. Hope tried not to react, but it was impossible, given that less than forty-eight hours ago she'd been surrounded by sweaty sheets while he used that carnal knowledge to give her five amazing orgasms.

Which was dumb. Stupid. And completely insane.

She had no business falling in bed with Colt Lomax—five orgasms or one. No business whatsoever. Hadn't she learned anything from the past? Every sweet kiss and caress he had given her had been followed by some mean-spirited prank. Yet all it had taken for her to forget were a few sentences: *I'm saying I want you, Hope Scroggs. Have wanted you ever since I can remember.* Not "I love you. I need you. I can't live without you." Just "I want you." And that had been enough to send her mind over the deep end and her libido off the scales.

Stupid. Stupid. Stupid.

But even knowing how stupid it was, Hope had to fight back the urge to slip off the bar stool and walk straight into those well-defined arms. And the feeling only intensified when he hung up the phone without even saying good-bye.

"Hey." The word was simple, but the deep, sexy underlying tones made her panties moist. Like steam off a Jacuzzi, heat rose from the spot where the soft material of her dress puddled in her lap.

"Hey," she squeaked.

"Y'all look mighty pretty today," he said.

There was a chorus of "thank yews," even though his gaze never left Hope. Trapped in those beautiful pools of gray, all she could do was sit there and stare back. Until Faith coughed and broke the connection.

After one sexy wink of an eye, Colt recapped the orange juice and slipped it back in the commercial-sized refrigerator. "Shirlene failed to mention she was havin' a group of lovely ladies over this afternoon. If I'd known, I would've cleaned up."

"Well, I don't know about the rest of the women here," Rachel Dean said as she rested her chin in one man hand and looked Colt up and down as if he was a big stick of butter. "But I don't mind a bit."

Colt flashed a smile at her before he asked, "Where is my ornery sister, anyway?"

"She had a phone call," Cindy Lynn piped up, her gaze glued to Colt's legs. Unable to stop herself, Hope shifted on the stool and kicked her hard in the shin. "Oww!" She threw Hope a dirty look as she leaned down to rub the spot.

"Sorry," Hope said. "I was just trying to cross my legs." She looked up to see Colt grinning like an idiot.

"Well, I guess I better let you ladies get back to what you were doing."

"Baby showers," Darla supplied. "We're plannin' baby showers."

"Really?" He shot a glance over at Hope.

In between orgasms, they had talked about a lot of things. The town's troubles. Music and books. Politics and religion. Colt's adventures on the road and Hope's adventures in Hollywood. Colt's passion for motorcycles and

Hope's passion for the town of Bramble. But the baby was one topic they had avoided.

"I'm sure it's nothin' that you would be interested in, Colt," Cindy Lynn said, still devouring him with her eyes.

To keep herself from slapping Cindy Lynn upside the head, Hope picked up a little cheesecake cup from the plate in front of her and popped it in her mouth.

"Oh, I don't know about that." Colt strolled over, and the thick cream cheese lodged in Hope's throat. "I think people might be surprised at what I find interestin'."

And then right there in front of the biggest gossips in Bramble, he reached across the counter and curled his fingers under Hope's chin, his eyes sparkling with devilry. "You missed some, honey." His thumb brushed across her lips in a long, heated stroke before he brought the digit back to his mouth and sucked it clean.

Heat infused Hope's body as he sent her another sizzling smile before he turned and strolled out of the kitchen. With her lips burning and her mind tumbling, she sat frozen to the bar stool, waiting for the shock to wear off and the questions to start.

But she'd overestimated the IQ of the planning committee.

"So do I get to do the poopy-diaper game or what?" Twyla asked.

Hope sat through another fifteen minutes of craziness before she had had enough. Slipping off the bar stool, she sent everyone a bright smile. "Excuse me, y'all, but I have to go to the bathroom."

Rachel waved one oversized hand. "You go right ahead, sugar. My bladder felt like the size of a pea when I was pregnant."

Hope continued smiling until she rounded the corner into the living room. Then, once out of sight, she dashed to the front door and slipped out. She had barely knocked on the door of the guesthouse when it was jerked open and she was pulled inside against Colt's damp, naked body, straight from the shower.

"I was hoping you'd come callin'." He nibbled along her neck, causing her legs to turn to jelly.

She ran her hands up through his thick hair and pulled him closer, relishing the feel of his hungry mouth against her neck and his hard chest against the tight nipples that pressed through her sweater. But when he reached for the edge of that sweater, she stopped him.

"So who were you talking to on the phone? Did you get a business to move here?" When his desire-filled eyes didn't clear, she tugged on his hair. "Come on, Lomax, don't keep me in suspense."

"At a time like this," he took her hand from his hair and pressed it to his hard-on, "is that all you can think about?"

She gave him a few lingering strokes that turned his eyes to liquid heat before she answered. "Not all, but we'll get to the other things I'm thinking about later."

The passion-filled eyes sparkled back at her. "In that case...yes, Desperado Customs is opening a shop here."

With a squeal, she threw herself back against him. "You did it! You came through!"

"Now, hold up, Hope." His face was serious when he pulled her away. "A small motorcycle custom shop isn't going to save the town if C-Corp doesn't buy Dalton."

"I know that, but it's a start." She cocked her head to one side. "Desperado? Isn't that the name you wrote in permanent marker on the back of that jacket you owned as a teenager?"

Although it was hard to tell in the shadowed entryway, it looked as if he blushed. The sight of such a tough guy blushing made her heart melt, and to hide her reaction, she leaned up on her tiptoes and kissed him. The depth of the tenderness she felt for this man took the sexual heat to a new level, turning the kiss into a greedy mating of uncontrollable need.

His hand slipped beneath her skirt, and she didn't hesitate to hike up a leg and give him full access. But when his warm fingers came in contact with wet heat, he groaned and pulled away from the kiss.

"You were sitting there the entire time without any panties?" he asked in a desire-roughened voice.

"Didn't you tell me it would make things easy if I left them off?" She leaned in and ran her tongue over his nipple.

Tipping his head back, he groaned up at the ceiling. "God, I love a woman who listens."

Before she could move to his other nipple, his hands dipped beneath her skirt and lifted her up. Her legs came around his waist, and he pressed deep inside her. The hard penetration took her breath away, but no more than the sweet thrusts that followed. His biceps flexed as he brought her hips forward, then back. With his hands gripping the flesh of her bottom and the tips of his fingers teasing the sensitive area deep inside the crevice, it didn't take long for her to go tumbling over the edge of an amazing orgasm. She tightened her legs and moaned out her release, while Colt followed right behind her.

Once their breathing had returned to normal, he

carried her into the bedroom, where he laid her down on rumpled sheets. Easing down beside her, he leaned over and gave her a quick kiss.

"I've missed you."

"Hmmm," she sighed. "I've missed you too."

He slipped a hand beneath her sweater. "I tried calling you all day yesterday, but your phone was busy." His hand skated over the lace of her bra.

"Ryan keeps calling me. He's worried that I won't be on the plane tomorrow." She drew a heart in the middle of his chest hair, but before she could do something really stupid like add initials, Colt grabbed her hand.

"You're leaving tomorrow?"

His question brought her out of her sexual haze and slammed her back to reality. A reality she'd been avoiding. She *was* leaving tomorrow. Leaving this town. Leaving her family. And leaving this man, who stared down at her with a look in his gray eyes that made it difficult to speak.

Her hand dropped from his neck, and she sat up. "First thing in the morning."

He followed her, his bare chest inches from her shoulder. "Why didn't you say anything?"

"I told you about the reality show." It was a lame answer, and she knew it. But it was better to keep things as uncomplicated as possible.

Unfortunately, it was too late for that.

He stared at her for a second longer before he rolled to his feet. "Yeah, I guess you did." Completely unconcerned with his nudity, he walked over to the sliding glass doors and stared out. "So if you're leaving tomorrow, what are you doing here?" He glanced back at her. "Or was this just a quickie before you left town?"

Before she could do more than sputter, he laughed, the sound harsh and brittle. "I thought things had changed, but I see that they haven't. You're still the same scared little girl, searching for the town's approval. And I'm still that poor Lomax kid, just waiting to be acknowledged."

Now angry, she jumped up from the bed. "Fine, you want me to acknowledge you? I'll run into town and scream at the top of my lungs that the baby is yours. But you better be ready for what happens next, Colt Lomax. Because if you thought shooting out the stained glass window of the First Baptist Church with a BB gun pissed them off, it will be nothing compared to how they'll react when they find out you impregnated me. And I don't think you'll like their solution. Not when it will include being chained to a town and a woman you couldn't get away from fast enough."

His eyes darkened. "Who's running now, Hope? Because it sure as hell isn't me."

Stunned, Hope stared back at him. But before she could open her mouth to find out what he meant, the front door crashed open. And Colt barely had enough time to grab a pair of jogging shorts and slip them on before Faith raced into the bedroom.

When she saw Hope, she seemed more relieved than surprised. "It's Shirlene. Something's wrong. She came out of the bedroom screaming at the top of her lungs for everyone to get out."

Their anger forgotten, Hope and Colt exchanged looks before they headed for the door.

By the time they reached the main house, the ladies of Bramble were gone. Only Shirlene remained, her tall frame pulled into a tight ball in one corner of the couch.

When they came through the back doors, she glanced up and her green eyes glittered with unshed tears.

"The craziest thing happened, y'all." Shirlene swallowed hard as a tiny droplet trickled down her cheek. "Lyle up and died on me."

Chapter Twenty-five

THE NEWS THAT Lyle Dalton had suffered a heart attack while celebrating the buyout of his company spread like wildfire through Texas. And business associates from all over the state converged on Bramble for the funeral. Besides oil men, there were land developers, technology leaders, media moguls, ranchers, and politicians. Even the governor stopped by for a short eulogy—one of many that were made during the two-hour church service.

When the service ended, a long line of limos, rental SUVs, and trucks headed out to Heavenly Haven Cemetery, where Pastor Robbins said a few last words before an honor guard gave a three-volley gun salute for the years that Lyle had served in the military. After the last shots echoed into the cloudy November sky and the flag was folded to the bugler's poignant rendition of "Taps," the crowd dispersed to give the family a chance for final good-byes.

Hope wandered over to a nearby oak tree to watch as Lyle's midnight blue coffin was lowered into the ground. Shirlene and Colt stood at the front of the group, both dressed in somber black. And although the style was the complete opposite of his faded jeans and T-shirts, Hope couldn't help but admire the figure Colt cut in the expensive suit.

After learning of Lyle's heart attack, Colt and Hope had worked together to get Lyle's body flown home from Houston, notify family and friends, and help with the funeral arrangements. And although they spoke cordially to one another, their argument in the guesthouse remained between them. It seemed that no matter how many bridges they had crossed since Colt returned, it would never be enough—something that brought an intense wave of sorrow to Hope's heart as she watched Colt pull Shirlene close and kiss her forehead.

"I always hoped that you would marry that boy," a gruff voice behind Hope said.

Startled out of her thoughts, Hope turned to find her daddy standing there. Unlike Colt's suit, Burl's black suit was faded and ill-fitting, the jacket stretching tight across his large linebacker shoulders and coming up short on his thick forearms.

Sending him a weak smile, she glanced over at Slate, who was talking with Harley, his arm hooked protectively around Faith. "You and the entire town, Daddy."

"I wasn't talkin' about Slate," he stated. "I was talkin' about Colt."

Her gaze snapped back to her father's deep blue eyes. "What?"

Looking down at his scuffed cowboy boots, he shrugged his shoulders. "Yeah, I guess it was a pretty crazy thought, seein' as how you two are a little like a lit match to dynamite."

Hope snorted. "That's putting it lightly, Daddy."

He grinned. "There were a few times I thought you were going to kill the poor boy."

"The poor boy? I wasn't the one flattening *his* bike tires, or putting gum on the door handles of *his* vehicle."

Her daddy chuckled, a sound that had always warmed her. "And maybe that's what got me to thinkin' about you two. Colt reminded me of myself when I was younger."

"You did things like that to Mama?"

"Worse. There was this one time that I—" He blushed. "Anyway I was pretty ornery. And there was nothing I liked better than gettin' your mama all riled up for a good fight."

Hope stared at him. "But I never heard you and Mama fighting."

"Probably because by the time you got old enough to know what was going on, we had learned to keep our fights behind closed doors." A smile creased his weathered face. "You remind me so much of your mama when she was younger—she was the feistiest little spitfire you'd ever want to meet." He shook his head. " 'Course she still is, when I forget to put down the toilet seat."

Hope grinned, but it faded when he continued.

"Now the crazy woman has got it in her head that you're thinkin' about givin' up the baby." His eyes, which were so much like her own, filled with a sadness that broke Hope's heart. "Thinks it has something to do with us givin' Faith away."

"Oh, Daddy," Hope moved into his waiting arms, burrowing her face against the familiar Dial-soap scent of him. She had cried so much in the last couple weeks, she thought she was all cried out. But as her tears soaked her daddy's suit jacket, she realized she'd been wrong.

"I thought I had it all figured out," she sobbed. "I'd

move to Hollywood and give the baby to Shirlene and everyone would be happy. But even if it makes perfect sense, I can't do it. I just can't give P-pumpkin Seed away."

Her daddy awkwardly patted her back. "Well, sometimes things don't have to make sense, honey. Sometimes they just have to feel right."

She pulled back and stared at him as he continued.

"And I'm not talkin' about fickle emotion. I'm talkin' about the kind of feelin' that settles right down in your soul—the kind that tells you you've made the right decision, even if it don't make no sense at all."

Since that was exactly how Hope was feeling after deciding to keep the baby, she figured her daddy was on to something. "And, I suppose, it wouldn't make any sense at all to give up a chance of fame and fortune in Hollywood to stay in a small Texan town with very few job opportunities?"

"Nope, that sure would be foolish." He winked at her. "But I'd rather be a happy fool than a miserable wise man."

Sighing, Hope rested her head back on his broad shoulder. "Damn, I wish I'd talked to you a few weeks ago, Daddy."

"I'm always here, baby girl."

They didn't say much after that. Instead, they stood silently and watched as Lyle's relatives dropped bloodred roses into the grave. Hope knew most of them from one gathering or another, except for Lyle's first wife, who had divorced him and moved to Houston when Hope was still a child. The woman was much older than Shirlene, but just as stunning, in a black suit that fit her tall svelte body to perfection. Her two grown sons had gotten her height and dark hair, while the teenage daughter was fair and short like Lyle. They didn't completely snub Shirlene, but they didn't exactly appear friendly either. Once they tossed their flowers in, they walked toward their limo without a backward glance, leaving Colt and Shirlene standing by the casket alone.

After giving her daddy one last hug, Hope started toward them. But she was delayed by Rachel Dean, who wanted to know if Hope thought Shirlene would like lasagna better than enchiladas. By the time she had assured Rachel that either one would be appreciated, Colt and Shirlene were no longer standing by the casket. Colt had moved over to talk with a distinguished-looking man and a redheaded woman, while Shirlene had walked to the far end of the cemetery.

When Hope reached her, she was standing in front of an old, crumbling headstone, a single long-stemmed rose clutched in her hand.

"Did you know my great-great-great-granddaddy was the very first sheriff of Bramble?" Shirlene said, as Hope came up to stand beside her. "Colt was named after him—not him exactly, but the man's favorite gun."

"I think you might've mentioned that," Hope said in a voice as soft as her sister's.

"I guess I did, didn't I?" Shirlene glanced over and sent her a smile that lacked her usual warmth and sparkle before she turned and headed along the row of headstones. Hope followed behind her to the gravestone on the very end, Shirlene's father's stone. There were no decorative scrolls, hearts, or pastoral scenes etched into the simple slab of stone, just the words *David Michael Lomax— Devoted Husband and Loving Father* carved above dates that spanned a mere twenty-four years.

Unconcerned with her expensive suit, Shirlene knelt down and rested the rose against the base. When Hope joined her on the cold ground, they both started clearing out the weeds that had cropped up around the stone.

"I don't remember him," Shirlene said as she worked. "When I was little, Colt would tell me stories of my daddy cradling me in his arms and singing to me, or carrying me around on his shoulders. But now I wonder if Colt didn't make it all up. He's willing to do just about anything to make me happy." She tossed the weeds off to the side before glancing over at Hope. "Even give away his unborn child."

Shocked, Hope fell back on her bottom. "Colt told you?"

"Faith. But I wouldn't be too angry at her. She can't help it if her face reads like a bestselling novel." Then, before Hope could figure out how to break the news to her friend that she'd changed her mind, Shirlene reached over and slugged her hard in the arm.

Placing a hand over the stinging spot, Hope glared at her. "What was that for?"

"For being stupid enough to come up with such a harebrained idea in the first place. What were you thinkin', Hog?"

"I was thinkin' about how much my best friend wanted a baby," she grumbled.

"And I appreciate the gesture." Shirlene scooted back to rest against Hootie Smith's grave marker with the scary-looking angel on top. "But I'm not one of your charity cases, Hope."

The anger fizzled out of her. "I wasn't doing it just for you, Shirl. I wanted my baby to have the best of everything—money, a big house, a mama who didn't have to work, and a dad—" She stopped and looked away.

"Man, Hollywood really screwed you up, Hog." Shirlene leaned her head back on the robes of the angel and closed her eyes. "The Hope Scroggs I knew wouldn't be worried about the things she couldn't give her child. Instead, she'd be figuring out how to get them. Besides, with the way you and my brother have been going at it, it doesn't look like you'll be without a daddy for very long."

"We have not being going at it!" When Hope realized how loudly she'd spoken, she glanced around. But most of the people were on the other side of the cemetery. Still, she lowered her voice and leaned in. "And even if we were, it didn't mean anything." She sniffed. "It was just... great sex."

Shirlene rolled her eyes. "And don't I feel sorry for you. Geez, Hope, pull your head out, would you? Colt has had a thing for you ever since I can remember."

"A thing?" Hope's heart skipped a beat. "He told you that?"

"He didn't tell me anything." Her gaze shifted over to the plain headstone with the single rose. "In case you haven't figured it out, we Lomaxes have trouble communicating our true feelings. Instead, we bury them beneath a tough exterior...or a quick wit. Unfortunately, some emotions refuse to stay buried and end up bubbling out in destructive ways—like rocks through windows or a smart-ass mouth."

When Shirlene looked back at Hope, her green eyes were even more sad. "Colt isn't going to tell you he loves you, Hope. Not because he doesn't, but because he can't. His only example of love came from a woman who couldn't stand up after one o'clock in the afternoon, let alone show her children any kind of affection. It wasn't so bad for me, at least I had Colt to shower me with love, but all he had was an ornery little sister."

Trying to think above her thumping heart, Hope leaned closer. "But if he loves me, then why did he pull all those pranks?"

"Maybe he was trying to get your attention."

She snorted. "Live ammo in a prop gun got my attention, all right."

"About that, honey..."

Hope's gaze snapped back to Shirlene, who suddenly looked like she had when Hope's mama had caught them smoking behind Shirlene's trailer. Shocked, Hope reared back and cracked her shoulder on Samuel Murdock's stone cross.

"You? You put the bullet in the gun? But why?"

Shirlene shrugged. "It wasn't enough that you won every award and contest there ever was. You had to go and take my part in the school play too? It just didn't seem fair."

Put that way, Hope couldn't very well argue the point. "I wish you hadn't gotten the flu, Shirl. It would've saved me a lot of grief." She looked across the cemetery to where Colt stood talking to Sheriff Winslow. "But if Colt cared about me, why did he leave town?"

One perfectly shaped eyebrow lifted. "Maybe because the girl he wanted had already made her choice."

"But I..."

Hope snapped her mouth closed. Shirlene was right; she had chosen Slate, if not in words, then in her refusal to correct an entire town's belief. And she was doing it again. Letting the town run around looking for a daddy, all because she was too scared to stand up for what she wanted, too scared of disappointing people who refused to see their sweetheart with a bad boy. Even if a bad boy was exactly who Hope wanted—had always wanted. A bad boy who had grown into a good man with a kind heart.

Unfortunately, her revelation might have come too late. In an attempt to shield her heart, she had said and done things that Colt might never forgive.

Hope turned her tearful eyes to Shirlene. "What am I going to do now, Shirl?"

With her head resting against Hootie's angel, Shirlene looked up into the overcast skies. Her smile was weak as she spoke just above a whisper.

"Funny, but I was going to ask the same thing."

Chapter Twenty-six

SINCE MOST FOLKS wanted to be home on Thanksgiving with a twenty-pound bird and a forty-six-inch TV, the Bramble Thanksgiving Day Parade was always held the Saturday before. The weather had finally turned the corner to winter, and frigid winds snapped the flag in front of the town hall and sent tumbleweeds—along with a few cowboy hats—careening down the cordoned-off street. It had been a while since Colt had attended a parade, but he knew the routine and picked out a spot along the parade route to park Shirlene's Navigator.

"This look okay to you?" He glanced over at Shirlene, and his heart tightened.

The woman who sat in the seat next to him might look like his sister in her tight jeans and flashy jewelry. But the lack of spirit in her eyes and the somber droop of her lips were nothing like his baby sister. And Colt didn't know what to do about it. Shirlene had always been the optimistic one in the family—the one who saw the glass as half full instead of half empty. And being the half-empty guy, he counted on her to keep his world balanced, so the reversal of their roles had him floundering like a trout on a hook.

The cold wind smacked him in the face as he climbed out of the SUV, and he zipped up his leather jacket to his throat before he walked around to the back.

"Good Lord, Shirlene, you think you brought enough?" He tried to tease a smile out of her as they unloaded the Navigator.

She paused and stared down at the thermos of coffee as if she didn't know what it was or how it had gotten in her hand. "I guess I did overpack, didn't I? Lyle always called me his 'Material Girl.' I guess he was right."

Colt's hand tightened around the aluminum of a chair as he tried to keep the concern from his voice. "There's nothing wrong with being prepared. If it hadn't been for you packing my lunches every night, I would've starved in high school."

"Doubtful." She reached in for the blankets. "I'm sure you would've found some girl to feed you."

"Yeah, but not a one of them would've known how to make peanut butter and Frosted Flake sandwiches."

"Losers," she said, and then carried the blankets and thermos around to the front of the truck.

Once they were seated with the blankets tucked around them and the coffee poured into thermal mugs, Colt didn't have a clue what to say. Sympathy had never been his strong suit. He thought about bringing up his meeting with Lyle's lawyers, but then figured that that would only depress his sister more. Although Lyle had sealed the deal with C-Corp, his personal finances were still in turmoil. And Colt wasn't sure, after paying debts and lawyers, if there would be any money left for Shirlene. Not that it mattered. His little sister would never go without.

"I hope you aren't going to get sick of me," Colt finally said. "With the custom motorcycle shop going up on the property next to Jones' Gas Station, I'll be in Bramble more often. So you don't have to worry about anything. I'll be around to take care of you."

Shirlene nodded. "And I appreciate that. But I think you've got other things to worry about. Like Hope's baby."

His gaze shot over to her. "How did you—" He stopped when the truth dawned on him. "So I guess Hope told you about her plan."

His sister nodded, and Colt actually felt sick to his stomach. For some strange reason, he still clung to the belief that Hope would change her mind—about Hollywood and the baby. Obviously, he'd been mistaken.

Aware of how much pain he was about to cause his sister, he took a deep breath before he turned to her.

"I love you, Shirlene. You know that, right?" When she nodded, he continued. "Your happiness means the world to me. But even knowing how happy a baby would make you, I can't give you mine. I love Pumpkin Seed and I'm keeping her."

Pushing the blanket down, Shirlene gifted him with the smile that had been absent for way too long. "Well, join the club, big brother, because Hope couldn't do it either. So I guess I'll have to be the best darned aunt little...Pumpkin Seed will ever have."

He blinked. "Hope couldn't do it?" And when Shirlene shook her head, all his pent-up emotions broke free, and he jumped from the chair and pulled his sister into his arms.

"I'm going to be a daddy, Shirl! I'm going to be a daddy."

Shirlene hugged him back. "And the best darned daddy in the state of Texas."

"So I guess you don't need no wife?"

The belligerent voice caused Colt to pull back from Shirlene and look over at the young boy standing in the familiar grubby jeans. At least today, he had on a coat.

Jesse's hostile gaze ran over Shirlene before he looked back at Colt. "Unless you want one that ain't so old."

"Old?" Shirlene's eyes narrowed on the kid. "Who you callin' old, pipsqueak?"

Colt bit back a grin. "Shirl, I'd like you to meet Jesse. Jesse this is my sister, Shirlene Dalton."

"Sister?" Jesse's face brightened before he held out one dirty hand. "Nice to meet ya, Shirl."

Shirlene cocked a brow at Colt before she replied. "Nice to meet you, Jess."

"Jesse."

"Ms. Dalton."

The young face scrunched up with annoyance before he turned back to Colt. "So anyway, since you ain't tied up with this one, I thought you'd like to meet my sister." Jesse glared at Shirlene. "Besides being younger, she's a whole lot prettier," he added.

Ignoring the look of outrage on his sister's face, Colt nodded. "I would love to meet your sister. But more importantly, I'd like to meet your mother."

"Well, you can't." Jesse shoved his hands in the front pockets of his jeans. "She's at work. But my sister is right over there."

He pointed across the street to where a teenage girl with glasses stood behind a stroller with a blanket-bundled baby inside and a toddler holding onto one of the curved handles. When the teenage girl's eyes narrowed on them, Jesse suddenly acted like a cat with a firecracker attached to its tail.

"Then again, maybe another time." He raced across the street before Colt could stop him.

"Where did you meet that ornery kid?" Shirlene asked as she sat back down and adjusted the blanket around her.

"He came to the garage." Colt watched as the girl lit into Jesse, her gaze flickering across to Colt and back again before she whirled the stroller around and headed down the street. Jesse took the hand of the toddler and followed at a slower pace, glancing back only once to wave at Colt.

"He lives out on Grover Road," Colt said.

"Figures." Shirlene snorted. "Ornery kids come from Grover Road."

As the kids disappeared around a corner, Colt looked back over at her and grinned. "They sure do."

Colt had about a million questions to ask his sister about Hope's decision to keep the baby. But about that time, Sheriff Winslow's patrol car came around the corner of Elm with siren blaring to start the parade. And figuring he had plenty of time for answers, Colt leaned back against the SUV to watch the parade. It turned out to be better than he'd remembered. Even without helium balloons or Broadway numbers, Bramble's beat out Macy's for sheer entertainment.

In the first few minutes, Sheriff Winslow snagged the gaping pocket of a lodge clown with the bumper of his patrol car and dragged him halfway down the parade route before Rye Pickett grabbed one of the clown's big red shoes and pulled him lose. Then some idiot put the

Four-H Club in front of the Jazzercising Ladies from Shady Meadows Retirement Village, and those old gals put on quite a show, trying to keep the green tennis balls on the ends of their walkers away from the huge steaming piles left behind by the horses. The marching band never broke stride, not even when Ms. Murphy's toy terrier attacked a band girl's flag and was whipped around for a full minute of "Love Shack" before he let go.

Luckily, Rossie Owen's grandson, Jimmy, was one hell of an outfielder and had no trouble reaching up and snagging the tiny dog before he hit the ground.

Finally the football team arrived, crowded onto a flatbed trailer covered in ugly purple flowers and huge Styrofoam guns that pointed out in all directions.

"What the hell?" Colt breathed, unable to take his eyes off the hideous float.

"It was the homecoming float," Shirlene stated as if that explained everything. And it did. For as long as Colt could remember, the homecoming floats had been damned hideous.

"Hey, Shirlene!" Austin Reeves, who cockily straddled the Colt Peacemaker, yelled to her from the float.

"Hey yourself, Austin!" Shirlene waved back. "I guess you think you're a stud now?"

"Pretty much!" Austin waved his straw cowboy hat over his head and released a big cowboy yee-haw, which had his teammates laughing and the crowd cheering.

Austin reminded Colt of a dark-headed Slate, a conquering hero who had the town by the tail. And Colt couldn't fault the kid for that. Nor could he fault Slate for enjoying all the glory that came with being a winning football coach in Texas. Standing with the rest of the coaches in the back of the pickup following the float, Slate smiled and waved like the golden-haired boy he was.

As the truck passed, he looked down at Colt. At one time, the situation would've been demeaning—the exalted hero looking down at "the poor Lomax kid." But now Colt realized that they were two different men who filled two different spots on this big rotating ball. And neither spot was any better or any worse than the other.

He nodded, and Slate nodded back.

A split second later, Colt's gaze got caught on Harley Sutter's convertible Cadillac, following the truck. Hope sat on the trunk of the Cadillac with her feet on the backseat, tossing out candy to the kids who raced along beside her.

Even after the news about the baby, Colt had thought Hope would be long gone by now—off to Hollywood to accomplish another one of her goals. But instead, there she was, looking much as she did twelve years earlier when riding atop the homecoming float. Her face was flushed with cold, her long hair blew out behind her, and her smile was bright as she waved to the whistling crowd.

"She's something else, isn't she," Shirlene said.

"Yes." Colt straightened and tried to restrain himself from running out into the street and jerking her from the car, a good half a block away, so he could ask her about her decision to keep the baby.

"Faith looks as pretty as a picture and that fat little pig sitting between them is a riot. But, if you notice, everyone's eyes are on Hope."

Since Colt hadn't even noticed Faith, or Sherman sitting next to Hope, he had to agree with his sister.

"It's a strange phenomenon," Shirlene continued.

"One I still haven't figured out. Somewhere between reciting Bible scriptures in church and winning ribbons at the county fair, Hope became something more than just a member of the town. She became a shining beacon of everything this town stands for and all its dreams for the future."

Colt pulled his eyes off the Cadillac and turned to his sister, although he couldn't think of a thing to say. His mind was too consumed with the truth Shirlene had spoken, a truth he hadn't understood until now: Hope's life hadn't been any easier than his. In fact, it had been harder. While he had had the weight of a mother and sister on his shoulders, Hope had the weight of an entire town.

"Do you love her?" Shirlene asked.

The question didn't shock him as much as he thought it would.

"I'm not sure I know what love is."

"Bullshit, Colt Lomax. You know exactly what love is, you're just too afraid to give yourself over to it. Too afraid you'll end up like Mama. But what you refuse to see is that love didn't put Mama on the road to self-destruction, Colt. Mama did that all by herself. And while it's always been easier to blame our crappy childhood on a twist of fate, fate doesn't control our lives..." She leaned up. "We do."

How in the hell did his little sister get so smart? And so pushy? Colt wondered.

"It might be too late," he said. "She's got her heart set on making it big in California."

Shirlene snorted. "Does that look like a woman who has her heart set on being anywhere but right where she is?"

Colt stared at the laughing woman who waved and

yelled out greetings to everyone she passed. The sight evoked the same wealth of emotions it always had, but this time he took his baby sister's advice and accepted love for what it was: a perfect emotion in an imperfect world.

"And what if she thinks I'm not good enough for her?" he said, more to himself than Shirlene.

"You'll never know until you try," Shirlene shot back. She paused. "And by the way, if you ever tell her the things I said about her, I'll deny every word."

Colt might've laughed if the Cadillac hadn't finally reached them. Everything inside him stilled when Hope's gaze caught his.

After searching for it for the last few weeks, it was finally there in the deep-blue depths of her eyes—something he only thought he'd see again in an old photograph. And just that quickly, Colt's heart jumped up to his throat as if he was free-falling from a fourteen-thousand-foot drop, and he wished he had a cowboy hat to wave over his head as he yelled yee-haw.

He wasn't aware of moving out to the curb. Or stepping into the street. He wasn't aware of anything but those eyes, which mirrored the same emotions churning deep inside of him.

"Colt?" Hope's voice penetrated his love bubble. "What are you doing?"

Finally becoming aware of his surroundings, he realized he was jogging next to the car. A younger Colt might've cared about looking like a fool in front of the entire town of Bramble, especially when some smartass yelled out, "Hey, Colt! If you're supposed to be a clown, you forgot your pooper-scooper!"

But this lovesick Colt couldn't have cared less.

"I need to talk to you," he said as he ran.

"Now?"

It was a good question, since they were in the middle of a parade.

"Yes. Right now."

She nodded as she leaned up over the front seat. "Stop the car, Kenny."

"Now, Hope, you know I can't do that," Kenny said. "Harley gave us strict orders to keep it at ten miles an hour. No more, and no less."

"I don't give a shit what Harley said, Kenny," Colt said as he placed a hand on the side door. "Stop the damned car."

"Please, Kenny," Faith joined in. "Colt needs to talk with Hope."

"No, sir, I ain't stoppin'." Kenny shook his head. "Not when it sounds like Colt wants to punch my head in."

"Well, if he doesn't punch your head in, Kenny Gene, I sure as heck will," Hope yelled, loud enough to draw the attention of the clown following the car in a little battery-powered Jeep. The hugely exaggerated foam cowboy hat and thick face paint couldn't camouflage the handlebar mustache or the mayor's big belly, swelling over the small steering wheel.

"Now, Colt," Harley said. "You sure have earned my respect in the last few weeks, but I still can't let you disrupt the parade with any more of your delinquent shenanigans."

"I need to talk with Hope," Colt said through gritted teeth.

Harley drove around in tiny circles behind the Cadillac. "Well, we only have less than a mile until we get to the school. You can talk to Hope then."

Except Colt didn't want to talk to Hope when he got to the school.

"Now, Harley. I need to talk to her now."

"What is going on here?" Rachel Dean pedaled up on her unicycle in face paint and a curly red wig, her man hands waggling in front of her. Colt had to give it to her. For a large woman, she was extremely skilled on the one-tire bike.

"Colt is bothering Hope again," Harley explained, as he tooted the horn of the little red Jeep and fired off a couple rounds from his cap gun.

"He is not bothering me!" Hope turned around and yelled at him.

"Now, Hope," Harley said. "I realize you've always had a soft spot for the underdog, and no one is more of an underdog than Colt Lomax—being how he was falsely accused and sent to prison and all. But I won't condone any more pranks."

For a moment, Colt thought about lifting Hope from the car. And if she hadn't been pregnant, he might've tried it. But the car was going a little too fast and the soles of his cowboy boots were a little too slick for him to chance it.

Sheriff Winslow pulled up behind with lights flashing and leaned out of his window. "Is there a problem?"

"No problem, Sam." Rachel backed up and then went forward as she tried to keep the same pace as the car. "Colt is just pullin' another prank on Hope."

"I'm not pulling a prank! I want to ask her something, is all."

"Well, go ahead and ask her, son," Harley said. "At this point, no one's stoppin' you."

"Fine!" For a runner, he suddenly felt extremely out

of shape. His heart was beating like the base drum up ahead, and his head reeled from lack of oxygen. But it didn't seem to matter anymore. All that mattered was the woman who looked at him with big questioning eyes.

"Hope," he started.

"Yes?" She scooted along the backseat as close as she could get to him. The baby pig snuffled and followed her, his snout pushing beneath her arm until his head rested on her lap.

Colt cleared his throat, but before he could speak, he stepped in a steaming pile left by the Four-H Club and almost took a header.

"Colt!" Hope grabbed his coat and held on while he got his footing. And once he was keeping pace again, she prompted. "So you were saying?"

He took a deep breath and dove in. "Marry me, Hope."

Up ahead, the horn of the semi truck pulling the float blasted, drowning out his words.

"What?" Hope leaned closer. "What did you say?"

"He said, 'Larry needs soap,'" Rachel supplied on her way around the car.

"Larry?" Kenny Gene questioned. "Is that Larry Lines who lives south of Big Springs? Because he empties septic tanks for a livin', and soap ain't gonna get rid of that smell."

"He didn't say 'Larry needs soap,'" Harley jumped in. "He said, 'Ferry the boat.'"

"Well, what in the heck does that mean?" Rachel asked, on her way around the other side.

"I said, marry me Hope!" Colt blurted the words out as loudly as one of Hope's hog calls. It was quite a feat, considering he was still running. There was a long, painful silence before everyone around them burst out laughing.

"And you said you wasn't pullin' no prank!" Rachel executed a jerky figure eight. "Why that's the biggest joke I've heard in a while. Hope Scroggs marrying Colt Lomax." She shook her orange corkscrews while Kenny banged on the steering wheel.

"Whoo-wee, Colt, that was a good one. Especially when Hope must've had a hun-nerd marriage proposals in the last week, and she ain't accepted a one." Kenny glanced back, and his eyes scrunched up at the corners. "Come to think of it, the only one you did accept was Slate's."

"Kenny, Slate didn't ask Hope to marry him," Harley clarified. "Hope asked Slate to marry her, but it was too late because Faith had already beat her to it."

The words caused Colt to stumble, and he had to hang on to the car or end up face-planted in the asphalt. When he righted himself, he expected to see Hope looking as confused as he was. But instead her face was painfully pale.

"You asked Slate to marry you?" It was difficult to talk around the huge lump in his throat.

"No." She shook her head. "I didn't ask him."

"No, she's right," Rachel jumped in again. "She just accepted his non-proposal."

Stunned, Colt tried to keep up, not only with the car but with the conversation.

"You came back to marry Slate?"

Her mouth opened, and then closed, then opened again. "I was confused . . . after that night I didn't know . . ."

"Did you know about the baby then?" The words felt like sawdust in his mouth.

"No!" She shook her head. "I swear I didn't, Colt."

But it didn't make any difference. All along, he thought she'd come back to Bramble to attend her sister's wedding, when in reality, she had come back to Bramble to marry Slate—right after she'd screwed the poor Lomax kid.

His feet slowed, and the car pulled away from him.

"Colt!" Hope called back to him. "It wasn't like that! It was a mistake!"

It was a mistake, all right.

A mistake to think that the Sweetheart of Bramble would ever love him.

Chapter Twenty-seven

"COLT!" HOPE YELLED as loud as her hog-calling lungs would allow.

But he didn't pay any attention as he walked away, his back straight and his dark hair waving in the wind. And with a sinking heart, she realized he wasn't coming back.

Not now.

Not ever.

"What are you doing?" Faith leaned over. "Go after him."

"It won't make any difference." Hope blinked back her tears. "There's no way I can ever explain."

"So you're not even going to try?"

Hope shook her head as she turned back around. Sherman rooted against her, and she hugged him close as the tears dripped in cold streaks down her cheeks.

"Well." Faith sat back and released her breath in one long agitated huff. "I guess I didn't realize my sister was such a chicken shit."

Hope's head came up, and her eyes narrowed. "A what?"

"A chicken shit," Kenny Gene supplied.

Just that quickly, anger joined pain, and Hope shot

Kenny a mean glare before she turned on her sister. "Oh, you should talk. You ran off with your tail between your legs as soon as I hit town."

"Only because I thought you were pregnant and needed a father for your child." Faith glared back at her. "But you're right, I was a chicken shit, but at least I let you talk some sense into me. Unlike you, who is just going to sit there and let the father of your child walk right out of your life without your doing one thing to stop him."

Kenny stretched around. "Colt ain't the father of Hope's baby, Faith. The entire town is bettin' on Matthew McConaughey."

"Shut up, Kenny!" They both yelled in unison.

Shrugging, Kenny turned back around.

"In case you don't remember," Hope continued, "I *did* accept Slate's proposal."

"Non-proposal," Rachel Dean clarified before she quickly unicycled away.

Exasperated, Hope spoke through her teeth. "I accepted Slate's non-proposal."

"So what?" Faith shrugged as if her twin sister hadn't wanted to marry her husband. "You were just on the rebound after Colt. Besides, when you had the chance to have Slate all to yourself, you didn't take it. Instead, you came and got me."

"Except I wasn't exactly happy about it, and everyone in town knows it."

"Of course, you weren't. Your safety net had been jerked out from under you by a sister you didn't even know you had." Faith reached out and took her hand. "But you don't need a safety net, Hope. All you need is enough guts to take a chance—to just step out on the wire."

Suddenly Hope realized it wasn't such a bad thing to have a twin sister after all. "But after everything I've done, how am I going to make him believe that I never loved Slate like that? That it was always him?"

"I don't know," Faith said, and Hope's shoulders slumped before her sister continued. "But aren't you Hope Scroggs, and isn't this Bramble, Texas?"

"Meaning?"

Faith smiled with so much evil devilry that it would've made a Disney villain proud.

Anything Hope wants... Hope gets.

It took more than a few seconds for her sister's thoughts to sink in. But once they did, Hope didn't waste any time screaming at the top of her lungs.

"Kenny Gene! If you don't stop this car right now, I'm going to jump out and hurt myself and the twins too!"

The car jerked to a stop and, as soon as it did, Hope handed off Sherman to Faith and hopped out. Unfortunately, Colt was already a good half of a mile down the street. She thought about running after him, but she didn't have more than a few minutes before he reached Shirlene's SUV.

"Uncle Harley!" she yelled.

He zipped over in the Jeep. "What, Hope?"

"As your goddaughter, I've never asked for much."

"No, honey, you ain't."

"Well, I'm asking now. I need your car."

Harley pulled off his big old hat and scratched at a spot on his forehead, leaving streaks in the white face paint. "Now, honey, why would you want this little old car when you can ride in my big old Cadillac?"

Hope glanced back at Colt's sweet behind. "Because

the man I love is getting away, and I've got to go after him."

Harley's eyes widened. "Now, are you sure about this, honey? Colt might be a converted convict, but, I hear tell, he doesn't have a pot to pee in or a window to throw it out of."

"I don't care," she said. And it was the truth. She didn't care if they had to live out on Grover Road in a tiny trailer with a leaky roof. As long as she was with Colt, she'd be happy. "Please, Uncle Harley."

Since she rarely used the word *please,* it only took Harley a second for his mustache to twitch up in a smile. "Well, in that case, honey." He waved Kenny Gene over. "Kenny, come help me out of here. Hope needs to go get her man."

It turned out to be harder to drive the little car than Hope had anticipated. Of course, her coat and the ugly purple maid-of-honor dress that Cindy Lynn, the parade coordinator, had insisted she wear didn't help matters. She ran up on the sidewalk more than a few times, scattering people like a bunch of startled chickens. But that didn't stop them from hurrying after her. Nor did it stop word from traveling. By the time she reached Colt, she had most of the town running behind her, quickly followed by the people in the parade—including the band, the football float, the coach's truck, and the mayor's Cadillac.

"Colt!" Hope tooted the horn.

His steps faltered, but he refused to stop.

"Colt, wait!" She sped up and circled around him. He adjusted his stride, but didn't stop, forcing her to talk and drive at the same time.

"I didn't come home to marry Slate. I came home

because I was heartsick and confused. I thought I was over the bad boy of Bramble who gave me sweet kisses, and then five seconds later ran my bra up the flagpole."

"Tiniest little bit of lace I've ever seen," Rachel Dean said, as she wheeled her way up.

Ignoring her, Hope continued. "But all it took was one look from those beautiful gray eyes and I was thirteen again, begging for whatever scraps you'd toss my way. And when you left that morning without saying a word, I couldn't deal with the rejection. So I did what I've always done to save face—I came running back to Slate. Except Slate had moved on and found someone else."

Making another circle around him, she glanced up at his face. But it didn't look any more understanding than it had a few seconds ago. His eyes still stared straight ahead, and his jaw was still as tight as one of Harley's western shirts. Still, she continued, like the rambling lovesick fool she was.

"And at first, I was mad. Slate was my backup plan, someone I counted on to be there when my life didn't work out the way I wanted. And when he wasn't there, I pouted like the spoiled brat I am. It took a while to realize what a mistake it would've been to marry Slate when I love someone else. And even if that someone doesn't love me, I still should've had enough guts to let him know how I feel—to let the entire town know how I feel." She took a deep breath and yelled as loudly as she could. "I love you, Colt Lomax!"

Hope thought the revelation would make him stop—or at least falter—but Colt kept on going as if he hadn't heard her. Completely defeated, she took her foot off the pedal and let the little Jeep coast to a stop. The town slowed with her, although their mouths kept going.

"Who does Hope love?" Twyla asked.

"Colt, you idiot," Cindy Lynn jumped in.

"Hope loves Colt?" Kenny said. "Well, ain't that a shocker."

"Not really," Rachel Dean said, as she pedaled up. "Not after seeing his hand up her shirt in the elevator."

"Come to think of it," Ms. Murphy huffed her way into the group, "there were all those suspicious times I caught them in the bibliography section, supposedly doing research for book reports."

"And there was that one time that I caught them beneath the bleachers," Sue Ellen offered. "And it didn't look like kissin' was the only thing going on."

"Well, well." Harley hooked his thumbs in his clown suspenders. "It seems we've solved the mystery of who impregnated our little Hope." He pointed at Sheriff Winslow, who had pulled up in his squad car. "Go get him, Sam."

"No!" Hope tried to stop him, but the siren drowned out her voice. And before she could even climb out of the Jeep, Sam had pulled up in front of Colt. She figured Colt was going to put up a fight, but instead he turned and walked back toward her, although he looked as angry as the sky above him.

"Now what exactly is goin' on here?" Shirlene said as she sashayed into the group.

"Colt asked Hope to marry him," Kenny stated with a broad smile on his face. "But then someone opened their big mouth and told him about her accepting Slate's proposal."

"Non-proposal," Rachel injected, as she whizzed around the group.

Shirlene got the gist and took over. "And I guess my big brother tapped into his stubborn streak and refuses to listen. Well," she shrugged, "I guess there's only one thing left to do." She glanced around the crowd until her gaze landed on Hope's daddy. "Burl, go get your gun."

"What?" Both Hope and Colt stared at Shirlene, but she only stared back with an innocence that didn't bode well.

"What else do you expect us to do? Our little Hope is knocked up, and if my ornery brother is the one who's responsible, then he needs to step up to the plate—or should I say the altar."

"Shirlene," Colt spoke through his teeth, "what the hell do you think you're doing?"

Her head tipped. "Are you saying that Pumpkin Seed isn't your baby?"

"Pumpkin Seed?" Rachel asked, as she continued to ride the unicycle as if she was competing for a Guinness world record. "Who's Pumpkin Seed?"

"Colt and Hope's baby," Faith supplied, as she struggled to control a wiggling pig. "Isn't that right, Hope?"

At that moment, Hope had a choice. She could deny it and spend the rest of her days without Colt, or she could accept what the town had given her and run with it.

Tipping up her chin, Hope took two steps closer to Colt. So close she could see the tiny specks of green in his gray irises.

"Yes. The baby's Colt's."

"Get my gun, Jenna," Hope's daddy said, not sounding the least bit angry.

Colt's eyes narrowed. "That's it? You're going to let your daddy force me into marrying you at gunpoint?"

She swallowed hard. "If that's what it takes to keep you, Colt Lomax, I sure as heck am. Especially considering you already asked me."

"I asked you before I knew about Slate."

"Well, too bad. You can't take it back now."

Hope tried to stare down his angry glare, but her nerves got the best of her and her knees started to shake uncontrollably. Especially when her mother returned with the gun and handed it to her grinning father.

"You can put the gun away, Burl," Colt said, his gaze never leaving Hope. "I'm not marrying Hope at gunpoint. No one can force me to do that."

Hope pressed her lips together and tried to act like her heart wasn't breaking. "I didn't expect that they could." Tears continued to form in her eyes until her vision was nothing but a watery blur. Which was why it took her a moment to realize that Colt was no longer standing in front of her.

"Hope Marie Scroggs."

Her gaze dropped down to the man who knelt on one knee. She brushed the tears from her eyes and looked again. But he was still there, his beloved gray eyes staring straight at her.

"I love you. And because of that love, I couldn't stay here and watch you marry Slate. So I left. But it didn't help. Because wherever I roamed, my thoughts were never far away from the Sweetheart of Bramble. I know I probably don't deserve you, but damned if I care. Marry me, Hope."

Unable to speak with the emotions clogging her throat, Hope flopped down on his knee and covered his face in kisses. When she pulled back, he was smiling.

"Yes," she breathed. "I'll marry you."

The townsfolk let out a rousing cheer. But the cheer fizzled when Rachel's cousin, Bear, shoved his way through the crowd, pushing a handsome man in front of him.

"I did it! I found him!" Bear beamed with pride, tobacco juice seeping from his wide grin.

For the first time in Bramble history, the townsfolk were struck speechless. Everyone just stood there staring as if they couldn't quite believe their eyes. Of course, it didn't take long for Kenny to find his voice.

"Well, hey, Matthew. Welcome to Bramble."

Epilogue

IT WAS A DREAM. It had to be. Where else but in a dream could you stand in front of a church filled to the rafters with all your family and friends and whisper your vows to the handsome outlaw you've loved for all your life? An outlaw who kissed you as if his life depended on it before he strolled you down the aisle and off to the town hall, where he fed you strawberry soda from his Solo cup and Josephine's Raspberry Jamboree Cake from his fingers, and sweet kisses from his lips before taking you in his strong arms and waltzing you toward happily-ever-after.

It was a dream.

Her dream.

"Hey, Hog!" Kenny Gene waltzed by with Twyla. "Is it true that you and Colt are buildin' a house out by Sutter Springs?"

"'Course it's true," Rachel Dean said, as she tromped by in the arms of Rossie Owens. "You can't expect a Hollywood movie star to live with her mama and daddy forever. Especially when she's got a husband and a couple babies on the way."

Hope ignored the conversation and snuggled back into her dream.

"Maybe I should start referring to the baby as Pumpkin Seeds." A deep, familiar voice rumbled above her head.

With a sigh of contentment, Hope pulled back and stared up at her handsome husband, who looked as sexy as a movie star in his crisp white tuxedo shirt. The black bow tie had long since been stripped off and the first few studs opened, so it was no trouble at all to slip her hand inside and touch all that smooth warm skin.

Preoccupied with the hollow at the base of his throat, it took her a while to answer. "I'm not having twins."

"And just what makes you think that?" Colt adjusted his hands on her waist so his thumbs could gently stroke her rounding belly. "Seeing as how the ultrasound isn't until next week."

"Call it woman's intuition—or just a strong feeling." Her fingers trailed along the edge of his collar, over his broad shoulder, down his hard biceps to his tattooed forearm. With his sleeve cuffed almost to his elbow, she was able to trace a fingernail along most of the rattlesnake. "Have I told you how sexy I think your tat is?"

"You might've mentioned it." There was a trace of humor in his voice.

"Of course, I could do without the pig."

The words were barely out of her mouth before Colt reached down and tipped her chin up. His eyes were heartbreakingly serious.

"Never. I'm never getting rid of my Homecoming Hog. Not in this lifetime or the next. And we better get that straight right here and now, Mrs. Lomax."

His words brought a brilliant smile to her face and a happy flutter to her stomach. She stretched up on her toes and gave him a kiss that ended the conversation for a good while. When she pulled back, she cradled his face in her hands, the two-carat diamond engagement ring flashing like the disco ball overhead.

"You spent too much money on the ring," she sighed.

Colt placed a kiss in her palm. "Please don't tell me, you *still* believe I'm broke."

She had, until she googled *Desperado Customs*. Then she sat in stunned silence staring at page after page of information about a certain motorcycle bum who had made it big.

Hope lowered her hands to his shoulders. "I'm sorry. I should've believed you. I guess I just didn't want to think you had made it when I had failed."

"Failed?" He shook his head. "Didn't you hear what Rachel Dean said? To the people of Bramble, you're a movie star—a movie star wealthy enough to pay for our house."

"A house way too big for just three people?"

"Three people," he sent her a sexy wink, "with more to come."

She tipped her head and shot him a sassy look. "So you plan on keeping me barefoot and pregnant, Colt Lomax?"

"Not barefoot." Colt glanced down at the pretty pink boots he'd given her as a wedding present.

"Well," she shrugged, "I can't say as I mind having a houseful of kids, as long as in between having babies I can go back to school to prepare myself for my next contest."

"Hog-callin' or pie-eatin'?" he said with a devilish grin.

"How about politickin'?"

For an answer, he swept her up in his arms and headed for the door.

"Colt Lomax, what are you doing?" she asked, not the least bit upset to find herself snuggled against his warm chest.

"I'm taking you to bed, Hog. If I'm going to be married to the next mayor of Bramble, I need to get while the gettin's good."

She giggled as the townsfolk took note of their departure.

"Hey, now," Harley yelled. "We aren't finished yet. I still need to make my speech."

"I'm sure it will keep, Harley," Colt said as he weaved around the tables.

"But you haven't throwed the bouquet." Twyla hurried after them, holding out the ugly silk arrangement.

Noticing Shirlene standing in one corner, Hope reached out and snagged it, heaving it as far as she could. The bouquet sailed through the air straight at Shirlene, who was forced to reach up and catch it or end up clocked in the head with five pounds of hot glue.

"Oh, no." Shirlene immediately dropped the flowers and shook her head.

"Too late, Shirl," Hope said, and sent her an evil smile. "You already caught it."

"She's right," Faith added, as she leaned over and picked up the bouquet. "Besides, who knows what waits for you just around the corner?"

"Trouble." Shirlene jerked the bouquet out of her hand. "No doubt, nothing but trouble."

Then Colt swept out the door, and Shirlene and Faith

were swallowed up by the herd of townsfolk who followed behind them. Beneath the town hall flagpole, an old Harley Knucklehead waited with a new custom seat Colt had made especially for two and a string of plastic baby bottles attached to the rusted back fender, along with a sign that read "Hitched Just In Time."

While Darla handed out the small bundles of birdseed and the townsfolk tried to figure out how to get the hot-glued pieces of tulle open, Colt slipped Hope's helmet on and snapped it beneath her chin.

"You sure you wouldn't rather drive away in my Escalade?"

Hope adjusted the helmet. "An Escalade when I just married a motorcycle bum? Not a chance."

Colt flashed her one of his smiles, which recently seemed to be getting more and more frequent, and then helped her into his leather jacket. It took some sweat and more than a few kicks to get the Knucklehead started, but finally the engine caught and throbbed to life as Colt hopped on and twisted the throttle.

Once he was satisfied, he helped her on and secured her hands around his waist before leaning back to ask, "So what's the plan?"

Snuggled up against his back, Hope contemplated the question before she rested her chin on his shoulder and whispered in his ear.

"To live happily ever after."

As the motorcycle eased down the sidewalk and off the curb, the townsfolk hurried after them, the unopened birdseed bundles still clutched in their hands.

"Well, who would've thunk it," Rachel Dean said as

she dabbed at the corners of her eyes with the sleeve of her Sunday-best dress.

"Makes sense," Harley replied, hitching up his pants. "Shoulda known our little Hope wouldn't fall for some foreigner from California."

"Though Matthew was awful understandin' about the mistake," Cindy Lynn said. "And he is from Austin."

"Austin's nice," Kenny Gene stated. "But there's no place better than Bramble."

There was a chorus of "sure ain't" as the Bad Boy of Bramble disappeared into the night with his sweetheart.

Chapter One

IF YOU THINK MY TRUCK IS BIG...

Faith Aldridge did a double take, but the bold black letters of the bumper sticker remained the same. Appalled, she read through the rest of the signs plastered on the tail end of the huge truck: DON'T MESS WITH TEXAS; REBEL BORN AND REBEL BRED AND WHEN I DIE I'LL BE REBEL DEAD; I LIVE BY THE THREE B'S: BEER, BRAWLS AND BROADS; CRUDE RUNS THROUGH MY VEINS.

She could agree with the last one. Whoever drove the mammoth-sized vehicle *was* crude. And arrogant. And chauvinistic. And a perfect example of the rednecks her aunt Jillian had warned her about. Not that her aunt Jillian had ever met a redneck, but she'd seen Jeff Foxworthy on television. And that was enough to make her fear for her niece's safety when traveling in a state filled with punch lines for the statement—

You might be a redneck if...

You have a bumper sticker that refers to the size of your penis.

The front tire of her Volvo hit yet another pothole,

pulling her attention away from the bumper stickers and back to her quest for an empty parking space. There was no defined parking in the small dirt lot but, even without painted lines, the occupants of the bar had formed fairly neat rows. All except for the crude redneck whose truck was blatantly parked on the sidewalk by the front door.

Someone should report him to the police.

Someone who wasn't intimidated by law enforcement officers and didn't worry about criminal retaliation.

Faith found an empty space at the very end of the lot and started to pull in when she noticed the beat-up door on the Ford Taurus next to her. Pulling back out, she inched closer to the cinder block wall, then turned off the car, unhooked her seat belt, and grabbed her purse from beneath her seat.

Ignoring the trembling in her hands, she pulled out the tube of lip gloss she'd purchased at a drugstore in Oklahoma City. But it was harder to ignore the apprehensive blue eyes that stared back at her from the tiny lit mirror on the visor. Harder, but not impossible. She liberally coated her lips with the glistening fuchsia of Passion Fruit, a color that didn't match her plain brown turtleneck or her conservative beige pants. Or even the bright red high heels she'd gotten at a Payless ShoeSource in Amarillo when she'd stopped for lunch.

A strong gust of warm wind whipped the curls around Faith's face as she stepped out of the car. She brushed back her hair and glanced up. Only a few wispy clouds marred the deep blue of the September sky. Still, it might be a good idea to get her jacket from the suitcase in the trunk, just in case it got colder when the sun went down. Of course, she didn't plan on staying at the bar past dark.

In fact, she didn't plan on staying at the bar at all. Just long enough to get some answers.

After closing the door, she pushed the button on her keychain twice until the Volvo beeped. Then, a few feet away, she pushed it again just to be sure. One of her fellow computer programmers said she had OCD—Overly Cautious Disorder. Her coworker was probably right. Although there was nothing cautious about walking into a bar filled with men who paraded their egomaniacal thoughts on the bumpers of their trucks. But she didn't have a choice. At seven o'clock on a Saturday night, this was the only place she'd found open in the small town.

As Faith walked past the truck parked by the door, she couldn't help but stare. Up close it looked bigger...and much dirtier. Mud clung to the huge, deep-treaded tires, hung like stalactites from the fender wells, splattered over the faded red paint and blotchy gray primer of the door, and flecked the side window. A window her head barely reached. And in the heels, she was a good five-foot-five inches. Well, maybe not five inches. Maybe closer to four. But it was still mind-boggling that a vehicle could be jacked up to such heights.

What kind of a brute owned it, anyway? Obviously, the kind who thought it went with his large penis. The kind who didn't think it was overkill to have not one, but two huge flags (one American and the other who knew) hanging limply from poles on either side of the back window. A back window that displayed a decal of a little cartoon boy peeing on the Toyota symbol, two blue-starred football helmet stickers, and a gun rack with one empty slot.

Faith froze.

On second thought, maybe she wouldn't ask questions

at this bar. Maybe she would drive down the main street again and try to find some other place open. Someplace that didn't serve alcohol to armed patrons. Someplace where she wouldn't end up Rebel Dead. Not that she was even close to being a rebel. Standing in the parking lot of Bootlegger's Bar in Bramble, Texas, was the most rebellious thing she'd ever done in her life. If she had a bumper sticker, it would read: CONFORMIST BORN, CONFORMIST BRED, AND WHEN SHE DIES SHE'LL BE CONFORMIST DEAD. But she just didn't want to be Conformist Dead yet.

Unfortunately, before she could get back to the leather-upholstered security of her Volvo, the battered door of the bar opened and two men walked out. Not walked, exactly. More like strutted—in wide felt cowboy hats and tight jeans with large silver belt buckles as big as brunch plates.

Faith ducked back behind the monster truck, hoping they'd walk past without noticing her. Except the sidewalk was as uneven as the parking lot and one pointy toe of her high heel got caught in a crack, forcing her to grab on to the tailgate or end up with her nose planted in the pavement. And as soon as her fingers hit the cold metal, an alarm went off—a loud howling that raised the hairs on her arms and had her stumbling back, praying that at least one of the men was packing so he could shoot the thing that had just risen up from the bed of the truck.

"For cryin' out loud, Buster. Shut up." One of the men shouted over the earsplitting noise.

The howling stopped as quickly as it had started. Shaken, Faith could only stare at the large, four-legged creature. With its mouth closed, the dog didn't look threatening as much as . . . cute. Soulful brown eyes looked back at her from a woolly face. While she recovered from her scare, it ambled over to the end of the truck and leaned its head out.

Faith stepped back. She wasn't good with dogs. Or cats, gerbils, birds, hamsters, or fish. Pretty much anything living. She had a rabbit once, but after only three months in her care, it died of a nervous condition.

"Hope?"

The name spoken by the tall, lean cowboy with the warm coffee-colored skin caused her stomach to drop, and she swiveled around to look behind her.

No one was there.

"Baby, is that you?" The man's Texas twang was so thick that it seemed contrived.

Faith started to shake her head, but he let out a whoop and had her in his arms before she could accomplish it. She was whirled around in a circle against his wiry body before he tossed her over to his friend, who had a soft belly and a chest wide enough to land a 747.

"Welcome home, Little Bit." The large man gave her a rough smack on the lips, the whiskers of his mustache and goatee tickling. He pulled back, and his blue eyes narrowed. "What the hell did you do to your hair?"

"She cut it, you idiot." With a contagious grin, the lean cowboy reached out and ruffled her hair. "That's what all them Hollywood types do. Cut off their crownin' glory like it's nothin' more than tangled fishin' line." He cocked his head. "But I guess it don't look so bad. It's kinda cute in a short, ugly kinda way. And I like the color. What's that called—streakin'?"

The man who still held her in his viselike grip grinned, tobacco juice seeping from the corner of his mouth. "No, Kenny, that's what we did senior year."

"Right." Kenny's dark eyes twinkled. "But it's like streakin'. Tintin'? Stripin'? Highlightin'! That's it!" He whacked her on the back so hard she wondered if he'd cracked a rib. "Shirlene did that. But it don't look as good as yours. She looked a little like a polecat when it was all said and done. Does she know you're back? Hot damn, she's gonna shit a brick when she sees you. She's missed you a lot."

His eyes lost some of their twinkle. "Of course, we all have. But especially Slate." He grabbed her arm and tugged her toward the door. "I can't wait to see his face when he sees you. Of course, he ain't real happy right now. The Dawgs lost last night—twenty-one to seven— but I'm sure you'll put an end to his depression."

Faith barely listened to the man's constant chatter as he dragged her through the door and into the dark, smoky depths of the bar. She felt light-headed, and emotion crept up the back of her throat. Did they really look so much alike that these men couldn't tell the difference? It made sense, but it was still hard to absorb. All this time, she thought she was an only child and to realize...

"Here." Kenny slapped his black cowboy hat down on her head and tipped it forward. "We don't want to start a stampede until Slate gets to see you. Not that anyone would recognize you in that getup." He shook his head as his gaze slid down her body to the tips of her high heels. "Please don't tell me you got rid of your boots, Hope. Gettin' rid of all that gorgeous hair's bad enough."

Faith opened her mouth with every intention of telling him she never owned a pair of western boots to get rid of, or had long gorgeous hair, for that matter. But before she could, he tucked her under his arm and dragged her past the long bar and around the crowded dance floor with his friend following obediently behind.

"So how's Hollywood treatin' ya?" Kenny yelled over the loud country music, then waved a hand at a group of women who called out his name. "It's been way too long since you came for a visit. But I bet you've been busy knockin' them Hollywood directors on their butts. Nobody can act like our little Hope. You flat killed me when you was Annie in *Annie Get Your Gun*. Of course, you did almost kill Colt—not that I blame you since he was the one who switched out that blank with live ammo. But the crowd sure went crazy when you shot out them stage lights. I still get chills just thinkin' about it."

Chills ran through Faith's body as well. Hollywood? Actor? Live ammo? Her mind whirled with the information she'd received in such a short span of time.

"Yep, things sure ain't been the same without you. I can barely go into Josephine's Diner without gettin' all misty-eyed. 'Course those onions Josie fries up will do that to a person. Still, nobody serves up chicken-fried steak as pretty as you did. Rachel Dean is a nice old gal, but them man hands of hers can sure kill an appetite."

Kenny glanced down at her, then stopped so suddenly his friend ran into him from behind. From beneath the wide brim of her hat, she watched his dark brows slide together.

"Hey, what's the matter with you, anyway? How come you're lettin' me haul you around without cussin' me up one side and down the other?"

Probably because Faith didn't cuss—up one side *or* down the other. And because she wasn't a pretty wait-ress who was brave enough to get on stage and perform in front of a crowd of people. Or move away from the familiarity of home for the bright lights of Hollywood.

Hollywood.

Hope was in Hollywood.

For a second, Faith felt an overwhelming surge of disappointment, but it was quickly followed by the realization that all the hundreds of miles traveled had not been in vain. This was where Hope had grown up. And where Faith would find answers to some of the questions that had plagued her for the last year.

Except once Kenny found out she wasn't Hope, she probably wouldn't get any more answers. She'd probably be tossed out of the bar without even a "y'all come back now, ya hear." She'd become a stranger. An uppity easterner with a weird accent, chopped-off ugly hair, and not one pair of cowboy boots to her name. A person who was as far from the popular Hometown Hope he'd described as Faith's Volvo was from the redneck's truck.

But what choice did she have? She had never been good at lying. Besides, once she opened her mouth, the truth would be out. Unless…unless she didn't open her mouth. Unless she kept her mouth shut and let everyone assume what they would. It wouldn't be a lie exactly, more of a fib. And fibs were okay, as long as they didn't hurt anyone. And who could possibly get hurt if she allowed these people to think she was someone else for just a little while longer?

Hope wasn't there.

And Faith wouldn't be, either, after tonight.

Swallowing down the last of her reservations, she tapped her throat and mouthed, "Laryngitis."

Those deep eyes grew more puzzled. "Huh?"

"My throat," she croaked in barely a whisper.

His brows lifted. "Oh! Your throat's hoarse. Well, that explains it." He gathered her back against his side and started moving again. "For a second, I thought I had someone else in my arms besides Miss Hog Caller of Haskins County five years runnin'." He chuckled deep in his chest. "'Course, Slate's gonna love this. He always said you talked too much."

"Hey, Kenny! What ya got there?" A skinny man stepped off the dance floor with a young woman in a tight T-shirt with the words "Keepin' It Country" stretched across her large breasts and an even tighter pair of jeans that pushed up a roll of white flesh over her tooled leather belt.

"None of your damned beeswax, Fletch." Kenny winked at the young woman. "Hey, Twyla."

She scowled. "I thought you was goin' home, Kenny Gene."

"I was, darlin', but I have to take care of something first."

"I got eyes, Kenny. And if this is the somethin' you need to take care of, then don't be callin' me to go to the homecomin' game with you. I got other plans."

"Now don't be gettin' all bent out of shape, honey," Kenny yelled at the woman's retreating back. "Man, that gal's got a temper," he chuckled. "Almost as bad as yours."

Faith didn't have a temper. At least not one anyone had witnessed.

"Now don't go and ruin the surprise, Hope. Let me do all the talkin'." He shot her a weak grin. "Sorry, I forgot about your voice. Man, is Slate gonna be surprised."

For the first time since allowing this man to take

charge of her life, Faith started to get worried. Surprises weren't always well received. Her mother had dropped a surprise a few months before she passed away, a surprise Faith was still trying to recover from.

But this was different. It sounded like this Slate and Hope had been good friends. He would probably whoop like Kenny had done, give her a big hug and possibly a little more razor burn—and hopefully a lot more information before she made her excuses and slipped out the door.

And no one would be the wiser. Except maybe Hope, if she came home before Faith found her. But that wouldn't happen. Faith had every intention of finding Hope as soon as possible. She might not be a rebel, but she was tenacious.

Tenacious but more than a little scared when Kenny pulled her inside a room with two pool tables, a gaggle of cowboy hats, and a sea of blue denim. The light in the room was better but the smoke thicker. The music softer but the conversation louder. They hesitated by the door for a few seconds as Kenny looked around; then Faith was hauled across the room to the far table where a man in a crumpled straw cowboy hat had just leaned over to take a shot.

Faith had barely taken note of the strong hand and lean forearm that stretched out of the rolled-up sleeve of the blue western shirt before Kenny whipped the hat off her head and pushed her forward.

"Lookie what the cat drug in, Slate!"

The loud conversation came to a dead halt, along with Faith's breath as every eye turned to her. But she wasn't overly concerned with the other occupants of the room. Only with the man who lifted his head, then froze with his fingers steepled over the skinny end of the pool cue. He remained that way for what seemed like hours. Or what seemed like hours to a woman whose knees had suddenly turned as limp as her hat hair.

Someone coughed, and slowly, he lifted his hand from the table and unfolded his body.

He was tall. At least, he looked tall to a woman who wasn't over five foot four in heels. His chest wasn't big enough to land a 747 on but it looked solid enough to hold up a weak-kneed woman. It tapered down to smooth flat cotton tucked into a leather belt minus the huge buckle. His jeans weren't tight or pressed with a long crease like most of the men in the room; instead the soft well-worn denim molded to his body, defining his long legs, muscular thighs, and slim hips.

The hand that wasn't holding the cue stick lifted to push the misshaped sweat-stained cowboy hat back on his high forehead, and a pair of hazel eyes stared back at her—a mixture of rich browns and deep greens. The eyes sat above a long, slim nose that boasted a tiny white scar across the bridge and a mouth that was almost too perfect to belong to a man. It wasn't too wide or too small, the top lip peaking nicely over the full bottom.

The corners hitched up in a smile.

"Hog?"

Hog?

Her mind was still trying to deal with the raw sensuality of the man who stood before her; there was no way it could deal with the whole "hog" thing. Especially when the man leaned his pool cue against the edge of the table and took a step toward her.

She prepared herself for the loud whoop and the rough

manhandling that would follow. But what she was not prepared for was the gentleness of the fingers that slid through her hair, or the coiled strength of the hand that pulled her closer, or the heat of the body that pressed up against hers. And she was definitely not prepared for the soft lips that swooped down to bestow a kiss.

It wasn't a long kiss or even a deep one. It was merely a touch. A teasing brush. A sweep of sweet, moist flesh against startled gloss. But it was enough. Enough to cause Faith's heart to bang against her ribs and her breath to leave her lungs.

Wow.

Her hands came up and pressed against the hard wall of his chest in an effort to balance her suddenly tipsy world. Her eyelids, which she hadn't even realized she'd closed, fluttered open. Unlike her, he didn't look passion-drugged. Just cocky and confident.

"Don't tell me I left you speechless, darlin'." The words drizzled off his tongue like honey off a spoon, with very little twang and a whole lot of southern sizzle.

She swallowed hard as Kenny spoke.

"She can't talk. She's got that there lar-in-gitis, probably from all that actin' she's been doin'."

A smirk a mile wide spread across Slate's devastating, handsome face. "Is that so? Well now, ain't that an interesting state of affairs."

"Who cares if she can talk, Coach." A man behind him yelled. "You call that a welcome-home kiss?"

Two other men joined in.

"Yeah, Slate, I kiss my cousin better than that."

"That's 'cause you're married to her."

"And you got a problem with that?"

"Shut up, you two," Kenny said. "Come on, Slate, remind her of what she's been missin' out on. Give her the good stuff."

A look of resignation entered those hazel eyes, a strange bedfellow for the dazzling grin. "Sorry, Hog," he whispered, right before he dipped his head for another taste. Except, this time, his lips were slightly parted, and the soft kiss brought with it the promise of wet heat.

If it hadn't been a year since she'd been kissed, she probably could've ignored the tremor that raced through her body and the zing that almost incinerated her panties. But it had been a year, a year filled with loss, pain, and revelation. A year that made a cautious conformist want to be something different. Something more like an arrogant rebel, Miss Hog Caller of Haskins County, or Annie Oakley with a loaded gun.

Or just a woman who gave a handsome cowboy a kiss he wouldn't forget anytime soon.

With a moan, she threw her arms around his neck, knocking off his cowboy hat and forcing him to stumble back a step. A chorus of whoops and whistles erupted, but didn't faze her one-track mind. Not when his lips opened wider, offering up all the good stuff. Teetering on the tiptoes of her high heels, she drove her fingers up into the silky waves of his hair, encasing his head and angling it so she had better access to the wet heat of his mouth. She dipped her tongue inside and sipped and tasted. But it still wasn't enough.

She wanted to consume this man. Wanted to slide her fingers over every square inch of fevered skin and sculptured muscles. Wanted to press her nose into the spot between his neck and shoulder and fill her lungs to capacity with the smoky laundry-detergent scent of him. But most of all, she wanted to stare into the rich fertile earth and endless sea of his eyes and see a reflection of her own desires—her own wants and needs.

Slowly, her eyes drifted open.

But it wasn't desire she saw in the hazel depths. And it wasn't cocky satisfaction. This time, it looked more like stunned disbelief. Obviously, Slate's relationship with Hope didn't involve sexual assault.

Stunned by her uncharacteristic behavior, Faith pulled away from his lips and dropped back down to her heels. What had she been thinking? Had she lost her mind? How could she throw herself at a complete stranger? And not just any complete stranger, but Hope's close friend? Her gaze settled on those perfect lips—lips that were slightly parted, wet, and smeared with glittery Passion Fruit—and it became crystal clear why she had lost her mind. The man was beyond hot. He was one sizzling stick of yummy, and she was a deprived child with a sweet tooth.

"Thatta way, Hope," a man on the other side of the pool table yelled. "You can take the girl out of the country but you can't take the country out of the girl!"

"Ooooo—wee, Coach! It looks like you was missed," someone else joined in.

"Does this mean you're stayin', Little Bit?" Kenny's friend stepped closer.

"Stayin'?" A voice came from the back. "With enthusiasm like that, I wouldn't let that woman out of my sight!"

"Is that true, Slate?" Kenny asked. "You gonna let Hope go back to Hollywood after that kind of greetin'?"

Slate blinked. Once. Twice. Three times. Slowly, the

shock receded from his eyes, but his shoulders remained tense. He cleared his throat twice before he spoke, but it still didn't sound as smooth or confident as it had.

"Well, I guess that depends."

"Depends on what?" someone asked.

"On whether or not she still likes me after she finds out I let The Plainsville Panthers whup our butts."

The room erupted in laughter, followed quickly with grumbled comments about hometown refs. Then a man with a huge belly and an even bigger handlebar mustache pushed his way over.

"All right, you've had your turn, Slate. Give someone else a chance to welcome our girl home."

For a fraction of a second, those hazel eyes narrowed, and the hands at her waist tightened. But then he released her and she was passed from one big bear hug to the next, accompanied with the greeting "Welcome home, Hope."

She wasn't Hope.

But, strangely enough, it felt like home.

THE DISH

Where authors give you the inside scoop!

♥ ♥ ♥ ♥ ♥ ♥ ♥ ♥ ♥ ♥ ♥ ♥ ♥ ♥ ♥ ♥ ♥

From the desk of Jami Alden

Dear Reader,

Whenever I start a new project, people inevitably ask me, "What's it about?" With BEG FOR MERCY, my answer seemed simple. This book is about Megan Flynn's desperate quest to get her wrongfully convicted brother off death row before he's executed. It's about a woman who is so determined she'll risk anything: her heart, when she begs Detective Cole Williams, the man who broke her heart when he arrested her brother, for help as she tracks down the real killer. And her life, when she herself becomes the target of a brutal killer's twisted desires.

But as I got further into Megan and Cole's journey, I realized that's *not* really what this book is about. Scratch beneath the surface, and you'll see that this book is really about faith. Not necessarily the religious kind, but the kind of faith you have in the people you love. It's also about the faith you have in yourself, in your gut, your instincts—whatever you want to call it. It's about listening to yourself and the truth that you cannot deny, even when the rest of the world tries to convince you that you're wrong.

No matter the evidence that points to her brother's guilt, Megan knows, deep down in her core, that her brother is not capable of the kind of brutal murder for which he was convicted. Nothing will convince her otherwise, her belief in her brother's innocence and faith in his true nature is absolutely unshakable.

It's so strong that it can even convince a skeptic like by the book, just the facts ma'am Detective Cole Williams to put aside everything he thinks he knows about this case. It will drive him to risk a career that means everything to him in order to help the woman he loves.

Megan and Cole's journey to happily ever after isn't an easy one, but nothing worth having comes easily. I hope you enjoy their story, and as you read, ask yourself, how deep is your faith in yourself and the people around you? How far would you go for someone you love?

Enjoy!

Jami Alden

www.jamialden.com
www.facebook.com/jamialden
twitter @jamialden

♥ ♥ ♥ ♥ ♥ ♥ ♥ ♥ ♥ ♥ ♥ ♥ ♥ ♥ ♥

From the desk of Carolyn Jewel

Dear Reader,

Paisley Nichols, the heroine of MY DANGEROUS
PLEASURE, is living her dream. She owns a bakery in
San Francisco's financial district, and she's making a go
of it. It's hard work and long hours, but she loves what
she does. I had some real life inspiration for her character. When I was a kid, my mother baked from scratch;
bread, cinnamon rolls, and delicious cookies, which my
siblings and I took for granted. It wasn't until much later
in life that I realized that not every mother baked like
that. Now I bake goodies for my son, and if I have to
taste test what I bake, well, that's a sacrifice I'm willing
to make.

My youngest brother worked as a pastry chef for a
while (he now does catering on the side) and there was
a time when he was training when he'd drive up from
Santa Barbara where he lived, spend the weekend at our
house, bake up a storm, and leave us with a refrigerator
full of whatever he was practicing at the time; crème
brûlée, chocolate souffle, chocolate mousse, and what
have you. When he got married, the restaurant threw a
party for him, and if you've never been around a slew of
professional chefs, let me tell you, you are missing out on
great food and lots of fun.

With my brother as an example, I got more ambitious

with my own baking. He taught me that quality ingredients make an enormous difference in the outcome, but there are also any number of little tips and tricks that get left out of many recipes that can transform a dessert from great to amazing or from decent looking to professional looking. For example, when making pie crust, use ice water, not room temperature water. Not even the *Joy of Cooking* mentions that crucial fact. Suddenly, my pie crusts were a success! I've also picked up and shared lots of recipes and tips from people on Twitter (I'm @cjewel).

Lest you think my story is nothing but sweetness and 70% (or higher) pure cocoa chocolate, Iskander, the demon hero of MY DANGEROUS PLEASURE, has a very dark side to him. He's been tasked with keeping Paisley safe from the mage who's stalking her, and when she develops some unusual magical abilities, his job gets even more difficult. There are people after them both, and they aren't very nice. But in between the enslaved demons and magic-using humans chasing them, Paisley and Iskander do find the time and place to indulge themselves with delicious sweets and each other.

Enjoy!

carolyn jewel

www.carolynjewel.com

♥ ♥ ♥ ♥ ♥ ♥ ♥ ♥ ♥ ♥ ♥ ♥ ♥ ♥ ♥

From the desk of Laurel McKee

Dear Reader,

I have a confession to make—I am totally addicted to dark, brooding, tortured heroes with complicated pasts! I blame *Jane Eyre*. This is still one of my all-time favorite books, and I first came across it when I was ten or eleven years old. It was a battered, old paperback copy from a box of books from a garage sale, and I stayed up all night reading it. I was shocked by the wife in the attic! And when I had finished, I started reading it all over again. I then snatched up every Gothic romance I could find. I guess I've never gotten over the "Mr. Rochester thing."

When I started writing the second book in The Daughters of Erin series, DUCHESS OF SIN, I had planned for Sir Grant Dunmore to be part of a love triangle in the story, who would probably die in the end. But as I wrote his scenes, he showed me that he was much more complicated than that. His scenes with Caroline seemed to take on a life of their own, and I wanted to find out more about him. I wanted to see what would happen between Grant and Caroline and where their unexpected attraction would take them. The answer became LADY OF SEDUCTION. And their passion for each other caused a *lot* of trouble for them, and fun for me!

I've loved spending time with the Blacknall sisters and their heroes, and I'm sorry to say good-bye to them in this book. But I'm very happy they've all found their happy-ever-afters. For excerpts, behind-the-book information on the history of this era, and some fun extras, you can visit my website at http://laurelmckee.net.

And if you'd like to put together your own Irish feast, here is a recipe for one of my favorite dishes—Shepherd's Pie! (The first two books featured Irish Soda Bread and Sticky Toffee Pudding, all great when served with a Guinness...)

Ingredients

- 1½ lbs ground round beef
- 1 onion chopped
- 1–2 cups vegetables—chopped carrots, corn, peas
- 1½–2 lbs potatoes (3 big ones)
- 8 tablespoons butter (1 stick)
- ½ cup beef broth
- 1 teaspoon Worcestershire sauce
- Salt, pepper, other seasonings of choice

1 Peel and quarter potatoes, boil in salted water until tender (about 20 minutes).
2 While the potatoes are cooking, melt 4 tablespoons butter (½ a stick) in large frying pan.
3 Sauté onions in butter until tender over medium heat (10 mins). If you are adding vegetables, add them according to cooking time. Put any carrots in with the onions. Add corn or peas either at the end of the cooking of the onions, or after the meat has initially cooked.

4 Add ground beef and sauté until no longer pink. Add salt and pepper. Add Worcesterchire sauce. Add half a cup of beef broth and cook, uncovered, over low heat for 10 minutes, adding more beef broth as necessary to keep moist.

5 Mash potatoes in bowl with remainder of butter, season to taste.

6 Place beef and onions in baking dish. Distribute mashed potatoes on top. Rough up with a fork so that there are peaks that will brown nicely. You can use the fork to make some designs in the potatoes as well.

7 Cook in 400 degree oven until bubbling and brown (about 30 minutes). Broil for last few minutes if necessary to brown.

Serves four.

Enjoy!

Laurel McKee

♥ ♥ ♥ ♥ ♥ ♥ ♥ ♥ ♥ ♥ ♥ ♥ ♥ ♥

From the desk of Katie Lane

Dear Reader,

There's something about a bad boy that's irresistible, something about a man who lives on the edge and plays by his own rules. And whether it was the time you caught the teenage rebel checking you out in your new

Christmas sweater—or the time the tatted biker sent you a blatantly sexual look as he cruised by on his custom bike—a run-in with a bad boy is like taking a ride on the world's biggest roller coaster; long after the ride's over, you're still shaky, breathless, and begging for more.

No doubt a portion of the blame lies with our mothers. (It's so easy to blame Mom.) Maternal warnings always include the things that turn out to be the most fun—wild parties, fast cars, and naughty boys. (All of which got me in plenty of trouble.) But I think most of our infatuation has to do with our desire to take a break from being the perfect daughter, the hardworking employee, the dependable wife, and the super mom. For one brief moment, we want to release our inner bad girl and jerk up that sweater Aunt Sally gave us and flash some cleavage. Or hop on that throbbing piece of machinery and take a ride on the wild side.

Even if it's only in our fantasies—or possibly a steamy romance novel—we want to throw caution to the wind and fearlessly proclaim...

MAKE MINE A BAD BOY.

Katie Lane

www.katielanebooks.com

Find out more about Forever Romance!

Visit us at
www.hachettebookgroup.com/publishing_forever.aspx

Find us on Facebook
http://www.facebook.com/ForeverRomance

Follow us on Twitter
http://twitter.com/ForeverRomance

NEW AND UPCOMING TITLES

Each month we feature our new titles
and reader favorites.

CONTESTS AND GIVEAWAYS

We give away galleys, autographed copies,
and all kinds of exclusive items.

AUTHOR INFO

You'll find bios, articles, and links to personal websites
for all your favorite authors—and so much more.

GET SOCIAL

Connect with your favorite authors, editors, and
other Forever fans, and share what's important to you.

THE BUZZ

Sign up for our monthly romance newsletter,
and be the first to read all about it.